Patricia Cornwell is one of the world's major international bestselling authors, translated into thirty-six languages across more than fifty countries. She is a founder of the Virginia Institute of Forensic Science and Medicine, a founding member of the National Forensic Academy, a member of the New York OCME Forensic Sciences Training Program's Advisory Board, and a member of the Harvard-affiliated McLean Hospital's National Council, where she is an advocate for psychiatric research.

In 2008 Cornwell won the Galaxy British Book Awards' Books Direct Crime Thriller of the Year – the first American ever to win this prestigious award. Her most recent bestsellers include *Scarpetta*, *Book of the Dead* and *The Front*. Her earlier works include *Postmortem* – the only novel to win five major crime awards in a single year – and *Cruel and Unusual*, which won the coveted Gold Dagger award in 1993. Dr. Kay Scarpetta herself won the 1999 Sherlock Award for the best detective created by an American writer.

Visit the author's website at www.patriciacornwell.com

ALSO BY PATRICIA CORNWELL

Patricia Cornwell

Cruel and Unusual

sphere

SPHERE

First published in Great Britain in 1993 by Little Brown and Company
Paperback edition published in 1994 by Warner Books
Reprinted 1994 (seven times), 1995 (three times), 1996 (twice), 1997 (four times), 1998
(three times), 1999, 2000, 2001
Reprinted by Time Warner Paperbacks in 2002
Reprinted 2003 (twice), 2004 (three times)
Reprinted by Time Warner Books in 2005, 2006
Reprinted by Sphere in 2007, 2008, 2009
This reissue published in 2010 by Sphere
Reprinted by Sphere in 2010, 2011, 2013, 2014

A CIP catalogue record for this book
is available from the British Library.

ISBN 978-0-7515-4453-4

Typeset in Garamond by M Rules
Printed and bound in Great Britain by
Clays Ltd, St Ives plc

Papers used by Sphere are from well-managed forests
and other responsible sources.

MIX
Paper from
responsible sources
FSC® C104740
www.fsc.org

Sphere
An imprint of
Little, Brown Book Group
100 Victoria Embankment
London EC4Y 0DY

An Hachette UK Company
www.hachette.co.uk

www.littlebrown.co.uk

THIS BOOK IS FOR
THE INIMITABLE DR. MARCELLA FIERRO.

(You taught Scarpetta well.)

Prologue

It is two weeks before Christmas. Four days before nothing at all. I lie on my bed staring at my dirty bare feet and the white toilet missing its seat, and when cockroaches crawl across the floor I don't jump anymore. I watch them the same way they watch me.

I close my eyes and breathe slow.

I remember raking hay in the heat of day and getting no pay compared to the way white folk live. I dream of roasting peanuts in a tin and when the tomatoes are in eating them like apples. I imagine driving the pickup truck, sweat shining on my face in that no-future place I swore I'd leave.

I can't use the john, blow my nose, or smoke without guards taking notes. There's no clock. I never know the weather. I open my eyes and see a blank wall going on forever. What's a man supposed to feel when he's about to be gone?

Like a sad, sad song. I don't know the words. I can't remember. They say it happened in September when the sky was like a robin's egg and leaves were on fire and falling to the ground. They say a beast got loose in the city. Now there's one less sound.

Killing me won't kill the beast. The dark is his friend, flesh and blood his feast. When you think it's safe to stop looking that's when you'd better start looking, brother.

One leads to another.

Ronnie Joe Waddell

1

The Monday I carried Ronnie Joe Waddell's meditation in my pocketbook, I never saw the sun. It was dark out when I drove to work that morning. It was dark again when I drove home. Small raindrops spun in my headlights, the night gloomy with fog and bitterly cold.

I built a fire in my living room and envisioned Virginia farmland and tomatoes ripening in the sun. I imagined a young black man in the hot cab of a pickup truck and wondered if his head had been full of murder back then. Waddell's meditation had been published in the *Richmond Times-Dispatch* and I had taken the clipping to work to add to his growing file. But the business of the day distracted me and his meditation had remained in my pocketbook. I had read it several times. I supposed it would always intrigue me that poetry and cruelty could reside in the same heart.

For the next few hours I paid bills and wrote Christmas cards while the television played mutely. Like the rest of Virginia's citizens, whenever an execution was scheduled I found out from the media whether all appeals had been exhausted or the governor had granted clemency. The news determined whether I went on to bed or drove downtown to the morgue.

At almost ten P.M. my telephone rang. I answered it expecting my deputy chief or some other member of my staff whose evening, like mine, was on hold.

"Hello?" asked a male voice I did not recognize. "I'm trying to reach Kay Scarpetta? Uh, the chief medical examiner, Dr. Scarpetta?"

"Speaking," I said.

"Oh, good. Detective Joe Trent with Henrico County. Found your number in the book. Sorry to bother you at home." He sounded keyed up. "But we've got a situation we really need your help with."

"What's the problem?" I asked, staring tensely at the TV. A commercial was playing. I hoped I wasn't needed at a scene.

"Earlier this evening, a thirteen-year-old white male was abducted after leaving a convenience store on Northside. He was shot in the head and there may be some sexual components involved."

My heart sank as I reached for paper and pen. "Where is the body?" I asked.

"He was found behind a grocery store on Patterson Avenue in the county. I mean, he's not dead. He hasn't regained consciousness but no one's saying right now whether he'll make it. I realize it's not your case since he's not dead. But he's got some injuries that are real odd. They're not like anything I've ever come across. I know you see a lot of different types of injuries.

4

I'm hoping you might have some idea how these were inflicted and why."

"Describe them for me," I said.

"We're talking about two areas. One on his inner right thigh, you know, up high near the groin. The other's in the area of his right shoulder. Chunks of flesh are missing—cut out. And there's weird cuts and scratches around the edges of the wounds. He's at Henrico Doctor's."

"Did you find the excised tissue?" My mind was racing through other cases, looking for something similar.

"Not so far. We've got men out there still searching. But it's possible the assault occurred inside a car."

"Whose car?"

"The assailant's. The grocery store parking lot where the kid was found is a good three or four miles from the convenience store where he was last seen. I'm thinking he got into somebody's car, maybe was forced to."

"You got photographs of the injuries before the doctors started working on him?"

"Yes. But they haven't done much. Because of the amount of skin missing, they'll have to do skin grafts—*full* grafts, is what they said, if that tells you anything."

It told me they had debrided the wounds, had him on intravenous antibiotics, and were waiting to do a gluteal graft. If, however, that was not the case and they had undermined the tissue around the injuries and sutured them, then there wasn't going to be much left for me to see.

"They haven't sutured his wounds," I said.

"That's what I've been told."

"Do you want me to take a look?"

"That would be really great," he said, relieved. "You should be able to see the wounds real well."

"When would you like me to do this?"

"Tomorrow would work."

"All right. What time? The earlier the better."

"Eight hundred hours? I'll meet you in front of the ER."

"I'll be there," I said as the anchorman stared grimly at me. Hanging up, I reached for the remote control and turned up the sound.

". . . Eugenia? Can you tell us if there's been any word from the governor?"

The camera shifted to the Virginia State Penitentiary, where for two hundred years the Commonwealth's worst criminals had been warehoused along a rocky stretch of the James River at the edge of downtown. Sign-carrying protesters and capital punishment enthusiasts gathered in the dark, their faces harsh in the glare of television lights. It chilled my soul that some people were laughing. A pretty, young correspondent in a red coat filled the screen.

"As you know, Bill," she said, "yesterday a telephone line was set up between Governor Norring's office and the penitentiary. Still no word, and that speaks volumes. Historically, when the governor doesn't intend to intervene, he remains silent."

"How are things there? Is it relatively peaceful so far?"

"So far, yes, Bill. I'd say several hundred people are standing vigil out here. And of course, the penitentiary itself is almost empty. All but several dozen of the inmates have already been transported to the new correctional facility in Greensville."

I turned off the TV and moments later was driving east with my doors locked and the radio on. Fatigue seeped through me like anesthesia. I felt dreary and numb. I dreaded executions. I dreaded waiting for someone to die, then running my scalpel through flesh as warm as mine. I was a physician with a law degree. I had been trained to know what gave life and what took it, what was right and what was wrong. Then experience had become my mentor, wiping its feet on that pristine part of myself that was idealistic and analytical. It is disheartening when a thinking person is forced to admit that many cliches are true. There is no justice on this earth. Nothing would ever undo what Ronnie Joe Waddell had done.

He had been on death row nine years. His victim had not been my case because she had been murdered before I had been appointed chief medical examiner of Virginia and had moved to Richmond. But I had reviewed her records. I was well aware of every savage detail. On the morning of September fourth, ten years before, Robyn Naismith called in sick at Channel 8, where she was an anchorwoman. She went out to buy cold remedies and returned home. The next day, her nude, battered body was found in her living room, propped against the TV. A bloody thumbprint recovered from the medicine cabinet was later identified as Ronnie Joe Waddell's.

There were a number of cars parked behind the morgue when I pulled in. My deputy chief, Fielding, was already there. So was my administrator, Ben Stevens, and morgue supervisor, Susan

Story. The bay door was open, lights inside dimly illuminating the tarmac beyond, and a capitol police officer was sitting in his marked car smoking. He got out as I parked.

"Safe to keep the bay door open?" I asked. He was a tall, gaunt man with thick white hair. Though I had talked to him many times in the past, I couldn't remember his name.

"Appears okay at the moment, Dr. Scarpetta," he said, zipping up his heavy nylon jacket. "I haven't seen any troublemakers around. But as soon as Corrections gets here I'll close it and make sure it stays closed."

"Fine. As long as you'll be right here in the meantime."

"Yes, ma'am. You can count on that. And we'll have a couple more uniform men back here in case there's a problem. Apparently there's a lot of protesters. I guess you read in the paper about that petition all those people signed and took to the governor. And I heard earlier today some bleeding hearts as far away as California are on a hunger strike."

I glanced around the empty parking lot and across Main Street. A car rushed past, tires swishing over wet pavement. Streetlights were smudges in the fog.

"Hell, not me. I wouldn't even miss a coffee break for Waddell." The officer cupped his hand around his lighter and began puffing on a cigarette. "After what he done to that Naismith girl. You know, I remember watching her on TV. Now, I like my women the same way I like my coffee—sweet and white. But I have to admit, she was the prettiest black girl I ever seen."

I had quit smoking barely two months ago, and it still made me crazy to watch someone else doing it.

"Lord, that must've been close to ten years ago," he went on. "I'll never forget the uproar, though. One of the worst cases we've ever had around here. You'd've thought a grizzly bear got hold of—"

I interrupted him. "You'll let us know what's going on?"

"Yes, ma'am. They'll radio me and I'll give you the word." He headed back to the shelter of his car.

Inside the morgue, fluorescent light bleached the corridor of color, the smell of deodorizer cloying. I passed the small office where funeral homes signed in bodies, then the X-ray room, and the refrigerator, which was really a large refrigerated room with double-decker gurneys and two massive steel doors. The autopsy suite was lit up, stainless steel tables polished bright. Susan was sharpening a long knife and Fielding was labeling blood tubes. Both of them looked as tired and unenthusiastic as I felt.

"Ben's upstairs in the library watching TV," Fielding said to me. "He'll let us know if there are any new developments."

"What's the chance this guy had AIDS?" Susan referred to Waddell as if he already were dead.

"I don't know," I said. "We'll double-glove, take the usual precautions."

"I hope they'll say something if he had it," she persisted. "You know, I don't trust it when they send these prisoners in. I don't think they care if they're HIV positive because it's not their problem. They're not the ones doing the posts and worrying about needle sticks."

Susan had become increasingly paranoid about such occupational hazards as exposure to radiation, chemicals, and diseases.

I could not blame her. She was several months pregnant, though it barely showed.

Slipping on a plastic apron, I went back into the locker room and put on greens, covered my shoes with booties, and got two packets of gloves. I inspected the surgical cart parked beside table three. Everything was labeled with Waddell's name, the date, and an autopsy number. The labeled tubes and cartons would go in the trash if Governor Norring interceded at the last minute. Ronnie Waddell would be deleted from the morgue log, his autopsy number assigned to whoever came in next.

At eleven P.M. Ben Stevens came downstairs and shook his head. All of us looked up at the clock. No one spoke. Minutes ticked by.

The capitol police officer walked in, portable radio in hand. I finally remembered his name was Rankin.

"He was pronounced at eleven-oh-five," he said. "Will be here in about fifteen minutes."

The ambulance beeped a warning as it backed into the bay, and when its rear doors swung open, enough Department of Corrections guards hopped out to control a small prison riot. Four of them slid out the stretcher bearing Ronnie Waddell's body. They carried it up the ramp and inside the morgue, metal clacking, feet scuffing, all of us getting out of the way. Lowering the stretcher to the tile floor without bothering to unfold the legs, they propelled it along like a sled on wheels, its passenger strapped in and covered with a bloodstained sheet.

"A nosebleed," one of the guards offered before I could ask the question.

"Who had a nosebleed?" I inquired, noting that the guard's gloved hands were bloody.

"Mr. Waddell did."

"In the ambulance?" I puzzled, for Waddell should not have had a blood pressure by the time he was loaded inside the ambulance.

But the guard was preoccupied with other matters and I did not get an answer. It would have to wait.

We transferred the body to the gurney positioned on top of the floor scale. Busy hands fumbled with unfastening straps and opening the sheet. The door to the autopsy suite quietly shut as the Department of Corrections guards left just as abruptly as they had appeared.

Waddell had been dead exactly twenty-two minutes. I could smell his sweat, his dirty bare feet, and the faint odor of singed flesh. His right pant leg was pushed up above his knee, his calf dressed in fresh gauze applied postmortem to his burns. He was a big, powerful man. The newspapers had called him the *gentle giant,* poetic Ronnie with soulful eyes. Yet there had been a time when he had used the large hands, the massive shoulders and arms before me to rip the life from another human being.

I pulled apart the Velcro fasteners of his light blue denim shirt, checking pockets as I undressed him. Searching for personal effects is pro forma and usually fruitless. Inmates are not supposed to carry anything with them to the electric chair, and I was very surprised when I discovered what appeared to be a letter in the back pocket of his jeans. The envelope had not been opened. Written in bold block letters across the front of it was

EXTREMELY CONFIDENTIAL. PLEASE BURY WITH ME!!

"Make a copy of the envelope and whatever's inside and submit the originals with his personal effects," I said, handing the envelope to Fielding.

He tucked it under the autopsy protocol on a clipboard, mumbling, "Jesus. He's bigger than I am."

"Amazing that anyone could be bigger than you are," Susan said to my bodybuilder deputy chief.

"Good thing he's not been dead long," he added. "Otherwise we'd need the Jaws of Life."

When musclebound people have been dead for hours, they are as uncooperative as marble statues. Rigor had not begun to set in. Waddell was limber as in life. He could have been asleep.

It required all of us to transfer him, facedown, to the autopsy table. He weighed two hundred and fifty-nine pounds. His feet protruded over the table's edge. I was measuring the burns to his leg when the buzzer sounded from the bay. Susan went to see who it was, and shortly Lieutenant Pete Marino walked in, trench coat unbuttoned, one end of the belt trailing along the tile floor.

"The burn to the back of his calf is four by one and a quarter by two and three-eighths," I dictated to Fielding. "It's dry, contracted, and blistered."

Marino lit a cigarette. "They're raising a stink about him bleeding," he said, and he seemed agitated.

"His rectal temp is one hundred and four," Susan said as she removed the chemical thermometer. "That's at eleven-forty-nine."

"You know why his face was bleeding?" Marino asked.

"One of the guards said a nosebleed," I replied, adding, "We need to turn him over."

"You saw this on the inner aspect of his left arm?" Susan directed my attention to an abrasion.

I examined it through a lens under a strong light. "I don't know. Possibly from one of the restraints."

"There's one on his right arm, too."

I took a look while Marino watched me and smoked. We turned the body, shoving a block under the shoulders. Blood trickled out of the right side of his nose. His head and chin had been shaved to an uneven stubble. I made the Y incision.

"There might be some abrasions here," Susan said, looking at the tongue.

"Take it out." I inserted the thermometer into the liver.

"Jesus," Marino said under his breath.

"Now?" Susan's scalpel was poised.

"No. Photograph the burns around his head. We need to measure those. Then remove the tongue."

"Shit," she complained. "Who used the camera last?"

"Sorry," Fielding said. "There was no film in the drawer. I forgot. By the way, it's your job to keep film in the drawer."

"It would help if you'd tell me when the film drawer's empty."

"Women are supposed to be intuitive. I didn't think I needed to tell you."

"I got the measurement of these burns around his head," Susan reported, ignoring his remark.

"Okay."

Susan gave him the measurements, then started work on the tongue.

Marino backed away from the table. "Jesus," he said again. "That always gets me."

"Liver temp's one hundred and five," I reported to Fielding.

I glanced up at the clock. Waddell had been dead for an hour. He hadn't cooled much. He was big. Electrocution heats you up. The brain temperatures of smaller men I had autopsied were as high as a hundred and ten. Waddell's right calf was at least that, hot to the touch, the muscle in total tetanus.

"A little abrasion at the margin. But nothing big-time," Susan pointed out to me.

"He bite his tongue hard enough to bleed that much?" Marino asked.

"No," I said.

"Well, they're already raising a stink about it." His voice rose. "I thought you'd want to know."

I paused, resting the scalpel on the edge of the table as it suddenly occurred to me. "You were a witness."

"Yeah. I told you I was going to be."

Everybody looked at him.

"Trouble's brewing out there," he said. "I don't want no one leaving this joint alone."

"What sort of trouble?" Susan asked.

"A bunch of religious nuts have been hanging out at Spring

14

Street since this morning. Somehow they got word about his bleeding, and when the ambulance drove off with his body they started marching in this direction like a bunch of zombies."

"Did you see it when he started bleeding?" Fielding asked him.

"Oh, yeah. They juiced him twice. The first time he made this loud hiss, like steam coming out of a radiator, and the blood started pouring out from under his mask. They're saying the chair might have malfunctioned."

Susan started the Stryker saw and no one competed with its loud buzzing as she cut through the skull. I continued examining the organs. Heart was good, coronaries terrific. When the saw stopped, I resumed dictating to Fielding.

"You got the weight?" he asked.

"Heart weighs five-forty, and he's got a single adhesion of the left upper lobe to the aortic arch. Even found four parathyroids, in case you didn't already get that."

"I got it."

I placed the stomach on the cutting board. "It's almost tubular."

"You sure?" Fielding moved closer to inspect. "That's bizarre. A guy this big needs a minimum of four thousand calories a day."

"He wasn't getting it, not lately," I said. "He doesn't have any gastric contents. His stomach is absolutely empty and clean."

"He didn't eat his last meal?" Marino asked me.

"It doesn't appear that he did."

"Do they usually?"

"Yes," I said, "usually."

We were finished by one A.M., and followed the funeral home attendants out to the bay, where the hearse was waiting. As we walked out of the building, darkness throbbed with red and blue lights. Radio static drifted on the cold, damp air, engines rumbled, and beyond the chainlink fence enclosing the parking lot was a ring of fire. Men, women, and children stood silently, faces wavering in candlelight.

The attendants wasted no time sliding Waddell's body into the back of the hearse and slamming the tailgate shut.

Somebody said something I did not get, and suddenly candles showered over the fence like a storm of falling stars and landed softly on the pavement.

"Goddam squirrels!" Marino exclaimed.

Wicks glowed orange and tiny flames dotted the tarmac. The hearse hastily began to back out of the bay. Flashguns were going off. I spotted the Channel 8 news van parked on Main Street. Someone was running along the sidewalk. Uniformed men were stamping out the candles, moving toward the fence, demanding that everyone clear the area.

"We don't want any problems here," an officer said. "Not unless some of you want to spend the night in lockup—"

"Butchers," a woman screamed.

Other voices joined in and hands grabbed the chain-link fence, shaking it.

Marino hurried me to my car.

A chant rose with tribal intensity. *"Butchers, butchers, butchers . . ."*

I fumbled with my keys, dropped them on the floor mat, snatched them up, and managed to find the right one.

"I'm following you home," Marino said.

I turned the heater on high but could not get warm. Twice I checked to make sure my doors were locked. The night took on a surreal quality, a strange asymmetry of light and dark windows, and shadows moved in the corners of my eyes.

We drank Scotch in my kitchen because I was out of bourbon.

"I don't know how you stand this stuff," Marino said rudely.

"Help yourself to whatever else there is in the bar," I told him.

"I'll tough it out."

I wasn't quite sure how to broach the subject, and it was obvious that Marino wasn't going to make it easy for me. He was tense, his face flushed. Strands of gray hair clung to his moist, balding head, and he was chain-smoking.

"Have you ever witnessed an execution before?" I asked.

"Never had a strong urge to."

"But you volunteered this time. So the urge must have been pretty strong."

"I bet if you put some lemon and soda water in this it wouldn't be half bad."

"If you want me to ruin good Scotch, I'll be glad to see what I can do."

He slid the glass toward me and I went to the refrigerator. "I've got bottled Key Lime juice, but no lemon." I searched shelves.

"That's fine."

I dribbled Key Lime juice into his glass, then added the Schweppes. Oblivious to the strange concoction he was sipping, he said, "Maybe you've forgotten, but the Robyn Naismith case was mine. Mine and Sonny Jones's."

"I wasn't around then."

"Oh, yeah. Funny, it seems like you've been here forever. But you know what happened, right?"

I was a deputy chief medical examiner for Dade County when Robyn Naismith was murdered, and I remembered reading about the case, following it in the news, and later seeing a slide presentation about it at a national meeting. The former Miss Virginia was a stunning beauty with a gorgeous alto voice. She was articulate and charismatic before the camera. She was only twenty-seven years old.

The defense claimed that Ronnie Waddell's intent was burglary, and Robyn's misfortune was to walk in on it after returning home from the drugstore. Allegedly, Waddell did not watch television and was unfamiliar with her name or brilliant future when he was ransacking her residence and brutalizing her. He was so hopped up on drugs, the defense argued, that he didn't know what he was doing. The jurors rejected Waddell's temporary insanity plea and recommended the death penalty.

"I know the pressure to catch her killer was incredible," I said to Marino.

"Friggin' unbelievable. We had this great latent print. We had bite marks. We had three guys doing a cold search through the files morning, noon, and night. I got no idea how many hours I put in on that damn case. Then we catch the bastard because he's driving around North Carolina with an expired inspection sticker." He paused, his eyes hard when he added, "Course, Jones wasn't around by then. Too damn bad he missed out on seeing Waddell get his reward."

"Do you blame Waddell for what happened to Sonny Jones?" I asked.

"Hey, what do you think?"

"He was a close friend."

"We worked Homicide together, fished together, was on the same bowling team."

"I know his death was hard for you."

"Yeah, well, the case wore him down. Working all hours, no sleep, never home, and that sure as hell didn't help matters with his wife. He kept telling me he couldn't take it no more and then he stopped telling me anything. One night he decides to eat his gun."

"I'm sorry," I said gently. "But I'm not sure you can blame Waddell for that."

"I had a score to settle."

"And was it settled when you witnessed his execution?"

At first Marino did not reply. He stared across the kitchen, his jaw rigidly set. I watched him smoke and drain his drink.

"Can I refresh that?"

"Yo. Why not."

I got up and did my thing again as I thought about the injustices and losses that had gone into the making of Marino. He had survived a loveless, impoverished childhood in the wrong part of New Jersey, and nursed an abiding distrust of anyone whose lot had been better. Not long ago his wife of

19

thirty years had left him, and he had a son nobody seemed to know anything about. Regardless of his loyalty to law and order and his record of excellent police work, it was not in his genetic code to get along with the brass. It seemed his life's journey had placed him on a hard road. I feared that what he hoped to find at the end was not wisdom or peace but paybacks. Marino was always angry about something.

"Let me ask you this, Doc," he said to me when I returned to the table. "How would you feel if they caught the assholes who killed Mark?"

His question caught me by surprise. I did not want to think about those men.

"Isn't there a part of you that wants to see the bastards hung?" he went on. "Doesn't a part of you want to volunteer for the firing squad so you could pull the trigger yourself?"

Mark died when a bomb placed in a trash can inside London's Victoria Station exploded at the moment he happened to walk past. My shock and grief had catapulted me beyond revenge.

"It's an exercise in futility for me to contemplate punishing a group of terrorists," I said.

Marino stared intensely at me. "That's what's known as one of your famous bullshit answers. You'd give them free autopsies if you could. And you'd want them alive and would cut real slow. I ever tell you what happened to Robyn Naismith's family?"

I reached for my drink.

"Her father was a doctor in northern Virginia, a real fine man," he said. "About six months after the trial, he came down

20

with cancer and a couple months after that was dead. Robyn was the only child. The mother moves to Texas, gets in a car wreck, and spends her days in a wheelchair with nothing but memories. Waddell killed Robyn Naismith's entire family. He poisoned every life he touched."

I thought of Waddell growing up on the farm, images from his meditation drifting through my mind. I envisioned him sitting on porch steps, biting into a tomato that tasted like the sun. I wondered what had gone through his mind the last second of his life. I wondered if he had prayed.

Marino stubbed out a cigarette. He was thinking about leaving.

"Do you know a Detective Trent with Henrico?" I asked.

"Joe Trent. Used to be with K-Nine and got transferred into the detective division after he made sergeant a couple months ago. Sort of a nervous Nellie, but he's all right."

"He called me about a boy—"

He cut me off. "Eddie Heath?"

"I don't know his name."

"A white male about thirteen years old. We're working on it. Lucky's is in the city."

"Lucky's?"

"The convenience store where he was last seen. It's off Chamberlayne Avenue, Northside. What did Trent want?" Marino frowned. "He gotten word that Heath ain't going to pull through and is making an appointment with you in advance?"

"He wants me to look at unusual injuries, possible mutilation."

"Christ. I hate it when it's kids." Marino pushed back his

chair and rubbed his temples. "Damn. Every time you get rid of one toad there's another to take his place."

After Marino left, I sat on the hearth in the living room watching coals shift in the fireplace. I was weary and felt a dull, implacable sadness that I did not have the strength to chase away. Mark's death had left a tear in my soul. I had come to realize, incredibly, just how much of my identity had been tied to my love for him.

The last time I saw him was on the day he flew to London, and we managed a quick lunch downtown before he headed to Dulles Airport. What I remembered most clearly about our last hour together was both of us glancing at our watches as storm clouds gathered and rain began to spit against the window beside our booth. He had a nick on his jaw from where he'd cut himself while shaving, and later, when I would see his face in my mind, I would envision that small injury and for some reason be undone by it.

He died in February while the war was ending in the Persian Gulf, and determined to put the pain behind me, I had sold my house and moved to a new neighborhood. What I accomplished was to uproot myself without really going anywhere, and the familiar plants and neighbors that once had given me comfort were gone. Redecorating my new home or redesigning the yard only added to my stress. Everything I did provided distractions for which I had no time, and I could imagine Mark shaking his head.

"For someone so logical . . ." he would smile and say.

"And what would you do?" I would tell him in my thoughts some nights when I could not sleep. "Just what the hell would you do if you were still here instead of me?"

Returning to the kitchen, I rinsed out my glass and went into my study to see what awaited me on my answering machine. Several reporters had called, so had my mother and Lucy, my niece. Three other messages were hang ups.

I would have loved an unlisted number but it was not possible. The police, Commonwealth's Attorneys, and the four hundred or so appointed medical examiners statewide had legitimate reasons to reach me after hours. To counter the loss of privacy, I used my answering machine to screen calls, and anyone who left threatening or obscene messages ran the risk of being tracked by Caller ID.

Pressing the review button on the ID box, I began scrolling through the numbers materializing on the narrow screen. When I found the three calls I was looking for, I was perplexed and unsettled. The number was curiously familiar by now. It had been appearing on my screen several times a week of late when the caller would hang up without leaving a message. Once, I had tried dialing the number back to see who answered and had gotten the high-pitched tone of what sounded like a fax machine or a computer modem. For whatever reason, this individual or thing had called my number three times between ten-twenty and eleven P.M., while I was at the morgue waiting for Waddell's body. That didn't make sense. Computerized telephone solicitations should not occur so frequently and at such a late hour, and if one modem trying to dial another was getting me instead, shouldn't someone have figured out by now that his computer was dialing a wrong number?

I woke up several times during the few hours left of the early morning. Every creak or shift of sound in the house made my pulse pick up. Red lights on the burglar alarm's control panel across from the bed glowed ominously, and when I turned or rearranged the covers, motion sensors I did not arm while I was home watched me silently with flashing red eyes. My dreams were strange. At five-thirty I turned on lamps and got dressed.

It was dark out and there was very little traffic as I drove to the office. The parking lot behind the bay was deserted and littered with dozens of small beeswax candles that brought to mind Moravian love feasts and other religious celebrations. But these candles had been used to protest. They had been used as weapons hours before. Upstairs, I fixed coffee and began going through the paperwork Fielding had left for me, curious about the contents of the envelope I'd found in Waddell's back pocket. I was expecting a poem, perhaps another meditation or a letter from his minister.

Instead, I discovered that what Waddell had considered "extremely confidential" and had wanted buried with him were cash register receipts. Inexplicably, five were for tolls; three others were for meals, including a fried chicken dinner ordered at a Shoney's two weeks earlier.

2

Detective Joe Trent would have looked quite youthful were it not for a beard and receding blond hair that was turning gray. He was trim and tall, a crisp trench coat belted tightly around his waist, his shoes perfectly shined. He blinked nervously as we shook hands and introduced ourselves on the sidewalk in front of Henrico Doctor's Emergency Center. I could tell he was upset by Eddie Heath's case.

"You don't mind if we talk out here a minute," he said, his breath turning white. "For privacy reasons."

Shivering, I tucked my elbows close to my sides as a Medflight helicopter made a terrific noise taking off from the helipad on a grassy rise not far from where we stood. The moon was a shaving of ice melting in the slate-gray sky, cars in the parking lots dirty from road salt and frigid winter rains. The early morning was stark and without color, the wind sharp like a slap, and I observed all this more keenly because of the nature of my business here. Had the temperature suddenly risen forty degrees and the sun begun to blaze I do not think I could have felt warm.

"What we got here is real bad, Dr. Scarpetta." He blinked. "I think you'll agree we don't want the details getting out."

"What can you tell me about this boy?" I asked.

"I've talked to his family and several other people who know him. As best I can ascertain, Eddie Heath is just your average kid—likes sports and has a paper route, has never gotten into any trouble with the police. His father works for the phone company and his mother sews for people out of the home. Apparently, last night, Mrs. Heath needed a can of cream of mushroom soup for a casserole she was fixing for dinner and asked Eddie to run over to the Lucky Convenience Store to get it."

"The store is how far from their house?" I asked.

"A couple of blocks, and Eddie's been there any number of times. The people working the counter know him by name."

"He was last seen at what time?"

"Around five-thirty P.M. He was in the store a few minutes and left."

"It would have been dark out," I said.

"Yes, it was." Trent stared off at the helicopter transfigured by distance into a white dragonfly softly thudding through clouds. "At approximately eight-thirty, an officer on routine patrol was checking the back of buildings along Patterson and saw the kid propped up against the Dumpster."

"Do you have photographs?"

"No, ma'am. When the officer realized the boy was alive, his first priority was getting help. We don't have pictures. But I've got a pretty detailed description based on the officer's observations. The boy was nude, and he was propped up, with his legs straight out and arms by his sides and head bent forward. His clothing was in a moderately neat pile on the pavement, along with a small bag containing a can of cream of mushroom soup and a Snickers bar. It was twenty-eight degrees out. We're thinking he may have been left there anywhere from minutes to half an hour before he was found."

An ambulance halted near us. Doors slammed and metal grated as attendants quickly lowered the legs of a stretcher to the ground and wheeled an old man through opening glass doors. We followed and in silence walked through a bright, antiseptic corridor busy with medical personnel and patients dazed by the misfortunes that had brought them here. As we rode the elevator up to the third floor, I wondered what trace evidence had been scrubbed away and tossed in the trash.

"What about his clothes? Was a bullet recovered?" I asked Trent as the elevator doors parted.

"I've got his clothes in my car and will drop them and his PERK off at the lab this afternoon. The bullet's still in his brain. They haven't gone in there yet. I hope like hell they swabbed him good."

The pediatric intensive care unit was at the end of a polished hallway, panes of glass in the double wooden doors covered with friendly dinosaur paper. Inside, rainbows decorated sky blue walls, and animal mobiles were suspended over hydraulic beds in the eight rooms arranged in a semicircle around the nurses' station. Three young women worked behind monitors, one of them typing on a keyboard and another talking on the phone. A slender brunette dressed in a red corduroy jumper and turtleneck sweater identified herself as the head nurse after Trent explained why we were here.

"The attending physician's not in yet," she apologized.

"We just need to look at Eddie's injuries. It won't take long," Trent said. "His family still in there?"

"They stayed with him all night."

We followed her through soft artificial light, past code carts and green tanks of oxygen that would not be parked outside the rooms of little boys and girls were the world the way it ought to be. When we reached Eddie's room, the nurse went inside and shut the door most of the way.

"Just for a few minutes," I overheard her say to the Heaths. "While we do the exam."

"What kind of specialist is it this time?" the father asked in an unsteady voice.

"A doctor who knows a lot about injuries. She's sort of like a police surgeon." The nurse diplomatically refrained from saying I was a medical examiner, or worse, a coroner.

After a pause, the father quietly said, "Oh. This is for evidence."

"Yes. How about some coffee? Maybe something to eat?"

Eddie Heath's parents emerged from the room, both of them considerably overweight, their clothes badly wrinkled from having been slept in. They had the bewildered look of innocent, simple people who have been told the world is about to end, and when they glanced at us with exhausted eyes I wished there were something I could say that would make it not so or at least a little better. Words of comfort died in my throat as the couple slowly walked off.

Eddie Heath did not stir on top of the bed, his head wrapped in bandages, a ventilator breathing air into his lungs while fluids dripped into his veins. His complexion was milky and hairless, the thin membrane of his eyelids a faint bruised blue in the low light. I surmised the color of his hair by his strawberry blond eyebrows. He had not yet emerged from that fragile prepubescent stage when boys are full-lipped and beautiful and sing more sweetly than their sisters. His forearms were slender, the body beneath the sheet small. Only the disproportionately large, still hands tethered by intravenous lines were true to his fledgling gender. He did not look thirteen.

"She needs to see the areas on his shoulder and leg," Trent told the nurse in a low voice.

She got two packets of gloves, one for her and one for me, and we put them on. The boy was naked beneath the sheet, his skin grimy in creases and fingernails dirty. Patients who are unstable cannot be thoroughly bathed.

Trent tensed as the nurse removed the wet-to-dry dressings from the wounds. "Christ," he said under his breath. "It looks even worse than it did last night. Jesus." He shook his head and backed up a step.

If someone had told me that the boy had been attacked by a shark, I might have gone along with it were it not for the neat edges of the wounds, which clearly had been inflicted by a sharp, linear instrument, such as a knife or razor. Sections of flesh the size of elbow patches had been excised from his right shoulder and right inner thigh. Opening my medical bag, I got out a ruler and measured the wounds without touching them, then took photographs.

"See the cuts and scratches at the edges?" Trent pointed. "That's what I was telling you about. It's like he cut some sort of pattern on the skin and then removed the whole thing."

"Did you find any anal tearing?" I asked the nurse.

"When I did a rectal temperature I didn't notice any tears, and no one noticed anything unusual about his mouth or throat when he was intubated. I also checked for old fractures and bruises."

"What about tattoos?"

"Tattoos?" she asked as if she'd never seen a tattoo.

"Tattoos, birthmarks, scars. Anything that someone may have removed for some reason," I said.

"I have no idea," the nurse said dubiously.

"I'll go ask his parents." Trent wiped sweat from his forehead. "They may have gone to the cafeteria."

"I'll find them," he said as he passed through the doorway.

"What are his doctors saying?" I asked the nurse.

"He's very critical and unresponsive." She stated the obvious without emotion.

"May I see where the bullet went in?" I asked.

She loosened the edges of the bandage around his head and pushed the gauze up until I could see the tiny black hole, charred around the edges. The wound was through his right temple and slightly forward.

"Through the frontal lobe?" I asked.

"Yes."

"They've done an angio?"

"There's no circulation to the brain, due to the swelling. There's no electroencephalic activity, and when we put cold water in his ears there was no caloric activity. It evoked no brain potentials."

She stood on the other side of the bed, gloved hands by her sides and expression dispassionate as she continued to relate the various tests conducted and maneuvers instigated to decrease intracranial pressure. I had paid my dues in ERs and ICUs and knew very well that it is easier to be clinical with a patient who has never been awake. And Eddie Heath would never be awake. His cortex was gone. That which made him human, made him think and feel, was gone and was never coming back. He had been left with vital functions, left with a brain stem. He was a breathing body with a beating heart maintained at the moment by machines.

I began looking for defense injuries. Concentrating on getting out of the way of his lines, I was unaware I was holding his hand until he startled me by squeezing mine. Such reflex movements are not uncommon in people who are cortically dead. It is the equivalent of a baby grabbing your finger, a reflex involving no thought process at all. I gently released his hand and took a deep breath, waiting for the ache in my heart to subside.

"Did you find anything?" the nurse asked.

"It's hard to look with all these lines," I said.

She replaced his dressings and pulled the sheet up to his chin. I took off my gloves and dropped them in the trash as Detective Trent returned, his eyes a little wild.

"No tattoos," he said breathlessly, as if he had sprinted to the cafeteria and back. "No birthmarks or scars, either."

Moments later we were walking to the parking deck. The sun

slipped in and out, and tiny snowflakes were blowing. I squinted as I stared into the wind at heavy traffic on Forest Avenue. A number of cars had Christmas wreaths affixed to their grilles.

"I think you'd better prepare for the eventuality of his death," I said.

"If I'd known that, I wouldn't have bothered you to come out. Damn, it's cold."

"You did exactly the right thing. In several days his wounds would have changed."

"They say all of December's going to be like this. Cold as hell and a lot of snow." He stared down at the pavement. "You have kids?"

"I have a niece," I said.

"I've got two boys. One of 'em's thirteen."

I got out my keys. "I'm over here," I said.

Trent nodded, following me. He watched in silence as I unlocked my gray Mercedes. His eyes took in the details of the leather interior as I got in and fastened my seat belt. He looked the car up and down as if appraising a gorgeous woman.

"What about the missing skin?" he asked. "You ever seen anything like that?"

"It's possible we're dealing with someone predisposed to cannibalism," I said.

I returned to the office and checked my mailbox, initialed a stack of lab reports, filled a mug with the liquid tar left in the bottom of the coffeepot, and spoke to no one. Rose appeared so quietly as I seated myself behind my desk that I would not have noticed her immediately had she not placed a newspaper clipping on top of several others centering the blotter.

"You look tired," she said. "What time did you come in this morning? I got here and found coffee made and you had already gone out somewhere."

"Henrico's got a tough one," I said. "A boy who probably will be coming in."

"Eddie Heath."

"Yes," I said, perplexed. "How did you know?"

"He's in the paper, too," Rose replied, and I noticed that she had gotten new glasses that made her patrician face less haughty.

"I like your glasses," I said. "A big improvement over the Ben Franklin frames perched on the end of your nose. What did it say about him?"

"Not much. The article just said that he was found off Patterson and that he had been shot. If my son were still young, no way I'd let him have a paper route."

"Eddie Heath was not delivering papers when he was assaulted."

"Doesn't matter. I wouldn't permit it, not these days. Let's see." She touched a finger to the side of her nose. "Fielding's downstairs doing an autopsy and Susan's off delivering several brains to MCV for consultation. Other than that, nothing happened while you were out except the computer went down."

"Is it still down?"

"I think Margaret's working on it and is almost done," Rose said.

"Good. When it's up again, I need her to do a search for me. Codes to look for would be *cutting, mutilation, cannibalism, bite*

33

marks. Maybe a free-format search for the words *excised, skin, flesh*—a variety of combinations of them. You might try *dismemberment,* too, but I don't think that's what we're really after."

"For what part of the state and what time period?" Rose took notes.

"All of the state for the past five years. I'm particularly interested in cases involving children, but let's not restrict ourselves to that. And ask her to see what the Trauma Registry's got. I spoke with the director at a meeting last month and he seemed more than willing for us to share data."

"You mean you also want to check victims who have survived?"

"If we can, Rose. Let's check everything to see if we find any cases similar to Eddie Heath's."

"I'll tell Margaret now and see if she can get started," my secretary said on her way out.

I began going through the articles she had clipped from a number of morning newspapers. Unsurprisingly, much was being made of Ronnie Waddell's allegedly bleeding from "his eyes, nose, and mouth." The local chapter of Amnesty International was claiming that his execution was no less inhumane than any homicide. A spokesman for the ACLU stated that the electric chair "may have malfunctioned, causing Waddell to suffer terribly," and went on to compare the incident to the execution in Florida in which synthetic sponges used for the first time had resulted in the condemned man's hair catching fire.

Tucking the news stories inside Waddell's file, I tried to anticipate what pugilistic rabbits his attorney, Nicholas Grueman, would pull out of his hat this time. Our confrontations, though infrequent, had become predictable. His true agenda, I was about to believe, was to impeach my professional competence and in general make me feel stupid. But what bothered me most was that Grueman gave no indication that he remembered I had once been his student at Georgetown. To his credit, I had despised my first year of law school, had made my only B, and missed out on *Law Review. I* would never forget Nicholas Grueman as long as I lived, and it did not seem right that he should have forgotten me.

I heard from him on Thursday, not long after I had been informed that Eddie Heath was dead.

"Kay Scarpetta?" Grueman's voice came over the line.

"Yes." I closed my eyes and knew from the pressure behind them that a raging front was rapidly advancing.

"Nicholas Grueman here. I've been looking over Mr. Waddell's provisional autopsy report and have a few questions."

I said nothing.

"I'm talking about Ronnie Joe Waddell."

"What can I help you with?"

"Let's start with his so-called *almost tubular* stomach. An interesting description, by the way. I'm wondering if that's your vernacular or a bona fide medical term? Am I correct in assuming Mr. Waddell wasn't eating?"

"I can't say that he wasn't eating at all. But his stomach had shrunk. It was empty and clean."

"Was it, perhaps, reported to you that he may have been on a hunger strike?"

"No such thing was reported to me." I glanced up at the clock and light stabbed my eyes. I was out of aspirin and had left my decongestant at home.

I heard pages flip.

35

"It says here that you found abrasions on his arms, the inner aspects of both upper arms," Grueman said.

"That's correct."

"And just what, exactly, is an *inner aspect?*"

"The inside of the arm above the antecubital fossa."

A pause. "The *antecubital fossa,*" he said in amazement.

"Well, let me see. I've got my own arm turned palm up and am looking at the inside of my elbow. Or where the arm folds, actually. That would be accurate, wouldn't it? To say that the inner aspect is the side where the arm folds, and the antecubital fossa, therefore, is where the arm folds?"

"That would be accurate."

"Well, well, very good. And to what do you attribute these injuries to the inner aspects of Mr. Waddell's arms?"

"Possibly to restraints," I said testily.

"Restraints?"

"Yes, as in the leather restraints associated with the electric chair."

"You said *possibly.* Possibly restraints?"

"That's what I said."

"Meaning, you can't say with certainty, Dr. Scarpetta?"

"There's very little in this life that one can say with certainty, Mr. Grueman."

"Meaning that it would be reasonable to entertain the possibility that the restraints that caused the abrasions could have been of a different variety? Such as the human variety? Such as marks left by human hands?"

"The abrasions I found are inconsistent with injuries inflicted by human hands," I said.

"And are they consistent with the injuries inflicted by the electric chair, with the restraints associated with it?"

"It is my opinion that they would be."

"*Your opinion,* Dr. Scarpetta?"

"I haven't actually examined the electric chair," I said sharply.

This was followed by a long pause, for which Nicholas Grueman had been famous in the classroom when he wanted a student's obvious inadequacy to hang in the air. I envisioned him hovering over me, hands clasped behind his back, his face expressionless as the clock ticked loudly on the wall. Once I had endured his silent scrutiny for more than two minutes as my eyes raced blindly over pages of the casebook opened before me. And as I sat at my solid walnut desk some twenty years later, a middle-aged chief medical examiner with enough degrees and certificates to paper a wall, I felt my face begin to burn. I felt the old humiliation and rage.

Susan walked into my office as Grueman abruptly ended the encounter with "Good day" and hung up.

"Eddie Heath's body is here." Her surgical gown was untied in back and clean, the expression on her face distracted. "Can he wait until the morning?"

"No," I said. "He can't."

The boy looked smaller on the cold steel table than he had seemed in the bright sheets of his hospital bed. There were no rainbows in this room, no walls or windows decorated with dinosaurs or color to cheer the heart of a child. Eddie Heath had come in naked with IV needles, catheter, and dressings still in place. They seemed sad remnants of what had held him to this world and then disconnected him from it, like string tailing a balloon blowing forlornly through empty air. For the better part of an hour I documented injuries and marks of therapy while Susan took photographs and answered the phone.

We had locked the doors leading into the autopsy suite, and beyond I could hear people getting off the elevator and heading home in the rapidly descending dark. Twice the buzzer sounded in the bay as funeral home attendants arrived to bring a body or take one away. The wounds to Eddie's shoulder and thigh were dry and a dark shiny red.

"God," Susan said, staring. "God, who would do something like that? Look at all the little cuts to the edges, too. It's like somebody cut crisscrosses and then removed the whole area of skin."

"That's precisely what I think was done."

"You think someone carved some sort of pattern?"

"I think someone attempted to eradicate something. And when that didn't work, he removed the skin."

"Eradicate what?"

"Nothing that was already there," I said. "He had no tattoos, birthmarks, or scars in those areas. If something wasn't already there, then perhaps something was added and had to be removed because of the potential evidentiary value."

"Something like bite marks."

"Yes," I said.

The body was not yet fully rigorous and was still slightly warm as I began swabbing any area that a washcloth might have missed. I checked axillas, gluteal folds, behind ears and inside them, and inside the navel. I clipped fingernails into clean white envelopes and looked for fibers and other debris in hair.

Susan continued to glance at me, and I sensed her tension. Finally she asked, "Anything special you're looking for?"

"Dried seminal fluid, for one thing," I said.

"In his axilla?"

"There, in any crease in skin, any orifice, anywhere."

"You don't usually look in all those places."

"I don't usually look for zebras."

"For what?"

"We used to have a saying in medical school. If you hear hoofbeats, look for horses. But in a case like this I know we're looking for zebras," I said.

I began going over every inch of the body with a lens. When I got to his wrists, I slowly turned his hands this way and that, studying them for such a long time that Susan stopped what she was doing. I referred to the diagrams on my clipboard, correlating each mark of therapy with the ones I had drawn.

"Where are his charts?" I glanced around.

"Over here." Susan fetched paperwork from a countertop. I began flipping through charts, concentrating particularly on emergency room records and the report filled in by the rescue squad. Nowhere did it indicate that Eddie Heath's hands had been bound. I tried to remember what Detective Trent had said to me when describing the scene where the boy's body had been found. Hadn't Trent said that Eddie's hands were by his sides?

"You find something?" Susan finally asked.

"You have to look through the lens to see. There. The

undersides of his wrists and here on the left one, to the left of the wrist bone. You see the gummy residue? The traces of adhesive? It looks like smudges of grayish dirt."

"Just barely. And maybe some fibers sticking to it," Susan marveled, her shoulder pressed against mine as she stared through the lens.

"And the skin's smooth," I continued to point out. "Less hair in this area than here and here."

"Because when the tape was removed, hairs would have been pulled out."

"Exactly. We'll take wrist hairs for exemplars. The adhesive and fibers can be matched back to the tape, if the tape is ever recovered. And if the tape that bound him is recovered, it can be matched back to the roll."

"I don't understand." She straightened up and looked at me. "His IV lines were held in place with adhesive tape. You sure that's not the explanation?"

"There are no needle marks on these areas of his wrists that would indicate marks of therapy," I said to her. "And you saw what was taped to him when he came in. Nothing to account for the adhesive here."

"True."

"Let's take photographs and then I'm going to collect this adhesive residue and let Trace see what they find."

"His body was outside next to a Dumpster. Seems like that would be a Trace nightmare."

"It depends on whether this residue on his wrists was in contact with the pavement." I began gently scraping the residue off with a scalpel.

"I don't guess they did a vacuuming out there."

"No, I'm sure they wouldn't have. But I think we can still get sweepings if we ask nicely. It can't hurt to try."

I continued examining Eddie Heath's thin forearms and wrists, looking for contusions or abrasions I might have missed. But I did not find any.

"His ankles look okay," Susan said from the far end of the table. "I don't see any adhesive or areas where the hair is gone. No injuries. It doesn't look like he was taped around his ankles. Just his wrists."

I could recall only a few cases in which a victim's tight bindings had left no mark on skin. Clearly, the strapping tape had been in direct contact with Eddie's skin. He should have moved his hands, wriggled as his discomfort had grown and his circulation had been restricted. But he had not resisted. He had not tugged or squirmed or tried to get away.

I thought of the blood drips on the shoulder of his jacket and the soot and stippling on the collar. I again checked around his mouth, looked at his tongue, and glanced over his charts. If he had been gagged, there was no evidence of it now, no abrasions or bruises, no traces of adhesive. I imagined him propped against the Dumpster, naked and in the bitter cold, his clothing piled by his side, not neatly, not sloppily, but casually from the way it had been described to me. When I tried to sense the emotion of the crime, I did not detect anger, panic, or fear.

"He shot him first, didn't he?" Susan's eyes were alert like those of a wary stranger you pass on a desolate, dark street. "Whoever did this taped his wrists together after he shot him."

41

"I'm thinking that."

"But that's so weird," she said. "You don't need to bind someone you've just shot in the head."

"We don't know what this individual fantasizes about." The sinus headache had arrived and I had fallen like a city under siege. My eyes were watering; my skull was two sizes too small.

Susan pulled the thick electrical cord down from its reel and plugged in the Stryker saw. She snapped new blades in scalpels and checked the knives on the surgical cart. She disappeared into the X-ray room and returned with Eddie's films, which she fixed to light boxes. She scurried about frenetically and then did something she had never done before. She bumped hard against the surgical cart she had been arranging and sent two quart jars of formalin crashing to the floor.

I ran to her as she jumped back, gasping, waving fumes from her face and sending broken glass skittering across the floor as her feet almost went out from under her.

"Did it get your face?" I grabbed her arm and hurried her toward the locker room.

"I don't think so. No. Oh, God. It's on my feet and legs. I think on my arm, too."

"You're sure it's not in your eyes or mouth?" I helped her strip off her greens.

"I'm sure."

I ducked inside the shower and turned on the water as she practically tore off the rest of her clothes.

I made her stand beneath a blast of tepid water for a very long time as I donned mask, safety glasses, and thick rubber gloves. I soaked up the hazardous chemical with formalin pillows, supplied by the state for biochemical emergencies like this. I swept up glass and tied everything inside double plastic bags. Then I hosed down the floor, washed myself, and changed into fresh greens. Susan eventually emerged from the shower, bright pink and scared.

"Dr. Scarpetta, I'm so sorry," she said.

"My only concern is you. Are you all right?"

"I feel weak and a little dizzy. I can still smell the fumes."

"I'll finish up here," I said. "Why don't you go home."

"I think I'll just rest for a while first. Maybe I'd better go upstairs."

My lab coat was draped over the back of a chair, and I reached inside a pocket and got out my keys. "Here," I said, handing them to her. "You can lie down on the couch in my office. Get on the intercom immediately if the dizziness doesn't go away or you start feeling worse."

She reappeared about an hour later, her winter coat on and buttoned up to her chin.

"How do you feel?" I asked as I sutured the Y incision.

"A little shaky but okay."

She watched me in silence for a moment, then added, "I thought of something while I was upstairs. I don't think you should list me as a witness in this case."

I glanced up at her in surprise. It was routine for anyone present during an autopsy to be listed as a witness on the official report. Susan's request wasn't of great importance, but it was peculiar.

"I didn't participate in the autopsy," she went on. "I mean, I helped with the external exam but wasn't present when you did

43

the post. And I know this is going to be a big case—if they ever catch anyone. If it ever goes to court. And I just think it's better if I'm not listed, since, like I said, I really wasn't present."

"Fine," I said. "I have no problem with that."

She placed my keys on a counter and left.

Marino was home when I tried him from my car phone as I slowed at a tollbooth about an hour later.

"Do you know the warden at Spring Street?" I asked him.

"Frank Donahue. Where are you?"

"In my car."

"I thought so. Probably half the truckers in Virginia are listening to us on their CBs."

"They won't hear much."

"I heard about the kid," he said. "You finished with him?"

"Yes. I'll call you from home. There's something you can do for me in the meantime. I need to look over a few things at the pen right away."

"The problem with looking over the pen is it looks back."

"That's why you're going with me," I said.

If nothing else, after two miserable semesters of my former professor's tutelage I had learned to be prepared. So it was on Saturday afternoon that Marino and I were en route to the state penitentiary. Skies were leaden, wind thrashing trees along the roadsides, the universe in a state of cold agitation, as if reflecting my mood.

"You want my private opinion," Marino said to me as we drove, "I think you're letting Grueman jerk you around."

"Not at all."

"Then why is it every time there's an execution and he's involved, you act jerked around?"

"And how would you handle the situation?"

He pushed in the cigarette lighter. "Same way you are. I'd take a damn look at death row and the chair, document everything, and then tell him he's full of shit. Or better yet, tell the press he's full of shit."

In this morning's paper Grueman was quoted as saying that Waddell had not been receiving proper nourishment and his body bore bruises I could not adequately explain.

"What's the deal, anyway?" Marino went on. "Was he defending these squirrels when you was in law school?"

"No. Several years ago he was asked to run Georgetown's Criminal Justice Clinic. That's when he began taking on death penalty cases pro bono."

"The guy must have a screw loose."

"He's very opposed to capital punishment and has managed to turn whoever he represents into a cause célèbre. Waddell in particular."

"Yo. Saint Nick, the patron saint of dirtbags. Ain't that sweet," Marino said. "Why don't you send him color photos of Eddie Heath and ask if he wants to talk to the boy's family? See how he feels about the pig who committed *that* crime."

"Nothing will change Grueman's opinions."

"He got kids? A wife? Anybody he cares about?"

45

"It doesn't make any difference, Marino. I don't guess you've got anything new on Eddie."

"No, and neither does Henrico. We've got his clothes and a twenty-two bullet. Maybe the labs will get lucky with the stuff you turned in."

"What about VICAP?" I asked, referring to the FBI's Violent Criminal Apprehension Program, in which Marino and FBI profiler Benton Wesley were regional team partners.

"Trent's working on the forms and will send them off in a couple days," Marino said. "And I alerted Benton about the case last night."

"Was Eddie the type to get into a stranger's car?"

"According to his parents, he wasn't. We're either dealing with a blitz attack or someone who earned the kid's confidence long enough to grab him."

"Does he have brothers and sisters?"

"One of each, both more than ten years older than him. I think Eddie was an accident," Marino said as the penitentiary came into view.

Years of neglect had faded its stucco veneer to a dirty, diluted shade of Pepto Bismol pink. Windows were dark and covered in thick plastic, tugged and torn by the wind. We took the Belvedere exit, then turned left on Spring Street, a shabby strip of pavement connecting two entities that did not belong on the same map. It continued several blocks past the penitentiary, then simply quit at Gambles Hill, where Ethyl Corporation's white brick headquarters roosted on a rise of perfect lawn like a great white heron at the edge of a landfill.

Drizzle had turned to sleet when we parked and got out of

the car. I followed Marino past a Dumpster, then a ramp leading to a loading dock occupied by a number of cats, their insouciance flickering with the wariness of the wild. The main entrance was a single glass door, and stepping inside what purported to be the lobby, we found ourselves behind bars. There were no chairs; the air was frigid and stale. To our right the Communication Center was accessible by a small window, which a sturdy woman in a guard's uniform took her time sliding open.

"Can I help you?"

Marino displayed his badge and laconically explained that we had an appointment with Frank Donahue, the warden. She told us to wait. The window shut again.

"That's Helen the Hun," Marino said to me. "I've been down here more times than I can count and she always acts like she don't know me. But then, I'm not her type. You'll get better acquainted with her in a minute."

Beyond barred gates were a dingy corridor of tan tile and cinder block, and small offices that looked like cages. The view ended with the first block of cells, tiers painted institutional green and spotted with rust. They were empty.

"When will the rest of the inmates be relocated?" I asked.

"By the end of the week."

"Who's left?"

"Some real Virginia gentlemen, the squirrels with segregation status. They're all locked up tight and chained to their beds in C Cell, which is that way." He pointed west. "We won't be walking through there, so don't get antsy. I wouldn't put you through that. Some of these assholes haven't seen a woman in years—and Helen the Hun don't count."

A powerfully built young man dressed in Department of Corrections blues appeared down the corridor and headed our way. He peered at us through bars, his face attractive but hard, with a strong jaw and cold gray eyes. A dark red mustache hid an upper lip that I suspected could turn cruel.

Marino introduced us, adding, "We're here to see the chair."

"Yeah, my name's Roberts and I'm here to give you the royal tour." Keys jingled against iron as he opened the heavy gates. "Donahue's out sick today." The clang of doors shutting behind us echoed off walls. "I'm afraid we got to search you first. If you'll step over there, ma'am."

He began running a scanner over Marino as another barred door opened and "Helen" emerged from the Communication Center. She was an unsmiling woman built like a Baptist church, her shiny Sam Browne belt the only indication she had a waist. Her close-cropped hair was mannishly styled and dyed shoe-polish black, her eyes intense when they briefly met mine. The name tag pinned on a formidable breast read "Grimes."

"Your bag," she ordered.

I handed over my medical bag. She rifled through it, then roughly turned me this way and that as she subjected me to a salvo of probes and pats with the scanner and her hands. In all, the search couldn't have lasted more than twenty seconds, but she managed to acquaint herself with every inch of my flesh, crushing me against her stiffly armored bosom like a wide-bodied spider as thick fingers lingered and she breathed loudly through her mouth. Then she brusquely nodded that I checked out okay as she returned to her lair of cinder block and iron.

Marino and I followed Roberts past bars and more bars,

through a series of doors that he unlocked and relocked, the air cold and ringing with the dull chimes of unfriendly metal. He asked us nothing about ourselves and made no references that I would call remotely friendly. His preoccupation seemed to be his role, which this afternoon was tour guide or guard dog, I wasn't sure which.

A right turn and we entered the first cell block, a huge drafty space of green cinder block and broken windows, with four tiers of cells rising to a false roof topped by coils of barbed wire. Sloppily piled along the middle of the brown tile floor were dozens of narrow, plastic-covered mattresses, and scattered about were brooms, mops, and ratty red barber chairs. Leather tennis shoes, blue jeans, and other odd personal effects littered high windowsills, and left inside many of the cells were televisions, books, and footlockers. It appeared that when the inmates had been evacuated they had not been allowed to take all of their possessions with them, perhaps explaining the obscenities scrawled in Magic Marker on the walls.

More doors were unlocked, and we found ourselves outside in the yard, a square of browning grass surrounded by ugly cell blocks. There were no trees. Guard towers rose from each corner of the wall, the men inside wearing heavy coats and holding rifles. We moved quickly and in silence as sleet stung our cheeks. Down several steps, we turned into another opening leading to an iron door more massive than any of the others I had seen.

"The east basement," Roberts said, inserting a key in the lock. "This is the place where no one wants to be."

We stepped inside death row.

Against the east wall were five cells, each furnished with an iron bed and a white porcelain sink and toilet. In the center of the room were a large desk and several chairs where guards sat around the clock when death row was occupied.

"Waddell was in cell two." Roberts pointed. "According to the laws of the Commonwealth, an inmate must be transferred here fifteen days prior to his execution."

"Who had access to him while he was here?" Marino asked.

"Same people who always have access to death row. Legal representatives, the clergy, and members of the death team."

"The death team?" I asked.

"It's made up of Corrections officers and supervisors, the identities of which are confidential. The team becomes involved when an inmate is shipped here from Mecklenburg. They guard him, set up everything from beginning to end."

"Don't sound like a very pleasant assignment," Marino commented.

"It's not an assignment, it's a choice," Roberts replied with the machismo and inscrutability of coaches interviewed after the big game.

"It don't bother you?" Marino asked. "I mean, come on, I saw Waddell go to the chair. It's got to bother you."

"Doesn't bother me in the least. I go home afterward, drink a few beers, go to bed." He reached in the breast pocket of his uniform shirt and pulled out a pack of cigarettes.

"Now, according to Donahue, you want to know everything that happened. So I'm going to walk you through it." He sat on top of the desk, smoking. "On the day of it, December thirteenth, Waddell was allowed a two-hour contact visit with members of his immediate family, which in this case was his mother. We put him in waist chains, leg irons, and cuffs and led him over to the visitors' side around one P.M.

"At five P.M., he ate his last meal. His request was sirloin steak, salad, a baked potato, and pecan pie, which we had prepared for him at Bonanza Steak House. He didn't pick the restaurant. The inmates don't get to do that. And, as is the routine, there were two identical meals ordered. The inmate eats one, a member of the death team eats the other. And this is all to make sure some overly enthusiastic chef doesn't decide to speed up the inmate's journey to the Great Beyond by spicing the food with something extra like arsenic."

"Did Waddell eat his meal?" I asked, thinking about his empty stomach.

"He wasn't real hungry—asked us to save it for him to eat the next day."

"He must have thought Governor Norring was going to pardon him," Marino said.

"I don't know what he thought. I'm just reporting to you what Waddell said when he was served his meal. Afterward, at seven-thirty, personal property officers came to his cell to take an inventory of his property and ask him what he wanted done with it. We're talking about one wristwatch, one ring, various articles of clothing and mail, books, poetry. At eight P.M., he was taken from his cell. His head, face, and right ankle were shaved. He was weighed, showered, and dressed in the clothing he would wear to the chair. Then he was returned to his cell.

"At ten-forty-five, his death warrant was read to him,

witnessed by the death team." Roberts got up from the desk. "Then he was led, without restraints, to the adjoining room."

"What was his demeanor at this point?" Marino asked as Roberts unlocked another door and opened it.

"Let's just say that his racial affiliation did not permit him to be white as a sheet. Otherwise, he would've been."

The room was smaller than I had imagined. About six feet from the back wall and centered on the shiny brown cement floor was the chair, a stark, rigid throne of dark polished oak. Thick leather straps were looped around the high slatted back, the two front legs, and the armrests.

"Waddell was seated and the first strap fastened was the chest strap," Roberts continued in the same indifferent tone. "Then the two arm straps, the belly strap, and the straps for the legs." He roughly plucked at each strap as he talked. "It took one minute to strap him in. His face was covered with the leather mask—and I'll show you that in a minute. The helmet was placed on his head, the leg piece attached to his right leg."

I got out my camera, a ruler, and photocopies of Waddell's body diagrams.

"At exactly two minutes past eleven, he received the first current—that's twenty-five hundred volts and six and a half amps. Two amps will kill you, by the way."

The injuries marked on Waddell's body diagrams correlated nicely with the construction of the chair and its restraints.

"The helmet attaches to this." Roberts pointed out a pipe running from the ceiling and ending with a copper wing nut directly over the chair.

I began taking photographs of the chair from every angle.

"And the leg piece attaches to this wing nut here."

The flashbulb going off gave me a strange sensation. I was getting jumpy.

"All this man was, was one big circuit breaker."

"When did he start to bleed?" I asked.

"The minute he was hit the first time, ma'am. And he didn't stop until it was completely over, then a curtain was drawn, blocking him from the view of the witnesses. Three members of the death team undid his shirt and the doc listened with his stethoscope and felt the carotid and pronounced him. Waddell was placed on a gurney and taken into the cooling room, which is where we're headed next."

"Your theory about the chair allegedly malfunctioning?" I said.

"Pure crap. Waddell was six-foot-four, weighed two hundred and fifty-nine pounds. He was cooking long before he sat in the chair, his blood pressure probably out of sight. After he was pronounced, because of the bleeding, the deputy director came over to take a look at him. His eyeballs hadn't popped out. His eardrums hadn't popped out. Waddell had a damn nosebleed, same thing people get when they strain too hard on the toilet."

I silently agreed with him. Waddell's nosebleed was due to the Valsalva maneuver, or an abrupt increase in intrathoracic pressure. Nicholas Grueman would not be pleased with the report I planned to send him.

"What tests had you run to make sure the chair was operating properly?" Marino asked.

"Same ones we always do. First, Virginia Power looks at the equipment and checks it out." He pointed to a large circuit box enclosed in gray steel doors in the wall behind the chair. "Inside this is twenty two-hundred-watt light bulbs attached to ply-board for running tests. We test this during the week before the execution, three times the day of it, and then once more in front of the witnesses after they've assembled."

"Yeah, I remember that," Marino said, staring at the glass-enclosed witness booth no more than fifteen feet away. Inside were twelve black plastic chairs arranged in three neat rows.

"Everything worked like a charm," Roberts said.

"Has it always?" I asked.

"To my knowledge, yes, ma'am."

"And the switch, where is that?"

He directed my attention to a box on the wall to the right of the witness booth. "A key cuts the power on. But the button's in the control room. The warden or a designee turns the key and pushes the button. You want to see that?"

"I think I'd better."

It wasn't much to look at, just a small cubicle directly behind the back wall of the room housing the chair. Inside was a large G.E. box with various dials to raise and lower the voltage, which went as high as three thousand volts. Rows of small lights affirmed that everything was fine or warned that things were not.

"At Greensville, it will all be computerized," Roberts added.

Inside a wooden cupboard were the helmet, leg piece, and two thick cables, which, he explained as he held them up, "attach to the wing nuts above and to one side of the chair, and then to this wing nut on top of the helmet and the one here on the leg piece." He did this without effort, adding, "Just like hooking up a VCR."

The helmet and leg piece were copper riddled with holes, through which cotton string was woven to secure the sponge lining inside. The helmet was surprisingly light, a patina of green tarnish at the edges of the connecting plates. I could not imagine having such a thing placed on top of my head. The black leather mask was nothing more than a wide, crude belt that buckled behind the inmate's head, a small triangle cut in it for the nose. It could have been on display in the Tower of London and I would not have questioned its authenticity.

We passed a transformer with coils leading to the ceiling, and Roberts unlocked another door. We stepped inside another room.

"This is the cooling room," he said. "We wheeled Waddell in here and transferred him to this table."

It was steel, rust showing at the joints.

"We let him cool down for ten minutes, put sandbags on his leg. That's them right there."

The sandbags were stacked on the floor at the foot of the table.

"Ten pounds each. Call it a knee-jerk reaction, but the leg's severely bent. The sandbags straighten it out. And if the burns are bad, like Waddell's were, we dress them with gauze. All done, and we put Waddell back on the stretcher and carried him out the same way you came in. Only we didn't bother with the stairs. No point in anybody getting a hernia. We used the food elevator and carried him out the front door, and loaded him in the ambulance. Then we hauled him into your place, just like we always do after our children ride the Sparky."

Heavy doors slammed. Keys jangled. Locks clicked. Roberts continued talking boisterously as he led us back to the lobby. I barely listened and Marino did not say a word. Sleet mixed with rain beaded grass and walls with ice. The sidewalk was wet, the cold penetrating. I felt queasy. I was desperate to take a long, hot shower and change my clothes.

"Lowlifes like Roberts are just one level above the inmates," Marino said as he started the car. "In fact, some of them aren't any better than the drones they lock up."

Moments later he stopped at a red light. Drops of water on the windshield shimmered like blood, were wiped away and replaced by a thousand more. Ice coated trees like glass.

"You got time for me to show you something?" Marino wiped condensation off the windshield with his coat sleeve.

"Depending on how important it is, I suppose I could make time." I hoped my obvious reluctance would inspire him to take me home instead.

"I want to retrace Eddie Heath's last steps for you." He flipped on the turn signal. "In particular, I think you need to see where his body was found."

The Heaths lived east of Chamberlayne Avenue, or on the wrong side of it, in Marino's words. Their small brick house was but several blocks from a Golden Skillet fried chicken restaurant and the convenience store where Eddie had walked to buy his mother a can of soup. Several cars, large and American, were parked in the Heaths' driveway, and smoke drifted out the chimney and disappeared in the smoky gray sky.

Aluminum glinted dully as the front screen door opened and an old woman bundled in a black coat emerged, then paused to speak to someone inside. Clinging to the railing as if the afternoon threatened to pitch her overboard, she made her way down the steps, glancing blankly at the white Ford LTD cruising past.

Had we continued east for another two miles, we would have entered the war zone of the federal housing projects.

"This neighborhood used to be all white," Marino said. "I remember when I first came to Richmond this was a good area to live. Lots of decent, hardworking folks who kept their yards real nice and went to church on Sunday. Times change. Me, I wouldn't let any kid of mine walk around out here after dark. But when you live in a place, you get comfortable. Eddie was comfortable walking around, delivering his papers, and running errands for his mother.

"The night it happened he came out the front door of his crib, cut through to Azalea, then took a right like we're doing as I speak. There's Lucky's on our left, next to the gas station." He pointed out a convenience store with a green horseshoe on the lighted sign. "That corner right over there is a popular hangout for drug drones. They trade crack for cash and fade. We catch the cockroaches, and two days later they're on another corner doing the same thing."

"A possibility Eddie was involved in drugs?" My question would have been somewhat farfetched back in the days when I began my career, but no longer. Juveniles now comprised approximately ten percent of all narcotics trafficking arrests in Virginia.

"No indication of it so far. My gut tells me he wasn't," Marino said.

He pulled into the convenience store's parking lot, and we sat gazing out at advertisements taped to plate glass and lights shining garishly through fog. Customers formed a long line by the counter as the harried clerk worked the cash register without looking up. A young black man in high tops and a leather coat stared insolently at our car as he sauntered out with a quart of beer and dropped change in a pay phone near the front door. A man, red-faced and in paint-spattered jeans, peeled cellophane off a pack of cigarettes as he trotted to his truck.

"I'm betting this is where he met up with his assailant," Marino said.

"How?" I said.

"I think it went down simple as hell. I think he came out of the store and this animal came right up to him and fed him a line to gain his confidence. He said something and Eddie went with him and got in the car."

"His physical findings would certainly support that," I said. "He had no defense injuries, nothing to indicate a struggle. No one inside the convenience store saw him with anyone?"

"No one I've talked to so far. But you see how busy this joint is, and it was dark out. If anybody saw anything, it was probably a customer coming in or returning to his car. I plan to get the media to run something so we can appeal to anyone who might have stopped here between five and six that night. And Crime Stoppers is going to do a segment on it, too."

"Was Eddie streetwise?"

"You get a squirrel who's smooth and even kids who know better can fall for it. I had a case back in New York where a ten-year-old girl walked to the local store to buy a pound of sugar. As she's leaving, this pedophile approaches her and says her father's sent him. He says her mom's just been rushed to the hospital and he's supposed to pick the girl up and take her there. She gets in his car and ends up a statistic." He glanced over at me. "All right, white or black?"

"In which case?"

"Eddie Heath's."

"Based on what you've said, the assailant is white."

Marino backed up and waited for a break in traffic. "No question the MO fits for white. Eddie's old man don't like blacks and Eddie didn't trust them, either, so it's unlikely a black guy gained Eddie's confidence. And if people notice a white boy walking with a white man—even if the boy looks unhappy—they think big brother and little brother or father and son." He turned right, heading west. "Keep going, Doc. What else?"

Marino loved this game. It gave him just as much pleasure when I echoed his thoughts as it did when he believed I was flat-out wrong.

"If the assailant is white, then the next conclusion I'd make is he's not from the projects, despite their close proximity."

"Race aside, why else might you conclude that the perp's not from the projects?"

"The MO again," I said simply. "Shooting someone in the head—even a thirteen-year-old—would not be unheard of in a street killing, but aside from that, nothing fits. Eddie was shot with a twenty-two, not with a nine- or ten-millimeter or large-caliber revolver. He was nude and he was mutilated, suggesting the violence was sexually motivated. As far as we know, he had nothing worth stealing and did not appear to have a life-style that put him at risk."

It was raining hard now, and streets were treacherous with cars moving at imprudent rates of speed with their headlights on. I supposed many people were headed to shopping malls, and it occurred to me that I had done little to prepare for Christmas.

The grocery store on Patterson Avenue was just ahead on our left. I could not remember its former name, and signs had been removed, leaving nothing but a bare brick shell with a number of windows boarded up. The space it occupied was poorly lit, and I suspected the police would not have bothered to check behind the building at all were there not a row of businesses to the left of it. I counted five of them: pharmacy, shoe repair, dry cleaner, hardware store, and Italian restaurant, all closed and deserted the night Eddie Heath was driven here and left for dead.

"Do you recall when this grocery store went out of business?" I asked.

"About the same time a bunch of other places did. When the war started in the Persian Gulf," Marino said.

He cut through an alleyway, the high beams of his head-lights licking brick walls and rocking when the unpaved ground got rough. Behind the store a chain-link fence separated an apron of cracked asphalt from a wooded area stirring darkly in the wind. Through the limbs of bare trees I could see streetlights in the distance and the illuminated sign for a Burger King.

Marino parked, headlights boring into a brown Dumpster cancerous with blistered paint and rust, beads of water running down its sides. Raindrops smacked against glass and drummed the roof, and dispatchers were busy dispatching cars to the scenes of accidents.

Marino pushed his hands against the steering wheel and hunched his shoulders. He massaged the back of his neck. "Christ, I'm getting old," he complained. "I got a rain slicker in the trunk."

"You need it more than I do. I won't melt," I said, opening my door.

Marino fetched his navy blue police raincoat and I turned my collar up to my ears. The rain stung my face and coldly tapped the top of my head. Almost instantly, my ears started getting numb. The Dumpster was near the fence, at the outer limits of the pavement, perhaps twenty yards from the back of the grocery store. I noted that the Dumpster opened from the top, not the side.

"Was the door to the Dumpster open or shut when the police got here?" I asked Marino.

"Shut." The hood of his raincoat made it difficult for him to look at me without turning his upper body. "You notice there's nothing to step up on." He shone a flashlight around the Dumpster. "Also, it was empty. Not a damn thing in it except rust and the carcass of a rat big enough to saddle up and ride."

"Can you lift the door?"

"Only a couple inches. Most of the ones made like this have

a latch on either side. If you're tall enough, you can lift the lid a couple inches and slide your hand down along the edge, continuing to raise the lid by bumping the latches in place a little at a time. Eventually you can get it open far enough to stuff a bag of trash inside. Problem is, the latches on this one don't catch. You'd have to open the lid all the way and let it flop over on the other side, and no way you're going to do that unless you climb up on something."

"You're what? Six-one or -two?"

"Yeah. If I can't open the Dumpster, he couldn't either. The favorite theory at the moment is he carried the body out of the car and leaned it up against the Dumpster while he tried to open the door—the same way you put a bag of garbage down for a minute to free your hands. When he can't get the door open, he hauls ass, leaving the kid and his crap right here on the pavement."

"He could have dragged him back there in the woods."

"There's a fence."

"It's not very high, maybe five feet high," I pointed out. "At the very least, he could have left the body *behind* the Dumpster. As it was, if you drove back here, the body was in plain sight."

Marino looked around in silence, shining the flashlight through the chain-link fence. Raindrops streaked through the narrow beam like a million small nails driven down from heaven. I could barely bend my fingers. My hair was soaked and icy water was trickling down my neck. We returned to the car and he switched the heater up high.

"Trent and his guys are all hung up on the Dumpster theory, the location of its door and so on," he said. "My personal opinion is the Dumpster's only role in this is it was a damn easel for the squirrel to prop his work of art against."

I looked out through the rain.

"The point is," he went on in a hard voice, "he didn't bring the kid back here to conceal the body but to make sure it was found. But the guys with Henrico just don't see it. I not only see it, I feel it like something breathing down the back of my neck."

I continued staring out at the Dumpster, the image of Eddie Heath's small body propped against it so vivid it was as if I had been present when he was found. The realization struck me suddenly and hard.

"When was the last time you went through the Robyn Naismith case?" I asked.

"It doesn't matter. I remember everything about it," Marino said, staring straight ahead. "I was waiting to see if it would cross your mind. It hit me the first time I came out here."

3

That night I built a fire and ate vegetable soup in front of it as freezing rain mixed with snow. I had switched off lamps and drawn draperies back from the sliding glass doors. Grass was frosted white, rhododendron leaves curled tight, winter-bare trees backlit by the moon.

The day had drained me, as if a greedy, dark force had sucked the light right out of my being. I felt the invasive hands of a prison guard named Helen, and smelled the stale stench of hovels that once had housed remorseless, hateful men. I remembered holding slides up to lamplight in a hotel bar in New Orleans at the American Academy of Forensic Sciences' annual meeting. Robyn Naismith's homicide was then unsolved, and to discuss what had been done to her as Mardi Gras revelers loudly drifted past had somehow seemed ghastly.

She had been beaten and bullied, and stabbed to death, it was believed, in her living room. But it was Waddell's postmortem acts that had shocked people most, his uncommon and creepy ritual. After she was dead, he undressed her. If he raped her, there was no evidence of it. His preference, it seemed, was to bite and repeatedly penetrate the fleshier parts of her body with a knife. When her friend from work stopped by to check on her, she found Robyn's battered body propped against the television, head drooping forward, arms by her sides, legs straight out, and clothing piled nearby. She looked like a bloody, life-size doll returned to its place after a session of make-believe and play that had turned into a horror.

The court testimony of a psychiatrist was that after Waddell had murdered her, he was overcome by remorse and had sat talking to her body for perhaps hours. A forensic psychologist for the Commonwealth speculated quite the opposite, that Waddell knew Robyn was a television personality and his act of propping her body against the television set was symbolic. He was watching her on TV again and fantasizing. He was returning her to the medium that had brought about their introduction, and this, of course, implied premeditation. The nuances and twists in the endless analyses got only more complicated with time.

The grotesque display of that twenty-seven-year-old anchorwoman's body was Waddell's special signature. Now a little boy was dead ten years later and someone had signed his work—on the eve of Waddell's execution—the same way.

I made coffee, poured it into a thermos, and carried it into my study. Sitting at my desk, I booted up my computer and dialed into the one downtown. I had yet to see the printout of the search Margaret had conducted for me, though I suspected it was one of the reports in the depressingly large stack of paperwork that had been in my box late Friday afternoon. The output file, however, would still be on the hard disk. At the UNIX log-in I typed my user name and password and was greeted by the flashing word *mail*. Margaret, my computer analyst, had sent me a message.

"Check flesh file," it read.

"That's really awful," I muttered, as if Margaret could hear.

Changing to the directory called Chief, where Margaret routinely directed output and copied files I had requested, I brought up the file she had named Flesh.

It was quite large because Margaret had selected from all manners of death and then merged the data with what she had generated from the Trauma Registry. Unsurprisingly, most of the cases the computer had picked up were accidents in which limbs and tissue had been lost in vehicular crashes and misadventures with machines. Four cases were homicides in which the bodies bore bite marks. Two of those victims had been stabbed, the other two strangled. One of the victims was an adult male, two were adult females, and one was a female only six years old. I jotted down case numbers and ICD-9 codes.

Next I began scanning screen after screen of the Trauma Registry's records of victims who had survived long enough to be admitted to a hospital. I expected the information to be a problem, and it was. Hospitals released patient data only after it had been as sterilized and depersonalized as operating rooms. For purposes of confidentiality, names, Social Security numbers, and other identifiers were stripped away. There was no common link as the person traveled through the paperwork labyrinth of rescue squads, emergency rooms, various police departments, and other agencies. The sorry end of the story was that data about a victim might reside in six different agency data bases and never be matched, especially if there had been any entry errors along the way. It was possible, therefore, for me to discover a case that aroused my interest without having much hope of figuring out who the patient was or if he or she had eventually died.

Making a note of Trauma Registry records that might prove interesting, I exited the file. Finally, I ran a list command to see what old data reports, memos, or notes in my directory I could remove to free up space on the hard disk. That was when I spotted a file I did not understand.

The name of it was tty07. It was only sixteen bytes in size and the date and time were December 16, this past Thursday, at 4:26 in the afternoon. The file's contents was one alarming sentence:

I can't find it.

Reaching for the phone, I started to call Margaret at home and then stopped. The directory Chief and its files were secure. Though anyone could change to my directory, unless he logged in with my user name and password, he should not be able to list the files in Chief or read them. Margaret should be the only person besides me who knew my password. If she had gone into my directory, what was it she could not find and who was she saying this to?

Margaret wouldn't, I thought, staring intensely at that one brief sentence on the screen.

Yet I was unsure, and I thought of my niece. Perhaps Lucy knew UNIX. I glanced at my watch. It was past eight on a Saturday night and in a way I was going to be heartbroken if I found Lucy at home. She should be out on a date or with friends. She wasn't.

"Hi, Aunt Kay." She sounded surprised, reminding me that I had not called in a while.

"How's my favorite niece?"

"I'm your only niece. I'm fine."

"What are you doing at home on a Saturday night?" I asked.

"Finishing a term paper. What are you doing at home on a Saturday night?"

For an instant, I did not know what to say. My seventeen-year-old niece was more adept at putting me in my place than anyone I knew.

"I'm mulling over a computer problem," I finally said.

"Then you've certainly called the right department," said Lucy, who was not given to fits of modesty. "Hold on. Let me move these books and stuff out of the way so I can get to my keyboard."

"It's not a PC problem," I said. "I don't guess you know anything about the operating system called UNIX, do you?"

"I wouldn't call UNIX an operating system, Aunt Kay. It's like calling it the weather when it's really the environment, which is comprised of the weather and all the elements and the edifices. Are you using A-T an' T?"

"Good God, Lucy. I don't know."

"Well, what are you running it on?"

"An NCR mini."

"Then it's A-T an' T."

"I think someone might have broken security," I said.

"It happens. But what makes you think it?"

"I found a strange file in my directory, Lucy. My directory and its files are secure—you shouldn't be able to read anything unless you have my password."

"Wrong. If you have root privileges, you're the superuser and can do anything you want and read anything you want."

"My computer analyst is the only superuser."

"That may be true. But there may be a number of users who have root privileges, users you don't even know about that came with the software. We can check that easily, but first tell me about the strange file. What's it called and what's in it?"

"It's called t-t-y-oh-seven and there's a sentence in it that reads: 'I can't find it.'"

I heard keys clicking.

"What are you doing?" I asked.

"Making notes as we talk. Okay. Let's start with the obvious. A big clue is the file's name, t-t-y-oh-seven. That's a device. In other words, t-t-y-oh-seven is probably somebody's terminal in your office. It's possible it could be a printer, but my guess is that whoever was in your directory decided to send a note to the device called t-t-y-oh-seven. But this person screwed up and instead of sending a note, he created a file."

"When you write a note, aren't you creating a file?" I puzzled.

"Not if you're just sending keystrokes."

"How?"

"Easy. Are you in UNIX now?"

"Yes."

"Type cat redirect t-t-y-q—"

"Wait a minute."

"And don't worry about the slash-dev—"

"Lucy, slow down."

"We're deliberately leaving out the dev directory, which is what I'm betting this person did."

"What comes after cat?"

"Okay. Cat redirect and the device—"

"Please slow down."

"You should have a four-eighty-six chip in that thing, Aunt Kay. Why's it so slow?"

"It's not the damn chip that's slow!"

"Oh, I'm sorry," Lucy said sincerely. "I forgot."

Forgot what?

"Back to the problem," she went on. "I'm assuming you don't have a device called t-t-y-q, by the way. Where are you?"

"I'm still on cat," I said, frustrated. "Then it's redirect . . . Damn. That's the caret pointing right?"

"Yes. Now hit return and your cursor will be bumped down to the next line, which is blank. Then you type the message you want echoed to t-t-y-q's screen."

"See Spot run," I typed.

"Hit return and then do a control C," Lucy said. "Now you can do an ls minus one and pipe it to p-g and you'll see your file."

I simply typed "ls" and caught a flash of something flying by.

"Here's what I think happened," Lucy resumed. "Someone was in your directory—and we'll get to that in a minute. Maybe they were looking for something in your files and couldn't find whatever it was. So this person sent a message, or tried to, to the device called t-t-y-oh-seven. Only he was in a hurry, and instead of typing cat redirect slash d-e-v slash t-t-y-oh-seven, he left out the dev directory and typed cat redirect t-t-y-oh-seven. So the keystrokes weren't echoed on t-t-y-oh-seven's screen at all. In other words, instead of sending a message to t-t-y-oh-seven, this person unwittingly created a file called t-t-y-oh-seven."

"If the person had typed in the proper command and sent the keystrokes, would the message have been saved?" I asked.

"No. The keystrokes would have appeared on t-t-y-oh-seven's screen, and would have stayed there until the user cleared it. But you would have seen no evidence of this in your directory or anywhere else. There wouldn't be a file."

"Meaning, we don't know how many times somebody might have sent a message from my directory, saying it was done correctly."

"That's right."

"How could someone have been able to read anything in my directory?" I went back to that basic question.

"You're sure no one else might have your password?"

"No one but Margaret."

"She's your computer analyst?"

"That's right."

"She wouldn't have given it to anyone?"

"I can't imagine that she would," I said.

"Okay. You could get in without the password if you have root privileges," Lucy said. "That's the next thing we'll check. Change to the etc directory and vi the file called Group and look for root group—that's r-o-o-t-g-r-p. See which users are listed after it."

I began to type.

"What do you see?"

"I'm not there yet," I said, unable to keep the impatience out of my voice.

She repeated her instructions slowly.

"I see three log-in names in the root group," I said.

"Good. Write them down. Then colon, q, bang, and you're out of Group."

"Bang?" I asked, mystified.

"An exclamation point. Now you've got to vi the password file—that's p-a-s-s-w-d—and see if any of those log-ins with root privileges maybe don't have a password."

"Lucy." I took my hands off the keyboard.

"It's easy to tell because in the second field you'll see the encrypted form of the user's password, if he has a password. If there's nothing in the second field except two colons, then he's got no password."

"Lucy."

"I'm sorry, Aunt Kay. Am I going too fast again?"

"I'm not a UNIX programmer. You might as well be speaking Swahili."

"You could learn. UNIX is really fun."

"Thank you, but my problem is I don't have time to learn right now. Someone broke into my directory. I keep very confidential documents and data reports in there. Not to mention, if someone is reading my private files, what else is he looking at and who is doing it and why?"

"The who part is easy unless the violator is dialing in by modem from the outside."

"But the note was sent to someone in my office—to a device in my office."

"That doesn't mean that an insider didn't get someone from the outside to break in, Aunt Kay. Maybe the person snooping doesn't know anything about UNIX and needed help to break into your directory, so they got a programmer from the outside."

"This is serious," I said.

"It could be. If nothing else, it sounds to me like your system isn't very secure."

"When's your term paper due?" I asked.

"After the holidays."

"Are you finished?"

"Almost."

"When does Christmas vacation start?"

"It starts Monday."

"How would you like to come up here for a few days and help me out with this?" I asked.

"You're kidding."

"I'm very serious. But don't expect much. I generally don't bother with much in the way of decorations. A few poinsettias and candles in the windows. Now, I *will* cook."

"No tree?"

"Is that a problem?"

"I guess not. Is it snowing?"

"As a matter of fact, it is."

"I've never seen snow. Not in person."

"You'd better let me talk to your mother," I said.

Dorothy, my only sibling, was overly solicitous when she got on the phone several minutes later.

"Are you still working so hard? Kay, you work harder than anyone I've ever met. People are so impressed when I tell them we're sisters. What's the weather like in Richmond?"

"There's a good chance we'll have a white Christmas."

"How special. Lucy ought to see a white Christmas at least once in her life. I've never seen one. Well, I take that back. There was the Christmas I went skiing out west with Bradley."

I could not remember who Bradley was. My younger sister's boyfriends and husbands were an endless parade I had stopped watching years ago.

"I'd very much like Lucy to spend Christmas with me," I said. "Would that be possible?"

"You can't come to Miami?"

"No, Dorothy. Not this year. I'm in the middle of several very difficult cases and have court scheduled virtually up to Christmas Eve."

"I can't imagine a Christmas without Lucy," she said with great reluctance.

"You've had Christmas without her before. When you went skiing out west with Bradley, for example."

"True. But it was hard," she said, nonplussed. "And every

time we've spent a holiday apart, I've vowed to never do it again."

"I understand. Maybe another time," I said, sick to death of my sister's games. I knew she couldn't get Lucy out the door fast enough.

"Actually, I'm on deadline for this newest book and will be spending most of the holiday in front of my computer anyway," she reconsidered quickly. "Maybe Lucy would be better off with you. I won't be much fun. Did I tell you that I now have a Hollywood agent? He's fantastic and knows everybody who's somebody out there. He's negotiating a contract with Disney."

"That's great. I'm sure your books will make terrific movies." Dorothy wrote excellent children's books and had won several prestigious awards. She was simply a failure as a human being.

"Mother's here," my sister said. "She wants to have a word with you. Now listen, it was so good to talk to you. We just don't do it enough. Make sure Lucy eats something besides salads, and I warn you that she'll exercise until it drives you mad. I worry that she's going to start looking masculine."

Before I could say anything, my mother was on the line.

"Why can't you come down here, Katie? It's sunny and you should see the grapefruit."

"I can't do it, Mother. I'm really sorry."

"And now Lucy won't be here, either? Is that what I heard? What am I supposed to do, eat a turkey by myself?"

"Dorothy will be there."

"What? Are you kidding? She'll be with Fred. I can't stand him."

Dorothy had gotten divorced again last summer. I didn't ask who Fred was.

"I think he's Iranian or something. He'll squeeze a penny until it screams and has hair in his ears. I know he's not Catholic, and Dorothy never takes Lucy to church these days. You ask me, that child's going to hell in a hand basket."

"Mother, they can hear you."

"No they can't. I'm in the kitchen by myself staring at a sink full of dirty dishes that I just know Dorothy expects me to do while I'm here. It's just like when she comes to my house, because she hasn't done a thing about dinner and is hoping I'll cook. Does she ever offer to bring anything? Does she care that I'm an old woman and practically a cripple? Maybe you can talk some sense into Lucy."

"In what way is Lucy lacking sense?" I asked.

"She doesn't have any friends except this one girl you have to wonder about. You should see Lucy's bedroom. It looks like something out of a science fiction movie with all these computers and printers and pieces and parts. It's not normal for a teenage girl to live inside her brain all the time like that and not get out with kids her own age. I worry about her just like I used to worry about you."

"I turned out all right," I said.

"Well, you spent far too much time with science books, Katie. You saw what it did to your marriage."

"Mother, I'd like Lucy to fly here tomorrow, if possible. I'll make the reservations from my end and take care of the ticket. Make sure she packs her warmest clothes. Anything she doesn't have, such as a winter coat, we can find here."

"She could probably borrow your clothes. When was the last time you saw her? Last Christmas?"

"I guess it was that long ago."

"Well, let me tell you. She's gotten bosoms since then. And the way she dresses? And did she bother to ask her grandmother's advice before cutting off her beautiful hair? No. Why should she bother telling me that—"

"I've got to call the airlines."

"I wish you were coming here. We could all be together." Her voice was getting funny. My mother was about to cry.

"I wish I could, too," I said.

Late Sunday morning I drove to the airport along dark, wet roads running through a dazzling world of glass. Ice loosened by the sun slipped from telephone lines, roofs, and trees, shattering to the ground like crystal missiles dropped from the sky. The weather report called for another storm, and I was deeply pleased, despite the inconvenience. I wanted quiet time in front of the fire with my niece. Lucy was growing up.

It did not seem so long ago that she was born. I would never forget her wide, unblinking eyes following my every move in her mother's house, or her bewildering fits of petulance and grief when I failed her in some small way. Lucy's open adoration touched my heart as profoundly as it frightened me. She had caused me to experience a depth of feeling I had not known before.

Talking my way past Security, I waited at the gate, eagerly searching passengers emerging from the boarding bridge. I was looking for a pudgy teenager with long, dark red hair and braces when a striking young woman met my eyes and grinned.

"Lucy," I exclaimed, hugging her. "My God. I almost didn't recognize you."

Her hair was short and deliberately messy, accentuating clear green eyes and good bones I did not know she had. There was not so much as a hint of metal in her mouth, and her thick glasses had been replaced by weightless tortoise-shell frames that gave her the look of a seriously pretty Harvard scholar. But it was the change in her body that astonished me most, for since I had seen her last she had been transformed from a chunky adolescent into a lean, leggy athlete dressed in snug, faded jeans several inches too short, a white blouse, a woven red leather belt, loafers, and no socks. She carried a book satchel, and I caught the sparkle of a delicate gold ankle bracelet. I was fairly certain she was wearing neither makeup nor bra.

"Where's your coat?" I asked as we headed to Baggage.

"It was eighty degrees when I left Miami this morning."

"You'll freeze walking out to the car."

"It's physically impossible for me to freeze while walking to your car unless you're parked in Chicago."

"Perhaps you have a sweater in your suitcase?"

"You ever notice that you talk to me the same way Grans talks to you? By the way, she thinks I look like a 'pet rocker.' That's her malapropism for the month. It's what you get when you cross a pet rock with a punk rocker."

"I've got a couple of ski jackets, corduroys, hats, gloves. You can borrow anything you wish."

She slipped her arm in mine and sniffed my hair. "You're still not smoking."

"I'm still not smoking and I hate being reminded that I'm still not smoking because then I think about smoking."

"You look better and don't stink like cigarettes. And you haven't gotten fat. Geez, this is a dinky airport," said Lucy, whose computer brain had formatting errors in the diplomacy sectors. "Why do they call it Richmond *International*?"

"Because it has flights to Miami."

"Why doesn't Grans ever come see you?"

"She doesn't like to travel and refuses to fly."

"It's safer than driving. Her hip is really getting bad, Aunt Kay."

"I know. I'm going to leave you to get your bags so I can pull the car in front," I said when we got to Baggage. "But first let's see which carousel it is."

"There are only three carousels. I bet I can figure it out."

I left her for the bright, cold air, grateful for a moment alone to think. The changes in my niece had thrown me off guard and I was suddenly more unsure than ever how to treat her. Lucy had never been easy. From day one she had been a prodigious adult intellect ruled by infantile emotions, a volatility accidentally given form when her mother had married Armando. My only advantage had been size and age. Now Lucy was as tall as I was and spoke with the low, calm voice of an equal. She was not going to run to her room and slam the door. She would no longer end a disagreement by screaming that she hated me or was glad I was not her mother. I imagined moods I could not anticipate and arguments I could not win. I had visions of her coolly leaving the house and driving off in my car.

We talked little during the drive, for Lucy seemed fascinated by the winter weather. The world was melting like an ice sculpture as another cold front appeared on the horizon in an ominous band of gray. When we turned into the neighborhood where I had moved since she had visited last, she stared out at expensive homes and lawns, at colonial Christmas decorations and brick sidewalks. A man dressed like an Eskimo was out walking his old, overweight dog, and a black Jaguar gray with road salt sprayed water as it slowly floated past.

"It's Sunday. Where are the children, or aren't there any?" Lucy said as if the observation incriminated me in some way.

"There are a few." I turned on my street.

"No bikes in the yards, no sleds or tree houses. Doesn't anybody ever go outside?"

"This is a very quiet neighborhood."

"Is that why you chose it?"

"In part. It's also quite safe, and hopefully buying a home here will prove to be a good investment."

"Private security?"

"Yes," I said as my uneasiness grew.

She continued staring out at the large homes flowing past. "I bet you can go inside and shut the door and never hear from anyone—never see anyone outside, either, unless they're walking their dog. But you don't have a dog. How many trick-or-treaters did you have on Halloween?"

"Halloween was quiet," I said evasively.

In truth, my doorbell had rung only once, when I was

working in my study. I could see in my video monitor the four trick-or-treaters on my porch, and picking up the handset, I started to tell them that I would be right there when I overheard what they were saying to each other.

"No, there isn't a dead body in there," whispered the tiny UVA cheerleader.

"Yes, there is," said Spiderman. "She's on TV all the time because she cuts dead people up and puts them in jars. Dad told me."

I parked inside the garage and said to Lucy, "We'll get you settled in your room and the first order of business after that is for me to build a fire and make a pot of hot chocolate. Then we'll think about lunch."

"I don't drink hot chocolate. Do you have an espresso maker?"

"Indeed I do."

"That would be perfect, especially if you have decaf French roast. Do you know your neighbors?"

"I know who they are. Here, let me get that bag and you take this one so I can unlock the door and deactivate the alarm. Lord, this is heavy."

"Grans insisted I bring grapefruit. They're pretty good but full of seeds." Lucy looked around as she stepped inside my house. "Wow. Skylights. What do you call this style of architecture, besides rich?"

Maybe her disposition would self-correct if I pretended not to notice.

"The guest bedroom is back this way," I said. "I could put you upstairs if you wish, but I thought you'd rather be down here near me."

"Down here is fine. As long as I'm close to the computer."

"It's in my study, which is next door to your room."

"I brought my UNIX notes, books, and a few other things." She paused in front of the sliding glass doors in the living room. "The yard's not as nice as your other one." She said this as if I had let down everyone I had ever known.

"I've got plenty of years to work on my yard. It gives me something to look forward to."

Lucy slowly scanned her surroundings, her eyes finally resting on me. "You've got cameras in your doors, motion sensors, a fence, security gates, and what else? Gun turrets?"

"No gun turrets."

"This is your Fort Apache, isn't it, Aunt Kay? You moved here because Mark's dead and there's nothing left in the world except bad people."

The comment ambushed me with terrific force, and instantly tears filled my eyes. I went into the guest bedroom and set down her suitcase, then checked towels, soap, and toothpaste in the bath. Returning to the bedroom, I opened the curtains, checked dresser drawers, rearranged the closet, and adjusted the heat while my niece sat on the edge of the bed, following my every move. In several minutes, I was able to meet her eyes again.

"When you unpack, I'll show you a closet you can rummage through for winter things," I said.

"You never saw him the way everybody else did."

"Lucy, we need to talk about something else." I switched on a lamp and made certain the telephone was plugged in.

"You're better off without him," she added with conviction.

"Lucy . . ."

"He wasn't there for you the way he should have been. He never would have been there because that's the way he was. And every time things didn't go right, you changed."

I stood in front of the window and looked out at dormant clematis and roses frozen to trellises.

"Lucy, you need to learn a little gentleness and tact. You can't just say exactly what you think."

"That's a funny thing to hear coming from you. You've always told me how much you hate dishonesty and games."

"People have feelings."

"You're right. Including me," she said.

"Have I somehow hurt your feelings?"

"How do you think I felt?"

"I'm not sure I understand."

"Because you didn't think about me at all. That's why you don't understand."

"I think about you all the time."

"That's like saying you're rich and yet you never give me a dime. What difference does it make to me what you've got hidden away?"

I did not know what to say.

"You don't call me anymore. You haven't come to see me once since he got killed." The hurt in her voice had been saved for a long time. "I wrote you and you didn't write back. Then you called me yesterday and asked me to come visit because you needed something."

"I didn't mean it like that."

"It's the same thing Mom does."

I shut my eyes and leaned my forehead against the cold glass. "You expect too much from me, Lucy. I'm not perfect."

"I don't expect you to be perfect. But I thought you were different."

"I don't know how to defend myself when you make a remark like that."

"You can't defend yourself!"

I watched a gray squirrel hop along the top of the fence bordering the yard. Birds were pecking seeds off the grass.

"Aunt Kay?"

I turned to her and never had I seen her eyes look so dejected.

"Why are men always more important than me?"

"They're not, Lucy," I whispered. "I swear."

My niece wanted tuna salad and *caffè latte* for lunch, and while I sat in front of the fire editing a journal article, she rummaged through my closet and dresser drawers. I tried not to think about another human being touching my clothes, folding something in a way I wouldn't or returning a jacket to the wrong hanger. Lucy had a gift for making me feel like the Tinman rusting in the forest. Was I becoming the rigid, serious adult I would have disliked when I was her age?

"What do you think?" she asked when she emerged from my bedroom at half past one. She was wearing one of my tennis warm-up suits.

"I think you spent a long time to come up with only that. And yes, it fits you fine."

"I found a few other things that are okay, but most of your

stuff is too dressy. All these lawyerly suits in midnight blue and black, gray silk with delicate pinstripes, khaki and cashmere, and white blouses. You must have twenty white blouses and just as many ties. You shouldn't wear brown, by the way. And I didn't see much in red, and you'd look good in red, with your blue eyes and grayish blond hair."

"Ash blond," I said.

"Ashes are gray or white. Just look in the fire. We don't wear the same size shoe, not that I'm into Cole-Haan or Ferragamo. I did find a black leather jacket that's really cool. Were you a biker in another life?"

"It's lambskin and you're welcome to borrow it."

"What about your Fendi perfume and pearls? Do you own a pair of jeans?"

"Help yourself." I started to laugh. "And yes, I have a pair of jeans somewhere. Maybe in the garage."

"I want to take you shopping, Aunt Kay."

"I'd have to be crazy."

"Please?"

"Maybe," I said.

"If it's all right, I want to go to your club to work out for a while. I'm stiff from the plane."

"If you'd like to play tennis while you're here, I'll see if Ted has any time to hit with you. My racquets are in the closet to the left. I just switched to a new Wilson. You can hit the ball a hundred miles an hour. You'll love it."

"No, thanks. I'd rather use the StairMaster and weights or go running. Why don't you take a lesson from Ted while I work out, and we can go together?"

Dutifully, I reached for the phone and dialed Westwood's pro shop. Ted was booked solid until ten o'clock. I gave Lucy directions and my car keys, and after she left, I read in front of the fire and fell asleep.

When I opened my eyes, I heard coals shift and wind gently touching the pewter wind chimes beyond the sliding glass doors. Snow was drifting down in large, slow flakes, the sky the color of a dusty blackboard. Lights in my yard had come on, the house so silent I was conscious of the clock ticking on the wall. It was shortly after four and Lucy had not returned from the club. I dialed the number for my car phone and no one answered. She had never driven in snow before, I thought anxiously. And I needed to go to the store to pick up fish for dinner. I could call the club and have her paged. I told myself that was ridiculous. Lucy had been gone barely two hours. She was not a child anymore. When it got to be four-thirty, I tried my car phone again. At five I called the club and they could not find her. I began to panic.

"Are you sure she's not on the StairMaster or maybe in the women's locker room taking a shower? Or maybe she stopped by the mixed grill?" I again asked the young woman in the pro shop.

"We've paged her four times, Dr. Scarpetta. And I've gone around looking. I'll check again. If I locate her, I'll have her call you immediately."

"Do you know if she ever showed up at all? She should have gotten there around two."

"Gosh. I just came on at four. I don't know."

I continued calling my car phone.

"The Richmond Cellular customer you have dialed does not answer . . ."

I tried Marino and he wasn't home or at headquarters. At six o'clock I stood in the kitchen staring out the window. Snow streaked down in the chalky glow of streetlights. My heart beat hard as I paced from room to room and continued calling my car phone. At half past six I had decided to file a missing person report with the police when the telephone rang. Running back to my study, I was reaching for the receiver when I noticed the familiar number eerily materializing on the Caller ID screen. The calls had stopped after the night of Waddell's execution. I had not thought about them since. Bewildered, I froze, waiting for the expected hang up to follow my recorded message. I was shocked when I recognized the voice that began to speak.

"I hate to do this to you, Doc . . ."

Snatching up the receiver, I cleared my throat and said in disbelief, "Marino?"

"Yeah," he said. "I got bad news."

4

Where are you?" I demanded, my eyes riveted to the number on the screen.

"East End, and it's coming down like a bitch," Marino said. "We got a DOA. White female. At a glance appears to be your typical CO suicide, car inside the garage, hose hooked up to the exhaust pipe. But the circumstances are a little weird. I think you better come."

"Where are you placing this call from?" I asked so adamantly that he hesitated. I could feel his surprise.

"The decedent's house. Just got here. That's the other thing. It wasn't secured. The back was unlocked."

I heard the garage door. "Oh, thank God. Marino, hold on," I said, flooded with relief.

Paper bags crackled as the kitchen door shut.

Placing my hand over the receiver, I called out, "Lucy, is that you?"

"No, Frosty the Snowman. You ought to see it coming down out there! It's awesome!"

Reaching for pen and paper, I said to Marino, "The decedent's name and address?"

"Jennifer Deighton. Two-one-seven Ewing."

I did not recognize the name. Ewing was off Williamsburg Road, not too far from the airport in a neighborhood unfamiliar to me.

Lucy walked into my study as I was hanging up the phone. Her face was rosy from the cold, eyes sparkling.

"Where in God's name have you been?" I snapped.

Her smile faded. "Errands."

"Well, we'll discuss this later. I've got to go to a scene."

She shrugged and returned my irritation. "So what else is new?"

"I'm sorry. It's not as if I have control over people dying."

Grabbing coat and gloves, I hurried out to the garage. I started the engine, buckled up, adjusted the heat, and studied my directions before remembering the automatic door opener attached to the visor. It's amazing how quickly an enclosed space will fill with fumes.

"Good God," I said severely to no one but my own distracted self as I quickly opened the garage door.

Poisoning by motor vehicle exhaust is an easy way to die. Young couples necking in the backseat, engine running and heater on, drift off in each other's arms and never wake up. Suicidal individuals turn cars into small gas chambers and leave their problems for others to solve. I had neglected to ask Marino if Jennifer Deighton lived alone.

The snow was already several inches deep, the night lit up by it. There was no traffic in my neighborhood and very little when I got on the downtown expressway. Christmas music played nonstop on the radio as my thoughts flew in a riot of bewilderment and alighted, one by one, on fear. Jennifer Deighton had been calling my number and hanging up, or someone using her telephone had. Now she was dead. The overpass curved above the east end of downtown, where railroad tracks crisscrossed the earth like sutured wounds, and concrete parking decks were higher than many of the buildings. Main Street station hulked out of the milky sky, tile roof frosted white, the clock in its tower a bleary Cyclops eye.

On Williamsburg Road I drove very slowly past a deserted shopping center, and just before the city turned into Henrico County, I found Ewing Avenue. Houses were small, with pickup trucks and old model American cars parked out front. At the 217 address, police cars were in the drive and on both sides of the street. Pulling in behind Marino's Ford, I got out with my medical bag and walked to the end of the unpaved driveway where the single-car garage was lit up like a Christmas crèche. The door was rolled up, police officers gathered inside around a beat-up beige Chevrolet. I found Marino squatting by the back door on the driver's side, studying a section of green garden hose leading from the exhaust pipe through a partially opened window. The interior of the car was filthy with soot, the smell of fumes lingering on the cold, damp air.

"The ignition's still switched on," Marino said to me. "The car ran out of gas."

The dead woman appeared to be in her fifties or early sixties.

She was slumped over on her right side behind the steering wheel, the exposed flesh of her neck and hands bright pink. Dried bloody fluid stained the tan upholstery beneath her head. From where I stood, I could not see her face. Opening my medical bag, I got out a chemical thermometer to take the temperature inside the garage, and put on a pair of surgical gloves. I asked a young officer if he could open the car's front doors.

"We were just about to dust," he said.

"I'll wait."

"Johnson, how 'bout dusting the door handles so the doc here can get in the car." He fixed dark Latin eyes on me. "By the way, I'm Tom Lucero. What we got here is a situation that doesn't completely add up. To begin with, it bothers me there's blood on the front seat."

"There are several possible explanations for that," I said. "One is postmortem purging."

He narrowed his eyes a little.

"When pressure in the lungs forces bloody fluid from the nose and mouth," I explained.

"Oh. Generally, that doesn't happen until the person's started to decompose, right?"

"Generally."

"Based on what we know, this lady's been dead maybe twenty-four hours and it's cold as a morgue fridge in here."

"True," I said. "But if she had her heater running, that in addition to the hot exhaust pouring in would have heated up the inside of the car, and it would have stayed quite warm until the car ran out of gas."

Marino peered through a window opaque with soot and said, "Looks like the heater's pushed all the way to hot."

"Another possibility," I continued, "is that when she became unconscious, she slumped over, striking her face on the steering wheel, the dash, the seat. Her nose could have bled. She could have bitten her tongue or split her lip. I won't know until I examine her."

"Okay, but how about the way she's dressed?" Lucero said. "Strike you as unusual that she'd walk out in the cold, come inside a cold garage, hook up the hose, and get into a cold car with nothing but a gown on?"

The pale blue gown was ankle-length, with long sleeves, and made of what looked like a flimsy synthetic material. There is no dress code for people who commit suicide. It would have been logical for Jennifer Deighton to put on coat and shoes before venturing outside on a frigid winter night. But if she had planned to take her life, she would have known she would not feel the cold long.

The ID officer had finished dusting the car doors. I retrieved the chemical thermometer. It was twenty-nine degrees inside the garage.

"When did you get here?" I asked Lucero.

"Maybe an hour and a half ago. Obviously, it was warmer in here before we opened the door, but not much. The garage isn't heated. Plus, the car hood was cold. I'm guessing the car ran out of gas and the battery went dead a number of hours before we were called."

Car doors opened and I took a series of photographs before going around to the passenger's side to look at her head. I braced myself for a spark of awareness, a detail that might ignite some long-buried memory. But there was not the faintest glimmer. I did not know Jennifer Deighton. I had never seen her before in my life.

Her bleached hair was dark at the roots and tightly wound in small pink curlers, several of which had been displaced. She was grossly overweight, though I could tell from her refined features that she may have been quite pretty in a younger, leaner life. I palpated her head and neck and felt no fractures. I placed the back of my hand against her cheek, then struggled to turn her. She was cold and stiff, the side of her face that had been resting against the seat, pale and blistered from the heat. It did not appear that her body had been moved after death, and the skin did not blanch when pressed. She had been dead at least twelve hours.

It wasn't until I was ready to bag her hands that I noticed something under her right index fingernail. I got out a flashlight for a better look, then retrieved a plastic evidence envelope and a pair of forceps. The tiny fleck of metallic green was embedded in the skin beneath the nail. Christmas glitter, I thought. I also found fibers of a gold tint, and as I studied each of her fingers I found more. Slipping the brown paper bags over her hands and securing them at the wrists with rubber bands, I went around to the other side of the car. I wanted to look at her feet. Her legs were fully rigorous and uncooperative as I pulled them free of the steering wheel and positioned them on the seat. Examining the bottoms of her thick dark socks, I found fibers clinging to the wool that looked similar to the ones I had noticed under her fingernails.

Absent was dirt, mud, or grass. An alarm was sounding in the back of my mind.

"Find anything interesting?" Marino asked.

"You found no bedroom slippers or shoes nearby?" I said.

"Nope," Lucero answered. "Like I told you, I thought it unusual she walked out of the house on a cold night with nothing but——"

I interrupted. "We've got a problem. Her socks are too clean."

"Shit," Marino said.

"We need to get her downtown." I backed away from the car.

"I'll tell the squad," Lucero volunteered.

"I want to see the inside of her house," I said to Marino.

"Yeah." He had taken his gloves off and was blowing on his hands. "I want you to see it, too."

While I waited for the squad, I moved about the garage, careful where I stepped and keeping out of the way. There wasn't much to see, just the usual clutter of items needed for the yard and odds and ends that had no other proper storage place. I scanned stacks of old newspapers, wicker baskets, dusty cans of paint, and a rusty charcoal grill that I doubted had been used in years. Sloppily coiled in a corner like a headless green garter snake was the hose from which the segment attached to the exhaust pipe appeared to have been cut. I knelt near the severed end without touching it. The plastic rim did not look sawn but severed at an angle by one hard blow. I spotted a linear cut in the cement floor nearby. Getting to my feet, I surveyed the tools hanging from a pegboard. There was an ax and a maul, both of them rusty and festooned with cobwebs.

The rescue squad was coming in with its stretcher and body pouch.

"Did you find anything inside her house that she might have used to cut the hose?" I asked Lucero.

"No."

Jennifer Deighton did not want to come out of the car, death resisting the hands of life. I moved to the passenger's side to help. Three of us secured her under the arms and waist while an attendant pushed her legs. When she was zipped up and buckled in, they carried her out into the snowy night and I trudged with Lucero along the driveway, sorry that I'd not taken the time to put on boots. We entered the ranch-style brick house through a back door that led into the kitchen.

It looked recently renovated, appliances black, counters and cabinets white, the wallpaper an Oriental pattern of pastel flowers against delicate blue. Heading toward the sound of voices, Lucero and I crossed a narrow hallway with a hardwood floor and stopped at the entrance of a bedroom where Marino and an ID officer were going through dresser drawers. For a long moment, I looked around at the peculiar manifestations of Jennifer Deighton's personality. It was as if her bedroom were a solar cell in which she captured radiant energy and converted it into magic. I thought again of the hang ups I had been getting, my paranoia growing by leaps and bounds.

Walls, curtains, carpet, linens, and wicker furniture were white. Oddly, on the rumpled bed not far from where both pillows were propped against the headboard a crystal pyramid anchored a single blank sheet of white typing paper. On the dresser and beside tabletops were more crystals, with smaller ones suspended from window frames. I could imagine rainbows dancing in the room and light glancing off prismatic glass when the sun poured in.

"Weird, huh?" Lucero asked.

"Was she a psychic of some sort?" I asked.

"Let's put it this way, she had her own business, most of it carried out right there." Lucero moved closer to an answering machine on a table by the bed. The message light was flashing, the number thirty-eight glowing red.

"*Thirty-eight* messages since eight o'clock last night," Lucero added. "I've skipped through a few of 'em. The lady was into horoscopes. Looks like people would call to find out if they were going to have a good day, win the lottery, or be able to pay off their charge cards after Christmas."

Opening the cover of the answering machine, Marino used his pocket knife to flip out the tape, which he sealed inside a plastic evidence envelope. I was interested in several other items on the small bedside table and moved closer to take a look. Next to a notepad and pen was a glass with an inch of clear liquid inside it. I bent close, smelling nothing. Water, I thought. Nearby were two paperback books, Pete Dexter's *Paris Trout* and Jane Roberts's *Seth Speaks*. I saw no other books in the bedroom.

"I'd like to take a look at these," I said to Marino.

"*Paris Trout*," he mused. "What's it about, fishing in France?"

Unfortunately, he was serious.

"They might tell me something about her state of mind before she died," I added.

"No problem. I'll have Documents check them for prints, then hand them over to you. And I think we'd better have Documents take a look at the paper, too," he added, referring to the sheet of blank paper on the bed.

"Right," Lucero said drolly. "Maybe she wrote a suicide note in disappearing ink."

"Come on," Marino said to me. "I want to show you a couple things."

He took me into the living room, where an artificial Christmas tree cowered in a corner, bent from copious gaudy ornaments and strangled by tinsel, lights, and angel hair. Gathered near its base were boxes of candy and cheeses, bubble bath, a glass jar of what looked like spiced tea, and a ceramic unicorn with blazing blue eyes and gilded horn. The gold shag carpet, I suspected, was the origin of the fibers I had noticed on the bottom of Jennifer Deighton's socks and under her finger-nails.

Marino slipped a small flashlight from a pocket and squatted.

"Take a look," he said.

I got down beside him as the beam of light illuminated metallic glitter and a bit of slender gold cord in the deep pile of the carpet around the base of the tree.

"When I got here, the first thing I checked was to see if she had any presents under the tree," Marino said, switching the flashlight off. "Obviously, she opened them early. And the wrapping paper and cards got disposed of right over there in the fireplace—it's full of paper ash, some pieces of foil-type paper still unburned. The lady across the street says she noticed smoke coming out of the chimney right before it got dark last night."

"Is this neighbor the one who called the police?" I asked.

"Yeah."

"Why?"

"That I'm not clear on. I got to talk to her."

"When you do, see if you can find out anything about this woman's medical history, if she had psychiatric problems, et cetera. I'd like to know who her physician is."

"I'm going over there in a few minutes. You can come with me and ask her yourself."

I thought of Lucy waiting for me at home as I continued taking in details. In the center of the room, my eyes stopped at four small square indentations in the carpet.

"I noticed that, too," Marino said. "Looks like someone brought a chair in here, probably from the dining room. There's four chairs around the dining room table. All of 'em have square legs."

"Another thing you might consider doing," I thought out loud, "is checking her VCR. See if she had programmed it to record anything. That might tell us something more about her, too."

"Good idea."

We left the living room, passing through the small dining room with an oak table and four straight-backed chairs. The braided rug on the hardwood floor looked either new or rarely walked on.

"Looks like the room she pretty much lived in was this one," Marino said as we crossed a hallway and entered what clearly was her office.

The room was crammed with the paraphernalia needed to

run a small business, including a fax machine, which I investigated immediately. It was turned off, the line connected to it plugged into a single jack in the wall. I looked around some more as my mystification grew. A personal computer, postage machine, various forms, and envelopes crowded a table and the desk. Encyclopedias and books on parapsychology, astrology, zodiac signs, and Eastern and Western religions lined bookcases. I noted several different translations of the Bible and dozens of ledgers with dates written on the spines.

Near the postage machine was a stack of what appeared to be subscription forms, and I picked up one. For three hundred dollars a year, you could call as often as once a day and Jennifer Deighton would spend up to three minutes telling you your horoscope "based on personal details, including the alignment of the planets at the moment of your birth." For an additional two hundred dollars a year, she would throw in "a weekly reading." Upon payment of the fee, the subscriber would receive a card with an identification code that was valid only as long as the annual fee continued to be paid.

"What a lot of horseshit," Marino said to me.

"I'm assuming she lived alone."

"That's the way it's looking so far. A woman alone running a business like this—a damn good way to attract the wrong person."

"Marino, do you know how many telephone lines she has?"

"No. Why?"

I told him about the hang ups I had been getting while he stared hard at me. His jaw muscles began to flex.

"I need to know if her fax machine and phone are on the same line," I concluded.

"Jesus Christ."

"If they are and she happened to have her fax machine turned on the night I dialed back the number that appeared on my Caller ID screen," I went on, "that would explain the tone I heard."

"Jesus friggin' Christ," he said, snatching the portable radio out of his coat pocket. "Why the hell didn't you tell me this before?"

"I didn't want to mention it when others were around."

He moved the radio close to his lips. "Seven-ten." Then he said to me, "If you were worried about hang ups, why didn't you say something weeks ago?"

"I wasn't that worried about them."

"Seven-ten," the dispatcher's voice crackled back.

"Ten-five eight-twenty-one."

The dispatcher sent out a broadcast for 821, the code for the inspector.

"Got a number I need you to dial," Marino said when he and the inspector connected on the air. "You got your cellular phone handy?"

"Ten-fo'."

Marino gave him Jennifer Deighton's number and then turned on the fax machine. Momentarily, it began a series of rings, beeps, and other complaints.

"That answer your question?" Marino asked me.

"It answers one question, but not the most important question," I said.

*

The name of the neighbor across the street who had notified the police was Myra Clary. I accompanied Marino to her small aluminum-sided house with its plastic Santa lit up on the front lawn and lights strung in the boxwoods. Marino barely had rung the bell when the front door opened and Mrs. Clary invited us in without asking who we were. It occurred to me that she probably had watched our approach from a window.

She showed us into a dismal living room where we found her husband huddled by the electric fire, lap robe over his spindly legs, his vacuous stare fixed on a man lathering up with deodorant soap on television. The pitiful custodial care of the years manifested itself everywhere. Upholstery was threadbare and soiled where human flesh had made repeated contact with it. Wood was cloudy from layers of wax, prints on walls yellowed behind dusty glass. The oily smell of a million meals cooked in the kitchen and eaten on TV trays permeated the air.

Marino explained why we were here as Mrs. Clary moved about nervously, plucking newspapers off the couch, turning down the television, and carrying dirty dinner plates into the kitchen. Her husband did not venture forth from his interior world, his head trembling on its stalklike neck. Parkinson's disease is when the machine shakes violently just before it conks out, as if it knows what is ahead and protests the only way it can.

"Nope, we don't need a thing," Marino said when Mrs. Clary offered us food and drink. "Sit down and try to relax. I know this has been a tough day for you."

"They said she was in her car breathing in those fumes. Oh, my," she said. "I saw how smoky the window was, looked like the garage had been on fire. I knew the worst right then."

"Who's *they?*" Marino asked.

"The police. After I called, I was watching for them. When they pulled up, I went straight over to see if Jenny was all right."

Mrs. Clary could not sit still in the wing chair across from the couch where Marino and I had settled. Her gray hair had strayed out of the bun on top of her head, face as wrinkled as a dried apple, eyes hungry for information and bright with fear.

"I know you already talked to the police earlier," Marino said, moving the ashtray closer. "But I want you to go through it chapter and verse for us, beginning with when you saw Jennifer Deighton last."

"I saw her the other day—"

Marino interrupted. "Which day?"

"Friday. I remember the phone rang and I went to the kitchen to answer it and saw her through the window. She was pulling into her driveway."

"Did she always park her car in the garage?" I asked.

"She always did."

"What about yesterday?" Marino inquired. "You see her or her car yesterday?"

"No, I didn't. But I went out to get the mail. It was late, tends to be that way this time of year. Three, four o'clock and still no mail. I guess it was close to five-thirty, maybe a little later, when I remembered to check the mailbox again. It was getting dark and I noticed smoke coming out of Jenny's chimney."

"You sure about that?" Marino asked.

She nodded. "Oh, yes. I remember it went through my mind it was a good night for a fire. But fires were always Jimmy's job. He never showed me how, you see. When he was good at something, that was his. So I quit on the fires and had the electric log put in."

Jimmy Clary was looking at her. I wondered if he knew what she was saying.

"I like to cook," she went on. "This time of year I do a lot of baking. I make sugar cakes and give them to the neighbors. Yesterday I wanted to drop one by for Jenny, but I like to call first. It's hard to tell when someone's in, especially when they keep their car in a garage. And you leave a cake on the doormat and one of the dogs around here gets it. So I tried her and got that machine. All day I tried and she didn't answer, and to tell you the truth, I was a little worried."

"Why?" I asked. "Did she have health problems, any sort of problems you were aware of?"

"Bad cholesterol. Way over two hundred's what she told me once. Plus high blood pressure, which she said ran in the family."

I had not seen any prescription drugs in Jennifer Deighton's house.

"Do you know who her doctor was?" I asked.

"I can't recall. But Jenny believed in natural cures. She told me when she felt poorly she'd meditate."

"Sounds like the two of you were pretty close," Marino said.

Mrs. Clary was plucking at her skirt, hands like hyperactive children. "I'm here all day except when I go to the store." She glanced at her husband, who was staring at the TV again.

"Now and then I'd go see her, you know, just being neighborly, maybe to drop by something I'd been cooking."

"Was she a friendly sort?" Marino asked. "She have a lot of visitors?"

"Well, you know she worked out of the house. I think she handled most of her business over the phone. But occasionally I'd see people going in."

"Anybody you knew?"

"Not that I recall."

"You notice anybody coming by to see her last night?" Marino asked.

"I didn't notice."

"What about when you went out to get your mail and saw the smoke coming out of her chimney? You get any sense she might have had company?"

"I didn't see a car. Nothing to make me think she had company."

Jimmy Clary had drifted off to sleep. He was drooling.

"You said she worked at home," I said. "Do you have any idea what she did?"

Mrs. Clary fixed wide eyes on me. She leaned forward and lowered her voice. "I know what folks said."

"And what was that?" I asked.

She pressed her lips together and shook her head.

"Mrs. Clary," Marino said. "Anything you could tell us might help. I know you want to help."

"There's a Methodist church two blocks away. You can see it. The steeple's lit up at night, has been ever since they built the church three or four years ago."

"I saw the church when I was driving in," Marino replied. "What's that got to do—"

"Well," she cut in, "Jenny moved here, I guess it was early September. And I've never been able to figure it out. The steeple light. You watch when you're driving home. Of course . . ." She paused, her face disappointed. "Maybe it won't do it anymore."

"Do what?" Marino asked.

"Go out and then come back on. The strangest thing I've ever seen. It's lit up one minute, and then you look out your window again and it's dark like the church isn't there. Then next thing you know, you look out again and the steeple's lit up just like it's always been. I've timed it. On for a minute, then off for two, on again for three. Sometimes it will burn for an hour. No pattern to it at all."

"What does this have to do with Jennifer Deighton?" I asked.

"I remember it was not long after she moved in, just weeks before Jimmy had his stroke. It was a cool night so he was building a fire. I was in the kitchen doing dishes and could see the steeple out the window lit up like it always was. And he came in to get himself a drink, and I said, 'You know what the Bible says about being drunk with the Spirit and not with wine.' And he said, 'I'm not drinking wine. I'm drinking bourbon. The Bible's never said a word about bourbon.' Then, right while he was standing there the steeple went dark. It was like the church vanished into thin air. I said, 'There you have it. The Word of the Lord. That's his opinion about you and your bourbon.'

105

"He laughed like I was the craziest thing, but he never touched another drop. Every night he'd stand in front of the window over the kitchen sink watching. One minute the steeple would be lit up, then it would be dark. I let Jimmy think it was God's doing—anything to keep him off the bottle. The church never behaved like that before Miss Deighton moved across the street."

"Has the light been going on and off lately?" I asked.

"Was still doing it last night. I don't know about now. To tell you the truth, I haven't looked."

"So you're saying that she somehow had an effect on the lights in the church steeple," Marino said mildly.

"I'm saying that more than one person on this street decided about her some time ago."

"Decided what?"

"About her being a witch," Mrs. Clary said.

Her husband had started snoring, making hideous strangling noises that his wife did not seem to notice.

"Sounds to me like your husband there started doing poorly about the time Miss Deighton moved here and the lights started acting funny," Marino said.

She looked startled. "Well, that's so. He had his stroke the end of September."

"You ever think there might be a connection? That maybe Jennifer Deighton had something to do with it, just like you're thinking she had something to do with the church lights?"

"Jimmy didn't take to her." Mrs. Clary was talking faster by the minute.

"You're saying the two of them didn't get along," Marino said.

"Right after she moved in, she came over a couple of times to ask him to help out with a few things around the house, man's work. I remember one time her doorbell was making a terrible buzzing sound inside the house and she appeared on the doorstep, scared she was about to have an electrical fire. So Jimmy went over there. I think her dishwasher flooded once, too, back then. Jimmy's always been real handy." She glanced furtively at her snoring husband.

"You still haven't made it clear why he didn't get along with her," Marino reminded her.

"He said he didn't like going over there," she said. "Didn't like the inside of her house, with all these crystals everywhere. And the phone would ring all the time. But what really gave him the willies was when she told him she read people's fortunes and would do it for him for nothing if he'd keep fixing things around her house. He said, and I remember this like it was yesterday, 'No, thank you, Miss Deighton. Myra's in charge of my future, plans every minute of it.'"

"I wonder if you might know of anybody who had a big enough problem with Jennifer Deighton to wish something bad on her, hurt her in some way," Marino said.

"You think somebody killed her?"

"There's a lot we don't know at this point. We have to check out every possibility."

She crossed her arms under her sagging bosom, hugging herself.

"What about her emotional state?" I inquired. "Did she ever

seem depressed to you? Do you know if she had any problems she couldn't seem to cope with, especially of late?"

"I didn't know her that well." She avoided my eyes.

"Did she go to any doctors that you're aware of?"

"I don't know."

"What about next of kin? Did she have family?"

"I have no idea."

"What about her phone?" I then said. "Did she answer it when she was home or did she always let the machine do it?"

"It's been my experience that when she was home, she answered it."

"Which is why you got worried about her earlier today when she wasn't answering the phone when you called," Marino said.

"That's exactly why."

Myra Clary realized too late what she had said.

"That's interesting," Marino commented.

A flush crept up her neck and her hands went still.

Marino asked, "How did you know she was home today?"

She did not answer. Her husband's breath rattled in his chest and he coughed, eyes blinking open.

"I guess I assumed. Because I didn't see her pull out. In her car . . ." Mrs. Clary's voice trailed off.

"Maybe you went over there earlier in the day?" Marino offered, as if trying to be helpful. "To deliver your cake or say hello and thought her car was in the garage?"

She dabbed tears from her eyes. "I was in the kitchen baking all morning and never saw her go out to get the paper or leave in her car. So mid-morning, when I went out, I went over there and rang the bell. She didn't answer. I peeked inside the garage."

"You telling me you saw the windows all smoked up and didn't think something was wrong?" Marino asked.

"I didn't know what it meant, what to do." Her voice went up several octaves. "Lord, Lord. I wish I'd called somebody then. Maybe she was—"

Marino cut in. "I don't know that she was still alive then, that she would have been." He looked pointedly at me.

"When you looked inside the garage, did you hear the car engine running?" I asked Mrs. Clary.

She shook her head and blew her nose.

Marino got up and tucked his notepad back in his coat pocket. He looked dejected, as if Mrs. Clary's spinelessness and lack of veracity deeply disappointed him. By now, there wasn't a role he played that I did not know well.

"I should have called earlier." Myra Clary directed this at me, her voice quavering.

I did not reply. Marino stared at the carpet.

"I don't feel good. I need to go lie down."

Marino slipped a business card out of his wallet and handed it to her. "Anything else comes to mind that you think I ought to know about, you give me a call."

"Yes, sir," she said weakly. "I promise I will."

"You doing the post tonight?" Marino asked me after the front door shut.

Snow was ankle-deep and still coming down.

"In the morning," I said, fishing keys out of my coat pocket.

"What do you think?"

"I think her unusual occupation put her at great risk for the wrong sort of person to come along. I also think her apparent isolated existence, as Mrs. Clary described it, and the fact that it appears she opened her Christmas presents early makes suicide an easy assumption. But her clean socks are a major problem."

"You got that right," he said.

Jennifer Deighton's house was lit up, and a flatbed truck with chains on its tires had backed into the driveway. Voices of men working were muted by the snow, and every car on the street was solid white and soft around the edges.

I followed Marino's gaze above the roof of Miss Deighton's house. Several blocks away, the church was etched against the pearl gray sky, the steeple shaped weirdly like a witch's hat. Arches in the arcade stared back at us with mournful, empty eyes when suddenly the light blinked on. It filled spaces and painted surfaces a luminescent ocher, the arcade an unsmiling but gentle face floating in the night.

I glanced over at the Clary house as curtains moved in the kitchen window.

"Jesus, I'm out of here." Marino headed across the street.

"You want me to alert Neils about her car?" I called after him.

"Yeah," he yelled back. "That'd be good."

My house was lit up when I got home and good smells came from the kitchen. A fire blazed and two places had been set on the butler's table in front of it. Dropping my medical bag on the couch, I looked around and listened. From my study across the hall came the faint, rapid clicking of keys.

"Lucy?" I called out, slipping off my gloves and unbuttoning my coat.

"I'm in here." Keys continued to click.

"What have you been cooking?"

"Dinner."

I headed for my study, where I found my niece sitting at my desk staring intensely at the computer monitor. I was stunned when I noticed the pound sign prompt. She was in UNIX. Somehow she had dialed into the computer downtown.

"How did you do that?" I asked. "I didn't tell you the dial-in command, user name, password, or anything."

"You didn't have to tell me. I found the file that told me what the *bat* command is. Plus, you've got some programs in here with your user name and password coded in so you don't get prompted for them. A good shortcut but risky. Your user name is Marley and password is *brain.*"

"You're dangerous." I pulled up a chair.

"Who's Marley?" She continued to type.

"We had assigned seating in medical school. Marley Scates sat next to me in labs for two years. He's a neurosurgeon somewhere."

"Were you in love with him?"

"We never dated."

"Was he in love with you?"

"You ask too many questions, Lucy. You can't just ask people anything you want."

"Yes I can. They don't have to answer."

"It's offensive."

"I think I've figured out how someone got into your directory, Aunt Kay. Remember I told you about users that came with the software?"

"Yes."

"There's one called demo that has root privileges but no password assigned to it. My guess is that this is what somebody used and I'll show you what probably happened." Her fingers flew over the keyboard without pause as she talked. "What I'm doing now is going into the system administrator's menu to check out the log-in accounting. We're going to search for a specific user. In this case, root. Now we'll hit g to go and boom. There it is." She ran her finger across a line on the screen.

"On December sixteenth at five-oh-six in the afternoon, someone logged in from a device called t-t-y-fourteen. This person had root privileges and we'll assume is the person who went into your directory. I don't know what he looked at. But twenty minutes later, at five-twenty-six, he tried to send the note 'I can't find it' to t-t-y-oh-seven and inadvertently created a file. He logged out at five-thirty-two, making the total time of the session twenty-six minutes. And it doesn't appear anything was printed, by the way. I took a look at the printer spooler log, which shows files printed. I didn't see anything that caught my attention."

"Let me make sure I've got this straight. Someone tried to send a note from t-t-y-fourteen to t-t-y-oh-seven," I said.

"Yes. And I checked. Both of those devices are terminals."

"How can we determine whose office those terminals are in?" I asked.

"I'm surprised there's not a list somewhere in here. But I haven't found it yet. If all else fails, you can check the cables leading to the terminals. Usually, they're tagged. And if you're interested in my personal opinion, I don't think your computer analyst is the spy. In the first place, she knows your user name and password and would have no need to log in with demo. Also, since I assume the mini is in her office, then I also assume she uses the system terminal."

"She does."

"The device name for your system terminal is t-t-y-b."

"Good."

"Another way to figure out who did this would be to sneak into someone's office when they aren't there but are logged in. All you've got to do is go into UNIX and type 'who am I' and the system will tell you."

She pushed back her chair and got up. "I hope you're hungry. We've got chicken breasts and a chilled wild rice salad made with cashews, peppers, sesame oil. And there's bread. Is your grill in working order?"

"It's after eleven and snowing outside."

"I didn't suggest that we eat outside. I simply would like to cook the chicken on the grill."

"Where did you learn to cook?"

We were walking to the kitchen.

"Not from Mother. Why do you think I was such a little fatso? From eating the junk she bought. Snacks, sodas, and pizza that tastes like cardboard. I have fat cells that will scream for the rest of my life because of Mother. I'll never forgive her."

"We need to talk about this afternoon, Lucy. If you hadn't

come home when you did, the police would have been looking for you."

"I worked out for an hour and a half, then took a shower."

"You were gone four and a half hours."

"I had groceries to buy and a few other errands."

"Why didn't you answer the car phone?"

"I assumed it was someone trying to reach you. Plus, I've never used a car phone. I'm not twelve years old, Aunt Kay."

"I know you're not. But you don't live here and have never driven here before. I was worried."

"I'm sorry," she said.

We ate by firelight, both of us sitting on the floor around the butler's table. I had turned off lamps. Flames jumped and shadows danced as if celebrating a magic moment in the lives of my niece and me.

"What do you want for Christmas?" I asked, reaching for my wine.

"Shooting lessons," she said.

5

Lucy stayed up very late working with the computer and I did not hear her stir when I woke up to the alarm early Monday morning. Parting the curtains in my bedroom window, I looked out at powdery flakes swirling in lights burning on the patio. The snow was deep and nothing was moving in my neighborhood. After coffee and a quick scan of the paper, I got dressed and was almost to the door when I turned around. No matter that Lucy was no longer twelve years old, I could not leave without checking on her.

Slipping inside her bedroom, I found her sleeping on her side in a tangle of sheets, the duvet half on the floor. It touched me that she was wearing a sweat suit that she had gotten out of one of my drawers. I had never had another human being wish to sleep in anything of mine, and I straightened the covers, careful not to wake her.

The drive downtown was awful, and I envied workers

whose offices were closed because of the snow. Those of us who had not been granted an unexpected holiday crept slowly along the interstate, skating with the slightest tap on the brakes as we peered through streaked windshields that the wipers could not keep clean. I wondered how I would explain to Margaret that my teenage niece thought our computer system was insecure. Who had gotten into my directory, and why had Jennifer Deighton been calling my number and hanging up?

I did not get to the office until half past eight, and when I walked into the morgue, I stopped midway in the corridor, puzzled. Parked at a haphazard angle near the stainless steel refrigerator door was a gurney bearing a body covered by a sheet. Checking the toe tag, I read Jennifer Deighton's name, and I looked around. There was no one inside the office or X-ray room. I opened the door to the autopsy suite and found Susan dressed in scrubs and dialing a number on the phone. She quickly hung up and greeted me with a nervous "Good morning."

"Glad you made it in." I unbuttoned my coat, regarding her curiously.

"Ben gave me a lift," she said, referring to my administrator, who owned a Jeep with four-wheel drive. "So far, we're the only three here."

"No sign of Fielding?"

"He called a few minutes ago and said he couldn't get out of his driveway. I told him we only have one case so far, but if more come in Ben can pick him up."

"Are you aware that our case is parked in the hall?"

She hesitated, blushing. "I was taking her over to X ray when the phone rang. Sorry."

"Have you weighed and measured her yet?"

"No."

"Let's do that first."

She hurried out of the autopsy suite before I could comment further. Secretaries and scientists who worked in the labs upstairs often entered and left the building through the morgue because it was convenient to the parking lot. Maintenance workers were in and out, too. Leaving a body unattended in the middle of a corridor was very poor form and could even jeopardize the case should chain of evidence be questioned in court.

Susan returned pushing the gurney, and we went to work, the stench of decomposing flesh nauseating. I fetched gloves and a plastic apron from a shelf, and clamped various forms in a clipboard. Susan was quiet and tense. When she reached up to the control panel to reset the computerized floor scale, I noticed her hands were shaking. Maybe she was suffering from morning sickness.

"Everything okay?" I asked her.

"Just a little tired."

"You sure?"

"Positive. She weighs one-eighty exactly."

I changed into my greens and Susan and I moved the body into the X-ray room across the hall, transferring it from the gurney to the table. Opening the sheet, I wedged a block under the neck to keep the head from lolling. The flesh of her throat was clean, spared from soot and burns because her chin had been tucked close to her chest while she was inside the car with the engine running. I did not see any obvious injuries, no bruises or broken fingernails. Her nose wasn't fractured. There were no cuts inside her lips and she hadn't bitten her tongue.

Susan took X rays and slipped them into the processor while I went over the front of the body with a lens. I collected a number of barely visible whitish fibers, quite possibly from the sheet or her bed covers, and found others similar to the ones on the bottoms of her socks. She wore no jewelry and was naked beneath her gown. I remembered the rumpled covers on her bed, the pillows propped against the headboard and glass of water on the table. The night of her death she had put curlers in her hair, gotten undressed, and at some point, perhaps, had been reading in bed.

Susan emerged from the developer room and leaned against the wall, supporting the small of her back with her hands.

"What's the story on this lady?" she asked. "Was she married?"

"It appears she lived alone."

"Did she work?"

"She ran a business out of her home." Something caught my eye.

"What sort of business?"

"Possibly fortune-telling of sorts." The feather was very small and sooty, clinging to Jennifer Deighton's gown in the area of her left hip. Reaching for a small plastic bag, I tried to recall if I'd noticed any feathers around her house. Perhaps the pillows on her bed were filled with feathers.

"Did you find any evidence she was into the occult?"

"Some of her neighbors seemed to think she was a witch," I said.

"Based on what?"

"There's a church near her house. Allegedly, the lights in the steeple starting going on and off after she moved in some months ago."

"You're kidding."

"I saw them go on myself when I was leaving the scene. The steeple was dark. Then suddenly it was lit up."

"Weird."

"It was weird."

"Maybe it's on a timer."

"Unlikely. Lights going on and off all night would not conserve electricity. If it's true they go on and off all night. I saw it happen only once."

Susan did not say anything.

"Possibly there's a short in the wiring." In fact, I thought as I continued to work, I would call the church. They might be unaware of the problem.

"Any strange stuff inside her house?"

"Crystals. Some unusual books."

Silence.

Then Susan said, "I wish you'd told me earlier."

"Pardon?" I glanced up. She was staring uneasily at the body. She looked pale.

"Are you sure you're feeling all right?" I asked.

"I don't like stuff like this."

"Stuff like what?"

"It's like someone having AIDS or something. I ought to be told up front. Especially now."

"It's unlikely this woman has AIDS or—"

"I should have been told. Before I touched her."

"Susan—"

"I went to school with a girl who was a witch."

I stopped what I was doing. Susan was rigid against the wall, hands pressed against her belly.

"Her name was Doreen. She belonged to a coven and our senior year she put a curse on my twin sister, Judy. Judy was killed in a car wreck two weeks before graduation."

Bewildered, I stared at her.

"You know how occult stuff creeps me out! Like that cow's tongue with needles stuck in it that the cops brought in a couple of months ago. The one wrapped up in a list of dead people's names. It was left on a grave."

"It was a prank," I reminded her calmly. "The tongue came from a grocery store, and the names were meaningless, copied from headstones in the cemetery."

"You shouldn't tamper with the satanic, prank or not." Her voice trembled. "I take evil just as seriously as God."

Susan was the daughter of a minister and had abandoned religion long ago. I'd never heard her so much as allude to Satan or mention God unless it was profanely. I'd never known her to be the least bit superstitious or unnerved by anything. She was about to cry.

"Tell you what," I said quietly. "Since it appears I'm going to be short-staffed today, if you'll answer the phones upstairs, I'll take care of things down here."

Her eyes filled with tears, and I immediately went to her.

"It's okay." Putting my arm around her, I walked her out of the room. "Come on," I said gently as she leaned against me, sobbing. "You want Ben to take you home?"

She nodded, whispering, "I'm sorry. I'm sorry."

"All you need is a little rest." I sat her in a chair inside the morgue office and reached for the phone.

Jennifer Deighton had inhaled no carbon monoxide or soot because by the time she had been placed inside her car she was no longer breathing. Her death was a homicide, an obvious one, and throughout the afternoon I impatiently left messages for Marino to call me. Several times I tried to check on Susan but her phone just rang and rang.

"I'm concerned," I said to Ben Stevens. "Susan's not answering her phone. When you drove her home, did she mention that she was planning to go somewhere?"

"She told me she was going to bed."

He was sitting at his desk, going through reams of computer printouts. Rock and roll played quietly from the radio on a bookcase, and he was drinking tangerine-flavored mineral water. Stevens was young, smart, and boyishly goodlooking. He worked hard, and played hard in singles bars, so I had been told. I was quite certain his job as my administrator would prove to be a short step on his way to someplace better.

"Maybe she unplugged her phone so she could sleep," he said, turning on his adding machine.

"Maybe that's it."

He launched into an update on our budget woes.

Late afternoon when it was beginning to get dark out, Stevens buzzed my line.

"Susan called. She said she won't be in tomorrow. And I've got a John Deighton on hold. Says he's Jennifer Deighton's brother."

Stevens transferred the call.

"Hello. They said you did my sister's autopsy," a man mumbled. "Uh, Jennifer Deighton's my sister."

"Your name, please?"

"John Deighton. I live in Columbia, South Carolina."

I glanced up as Marino appeared in my office doorway, and motioned for him to take a chair.

"They said she hooked up a hose to her car and killed herself."

"Who said that?" I asked. "And could you speak up, please?"

He hesitated. "I don't remember the name, should've wrote it down but I was too shocked."

The man didn't sound shocked. His voice was so muffled I barely could hear what he was saying.

"Mr. Deighton, I'm very sorry," I said. "But you will have to request any information regarding her death in writing. I will also need, included with your written request, some verification that you are next of kin."

He did not respond.

"Hello?" I asked. "Hello?"

I was answered by a dial tone.

"That's strange," I said to Marino. "Are you familiar with a John Deighton who claims to be Jennifer Deighton's brother?"

"That's who that was? Shit. We're trying to reach him."

"He said someone's already notified him about her death."

"You know where he was calling from?"

"Columbia, South Carolina, supposedly. He hung up on me."

Marino didn't seem interested. "I just came from Vander's office," he said, referring to Neils Vander, the chief fingerprints examiner. "He checked out Jennifer Deighton's car, plus the books that were beside her bed and a poem that was stuck inside one of 'em. As for the sheet of blank paper that was on her bed, he hasn't gotten to that yet."

"Anything so far?"

"He lifted a few. Will run them through the computer if there's a need. Probably most of the prints are hers. Here." He placed a small paper bag on my desk. "Happy reading."

"I think you're going to want those prints run without delay," I said grimly.

A shadow passed over Marino's eyes. He massaged his temples.

"Jennifer Deighton definitely did not commit suicide," I informed him. "Her CO was less than seven percent. She had no soot in her airway. The bright pink tint of her skin was due to exposure to cold, not CO poisoning."

"Christ," he said.

Shuffling through the paperwork in front of me, I handed him a body diagram, then opened an envelope and withdrew Polaroid photographs of Jennifer Deighton's neck.

"As you can see," I went on, "there are no injuries externally."

"What about the blood on the car seat?"

"A postmortem artifact due to purging. She was beginning to decompose. I found no abrasions or contusions, no fingertip

123

bruises. But here"—I showed him a photograph of her neck at autopsy—"she's got irregular hemorrhages in the sternoclei-domastoid muscles bilaterally. She's also got a fracture of the right cornua of the hyoid. Her death was caused by asphyxia, due to pressure applied to the neck—"

Marino interrrupted, loudly. "You suggesting she got yoked?"

I showed him another photograph. "She's also got some facial perechia, or pinpoint hemorrhages. These findings are consistent with yoking, yes. She's a homicide, and I might suggest that we keep this out of the newspapers as long as possible."

"You know, I didn't need this." He looked up at me with bloodshot eyes. "I got eight uncleared homicides sitting on my desk even as we speak. Henrico don't got shit on Eddie Heath, and the kid's old man calls me almost every day. Not to mention, they're having a damn drug war in Mosby Court. Merry friggin' Christmas. I didn't need this."

"Jennifer Deighton didn't need this either, Marino."

"Keep going. What else did you find?"

"She did have high blood pressure, as her neighbor Mrs. Clary suggested."

"Huh," he said, shifting his eyes away from me. "How could you tell?"

"She had left ventricular hypertrophy, or thickening of the left side of the heart."

"High blood pressure does that?"

"It does. I should find fibrinoid changes in the renal microvasculature or early nephrosclerosis. I suspect the brain will show hypertensive changes, too, in the cerebral arterioles, but I won't be able to say with certainty until I can take a look under the scope."

"You're saying kidney and brain cells get killed off when you got high blood pressure?"

"In a manner of speaking."

"Anything else?"

"Nothing significant."

"What about gastric contents?" Marino asked.

"Meat, some vegetables, partially digested."

"Alcohol or drugs?"

"No alcohol. Drug screens are under way."

"No sign of rape?"

"No injuries or other evidence of sexual assault. I swabbed her for seminal fluid but won't get those reports for a while. Even then, you can't always be sure."

Marino's face was unreadable.

"What are you after?" I finally asked.

"Well, I'm thinking about how this thing was staged. Someone went to a lot of trouble to make us think she gassed herself. But then the lady's dead before he even gets her into her car. What I'm considering is that he didn't mean to whack her inside the house. You know, he applies a choke hold, uses too much force, and she dies. So, maybe he didn't know her health was bad and that's how it happened."

I started shaking my head. "Her high blood pressure has nothing to do with it."

"Explain how she died, then."

"Say the assailant is right-handed, he brought his left arm around the front of her neck and used his right hand to pull the left wrist toward the right." I demonstrated. "This placed pressure eccentrically on her neck, resulting in fracture of the right greater comua of the hyoid bone. The pressure collapsed her upper airway and put pressure on the carotid arteries. She would have gotten hypoxic, or air hungry. Sometimes pressure on the neck produces bradycardia, a drop in the heart rate, and the victim has an arrhythmia."

"Could you tell from her autopsy if the assailant started using a choke hold that ended up a yoking? If he was just trying to subdue her and used too much force, in other words?"

"I can't tell you that from medical findings."

"But it's possible."

"It's within the realm of possibility."

"Come on, Doc," Marino said, exasperated. "Get off the witness stand for a minute, okay? Somebody else in this office besides you and me?"

No one was. But I was unnerved. Most of my staff had not shown up for work today, and Susan had acted bizarrely. Jennifer Deighton, a stranger, apparently had been trying to call me, then was murdered, and a man who claimed to be her brother had just hung up on me. Not to mention, Marino's mood was foul. When I felt a loss of control, I became very clinical.

"Look," I said, "he very well may have used a choke hold to subdue her and ended up applying too much force, yoking her by mistake. In fact, I'll even go so far as to suggest that he simply thought he'd knocked her out and didn't know she was dead when he placed her inside her car."

"So we're dealing with a dumb shit."

"I wouldn't conclude that if I were you. But if he gets up

tomorrow morning and reads in the paper that Jennifer Deighton was murdered, he may be in for the surprise of his life. He's going to wonder what he did wrong. Which is why I recommended we keep this away from the press."

"I got no problem with that. By the way, just because you didn't know Jennifer Deighton don't mean she didn't know you."

I waited for him to explain.

"I've been thinking about your hang ups. You're on TV, in the papers. Maybe she knew someone was after her, didn't know where to turn, and reached out to you for help. When she got your machine, she was too paranoid to leave a message."

"That's a very depressing thought."

"Almost everything we think in this joint is depressing." He got up from his chair.

"Do me a favor," I said. "Check her house. Tell me if you find any feather pillows, down-filled jackets, feather dusters, anything relating to feathers."

"Why?"

"I found a small feather on her gown."

"Sure. I'll let you know. Are you leaving?"

I glanced past him as I heard the elevator doors open and shut. "Was that Stevens?" I asked.

"Yeah."

"I've got a few more things to do before I go home," I said.

After Marino got on the elevator, I went to a window at the end of the hall that overlooked the parking lot in back. I wanted to make sure Ben Stevens's Jeep was gone. It was, and I watched as Marino emerged from the building, picking his way through crushed snow lit up by street lamps. He trudged to his car and stopped to vigorously shake snow off his feet, like a cat that's stepped in water, before sliding behind the wheel. God forbid that anything should violate the freshened air and Armor All of his inner sanctum. I wondered if he had plans for Christmas and was dismayed that I had not thought to invite him in for dinner. This would be his first Christmas since he and Doris had divorced.

As I made my way back down the empty hall, I ducked into each office along the way to check computer terminals. Unfortunately, no one was logged in, and the only cable tagged with a device number was Fielding's. It was neither tty07 nor tty14. Frustrated, I unlocked Margaret's office and switched on the light.

Typically, it looked as if a fierce wind had blown through, scattering papers across her desk, tipping books over in the bookcase and knocking others on the floor. Stacks of continuous-paper printouts spilled over like accordions, and indecipherable notes and telephone numbers were taped to walls and terminal screens. The minicomputer hummed like an electronic insect and lights danced across banks of modems on a shelf. Sitting in her chair before the system terminal, I slid open a drawer to my right and began rapidly walking my fingers through file tabs. I found several with promising labels such as "users" and "networking," but nothing I perused told me what I needed to know. Looking around as I thought, I noticed a thick bundle of cables that ran up the wall behind the computer and disappeared through the ceiling. Each cable was tagged.

Both tty07 and tty14 were connected directly to the computer. Unplugging tty07 first, I roamed from terminal to terminal to see which had been disconnected as a result. The terminal in Ben Stevens's office was down, then up again when I reconnected the cable. Next I set about to trace tty14, and was perplexed when the unplugging of that cable seemed to illicit no response. Terminals on the desks of my staff continued to work without pause. Then I remembered Susan. Her office was downstairs in the morgue.

Unlocking her door, I noticed two details the instant I walked into her office. There were no personal effects, such as photographs and knickknacks, to be seen, and on a bookshelf over the desk were a number of UNIX, SQL, and WordPerfect reference guides. I vaguely recalled that Susan had signed up for several computer courses last spring. Flipping a switch to turn on her monitor, I tried to log in and was baffled when the system responded. Her terminal was still connected; it could not be tty14. And then I realized something so obvious that I might have laughed were I not horrified.

Back upstairs, I paused in my office doorway, looking in as if someone I had never met worked here. Pooled around the workstation on my desk were lab reports, call sheets, death certificates, and page proofs of a forensic pathology textbook I was editing, and the return bearing my microscope didn't look much better. Against a wall were three tall filing cabinets, and across from them a couch situated far enough away from bookcases that you could easily go around it to reach books on lower shelves. Directly behind my chair was an oak credenza I had found years earlier in the state's surplus warehouse. Its drawers had locks, making it a perfect repository for my pocketbook and active cases that were unusually sensitive. I kept the key under my phone, and I thought again of last Thursday when Susan had broken jars of formalin while I was doing Eddie Heath's autopsy.

I did not know the device number of my terminal, for there had never been occasion when it mattered. Seating myself at my desk and sliding out the keyboard drawer, I tried to log in but my keystrokes were ignored. Disconnecting tty14 had disconnected me.

"Damn," I whispered as my blood ran cold. "Damn!"

I had sent no notes to my administrator's terminal. It was not I who had typed "I can't find it." In fact, when the file was accidentally created late last Thursday afternoon, I was in the morgue. But Susan wasn't. I had given her my keys and told her to lie down on the couch in my office until she recovered from the formalin spill. Was it possible that she not only had broken into my directory but also had gone through files and the paperwork on my desk? Had she attempted to send a note to Ben Stevens because she couldn't find what they were interested in?

One of the trace evidence examiners from upstairs suddenly appeared in my doorway, startling me.

"Hello," he muttered as he looked through paperwork, his lab coat buttoned up to his chin. Pulling out a multiple-page report, he walked in and handed it to me.

"I was getting ready to leave this in your box," he said. "But since you're still here, I'll give it to you in person. I've finished examining the adhesive residue you lifted from Eddie Heath's wrists."

"Building materials?" I asked, scanning the first page of the report.

"That's right. Paint, plaster, wood, cement, asbestos, glass. Typically, we find this sort of debris in burglary cases, often on the suspects' clothing, in their cuffs, pockets, shoes, and so on."

"What about on Eddie Heath's clothes?"

"Some of this same debris was on his clothes."

"And the paints? Tell me about them."

"I found bits of paint from five different origins. Three of them are layered, meaning something was painted and repainted a number of times."

"Are the origins vehicular or residential?" I inquired.

"Only one is vehicular, an acrylic lacquer typically used as a top coat in cars manufactured by General Motors."

It could have come from the vehicle used to abduct Eddie Heath, I thought. And it could have come from anywhere.

"The color?" I inquired.

"Blue."

"Layered?"

"No."

"What about the debris from the area of pavement where the body was found? I asked Marino to get sweepings to you and he said he would."

"Sand, dirt, bits of paving material, plus the miscellaneous debris you might expect around a Dumpster. Glass, paper, ash, pollen, rust, plant material."

"That's different from what you found adhering to the residue on his wrists?"

"Yes. It would appear to me that the tape was applied and removed from his wrists in a location where there's debris from building materials and birds."

"Birds?"

"On the third page of the report," he said. "I found a lot of feather parts."

Lucy was restless and rather irritable when I got home. Clearly, she had not had enough to occupy her during the day, for she had taken it upon herself to rearrange my study. The laser printer had been moved, as had the modem and all of my computer reference guides.

"Why did you do this?" I asked.

She was in my chair, her back to me, and she replied without turning around or slowing her fingers on the keyboard. "It makes more sense this way."

"Lucy, you can't just go into someone else's office and move everything around. How would you feel if I did that to you?"

"There would be no reason to rearrange anything of mine. It's all arranged very sensibly." She stopped typing and swiveled around. "See, now you can reach the printer without getting up from the chair. Your books are right here within reach, and the modem is out of your way completely. You shouldn't set books, coffee cups, and things on top of a modem."

"Have you been in here all day?" I asked.

"Where else would I be? You took the car. I went jogging

132

around your neighborhood. Have you ever tried to run on snow?"

Pulling up a chair, I opened my briefcase and got out the paper bag Marino had given me. "You're saying you need a car."

"I feel stranded."

"Where would you like to go?"

"To your club. I don't know where else. I'd simply like the option. What's in the bag?"

"Books and a poem Marino gave me."

"Since when is he a member of the literati?" She got up and stretched. "I'm going to make a cup of herbal tea. Would you like some?"

"Coffee, please."

"It's bad for you," she said as she left the room.

"Oh, hell," I muttered irritably as I pulled the books and poem out of the bag and red fluorescent powder got all over my hands and clothes.

Neils Vander had done his usual thorough examination, and I had forgotten his passion for his new toy. Several months ago he had acquired an alternate light source and had retired the laser to the scrap heap. The Luma-Lite, with its "state-of-the-art three-hundred-and-fifty-watt high-intensity blue enhanced metal vapor arc lamp," as Vander lovingly described it whenever the subject came up, turned virtually invisible hairs and fibers a burning orange. Semen stains and street drug residues jumped out like solar flares, and best of all, the light could pick up fingerprints that never would have been seen in the past.

Vander had gone the gamut on Jennifer Deighton's paperback novels. They had been placed in the glass tank and exposed to vapors from Super Glue, the cyanoacrylate ester that reacts to the components of perspiration transferred by human skin. Then Vander had dusted the slick covers of the books with the red fluorescent powder that was now all over me. Finally, he had subjected the books to the cool blue scrutiny of the Luma-Lite and purpled pages with Ninhydrin. I hoped he would be rewarded for all of his trouble. My reward was to go into the bathroom and clean up with a wet washcloth.

Flipping through *Paris Trout* was unrevealing. The novel told the story of the heartless murder of a black girl, and if that was significant to Jennifer Deighton's own story, I could not imagine why. *Seth Speaks* was a spooky account of someone supposedly from another life communicating through the author. It did not really surprise me that Miss Deighton, with her otherworldly inclinations, might read such a thing. What interested me most was the poem.

It was typed on a sheet of white paper smudged purple with Ninhydrin and enclosed in a plastic bag:

JENNY

Jenny's kisses many
   warmed the copper penny
   wedded to her neck
   with cotton string.
It was in the spring
   when he had found it
   on the dusty drive
   beside the meadow
   and given it to her.

> No words of passion
>> spoken.
> He loved her
>> with a token.
> The meadow now is brown
>> and overgrown with brambles.
>> He is gone.
> The coin asleep
>> is cold
>>> down deep
>> in a woodland
> wishing pond.

There was no date, no name of the author. The paper was creased from having been folded in quarters. I got up and went into the living room, where Lucy had set coffee and tea on the table and was stirring the fire.

"Aren't you hungry?" she asked.

"As a matter of fact, I am," I said, glancing over the poem again and wondering what it meant. Was "Jenny" Jennifer Deighton? "What would you like to eat?"

"Believe it or not, steak. But only if it's good and the cows haven't been fed a bunch of chemicals," Lucy said. "Is it possible you could bring home a car from work so I could use yours this week?"

"I generally don't bring home the state car unless I'm on call."

"You went to a scene last night when you supposedly weren't on call. You're always on call, Aunt Kay."

"All right," I said. "Why don't we do this. We'll go get the

135

best steak in town. Afterward, we'll stop by the office and I'll drive the wagon home and you can take my car. There's still a little ice on the roads in spots. You have to promise to be extra careful."

"I've never seen your office."

"I'll show it to you if you wish."

"No way. Not at night."

"The dead can't hurt you."

"Yes, they can," Lucy said. "Dad hurt me when he died. He left me to be raised by Mom."

"Let's get our coats."

"Why is it that every time I bring up anything germane to our dysfunctional family, you change the subject?"

I headed to my bedroom for my coat. "Do you want to borrow my black leather jacket?"

"See, you're doing it again," she screamed.

We argued all the way to Ruth's Chris Steak House, and by the time I parked the car I had a headache and was completely disgusted with myself. Lucy had provoked me into raising my voice, and the only other person who could routinely do that was my mother.

"Why are you being so difficult?" I said in her ear as we were shown to a table.

"I want to talk to you and you won't let me," she said.

A waiter instantly appeared for drink orders.

"Dewar's and soda," I said.

"Sparkling water with a twist," Lucy said. "You shouldn't drink and drive."

"I'm having only one. But you're right. I'd be better off not having any. And you're being critical again. How can you expect to have friends if you talk to people this way?"

"I don't expect to have friends." She stared off. "It's others who expect me to have friends. Maybe I don't want any friends because most people bore me."

Despair pressed against my heart. "I think you want friends more than anyone I know, Lucy."

"I'm sure you think that. And you probably also think I should get married in a couple of years."

"Not at all. In fact, I sincerely hope you won't."

"While I was roaming around inside your computer today, I saw the file called 'flesh.' Why do you have a file called that?" my niece asked.

"Because I'm in the middle of a very difficult case."

"The little boy named Eddie Heath? I saw his record in the case file. He was found with no clothes on, next to a Dumpster. Someone had cut out parts of his skin."

"Lucy, you shouldn't read case records," I said as my pager went off. I unclipped it from the waistband of my skirt and glanced at the number.

"Excuse me for a moment," I said, getting up from the table as our drinks arrived.

I found a pay phone. It was almost eight P.M.

"I need to talk to you," said Neils Vander, who was still at the office. "You might want to come down here and bring by Ronnie Waddell's ten print cards."

"Why?"

"We've got an unprecedented problem. I'm about to call Marino, too."

"All right. Tell him to meet me at the morgue in a half hour."

When I returned to the table, Lucy knew by the look on my face that I was about to ruin another evening.

"I'm so sorry," I said.

"Where are we going?"

"To my office, then to the Seaboard Building." I got out my billfold.

"What's in the Seaboard Building?"

"It's where the serology, DNA, and fingerprint labs moved not so long ago. Marino's going to meet us," I said. "It's been a long time since you've seen him."

"Jerks like him don't change or get better with time."

"Lucy, that's unkind. Marino is not a jerk."

"He was last time I was here."

"You weren't exactly nice to him, either."

"I didn't call him a smartass brat."

"You called him a number of other names, as I recall, and were continually correcting his grammar."

A half hour later, I left Lucy inside the morgue office while I hurried upstairs. Unlocking the credenza, I retrieved Waddell's case file, and no sooner had I boarded the elevator when the buzzer sounded from the bay. Marino was dressed in jeans and a dark blue parka, his balding head warmed by a Richmond Braves baseball cap.

"You two remember each other, don't you?" I said. "Lucy's visiting me for Christmas and is helping out with a computer problem," I explained as we walked out into the cold night air.

The Seaboard Building was across the street from the parking lot behind the morgue and cater-cornered to the front of Main Street Station, where the Health Department's administrative offices had relocated while its former building was being stripped of asbestos. The clock in Main Street Station's tower floated high above us like a hunter's moon, and red lights atop high buildings blinked slow warnings to low-flying planes. Somewhere in the dark, a train lumbered along its tracks, the earth rumbling and creaking like a ship at sea.

Marino walked ahead of us, the tip of his cigarette glowing at intervals. He did not want Lucy here, and I knew she sensed it. When he reached the Seaboard Building, where supplies had been loaded onto boxcars around the time of the Civil War, I rang the bell outside the door. Vander appeared almost immediately to let us in.

He did not greet Marino or ask who Lucy was. If a creature from outer space were to accompany someone he trusted, Vander would not ask any questions or expect to be introduced. We followed him up a flight of stairs to the second floor, where old corridors and offices had been repainted in shades of gunmetal gray and refurnished with cherry-finished desks and bookcases and teal upholstered chairs.

"What are you working on so late?" I asked as we entered the room housing the Automated Fingerprint Identification System, known as AFIS.

"Jennifer Deighton's case," he said.

"Then what do you want with Waddell's ten print cards?" I asked, perplexed.

139

"I want to be sure it was Waddell you autopsied last week," Vander said bluntly.

"What the hell are you talking about?" Marino looked at him in astonishment.

"I'm getting ready to show you." Vander seated himself before the remote input terminal, which looked like an everyday PC. It was connected by modem to the State Police computer, on which resided a data base of more than six million fingerprints. He hit several keys, activating the laser printer.

"Perfect scores are few and far between, but we got one here." Vander began typing, and a bright white fingerprint filled the screen. "Right index finger, plain whorl." He pointed to the vortex of lines swirling behind glass. "A damn good partial recovered from Jennifer Deighton's house."

"Where in her house?" I asked.

"From a dining room chair. At first I wondered if there was some mistake. But apparently not." Vander continued staring at the screen, then resumed typing as he talked. "The print comes back to Ronnie Joe Waddell."

"That's impossible," I said, shocked.

"You would think so," Vander replied abstractedly.

"Did you find anything in Jennifer Deighton's house that might indicate she and Waddell were acquainted?" I asked Marino as I opened Waddell's case file.

"No."

"If you've got Waddell's prints from the morgue," Vander said to me, "we'll see how they compare to what's in AFIS."

I pulled out two manila envelopes, and it struck me wrong

immediately that both weren't heavy and thick. I felt my face get hot as I opened each and found the expected photographs inside and nothing else. There was no envelope containing Waddell's ten print cards. When I looked up, everybody was looking at me.

"I don't understand this," I said, conscious of Lucy's uneasy stare.

"You don't have his prints?" Marino asked in disbelief.

I rifled through the file again. "They're not here."

"Susan usually does it, right?" he said.

"Yes. Always. She was supposed to make two sets. One for Corrections and one for us. Maybe she gave them to Fielding and he forgot to give them to me."

I got out my address book and reached for the phone. Fielding was home and knew nothing about the fingerprint cards.

"No, I didn't notice her printing him, but I don't notice half of what other people are doing down there," he said. "I just assumed she'd given the cards to you."

Dialing Susan's number next, I tried to remember seeing her get out the spoon and print cards, or rolling Waddell's fingers on the ink pad.

"Do you remember seeing Susan print Waddell?" I asked Marino as Susan's phone continued to ring.

"She didn't do it while I was there. I would have offered to help if she had."

"No answer." I hung up.

"Waddell was cremated," Vander said.

"Yes," I said.

We were silent for a moment.

Then Marino said to Lucy with unnecessary brusqueness, "You mind? We need to talk alone for a minute."

"You can sit in my office," Vander said to her. "Down the hall, last one on the right."

When she was gone, Marino said, "Waddell's supposedly been locked up ten years, and there's no way the print we got from Jennifer Deighton's chair was left ten years ago. She didn't even move into her house on Southside until a few months ago, and the dining room furniture looks brand-new. Plus, there were indentations on the carpet in the living room that make it appear a dining room chair was carried in there, maybe on the night she died. That's why I wanted the chairs dusted to begin with."

"An uncanny possibility," Vander said. "At this moment, we can't prove that the man who was executed last week was Ronnie Joe Waddell."

"Perhaps there is some other explanation for how Waddell's print ended up on a chair in Jennifer Deighton's house," I said. "For example, the penitentiary has a wood shop that makes furniture."

"Unlikely as hell," Marino said. "For one thing, they don't do woodworking or make license plates on death row. And even if they did, most civilians don't end up with prison-made furniture in their house."

"All the same," Vander said to Marino, "it would be interesting if you could track down who and where she bought her dining room set from."

"Don't worry. It's a top priority."

"Waddell's complete past arrest record, including his prints, should all be in one file at the FBI," Vander added. "I'll get a copy of their print card and retrieve the photograph of the thumbprint from Robyn Naismith's case. Where else was Waddell arrested?"

"Nowhere else," Marino said. "The only jurisdiction that will have his records should be Richmond."

"And this print found on a dining room chair is the only one you've identified?" I asked Vander.

"Of course, a number of those lifted came back to Jennifer Deighton," he said. "Particularly on the books by her bed and the folded sheet of paper—the poem. And a couple of unknown partials from her car, as you might expect, maybe left by whoever loaded groceries into her trunk or filled her tank with gas. That's all for now."

"And no luck with Eddie Heath?" I asked.

"There wasn't much to examine. The paper bag, can of soup, candy bar. I tried the Luma-Lite on his shoes and clothes. No luck."

Later, he walked us out through the bay, where locked freezers stored the blood of enough convicted felons to fill a small city, the samples awaiting entry into the Commonwealth's DNA data bank. Parked in front of the door was Jennifer Deighton's car, and it looked more pathetic than I remembered, as if it had gone into a dramatic decline since the murder of its owner. Metal along the sides was creased and dented from being repeatedly struck by other car doors. Paint was rusting in spots and scraped and gouged in others, and the vinyl top was peeling. Lucy paused to peer inside a sooty window.

"Hey, don't touch nothing," Marino said to her.

She looked levelly at him without a word, and all of us went outside.

Lucy drove off in my car and went straight to the house without waiting for Marino or me. When we walked in, she was already in my study with the door shut.

"I can see she's still Miss Congeniality," Marino said.

"You don't win any prizes tonight, either." I opened the fireplace screen and added several logs.

"She'll keep her mouth shut about what we were talking about?"

"Yes," I said wearily. "Of course."

"Yeah, well, I know you trust her, since you're her aunt. But I'm not sure it was a good idea for her to hear all that, Doc."

"I do trust Lucy. She means a lot to me. You mean a lot to me. I hope the two of you will become friends. The bar is open, or I'll be glad to put on a pot of coffee."

"Coffee would be good."

He sat on the edge of the hearth and got out his Swiss Army knife. While I made coffee, he trimmed his nails and tossed the shavings into the fire. I tried Susan's number again, but there was no answer.

"I don't think Susan took his prints," Marino said when I set the coffee tray on the butler's table. "I've been thinking while you were in the kitchen. I know she didn't do it while I was at the morgue that night, and I was there most of the time. So unless it was done right when the body was brought in, forget it."

"It wasn't done then," I said, getting more unnerved. "Corrections was out of there in minutes. The entire scene was very distracting. It was late and everybody was tired. Susan forgot, and I was too busy with what I was doing to notice."

"You hope she forgot."

I reached for my coffee.

"Something's going on with her, based on what you've been telling me. I wouldn't trust her as far as I could throw her," he said.

Right now I didn't.

"We need to talk to Benton," he said.

"You saw Waddell on the table, Marino. You saw him executed. I can't believe we can't say it was him."

"We can't say it. We could compare mug shots and your morgue photos and still not say it. I hadn't seen him since he got popped more than ten years ago. The guy they walked out to the chair was about eighty pounds heavier. His beard, mustache, and head had been shaved. Sure, there was enough resemblance that I just assumed. But I can't swear it was him."

I recalled Lucy's walking off the plane the other night. She was my niece. I had seen her but a year ago, and still I almost had not recognized her. I knew all too well how unreliable visual identifications can be.

"If someone switched inmates," I said. "And if Waddell is free and someone else was put to death, please tell me why."

Marino spooned more sugar into his coffee.

"A motive, for God's sake. Marino, what would it be?"

He looked up. "I don't know why."

Just then, the door to my study opened and both of us turned as Lucy walked out. She came into the living room and sat on the side of the hearth opposite Marino, who had his back to the fire, elbows on his knees.

"What can you tell me about AFIS?" she asked me as if Marino were not in the room.

"What is it you wish to know?" I said.

"The language. And is it run on a mainframe."

"I don't know the technical details. Why?"

"I can find out if files have been altered."

I felt Marino's eyes on me.

"You can't break into the State Police computer, Lucy."

"I probably could, but I'm not necessarily advocating that. There may be some other way to gain access."

Marino turned to her. "You're saying you could tell if Waddell's records was changed in AFIS?"

"Yes. I'm saying I could tell if his records *were* changed."

Marino's jaw muscles flexed. "Seems to me if someone was slick enough to do it, they'd be slick enough to make sure some computer nerd didn't catch on."

"I'm not a computer nerd. I'm not a nerd of any description." They fell silent, parked on either end of the hearth like mismatched bookends.

"You can't go into AFIS," I said to Lucy.

She looked impassively at me.

"Not alone," I added. "Not unless there is a safe way to grant you access. And even if there is, I think I'd rather you stay out of it."

"I don't think you'd really rather that. If something was tampered with, you know I'd find out, Aunt Kay."

"The kid's got a god complex." Marino got up from the hearth.

Lucy said to him, "Could you hit the twelve on the clock over there on the wall? If you drew your gun right this minute and took aim?"

"I ain't interested in shooting up your aunt's house in order to prove something to you."

"Could you hit the twelve from where you're standing?"

"You're damn right."

"You're positive."

"Yeah, I'm positive."

"The lieutenant's got a god complex," Lucy said to me.

Marino turned to the fire, but not before I caught a flicker of a smile.

"All Neils Vander has is a workstation and printer," Lucy said. "He's connected to the State Police computer by modem. Has that always been the case?"

"No," I replied. "Before he moved into the new building, there was much more equipment involved."

"Describe it."

"Well, there were several different components. But the actual computer was much like the one Margaret has in her office." Realizing Lucy had not been inside Margaret's office, I added, "A mini."

Firelight cast moving shadows on her face. "I'll bet AFIS is a mainframe that isn't a mainframe. I'll bet it's a series of minis strung together, all of it connected by UNIX or some other multiuser, multitasking environment. If you got me access to the system, I could probably do it from your terminal here in the house, Aunt Kay."

"I don't want anything traced back to me," I said with feeling.

"Nothing would be traced back to you. I would dial into your computer downtown, then go through a series of gateways, set up a really complicated link. By the time all was said and done, I'd be very hard to track."

Marino headed to the bathroom.

"He acts like he lives here," Lucy said.

"Not quite," I replied.

Several minutes later, I walked Marino out. The crusty snow of the lawn seemed to radiate light, and the air was sharp in my lungs like the first hit of a menthol cigarette.

"I'd love it if you would join Lucy and me for Christmas dinner," I said from the doorway.

He hesitated, looking at his car parked on the street. "That's mighty nice of you, but I can't make it, Doc."

"I wish you did not dislike Lucy so much," I said, hurt.

"I'm tired of her treating me like a dumb shit who was born in a barn."

"Sometimes you act like a dumb shit who was born in a barn. And you haven't tried very hard to earn her respect."

"She's a spoiled Miami brat."

"When she was ten, she was a Miami brat," I said. "But she's never been spoiled. In fact, quite the opposite is true. I want you two to get along. I want that for my Christmas present."

"Who said I was giving you a Christmas present?"

"Of course you are. You're going to give me what I've just requested. And I know exactly how to make it happen."

"How?" he asked suspiciously.

"Lucy wants to learn to shoot and you just told her you could shoot the twelve off a clock. You could give her a lesson or two."

"Forget it," he said.

6

The next three days were typical for the holiday season. No one was in or returning telephone calls. Parking lots had spaces to spare, lunch hours were long, and office errands involved clandestine stops at stores, the bank, and the post office. For all practical purposes, the Commonwealth had shut down before the official holiday began. But Neils Vander was not typical by any standard. He was oblivious to time and place when he called me Christmas Eve morning.

"I'm getting started on an image enhancement over here that I think you might be interested in," he said. "The Jennifer Deighton case."

"I'm on my way," I said.

Heading down the hallway, I almost ran into Ben Stevens as he emerged from the men's room.

"I have a meeting with Vander," I said. "I shouldn't be long, and I've got my pager."

"I was just coming to see you," he said.

Reluctantly, I paused to hear what he had on his mind. I wondered if he detected that it was a struggle for me to act relaxed around him. Lucy continued to monitor our computer from my terminal at home to see if anyone attempted to access my directory again. So far, no one had.

"I had a talk with Susan this morning," Stevens said.

"How is she?"

"She's not coming back to work, Dr. Scarpetta."

I was not surprised, but I was stung that she could not tell me this herself. By now I had tried at least half a dozen times to get hold of her, and either no one answered or her husband did and offered some excuse for why Susan couldn't come to the phone.

"That's it?" I asked him. "She's simply not coming back? Did she give a reason?"

"I think she's having a tougher time with the pregnancy than she thought. I guess the job's just too much right now."

"She'll need to send a letter of resignation," I said, unable to keep the anger from my voice. "And I'll leave it to you to work out the details with Personnel. We'll need to begin looking for a replacement immediately."

"There's a hiring freeze," he reminded me as I walked off.

Outside, snow plowed along roadsides had frozen into mounds of filthy ice impossible to park on or walk across, and the sun burned wanly through portentous clouds. A streetcar carried a small brass band past, and I climbed granite steps gritty with salt as "Joy to the World" moved on. A Forensics police officer let me inside the Seaboard Building, and upstairs

I found Vander inside a room bright with color monitors and ultraviolet lights. Seated at the image enhancer's workstation, he was staring intensely at something on the screen as he manipulated a mouse.

"It's not blank," he announced without so much as a "how are you." "Someone wrote something on a piece of paper that was on top of this one, or close to on top of this one. If you look hard, you can barely make out impressions."

Then I began to understand. Centered on the light table to his left was a clean sheet of white paper, and I leaned closer to take a look. The impressions were so faint that I wasn't sure if I was imagining them.

"The sheet of paper found under the crystal on Jennifer Deighton's bed?" I asked, getting excited.

He nodded, moving the mouse some more, adjusting the gray tones.

"Is this live?"

"No. The video camera's already captured the impressions and they're saved on the hard disk. But don't touch the paper. I haven't processed it for prints yet. I'm just getting started, keep your fingers crossed. Come on, come on." He was talking to the enhancer now. "I know the camera saw it fine. You gotta help us out here."

Computerized methods of image enhancement are a lesson in contrasts and conundrums. A camera can differentiate more than two hundred shades of gray, the human eye less than forty. Just because something isn't there doesn't mean it isn't there.

"Thank God with paper you don't have to worry about background noise," Vander went on as he worked. "Speeds things up considerably when you don't have to worry about that. Had a time of it the other day with a bloody print left on a bed sheet. The weave of the fabric, you know. Not so long ago the print would have been worthless. Okay." Another tint of gray washed over the area he was working on. "Now we're getting somewhere. You see it?" He pointed at slender, ghostly shapes on the upper half of the screen.

"Barely."

"What we're trying to enhance here is shadow versus eradicated writing, because nothing was written and erased here. The shadow was produced when oblique light hit the flat surface of this paper and the indentations in it—at least the video camera perceived shadow loud and clear. You and I can't see it without help. Let's try a little more enhancement of the verticals." He moved the mouse. "Darken the horizontals just a tad. Good. It's coming. Two-oh-two, dash. We've got part of a phone number."

I pulled a chair close to him and sat down. "The area code for D.C.," I said.

"I'm making out a four and a three. Or is that an eight?"

I squinted. "I think it's a three."

"That's better. You're right. Definitely a three."

He continued to work for a while and more numbers and words became visible on the screen. Then he sighed and said, "Rats. I can't get the last digit. It's just not there, but look at this before the D.C. area code. 'To' followed by a colon. And right under it is 'from' followed by another colon and another number. Eight-oh-four. That's local. This number's very unclear. A five and maybe a seven, or is that a nine?"

"I think that's going to be Jennifer Deighton's number," I said. "Her fax machine and telephone are on the same line—she had a fax machine in her office, a single-sheet feed that uses ordinary typing paper. It appears she wrote out a fax on top of this sheet of paper. What did she send? A separate document? There's no message here."

"We're not finished yet. We're getting what looks like the date now. An eleven? No, that's a seven. December seventeenth. I'm going to move down."

He moved the mouse and the arrows slid down the screen. Hitting a key, he enlarged the area he wanted to work on, then began painting it with shades of gray. I sat very still while shapes began to slowly materialize out of a literary limbo, curves here, dots there, and t's boldly crossed. Vander worked silently. We barely blinked or breathed. We sat like this for an hour, words gradually getting sharper, one shade of gray contrasting with another, molecule by molecule, bit by bit. He willed them, coaxed them into existence. It was incredible. It was all there.

Exactly one week ago, barely two days before her murder, Jennifer Deighton had faxed the following message to a number in Washington, D.C.:

Yes, I'll cooperate, but it's too late, too late, too late. Better you should come here. This is all so wrong!

When I finally looked up from the screen as Vander hit the print button, I was light-headed. My vision was temporarily blurred, adrenaline surging.

"Marino needs to see this immediately. Hopefully, we can figure out whose fax number this is, the Washington number. We've got all but the last digit. How many fax numbers can there be in Washington that are exactly like this except for the last digit?"

"Digits zero through nine." Vander raised his voice above the printer's rat-a-tat-tat. "At the most, there could be only ten. Ten numbers, fax or otherwise, exactly like this one except for the last digit."

He gave me a printout. "I'll clean it up some more and get you a better copy later," he said. "And there's one more thing. I'm not having any luck getting my hands on Ronnie Waddell's print, the photo of the bloody thumbprint recovered from Robyn Naismith's house. Every time I call Archives, I'm told they're still looking for his file."

"Remember what time of year it is. I'll bet there's hardly anybody there," I said, unable to dispel a sense of foreboding.

Back in my office, I got hold of Marino and explained what the image enhancer had discovered.

"Hell, you can forget the phone company," he said. "My contact there's already left for vacation, and nobody else is going to do shit on Christmas Eve."

"There's a chance we can figure out who she sent the fax to on our own," I said.

"I don't know how, short of sending a fax that reads 'Who are you?' and then hoping you get a fax back that reads 'Hi. I'm Jennifer Deighton's killer.' "

"It depends on if the person has a label programmed into his fax machine," I said.

"A *label*?"

"Your more sophisticated fax machines allow you to program your name or company name into the system. This label will be printed on anything you fax to someone else. But what's more significant is that the label of the person receiving the fax will also appear in the character-display window of the machine sending the fax. In other words, if I send a fax to you, in the character display of my fax machine I'll see 'Richmond Police Department' right above the fax number I've just dialed."

"You got access to a fancy fax machine? The one we got in the squad room sucks."

"I've got one here at the office."

"Well, tell me what you find out. I've gotta hit the street."

Quickly, I made up a list of ten telephone numbers, each one beginning with the six digits Vander and I had been able to make out on the sheet of paper found on Jennifer Deighton's bed. I completed each number with a zero, a one, a two, a three, and so on, then began trying them out. Only one of them was answered by an inhuman, high-pitched tone.

The fax machine was located in my computer analyst's office, and Margaret, fortunately, had begun her holiday early, too. I shut her door and sat down at her desk, thinking as the mini-computer hummed and modem lights blinked. Labels worked both ways. If I began a transmission, the label for my office was going to appear in the character-display window of the fax machine I had dialed. I would have to kill the process fast, before the transmission was completed. I hoped that by the time anyone checked the machine to see what was going on,

"Office of the Chief Medical Examiner" and our number would have vanished from the window.

Inserting a blank sheet of paper into the tray, I dialed the Washington number and waited as the transmission began. Nothing materialized in the character-display window. Damn. The fax machine I had dialed did not have a label. So much for that. I killed the process and returned to my office, defeated.

I had just sat down at my desk when the telephone rang.

"Dr. Scarpetta," I answered.

"Nicholas Grueman here. Whatever you just tried to fax, it didn't transmit."

"Excuse me?" I said, stunned.

"I got nothing on this end but a blank sheet of paper with the name of your office stamped on it. Uh, error code zero-zero-one, 'please send again,' it says."

"I see," I said as the hairs on my arms raised.

"Perhaps you were trying to send an amendment to your record? I understand you took a look at the electric chair."

I did not reply.

"Very thorough of you, Dr. Scarpetta. Perhaps you learned something new about those injuries we discussed, the abrasions to the inner aspects of Mr. Waddell's arms? The *antecubital fossas*?"

"Please give me your fax number again," I said quietly.

He recited it for me. The number matched the one on my list.

"Is the fax machine in your office or do you share it with other attorneys, Mr. Grueman?"

"It's right next to my desk. No need to mark anything for

157

my attention. Just send it on—and *do* put a rush on it please, Dr. Scarpetta. I was thinking of going home soon."

I left the office a little later, frustration having driven me out the door. I could not get Marino. There was nothing more I could do. I felt caught in a web of bizarre connections, clueless as to the point in common they shared.

On impulse I pulled into a lot of West Cary where an old man was selling wreaths and Christmas trees. He looked like a lumberjack from a fable as he sat on a stool in the midst of his small forest, the cold air fragrant with evergreen. Perhaps my shunning of the Christmas spirit finally had gotten to me. Or maybe I simply wanted a distraction. At this late date, there wasn't much of a selection, those trees passed over, misshapen or dying, each destined to sit out the season, I suspected, except for the one I chose. It would have been lovely were it not scoliotic. Decorating it proved more an orthopedic challenge than a festive ritual, but with ornaments and strands of lights strategically hung and wire straightening the problem places, it stood proudly in my living room.

"There," I said to Lucy as I stepped back to admire my work. "What do you think?"

"I think it's weird that you suddenly decided to get a tree on Christmas Eve. When was the last time you had one?"

"I suppose when I was married."

"Is that where the ornaments came from?"

"Back then I went to a lot of trouble at Christmas."

"Which is why you don't anymore."

"I'm much busier than I was back then," I said.

Lucy opened the fireplace screen and rearranged logs with the poker. "Did you and Mark ever spend Christmas together?"

"Don't you remember? We came down to see you last Christmas."

"No, you didn't. You came for three days *after* Christmas and flew home on New Year's Day."

"He was with his family on Christmas Day."

"You weren't invited?"

"No."

"Why not?"

"Mark came from an old Boston family. They had certain ways of doing things. What did you decide about this evening? Did my jacket with the black velvet collar fit?"

"I haven't tried anything. Why do we have to go to all these places?" Lucy said. "I won't know anybody."

"It's not that bad. I simply have to drop off a present to someone who's pregnant and probably not coming back to work. And I need to show the flag at a neighborhood party. I accepted the invitation before I knew you were going to be visiting. You certainly don't have to come with me."

"I'd rather stay here," she said. "I wish I could get started on AFIS."

"Patience," I told her, though I did not feel patient at all.

In the late afternoon, I left another message with the dispatcher and decided that either Marino's pager wasn't working or he was too busy to find a pay phone. Candles glowed in my neighbors' windows, an oblong moon shining high above trees. I played that Christmas music of Pavarotti and the New York

Philharmonic, doing what I could to get into the proper frame of mind as I showered and dressed. The party I was to attend did not begin until seven. That gave me enough time to drop off Susan's gift and have a word with her.

She surprised me by answering the phone, and sounded reluctant and tense when I asked if I could drop by.

"Jason's out," she said, as if that mattered somehow. "He went to the mall."

"Well, I have a few things for you," I explained.

"What things?"

"Christmas things. I'm supposed to go to a party, so I won't stay long. Is that all right?"

"I guess. I mean, that's nice."

I had forgotten she lived in Southside, where I rarely went and was inclined to get lost. Traffic was worse than I had feared, the Midlothian Turnpike choked with last-minute shoppers prepared to run you off the road as they ran their Happy Holidays errands. Parking lots swarmed with cars, stores and malls so garishly lit up it was enough to make you blind. Susan's neighborhood was very dark and twice I had to pull over and turn on the interior light to read her directions. After much riding around, I finally found her tiny ranch-style house sandwiched between two others that looked exactly like it.

"Hi," I said, peering at her through leaves of the pink poinsettia in my arms.

She nervously locked the door and showed me to the living room. Pushing books and magazines aside, she set the poinsettia on the coffee table.

"How are you feeling?" I asked.

"Better. Would you like something to drink? Here, let me take your coat."

"Thanks. Nothing to drink. I can't stay but a minute." I handed her a package. "A little something I picked up when I was in San Francisco last summer." I sat on the couch.

"Wow. You really do your shopping early." She avoided my eyes as she curled up in a wing chair. "You want me to open it now?"

"Whatever you'd like."

She carefully sliced through tape with a thumbnail and slipped off the satin ribbon intact. Smoothing the paper into a neat rectangle, as if she planned to reuse it, she placed it in her lap and opened the black box.

"Oh," she said under her breath, unfolding the red silk scarf.

"I thought it would look good with your black coat," I said. "I don't know about you, but I don't like wool against my skin."

"This is beautiful. It's really thoughtful of you, Dr. Scarpetta. I've never had anybody bring me something from San Francisco before."

The expression of her face pricked my heart, and suddenly my surroundings came into sharper focus. Susan was wearing a yellow terry cloth robe, frayed at the cuffs, and a pair of black socks that I suspected belonged to her husband. Furniture was scarred and cheap, upholstery shiny. The artificial Christmas tree near the small TV was scantily decorated and missing several limbs. There were few presents underneath. Propped against a wall was a folded crib that was clearly secondhand.

Susan caught me glancing around and looked ill at ease.

"Everything is so immaculate," I said.

"You know how I am. Obsessive-compulsive."

"Thankfully. If a morgue can look terrific, ours does."

She carefully folded the scarf and returned it to its box. Pulling her robe more tightly around her, she stared silently at the poinsettia.

"Susan," I said gently, "do you want to talk about what's going on?"

She did not look at me.

"It's not like you to get upset as you did the other morning. It's not like you to miss work and then quit without so much as calling me."

She took a deep breath. "I'm really sorry. I just can't seem to handle things too well these days. I really react. Like when I was reminded of Judy."

"I know your sister's death must have been terrible for you."

"We were twins. Not identical. Judy was a lot prettier than me. That was part of the problem. Doreen was jealous of her."

"Doreen was the girl who claimed to be a witch?"

"Yes. I'm sorry. I just don't want to be around anything like that. Especially now."

"It might make you feel better to know that I called the church near Jennifer Deighton's house and was told that the steeple is illuminated with sodium vapor lights that started going bad several months ago. Apparently, no one was aware that the lights hadn't been properly repaired. That seems to be the explanation for why they blink on and off."

"When I was growing up in the church," she said, "there were pentecostals in the congregation who believed in speaking

162

in tongues and casting out demons. I remember this man coming to dinner and talking about his encounter with demons, about lying in bed at night and hearing something breathing in the dark and books flying off shelves and slamming around the room. I was scared to death by stuff like that. I couldn't even see *The Exorcist* when it came out."

"Susan, we have to be objective and clearheaded on the job. We can't let our backgrounds, beliefs, or phobias interfere."

"You didn't grow up the daughter of a minister."

"I grew up Catholic," I said.

"Nothing's the same as growing up the daughter of a fundamentalist minister," she challenged, blinking back tears.

I did not argue.

"I think I've gotten free of old stuff, then it grabs me around the throat," she went on with difficulty. "Like there's this other person inside who messes with me."

"How are you being messed with?"

"Some things have gotten ruined."

I waited for her to elaborate, but she would not. She stared down at her hands, her eyes miserable. "It's just too much pressure," she muttered.

"What is too much pressure, Susan?"

"Work."

"How is it any different than it's ever been?" I assumed she would say that expecting a child made everything different.

"Jason doesn't think it's healthy for me. He's always thought that."

"I see."

"I come home and tell him what my day was like, and he has

a real hard time with it. He says, 'Don't you realize how awful this is? There's no way it can be good for you.' He's right. I can't always shake it off anymore. I'm tired of decomposed bodies and people raped, cut up, and shot. I'm tired of dead babies and people killed in their cars. I don't want any more violence." She looked at me, her lower lip trembling. "I don't want any more death."

I thought of how difficult it was going to be to replace her. With someone new, days would be slow, the learning curve long. Worse were the perils of interviewing applicants and screening out the weirdos. Not everyone eager to work in a morgue is the paragon of normalcy. I liked Susan and I felt hurt and deeply troubled. She was not being honest with me.

"Is there anything else you'd like to tell me about?" I asked, my eyes not leaving her.

She glanced at me and I saw fear. "I can't think of anything."

I heard a car door shut.

"Jason's home," she barely said.

Our conversation had ended, and as I got up I said quietly to her, "Please contact me if you need anything, Susan. A reference, or just to talk. You know where I am."

I spoke to her husband only briefly on my way out. He was tall and well built, with curly brown hair and distant eyes. Though he was polite, I could tell he was not pleased to discover me in his house. As I drove across the river, I was shaken by the image that this struggling young couple must have of me. I was the *boss* dressed in a designer suit arriving in her Mercedes to deliver token gifts on Christmas Eve. The alienation of Susan's loyalty touched my deepest insecurities. I was no longer sure of my relationships or how I was perceived. I feared I had failed some test after Mark was killed, as if my reaction to that loss held the answer to a question in the lives of those around me. After all, I was supposed to handle death better than anyone. Dr. Kay Scarpetta, the expert. Instead, I had withdrawn, and I knew others felt the coolness around my edges no matter how friendly or thoughtful I tried to be. My staff no longer confided in me. Now it appeared security in my office had been violated, and Susan had quit.

Taking the Cary Street exit, I turned left into my neighborhood and headed for the home of Bruce Carter, a district court judge. He lived on Sulgrave, several blocks from me, and suddenly I was a child in Miami again, staring at what had seemed mansions to me then. I remembered going door-to-door with a wagon full of citrus fruit, knowing that the elegant hands doling out change belonged to unreachable people who felt pity. I remembered returning home with a pocket full of pennies and smelling the sickness in the bedroom where my father lay dying.

Windsor Farms was quietly rich, with Georgian and Tudor houses neatly arranged along streets with English names, and estates shadowed by trees and surrounded by serpentine brick walls. Private security jealously guarded the privileged, for whom burglar alarms were as common as sprinklers. Unspoken covenants were more intimidating than those in print. You did not offend your neighbors by putting up clotheslines or dropping by unannounced. You did not have to drive a Jaguar, but if your means of transportation was a rusting pickup truck or a morgue wagon, you kept it out of sight inside the garage.

At quarter past seven, I parked behind a long line of cars in front of a white-painted brick house with a slate roof. White lights were caught like tiny stars in boxwoods and spruces, and a fragrant fresh wreath hung on the red front door. Nancy Carter embraced my arrival with a gorgeous smile and arms extended to take my coat. She talked nonstop above the indecipherable language of crowds as light winked off the sequins of her long red gown. The judge's wife was a woman in her fifties refined by money into a work of well-bred art. In her youth, I suspected, she had not been pretty.

"Bruce is somewhere . . ." She glanced about. "The bar's over there."

She directed me to the living room, where the bright holiday attire of guests blended wonderfully with a large vibrant Persian rug that I suspected cost more than the house I had just visited on the other side of the river. I spotted the judge talking to a man I did not know. I scanned faces, recognizing several physicians and attorneys, a lobbyist, and the governor's chief of staff. Somehow I ended up with a Scotch and soda, and a man I had never seen before was touching my arm.

"Dr. Scarpetta? Frank Donahue," he introduced himself loudly. "A Merry Christmas to you."

"And to you," I said.

The warden, who allegedly had been ill the day Marino and I had toured the penitentiary, was small, with coarse features and thick graying hair. He was dressed like a parody of an English toastmaster in bright red tails, a ruffled white dress shirt, and a red bow tie twinkling with tiny electric lights. A glass of straight whiskey tilted perilously in one hand as he offered me the other.

He leaned close to my ear. "I was disappointed I was unable to show you around the day you came to the pen."

"One of your officers took good care of us. Thank you."

"I guess that would have been Roberts."

"I think that was his name."

"Well, it's unfortunate that you had to go to the trouble." His eyes roamed the room and he winked at someone behind me. "A lot of horse crap was what it was. You know, Waddell'd had a couple of nosebleeds in the past, and high blood pressure. Was always complaining about something. Headaches. Insomnia."

I bent my head, straining to hear.

"These guys on death row are consummate con artists. And to be honest, Waddell was one of the worst."

"I wouldn't know," I said, looking up at him.

"That's the trouble, nobody knows. No matter what you say, nobody knows except those of us who are around these guys every day."

"I'm sure."

"Waddell's so-called reformation, him turning into such a sweetheart. Sometime let me tell you about that, Dr. Scarpetta, about the way he used to brag to other inmates about what he did to that poor Naismith girl. Thought he was a real cock of the walk because he *did* a celebrity."

The room was airless and too warm. I could feel his eyes crawl over my body.

"Of course, I don't guess much surprises you, either," he said.

"No, Mr. Donahue. There isn't much that surprises me."

"To be honest, I don't know how you look at what you do every day. Especially this time of year, people killing each other and themselves, like that poor lady who committed suicide in her garage the other night after opening her Christmas presents early."

His remark caught me like an elbow in the ribs. There had been a brief story in the morning paper about Jennifer's Deighton's death, and a police source had been quoted as saying that it appeared she had opened her Christmas presents early. This might imply she had committed suicide, but there had been no statement to that effect.

"Which lady are you referring to?" I asked.

"Don't recall the name." Donahue sipped his drink, his face flushed, eyes bright and constantly moving. "Sad, real sad. Well, you'll have to visit us at our new digs in Greensville one of these days." He smiled broadly, then left me for a bosomy matron in black. He kissed her on the mouth and both of them started laughing.

I went home at the earliest opportunity, to find a fire blazing and my niece stretched out on the couch, reading. I noted several new presents under the tree.

"How was it?" she asked with a yawn.

"You were wise to stay home," I said. "Has Marino called?"

"Nope."

I tried him again, and after four rings he answered irritably.

"I hope I didn't get you too late," I apologized.

"I hope not, either. What's wrong now?"

"A lot of things are wrong. I met your friend Mr. Donahue at a party this evening."

"What a thrill."

"I wasn't impressed, and maybe I'm just paranoid, but I thought it odd he brought up Jennifer Deighton's death."

Silence.

"The other little twist," I went on, "is it appears Jennifer Deighton faxed a note to Nicholas Grueman less than two days before her murder. In it she sounded upset, and I got the impression he wanted to meet with her. She suggested he come to Richmond."

Still Marino said nothing.

"Are you there?" I asked.

"I'm thinking."

"Glad to hear it. But maybe we should think together. Sure I can't change your mind about dinner tomorrow?"

He took a deep breath. "I'd like to, Doc. But I . . ."

A female voice in the background said, "Which drawer's it in?"

Marino evidently placed his hand over the receiver and mumbled something. When he got back to me he cleared his throat.

"I'm sorry," I said. "I didn't know you had company."

"Yeah." He paused.

"I would be delighted if you and your friend would come to dinner tomorrow," I offered.

"The Sheraton's got this buffet. We was going to go to that."

"Well, there's something for you under the tree. If you change your mind, give me a call in the morning."

"I don't believe it. You broke down and got a tree? Bet it's an ugly little sucker."

"The envy of the neighborhood, thank you very much," I said. "Wish your friend a Merry Christmas for me."

7

I woke up the next morning to church bells chiming and draperies glowing with the sun. Though I'd had very little to drink the night before, I felt hung over. Lingering in bed, I fell back to sleep and saw Mark in my dreams.

When I finally got up, the kitchen was fragrant with vanilla and oranges. Lucy was grinding coffee beans.

"You're going to spoil me, and then what will I do? Merry Christmas." I kissed the top of her head, noticing an unusual bag of cereal on the counter. "What's this?"

"Cheshire muesli. A special treat. I brought my own supply. It's best with plain yogurt if you've got it, which you don't. So we'll have to settle for skim milk and bananas. Plus, we have fresh orange juice and decaffeinated French vanilla coffee. I guess we should call Mom and Grans."

While I dialed my mother's number from the kitchen, Lucy went into my study to use that extension. My sister was already at my mother's, and soon the four of us were on the line, my mother complaining at great length about the weather. It was storming fiercely in Miami, she said. Torrential rains accompanied by punishing winds had begun late Christmas Eve, the morning celebrated by a grand illumination of lightning.

"You shouldn't be on the phone during an electrical storm," I said to them. "We'll call back later."

"You're so paranoid, Kay," Dorothy chided. "You look at everything in terms of how it might kill somebody."

"Lucy, tell me about your presents," my mother interjected.

"Grans, we haven't opened them yet."

"Wow. That was really close," Dorothy exclaimed above crackling static. "The lights just flickered."

"Mom, I hope you don't have a file open on your computer," Lucy said. "Because if you do, you probably just lost whatever you were working on."

"Dorothy, did you remember to bring butter?" my mother asked.

"Damn. I knew there was something . . ."

"I must have reminded you three times last night."

"I've told you I can't remember things when you call me while I'm writing, Mother."

"Can you imagine? Christmas Eve and would you go to mass with me? No. You stay home working on that book and then forget to bring the butter."

"I'll go out and get some."

"And just what do you think will be open on Christmas morning?"

"Something will be."

I looked up as Lucy walked into the kitchen.

"I don't believe it," she whispered to me as my mother and sister continued to argue with each other.

After I hung up, Lucy and I went into my living room, where we were returned to a quiet winter morning in Virginia, bare trees still and patches of snow pristine in the shade. I did not think I could ever live in Miami again. The change of seasons was like the phases of the moon, a force that pulled me and shifted my point of view. I needed the full with the new and the nuances in between, days to be short and cold in order to appreciate spring mornings.

Lucy's present from her grandmother was a check for fifty dollars. Dorothy gave money as well, and I felt rather ashamed when Lucy opened the envelope from me and added my check to the others.

"Money seems so impersonal," I apologized.

"It's not impersonal to me because it's what I want. You just bought another meg of memory for my computer." She handed me a small, heavy gift wrapped in red-and-silver paper, and could not suppress her joy when she saw the look on my face as I opened the box and parted layers of tissue paper.

"I thought you could keep your court schedule in it," she said. "It matches your motorcycle jacket."

"Lucy, it's gorgeous." I touched the black lambskin binding of the appointment book and smoothed open its creamy pages. I thought of the Sunday she had come to town, of how late she had stayed out when I'd let her take my car to the club. I bet the sneak had gone shopping.

"And this other present here is just refills for the address

173

section and the next calendar year." She set a smaller gift in my lap as the telephone rang.

Marino wished me a Merry Christmas and said he wanted to drop by with my "present."

"Tell Lucy she'd better dress warmly and not to wear anything tight," he said irritably.

"What are you talking about?" I puzzled.

"No tight jeans or she won't be able to get cartridges in and out of her pockets. You said she wanted to learn how to shoot. Lesson one is this morning before lunch. If she misses class, it's her damn problem. What time are we eating?"

"Between one-thirty and two. I thought you were tied up."

"Yeah, well, I untied myself. I'll be over in about twenty minutes. Tell the brat it's cold as hell outside. You want to come with us?"

"Not this time. I'll stay here and cook."

Marino's disposition was no more pleasant when he arrived at my door, and he made a great production of checking my spare revolver, a Ruger .38 with rubber grips. Depressing the thumb latch, he pushed open the cylinder and slowly spun it around, peering into each chamber. He pulled back the hammer, looked down the barrel, and then tried the trigger. While Lucy watched him in curious silence, he pontificated on the residue buildup left by the solvent I used and informed me that my Ruger probably had "spurs" that needed filing. Then he drove Lucy away in his Ford.

When they returned several hours later, their faces were rosy from the cold and Lucy proudly sported a blood blister on her trigger finger.

"How did she do?" I asked, drying my hands on my apron.

"Not bad," Marino said, looking past me. "I smell fried chicken."

"No, you don't." I took their coats. "You smell *cotoletta di tacchino alla bolognese.*"

"I did better than 'not bad,' " Lucy said. "I only missed the target twice."

"Just keep dry firing until you stop slapping the trigger. Remember, crawl the hammer back."

"I've got more soot on me than Santa after he's come down the chimney," Lucy said cheerfully. "I'm going to take a shower."

In the kitchen I poured coffee as Marino inspected a counter crowded with Marsala, fresh-grated Parmesan, prosciutto, white truffles, sauteed turkey fillets, and other assorted ingredients that were going into our meal. We went into the living room, where the fire was blazing.

"What you did was very kind," I said. "I appreciate it more than you'll ever know."

"One lesson's not enough. Maybe I can work with her a couple more times before she goes back to Florida."

"Thank you, Marino. I hope you didn't go to a lot of bother and sacrifice to change your plans."

"It was no big deal," he said curtly.

"Apparently, you decided against dinner at the Sheraton," I probed. "Your friend could have joined us."

"Something came up."

"Does she have a name?"

"Tanda."

"That's an interesting name."

Marino's face was turning crimson.

"What's Tanda like?" I asked.

"You want to know the truth, she ain't worth talking about."
Abruptly, he got up and headed down the hall to the bathroom.

I'd always been careful not to quiz Marino about his personal
life unless he invited me to do so. But I could not resist this time.

"How did you and Tanda meet?" I asked when he returned.

"The FOP dance."

"I think it's terrific that you're getting out and meeting new
people."

"It sucks, if you really want to know. I haven't dated nobody
in more than thirty years. It's like Rip Van Wrinkle waking up
in another century. Women are different from what they used
to be."

"How so?" I tried not to smile. Clearly, Marino did not think
any of this was amusing.

"They're not simple anymore."

"Simple?"

"Yeah, like Doris. What we had wasn't complicated. Then
after thirty years she suddenly splits and I have to start over. I
go to this friggin' dance at the FOP because some of the guys
talk me into it. I'm minding my own business when Tanda
comes up to my table. Two beers later, she asks me for my
phone number, if you can believe that."

"Did you give it to her?"

"I say, 'Hey, if you want to get together, you give me your
number. I'll do the calling.' She asks me which zoo I escaped
from, then invites me bowling. That's how it started. How it

ended is her telling me she rear-ended somebody a couple weeks back and was charged with reckless driving. She wanted me to fix it."

"I'm sorry." I fetched his present from under the tree and handed it to him. "I don't know if this will help your social life or not."

He unwrapped a pair of Christmas-red suspenders and compatible silk tie.

"That's mighty nice, Doc. Geez." Getting up, he muttered in disgust, "Damn water pills," and headed to the bathroom again. Several minutes later, he returned to the hearth.

"When was your last checkup?" I asked.

"A couple weeks ago."

"And?"

"And what do you think?" he said.

"You have high blood pressure, that's what I think."

"No shit."

"What, specifically, did your doctor tell you?" I asked.

"It's one-fifty over one-ten, and my damn prostate's enlarged. So I'm taking these water pills. Up and down all the time feeling like I gotta go and half the time I can't. If things don't get better, he says he's gonna turp me."

A turp was a transurethral resection of the prostate. That wasn't serious, though it wasn't much fun. Marino's blood pressure worried me. He was a prime candidate for a stroke or a heart attack.

"Plus, my ankles swell," he went on. "My feet hurt and I get these damn headaches. I've gotta quit smoking, give up coffee, lose forty pounds, cut down on stress."

"Yes, you've got to do all of those things," I said firmly. "And it doesn't look to me like you're doing any of them."

"We're only talking about changing my whole life. And you're one to talk."

"I don't have high blood pressure and I quit smoking exactly two months and five days ago. Not to mention, if I lost forty pounds I wouldn't be here."

He glared into the fire.

"Listen," I said. "Why don't we work on this together? We'll both cut back on coffee and get into exercise routines."

"I can just see you doing aerobics," he said sourly.

"I'll play tennis. You can do aerobics."

"Anybody so much as waves a pair of tights near me, they're dead."

"You're not being very cooperative, Marino."

He impatiently changed the subject. "You got a copy of the fax you told me about?"

I went to my study and returned with my briefcase. Snapping it open, I handed him the printout of the message Vander had discovered with the image enhancer.

"This was on the blank sheet of paper we found on Jennifer Deighton's bed, right?" he asked.

"That's correct."

"I still can't figure out why she had a blank sheet of paper on her bed with a crystal on top of it. What were they doing there?"

"I don't know," I said. "What about the messages on her answering machine? Anything?"

"We're still running them down. We've got a lot of people

to interview." He slipped a pack of Marlboros out of his shirt pocket and blew out a loud breath of air. "Damn." He slapped the pack on top of the coffee table. "You're going to nag me every time I light up one of these now, aren't you?"

"No, I'll just stare at it. But I won't say a word."

"You remember that interview of you that was on PBS a couple months back?"

"Vaguely."

"Jennifer Deighton taped it. The tape was in her VCR and we started playing it and there you were."

"What?" I asked, amazed.

"Of course, you weren't the only thing featured on that particular program. There was also some crap about an archaeology dig and a Hollywood movie they filmed around here."

"Why would she tape me?"

"It's just another piece that's not fitting with anything else yet. Except the calls made from her phone—the hang ups. It looks like Deighton was thinking about you before she was whacked."

"What else have you found out about her?"

"I gotta smoke. You want me to go outside?"

"Of course not."

"It gets weirder," he said. "While going through her office, we came across a divorce decree. Appears she was married in 1961, got divorced two years later, and changed her name back to Deighton. Then she moved from Florida to Richmond. The name of her ex is Willie Travers, and he's one of these health nut types—you know, into *whole* health. Hell, I can't think of the name."

"Holistic medicine?"

"That's it. Still lives in Florida, Fort Myers Beach. I got him on the phone. Hard as hell to get much out of him, but I managed to find out a few things. He says he and Miss Deighton continued feeling friendly toward each other after they split and, in fact, continued seeing each other."

"He came up here?"

"Travers said she'd go down there to see him, in Florida. They'd get together, as he put it, 'for old times' sake.' Last time she was down there was this past November, around Thanksgiving. I also pried out of him a little bit about Deighton's brother and sister. The sister's a lot younger, married, lives out West. The brother's the eldest, in his mid-fifties, and manages a grocery store. He had throat cancer a couple years back and his voice box was cut out."

"Wait a minute," I said.

"Yeah. You know what that sounds like. You'd know it if you heard it. No way the guy who called you at the office was John Deighton. It was somebody else who had personal reasons for being interested in Jennifer Deighton's autopsy findings. He knew enough to get the name right. He knew enough to get it straight that he's supposed to be from Columbia, South Carolina. But he didn't know about the real John Deighton's health problems, didn't know he should sound like he's talking through a machine."

"Does Travers know his ex-wife's death is a homicide?" I asked.

"I told him the medical examiner is still running tests."

"And he was in Florida when she died?"

"Allegedly. I'd like to know where your friend Nicholas Grueman was when she died."

"He has never been a friend," I said. "How will you approach him?"

"I won't for a while. You only get one shot with someone like Grueman. How old is he?"

"Somewhere in his sixties," I said.

"He a big guy?"

"I haven't seen him since I was in law school." I got up to stir the fire. "Back then Grueman's build was trim bordering on thin. I would describe his height as average."

Marino did not say anything.

"Jennifer Deighton weighed one-eighty," I reminded him. "It appears her killer yoked her and then carried her body out to her car."

"All right. So maybe Grueman had help. You want a farout scenario? Try this one on for size. Grueman represented Ronnie Waddell, who wasn't exactly a pencil-neck. Or maybe we should say, *isn't* exactly a pencil-neck. Waddell's print was found inside Jennifer Deighton's house. Maybe Grueman did go to see her and he didn't go alone."

I stared into the fire.

"By the way, I didn't see nothing in Jennifer Deighton's house that could have been the source of the feather you found," he added. "You asked me to check."

Just then, his pager sounded. Snapping it off his belt, he squinted at the narrow screen.

"Damn," he complained, heading into the kitchen with the phone.

"What's going . . . *What?*" I heard him say. "Oh, Christ. You sure?" He was silent for a moment. He sounded very tense when he said, "Don't bother. I'm standing fifteen feet from her."

Marino ran a red light at West Cary and Windsor Way, and headed east. Grille lights flashed and scanner lights danced in the white Ford LTD. Ten-codes crackled over the radio as I envisioned Susan curled up in the wing chair, her terry cloth robe pulled tightly around her to ward off a chill that had nothing to do with the temperature in the room. I remembered the expression on her face shifting constantly like clouds, her eyes revealing no secrets to me.

I was shivering and could not seem to catch my breath. My heart beat hard in my throat. Police had found Susan's car in an alleyway off Strawberry Street. She was in the driver's seat, dead. It was unknown what she had been doing in that part of town or what might have motivated her assailant.

"What else did she say when you talked with her last night?" Marino asked.

Nothing significant would come to mind. "She was tense," I said. "Something was bothering her."

"What? You got any guesses?"

"I don't know what." My hands shook as I fumbled with my medical bag and checked the contents again. Camera, gloves, and everything else were accounted for. I remembered Susan once saying that if anyone tried to abduct or rape her, they'd have to kill her first.

There had been a number of late afternoons when it was just the two of us cleaning up and filling out paperwork. We had had many personal conversations about being a woman and loving men, and what it would be like to be a mother. Once we had talked about death and Susan confessed she was afraid of it.

"I'm not talking about hell, either, the fire and brimstone my father preaches about—I'm not afraid of that," she said adamantly. "I'm just afraid of this being all there is."

"This isn't all there is," I said.

"How do you know?"

"Something's gone. You look at their faces and you can tell. Their energy has departed. The spirit didn't die. Just the body did."

"But how do you know?" she asked again.

Easing up on the accelerator, Marino turned onto Strawberry Street. I glanced in my side mirror. Another police car was behind us, light bar flashing red and blue. We passed restaurants and a small grocery store. Nothing was open, and the few cars out pulled over to let us pass. Near the Strawberry Street Cafe, the narrow street was lined with cruisers and unmarked units, and an ambulance was blocking the entrance of an alleyway. Two television trucks had parked a little farther down. Reporters moved restlessly along the perimeter cordoned off in yellow tape. Marino parked and our doors opened at the same time. Instantly, cameras pointed our way.

I watched where Marino stepped and was right behind him. Shutters whirred, film advanced, and microphones were raised. Marino's long strides did not pause and he did not answer anyone. I averted my face. Rounding the ambulance, we ducked under the tape. The old burgundy Toyota was parked head-in midway along a narrow stretch of cobblestone covered with churned-up, dirty snow. Ugly brick walls pressed in from either side and blocked out the low sun's slanted rays. Police were taking photographs, talking, and looking around. Water slowly dripped from roofs and rusting fire escapes. The smell of garbage wafted on the damp, stirring air.

It barely registered that the young Latin-looking officer talking on a portable radio was someone I had recently met. Tom Lucero watched us as he mumbled something and got off the air. From where I stood, all I could see through the Toyota's open driver's door was a left hip and arm. A shock went through me as I recognized the black wool coat, the brush-gold wedding band, and black plastic watch. Wedged between the windshield and the dash was her red medical examiner's plate.

"Tags come back to Jason Story. I guess that's her husband," Lucero said to Marino. "She's got identification on her in her purse. The name on the driver's license is Susan Dawson Story, a twenty-eight-year-old white female."

"What about money?"

"Eleven dollars in her billfold and a couple of credit cards. Nothing so far to suggest robbery. You recognize her?"

Marino leaned forward to get a better look. His jaw muscles bunched. "Yeah. I recognize her. This how the car was found?"

"We opened the driver's door. That's it," Lucero said, stuffing the portable radio in a pocket.

"The engine was off, doors unlocked?"

"They were. Like I told you on the phone, Fritz spotted the car while on routine patrol. Uh, around fifteen hundred hours, and he noticed the M.E.'s tag in the window." He glanced at me. "If you go around to the passenger's side and look in, you can see blood in the area of her right ear. Someone did a real neat job."

Marino backed away and scanned the messy snow. "Don't look like we'll have much luck with footprints."

"You got that right. It's melting like ice cream. Was when we got here."

"Any cartridge cases?"

"Zip."

"Her family know?"

"Not yet. I thought you might want to handle this one," Lucero said.

"Just make damn sure who she is and where she worked don't leak out to the media before the family knows. Jesus." Marino turned his attention to me. "What do you want to do here?"

"I don't want to touch anything inside the car," I muttered, surveying the surroundings as I got out my camera. I was alert and thinking clearly but my hands would not stop shaking. "Give me a minute to look, then let's get her on a stretcher."

"You guys ready for the doc?" Marino asked Lucero.

"We're ready."

Susan was dressed in faded blue jeans and scuffed lace-up boots, her black wool coat buttoned to her chin. My heart constricted as I noticed the red silk scarf peeking out of her collar. She wore sunglasses and leaned back in the driver's seat as if she had gotten comfortable and dozed off. On the light gray upholstery behind her neck was a reddish stain. I moved around to the other side of the car and saw the blood Lucero had mentioned. As I began taking photographs, I paused, then leaned closer to her face, detecting the faint fragrance of a distinctive masculine cologne. Her seat belt, I noted, was unfastened.

I did not touch her head until the squad had arrived and Susan's body was on a stretcher inside the back of an ambulance. I climbed in and spent several minutes looking for bullet wounds. I found one in the right temple, another in the hollow at the back of the neck, just below the hairline. I ran my gloved fingers through her chestnut hair, looking for more blood and not finding it.

Marino climbed into the back of the ambulance. "How many times was she shot?" he asked me.

"I've found two entrances. No exits, though I can feel one bullet beneath the skin over her left temporal bone."

He glanced tensely at his watch. "The Dawsons don't live too far from here. In Glenburnie."

"The Dawsons?" I peeled off my gloves.

"Her parents. I've got to talk to them. Now. Before some toad leaks something and they end up hearing about this on the damn radio or TV. I'll get a marked unit to take you home."

"No," I said. "I'll go with you. I think I should."

Streetlights were coming on as we drove away. Marino stared hard at the road, his face dangerously red.

"Damn!" he blurted, pounding his fist on the steering wheel. "Goddam! Shooting her in the head. *Shooting a pregnant woman.*"

I stared out the side window, my shattered thoughts filled with fragmented images and distortion.

I cleared my throat. "Has her husband been located?"

"No answer at their crib. Maybe he's with her parents. God, I hate this job. Christ, I don't want to do this. Merry friggin' Christmas. I knock on your door and you're screwed because I'm going to tell you something that will ruin your life."

"You have not ruined anybody's life."

"Yeah, well, get ready, 'cause I'm about to."

He turned onto Albemarle. Supercans had been rolled to the edge of the street and were surrounded by leaf bags bulging with Christmas trash. Windows glowed warmly, multi-colored tree lights filling some of them. A young father was pulling his small son along the sidewalk on a fishtailing sled. They smiled and waved at us as we passed. Glenburnie was the neighborhood of middle-class families, of young professionals, single, married, and gay. In the warm months, people sat on their porches and cooked out in their yards. They had parties and hailed each other from the street.

The Dawsons' modest house was Tudor style, comfortably weathered with neatly pruned evergreens in front. Windows upstairs and down were lit up, an old station wagon parked by the curb.

The bell was answered by a woman's voice on the other side of the door. "Who is it?"

"Mrs. Dawson?"

"Yes?"

"Detective Marino, Richmond P.D. I need to talk with you," he said loudly, holding his badge up to the peephole.

Locks clicked free as my pulse raced. During my various medical rotations, I had experienced patients screaming in pain as they begged me not to let them die. I had reassured them falsely, "You're going to be just fine," as they died gripping my hand. I had said "I'm sorry" to loved ones desperate in small, airless rooms where even chaplains felt lost. But I had never delivered death to someone's door on Christmas Day.

The only resemblance I could see between Mrs. Dawson and her daughter was the strong curve of their jaws. Mrs. Dawson was sharp-featured, with short, frosted hair. She could not have weighed more than a hundred pounds and reminded me of a frightened bird. When Marino introduced me, panic filled her eyes.

"What's happened?" she barely said.

"I'm afraid I have very bad news for you, Mrs. Dawson," Marino said. "It's your daughter, Susan. I'm afraid she's been killed."

Small feet sounded in a nearby room, and a little girl appeared in a doorway to the right of us. She stopped and regarded us with wide blue eyes.

"Hailey, where's Grandpa?" Mrs. Dawson's voice quavered, her face ashen now.

"Upstairs." Hailey was a tiny tomboy in blue jeans and leather sneakers that looked brand-new. Her blond hair shone like gold and she wore glasses to straighten a lazy left eye. I guessed she was, at the most, eight.

"You go tell him to come downstairs," Mrs. Dawson said. "And you and Charlie stay up there until I come get you."

The child hesitated in the doorway, inserting two fingers into her mouth. She stared warily at Marino and me.

"Hailey, go on now!"

Hailey left with an abrupt burst of energy.

We sat in the kitchen with Susan's mother. Her back did not touch the chair. She did not weep until her husband walked in minutes later.

"Oh, Mack," she said in a weak voice. "*Oh, Mack.*" She began to sob.

He put his arm around her, pulling her close. His face blanched and he pressed his lips together as Marino explained what had happened.

"Yes, I know where Strawberry Street is," Susan's father said. "I don't know why she would have gone there. To my knowledge, it's not an area where she normally went. Nothing would have been open today. I don't know."

"Do you know where her husband, Jason Story, is?" Marino asked.

"He's here."

"Here?" Marino glanced around.

"Upstairs, asleep. Jason's not feeling well."

"The children are whose?"

"Tom and Marie's. Tom's our son. They're visiting for the holidays and left early this afternoon. For Tidewater. To visit friends. They should be home anytime." He reached for his wife's hand. "Millie, these people have a lot of questions to ask. You'd better get Jason."

"I tell you what," Marino said. "I'd rather talk to him alone for a minute. Maybe you could take me to him?"

189

Mrs. Dawson nodded, hiding her face in her hands.

"I think you best check on Charlie and Hailey," her husband said to her. "See if you can get your sister on the phone. Maybe she can come."

His pale blue eyes followed his wife and Marino out of the kitchen. Susan's father was tall, with fine bones, his dark brown hair thick, with very little gray. His gestures were economical, his emotions well contained. Susan had gotten her looks from him and perhaps her disposition.

"Her car is old. She has nothing of value to steal, and I know she would not have been involved. Not in drugs or anything." He searched my face.

"We don't know why this happened, Reverend Dawson."

"She was pregnant," he said, the words catching in his throat. "How could anyone?"

"I don't know," I said. "I don't know how."

He coughed. "She did not own a gun."

For a moment, I did not know what he meant. Then I realized, and reassured him, "No. The police did not find a gun. There's no evidence she did this to herself."

"The police? You aren't the police?"

"No. I'm the chief medical examiner. Kay Scarpetta."

He stared numbly at me.

"Your daughter worked for me."

"Oh. Of course. I'm sorry."

"I don't know how to comfort you," I said with difficulty.

"I haven't begun to deal with this myself. But I'm going to do everything possible to find out what happened. I want you to know that."

"Susan spoke of you. She always wanted to be a doctor." He averted his gaze, blinking back tears.

"I saw her last night. Briefly, at her home." I hesitated, reluctant to probe the soft places of their lives. "Susan seemed troubled. And she has not been herself at work of late."

He swallowed, fingers laced tightly on top of the table. His knuckles were white.

"We need to pray. Would you pray with me, Dr. Scarpetta?" He held out his hand. "Please."

As his fingers wrapped firmly around mine, I could not help but think of Susan's obvious disregard for her father and distrust for what he represented. Fundamentalists frightened me, too. I felt anxious shutting my eyes and holding hands with the Reverend Mack Dawson as he thanked God for a mercy I saw no evidence of and claimed promises too late for God to keep. Opening my eyes, I withdrew my hand. For an uneasy moment I feared that Susan's father sensed my skepticism and would question my beliefs. But the fate of my soul was not foremost on his mind.

A loud voice sounded from upstairs, a muffled protest I could not make out. A chair scraped across the floor. The telephone rang and rang, and the voice rose again in a primal outcry of rage and pain. Dawson closed his eyes. He muttered something under his breath that seemed rather strange. I thought he said, "Stay in your room."

"Jason has been here the entire time," he said. I could see his pulse pounding in his temples. "I realize he can speak for himself. But I just want you to know this from me."

"You mentioned he's not feeling well."

"He woke up with a cold, the beginning of one. Susan took

his temperature after lunch and encouraged him to go to bed. He would never hurt . . . Well." He coughed again. "I know the police have to ask, have to consider domestic situations. But that's not the case here."

"Reverend Dawson, what time did Susan leave the house today, and where did she say she was going?"

"She left after dinner, after Jason went to bed. I think that would have been around one-thirty or two. She said she was going over to a friend's house."

"Which friend?"

He stared past me. "A friend she went to high school with. Dianne Lee."

"Where does Dianne live?"

"Northside, near the seminary."

"Susan's car was found off Strawberry Street, not in Northside."

"I suppose if somebody . . . She could have ended up anywhere."

"It would be helpful to know if she ever made it to Dianne's house, and whose idea the visit was," I said.

He got up and started opening kitchen drawers. It took him three tries to find the telephone directory. His hands trembled as he turned pages and dialed a number. Clearing his throat several times, he asked to speak to Dianne.

"I see. What was that?" He listened for a moment. "No, no." His voice shook. "Things are not all right."

I sat quietly as he explained, and I imagined him many years earlier praying and talking on the phone as he dealt with the death of his other daughter, Judy. When he returned to the table, he confirmed what I feared. Susan had not visited her friend that afternoon, nor had there been any plan for her to do so. Her friend was not in town.

"She's with her husband's family in North Carolina," Susan's father said. "She's been there several days. Why would Susan lie? She didn't have to. I've always told her no matter what, she didn't have to lie."

"It would seem she did not want anyone to know where she was going or who she was going to see. I know that raises unhappy speculations, but we need to face them," I said gently.

He stared down at his hands.

"Were she and Jason getting along all right?"

"I don't know." He fought to regain his composure. "Dear Lord, not again." Again he whispered curiously. "Go to your room. Please go." Then he looked up at me with bloodshot eyes. "She had a twin sister. Judy died when they were in high school."

"In a car accident, yes. Susan told me. I'm so sorry."

"She's never gotten over it. She blamed God. She blamed me."

"I did not get that impression," I said. "If she blamed anyone, it seemed to be a girl named Doreen."

Dawson slipped out a handkerchief and quietly blew his nose. "Who?" he asked.

"The girl in high school who allegedly was a witch."

He shook his head.

"She supposedly put a curse on Judy?" But it was pointless to explain further. I could tell that Dawson did not know what I was talking about. We both turned as Hailey walked into the kitchen. She was cradling a baseball glove, her eyes frightened.

"What have you got there, darling?" I asked, trying to smile.

She came close to me. I could smell the new leather. The glove was tied with string, a softball in the sweet spot like a large pearl inside an oyster.

"Aunt Susan gave it to me," she said in a small voice. "You got to break it in. I have to put it under my mattress. Aunt Susan says I have to for a week."

Her grandfather reached for her and lifted her onto his lap. He buried his nose in her hair, holding her tight. "I need for you to go to your room for a little while, sugar. Will you do that for me so I can take care of things? Just for a while?"

She nodded, her eyes not leaving me.

"What are Grandma and Charlie doing?"

"Don't know." She slid off his lap and reluctantly left us.

"You said that before," I said to him.

He looked lost.

"You told her to go to her room," I said. "I heard you say that earlier, mutter something about going to your room. Who were you talking to?"

He dropped his eyes. "The child is self. Self feels intensely, cries, cannot control emotions. Sometimes it is best to send self to his room as I just did Hailey. To hold together. A trick I learned. When I was a boy I learned, had to; my father did not react well if I cried."

"It is all right to cry, Reverend Dawson."

His eyes filled with tears. I heard Marino's footsteps on the stairs. Then he strode into the kitchen and Dawson said the phrase again, in anguish, under his breath.

Marino looked at him, baffled. "I think your son's home," he said.

Susan's father began to weep uncontrollably as car doors slammed shut out front in the wintry darkness and laughter sounded from the porch.

Christmas dinner went into the trash, the evening spent pacing about the house and talking on the phone while Lucy stayed inside my study with the door shut. Arrangements had to be made. Susan's homicide had thrown the office into a state of crisis. Her case would have to be sealed, photographs kept away from those who had known her. The police would have to go through her office and her locker. They would want to interview members of my staff.

"I can't be down there," Fielding, my deputy chief, told me over the phone.

"I realize that," I said, a lump forming in my throat. "I neither expect nor want anyone down there."

"And you?"

"I have to be."

"Christ. I can't believe this has happened. I just can't believe it."

Dr. Wright, my deputy chief in Norfolk, kindly agreed to drive to Richmond early the next morning. Because it was Sunday, no one else was in the building except for Vander, who had come to assist with the Luma-Lite. Had I been emotionally capable of doing Susan's autopsy, I would have refused. The worst thing I could do for her was to jeopardize her case by having the defense question the objectivity and judgment of an expert witness who also happened to be her boss. So I sat at a desk in the morgue while Wright worked. From time to time he commented to me above the clatter of steel instruments and running water as I stared at the cinder-block wall. I did not touch any of her paperwork or label a single test tube. I did not turn around to look.

Once I asked him, "Did you smell anything on her or her clothes? A cologne of some sort?"

He stopped what he was doing and I heard him walk several steps. "Yes. Definitely around the collar of her coat and on the scarf."

"Does it smell like men's cologne to you?"

"Hmm. I think so. Yes, I'd say the fragrance is masculine. Perhaps her husband wears cologne?" Wright was near retirement age, a balding, potbellied man with a West Virginian accent. He was a very capable forensic pathologist and knew exactly what I was contemplating.

"Good question," I said. "I'll ask Marino to check it. But her husband was ill yesterday and went to bed after lunch. That doesn't mean he didn't have on cologne. It doesn't mean her brother or father didn't have on cologne that got on her collar when they hugged her."

"This looks small-caliber. No exit wounds."

I closed my eyes and listened.

"The wound in her right temple is three-sixteenths of an inch with half an inch of smoke—an incomplete pattern. A little bit of stippling and some powder but most will be lost in her hair. There's some powder in the temporalis muscle. Nothing much in bone or dura."

"Trajectory?" I asked.

"The bullet goes through the posterior aspect of the right frontal lobe, travels across anterior to basal ganglia and strikes the left temporal bone, and gets hung up in muscle under the skin. And we're talking about a plain lead bullet, uh, copper coated but not jacketed."

"And it didn't fragment?" I asked.

"No. Then we've got this second wound here at the nape of the neck. Black, burned abraded margin with muzzle mark. A little laceration about one-sixteenth of an inch at the edges. Lots of powder in the occipital muscles."

"Tight contact?"

"Yes. Looks to me like he pressed the barrel hard against her neck. The bullet enters at the junction of the foramen magnum and C-one and takes out the cervical-medullary junction. Travels right up into the pons."

"What about the angle?" I asked.

"It's angled up quite a bit. I'd say that if she was sitting in the car at the time she received this wound, she was slumped forward or had her head bowed."

"That's not the way she was found," I said. "She was leaning back in the seat."

"Then I guess he positioned her that way," Wright commented. "After he shot her. And I'd say that this shot that went through the pons was fired last. I would speculate she was already incapacitated, maybe slumped over when she was shot the second time."

At intervals I could handle it, as if we were not referring to anyone I knew. Then a tremor would go through me, tears fighting to break free. Twice I had to walk outside and stand in the parking lot in the cold. When he got to the ten-week-old fetus in her womb, a girl, I retreated to my office upstairs. According to Virginia law, the unborn child was not a person and therefore could not have been murdered because you cannot murder a nonperson.

"Two for the price of one," Marino said bitterly over the phone later in the day.

"I know," I said, digging a bottle of aspirin out of my pocketbook.

"In court the damn jurors won't be told she was pregnant. It won't be admissible, don't count he murdered a pregnant woman."

"I know," I said again. "Wright's about done. Nothing significant turned up during her external exam. No trace to speak of, nothing that jumped out. What's going on at your end?"

"Susan was definitely going through something," Marino said.

"Problems with her husband?"

"According to him, her problem was with you. He claims you were doing weird shit like calling her a lot at home, hassling her. And sometimes she'd come home from work acting half crazy, like she was scared shitless about something."

"Susan and I did not have a problem." I swallowed three aspirin with a mouthful of cold coffee.

"I'm just telling you what the guy's saying. Other thing is—and I think you'll find this interesting—looks like we got us another feather. Not that I'm saying it links Deighton and this one, Doc, or that I'm necessarily thinking that way. But damn. Maybe we're dealing with some squirrel who wears down-filled gloves, a jacket. I don't know. It's just not typical. Only other time I've ever found feathers was when this drone broke into a crib by smashing out a window and cut his down jacket on broken glass."

My head hurt so much I felt sick to my stomach.

"What we found in Susan's car is real small—a little piece of white down," he went on. "It was clinging to the upholstery of the passenger's door. On the inside, near the floor, a couple inches below the armrest."

"Can you get that to me?" I asked.

"Yeah. What are you going to do?"

"Call Benton."

"I've been trying, dammit. I think he and the wife went out of town."

"I need to ask him if Minor Downey can help us."

"You talking about a person or a fabric softener?"

"Minor Downey with hairs and fibers at the FBI labs. His specialty is feather analysis."

"And his name's *Downey,* it really is?" Marino was incredulous.

"It really is," I said.

8

The telephone rang for a long time at the FBI's Behavioral Science Unit, located in the subterranean reaches of the Academy at Quantico. I could envision its bleak, confusing hallways and offices cluttered with the mementos of polished warriors like Benton Wesley, who had gone skiing, I was told.

"In fact, I'm the only one here at the moment," said the courteous agent who answered the phone.

"This is Dr. Kay Scarpetta and it's urgent that I reach him."

Benton Wesley returned my call almost immediately.

"Benton, where are you?" I raised my voice above terrible static.

"In my car," he said. "Connie and I spent Christmas with her family in Charlottesville. We're just west of there on our way to Hot Springs. I heard about what happened to Susan Story. God, I'm sorry. I was going to call you tonight."

"You're breaking up. I almost can't hear you."

"Hold on."

I waited impatiently for a good minute. Then he was back.

"That's better. We were in a low area. Listen, what do you need from me?"

"I need the Bureau's help with analysis of some feathers."

"No problem. I'll call Downey."

"I need to talk," I said with great reluctance, for I knew I was putting him on the spot. "I don't feel it can wait."

"Hold on."

This time the pause was not due to static. He was conferring with his wife.

"Do you ski?" His voice came back.

"It depends on who you ask."

"Connie and I are on our way to the Homestead for a couple of days. We could talk there. Can you get away?"

"I'll move heaven and earth to, and I'll bring Lucy."

"That's good. She and Connie can pal around while you and I talk. I'll see about your room when we check in. Can you bring something for me to look at?"

"Yes."

"Including whatever you've got on the Robyn Naismith case. Let's cover every base and every imagined one."

"Thank you, Benton," I said gratefully. "And please thank Connie."

I decided to leave the office immediately, and offered little explanation.

"It will be good for you," Rose said, jotting down the Homestead's number. She did not understand that my intention was not to unwind at a five-star resort. For an instant, her eyes were bright with tears as I told her to let Marino know where I was so he could contact me immediately if there were any new developments in Susan's case.

"Please don't release my whereabouts to anyone else," I added.

"Three reporters have called in the last twenty minutes," she said. "Including the *Washington Post.*"

"I'm not discussing Susan's case right now. Tell them the usual, that we're waiting on lab results. Just tell them I'm out of town and unavailable."

I was haunted by images as I drove west toward the mountains. I pictured Susan in her baggy scrubs, and the faces of her mother and father as Marino told them their daughter was dead.

"Are you feeling okay?" Lucy asked. She had been looking at me every other minute since we left my house.

"I'm just preoccupied," I replied, concentrating on the road. "You're going to love skiing. I have a feeling you'll be good at it."

She silently gazed out the windshield. The sky was a washed-out denim blue, mountains rising in the distance dusted with snow.

"I'm sorry about this," I added. "It seems that every time you visit, something happens and I can't give you my full attention."

"I don't need your full attention."

"Someday you'll understand."

"Maybe I'm the same way about my work. In fact, maybe I learned from you. I'll probably be successful like you, too."

My spirit felt as heavy as lead. I was grateful that I was wearing sunglasses. I did not want Lucy to see my eyes.

"I know you love me. That's what counts. I know my mother doesn't love me," my niece said.

"Dorothy loves you as much as she is able to love anyone."

"You're absolutely right. As much as she is able to, which isn't much because I'm not a man. She only loves men."

"No, Lucy. Your mother doesn't really love men. They are a symptom of her obsessive quest of finding somebody who will make her whole. She doesn't understand that she has to make herself whole."

"The only thing 'whole' in the equation is she picks assholes every time."

"I agree that her batting average hasn't been good."

"I'm not going to live like that. I don't want to be anything like her."

"You aren't," I said.

"I read in the brochure they have skeet shooting where we're going."

"They have all sorts of things."

"Did you bring one of the revolvers?"

"You don't shoot skeet with a revolver, Lucy."

"You do if you're from Miami."

"If you don't stop yawning, you're going to get me started."

"Why didn't you bring a gun?" she persisted.

The Ruger was in my suitcase, but I did not intend to tell her that. "Why are you so worried about whether I brought a gun?" I asked.

"I want to be good at it. So good I can shoot the twelve off the clock every time I try," she said sleepily.

My heart ached as she rolled up her jacket and used it as a

pillow. She lay next to me, the top of her head touching my thigh as she slept. She did not know how strongly tempted I was to send her back to Miami this minute. But I could tell she sensed my fear.

The Homestead was situated on fifteen thousand acres of forest and streams in the Allegheny Mountains, the main section of the hotel dark red brick with white-pillared colonnades. The white cupola had a clock on each of its four sides that always agreed on the time and could be read for miles, and tennis courts and golf greens were solid white with snow.

"You're in luck," I said to Lucy as gracious men in gray uniforms stepped our way. "The ski conditions are going to be terrific."

Benton Wesley had accomplished what he had promised, and we found a reservation waiting for us when we got to the front desk. He had booked a double room with glass doors opening onto a balcony overlooking the casino, and on top of a table were flowers from Connie and him. "Meet us on the slopes," the card read. "We scheduled a lesson for Lucy at three-thirty."

"We've got to hurry," I said to Lucy as we flung open suitcases. "You've got your first ski lesson in exactly forty minutes. Try these." I tossed her a pair of red ski pants, which were followed by jacket, socks, mittens, and sweater flying through the air and landing on her bed. "Don't forget your butt pack. Anything else you need we'll have to get later."

"I don't have any ski glasses," she said, pulling a bright blue turtleneck over her head. "I'll go snow-blind."

"You can use my goggles. The sun will be going down soon anyway."

By the time we caught the shuttle to the slopes, rented equipment for Lucy, and connected her with the instructor at the rope tow, it was twenty-nine minutes past three. Skiers were brilliant spots of color moving downhill, and it was only when they got close that they turned into people. I leaned forward in my boots, skis firmly wedged against the slope as I scanned lines and lifts, my hand shielding my eyes. The sun was nearing the top of trees, the snow dazzled by its touch, but shadows were spreading and the temperature was dropping quickly.

I spotted the man and woman simply because their parallel skiing was so graceful, poles lifted like feathers and barely flicking snow as they soared and turned like birds. I recognized Benton Wesley's silver hair and raised my hand. Glancing back at Connie and yelling something I could not hear, he pushed off and schussed downhill like a knife, skis so close together I doubted you could fit a piece of paper between them.

When he stopped in a spray of snow and pushed back his goggles, it suddenly occurred to me that if I did not know him I would have been watching him anyway. Black ski pants hugged well-muscled legs I had never known were beneath the trousers of his conservative suits, and the jacket he wore reminded me of a Key West sunset. His face and eyes were brightened by the cold, making his sharp features more striking than formidable. Connie eased to a stop beside him.

"It's wonderful that you're here," Wesley said, and I could

never see him or hear his voice without being reminded of Mark. They had been colleagues and best friends. They could have passed for brothers.

"Where's Lucy?" Connie asked.

"Conquering the rope tow even as we speak." I pointed.

"I hope you didn't mind my signing her up for a lesson."

"Mind? I can't thank you enough for being so thoughtful. She's having the time of her life."

"I think I'll stand right here and watch her for a while," Connie said. "Then I'll be ready for something hot to drink and I have a feeling Lucy will be, too. Ben, you look like you haven't had enough."

Wesley said to me, "You up for a few quick runs?"

We exchanged remarks about nonessential matters as we moved through the line, and then were silent when the lift swung around and seated us. Wesley lowered the bar as the cable slowly pulled us toward the mountaintop. The air was numbing and deliciously clean, and filled with the quiet sounds of skis swishing and dully slapping hard-packed snow. Snow from snow machines drifted like smoke through the woods between slopes.

"I talked to Downey," he said. "He'll see you at headquarters just as soon as you can get there."

"That's good news," I said. "Benton, what have you been told?"

"Marino and I have talked several times. It appears you have several cases going on right now that aren't connected by evidence, necessarily, but by a peculiar coincidence in timing."

"I think we're dealing with more than coincidence. You

know about Ronnie Waddell's print turning up in Jennifer Deighton's house."

"Yes." He stared off at a stand of evergreens backlit by the setting sun. "As I've told Marino, I'm hoping there's a logical explanation for how Waddell's print got there."

"The logical explanation may very well be that he was, at some point, inside her house."

"Then we're dealing with a situation so bizarre as to defy description, Kay. A death row convict is out on the street killing again. And we're supposed to assume someone else took his place in the chair on the night of December thirteenth. I doubt there would have been many volunteers."

"You wouldn't think so," I said.

"What do you know about Waddell's criminal history?"

"Very little."

"I interviewed him years ago, in Mecklenburg."

I glanced over at him with interest.

"I'll preface my next remarks by saying that he was not particularly cooperative in that he would not discuss Robyn Naismith's murder. He claimed that if he killed her, he didn't remember it. Not that this is unusual. Most of the violent offenders I have interviewed either claim to have poor recall, or they deny that they committed the crimes. I had a copy of Waddell's Assessment Protocol faxed to me before you got here. We'll go over it after dinner."

"Benton, I'm already glad I'm here."

He stared straight ahead, our shoulders barely touching. The slope beneath us got steeper as we rode in silence for a while. Then he said, "How are you, Kay?"

"Better. There are still moments."

"I know. There will always be moments. But fewer of them, I hope. Days, perhaps, where you don't feel it."

"Yes," I said. "There are days when I don't."

"We've got a very good lead on the group responsible. We think we know who placed the bomb."

We raised the tips of our skis and leaned forward as the lift eased us out like baby birds nudged from the nest. My legs were stiff and cold from the ride, and trails in the shade were treacherous with ice. Wesley's long white skis vanished against the snow and caught light at the same time. He danced down the slope in dazzling puffs of diamond dust, pausing every now and then to look back. I waved him on by barely lifting a pole as I made languid parallel turns and floated over moguls. Halfway into the run I was limber and warm, thoughts flying free.

When I returned to my room as it was getting dark, I discovered Marino had left a message that he would be at headquarters until five-thirty and for me to call ASAP.

"What's going on?" I said when he answered.

"Nothing that's going to make you sleep better. For starters, Jason Story's badmouthing you to anyone who will stand still long enough to listen—including reporters."

"His rage has to go somewhere," I said, my mood darkening again.

"Well, what he's doing ain't good, but it also ain't the worst of our problems. We can't locate ten print cards for Waddell."

"Not *anywhere*?"

"You got it. We've checked his files at Richmond P.D., the

State Police, and the FBI. That's every jurisdiction that should have them. No cards. Then I contacted Donahue at the pen to see if I could track down Waddell's personal effects, such as books, letters, hairbrush, toothbrush—anything that might be a source for latent prints. And guess what? Donahue says the only things Waddell's mother wanted were his watch and ring. Everything else Corrections destroyed."

I sat heavily on the edge of the bed.

"And I saved the best for last, Doc. Firearms hit paydirt and you ain't going to believe it. The bullets recovered from Eddie Heath and Susan Story was fired from the same gun, a twenty-two."

"Dear God," I said.

Downstairs in the Homestead Club, a band was playing jazz, but the audience was small and the music was not too loud to talk over. Connie had taken Lucy to a movie, leaving Wesley and me at a table in a deserted corner of the dance floor. Both of us were sipping cognac. He did not seem as physically tired as I was, but tension had returned to his face.

Reaching behind him, he took another candle from an unoccupied table and set it by two others he had claimed. The light was unsteady but adequate, and though we did not get long stares from guests, we did get glances. I supposed it seemed a strange place to work, but the lobby and dining room were not private enough, and Wesley was much too circumspect to suggest we meet in his room or mine.

"There would seem to be a number of conflicting elements

here," he said. "But human behavior is not set in stone. Waddell was in prison for ten years. We don't know how he might have changed. I would categorize Eddie Heath's murder as a sexually motivated homicide while, at first glance, Susan Story's homicide appears to be an execution, a hit."

"As if two different perpetrators are involved," I said, toying with my cognac.

He leaned forward, idly flipping through Robyn Naismith's case file. "It's interesting," he said, without looking up. "You hear so much about modus operandi, about the offender's signature. He always selects this type of victim or chooses this sort of location and prefers knives, and so on. But, in fact, this isn't always the case. Nor is the emotion of the crime always obvious. I said that Susan Story's homicide, *at first glance,* does not appear to be sexually motivated. But the more I've thought about it, the more I believe there is a sexual component. I think this killer is into piquerism."

"Robyn Naismith was stabbed multiple times," I said.

"Yes. I'd say that what was done to her is a textbook example. There was no evidence of rape—not that this means it didn't occur. But no semen. The repeated plunging of the knife in her abdomen, buttocks, and breasts was a substitute for penile penetration. Obvious piquerism. Biting is less obvious, not at all related to any oral components of the sexual act, it is my opinion, but again, a substitute for penile penetration. Teeth sinking into flesh, cannibalism, like John Joubert did to the newspaper delivery boys he murdered in Nebraska. Then we have bullets. You would not associate shootings with piquerism unless you thought about it for a moment. Then the dynamics, in some instances, become clear. Something penetrating flesh. That was the Son of Sam's thing."

"There's no evidence of piquerism in Jennifer Deighton's death."

"True. This goes back to what I was saying. There isn't always a clear pattern. Certainly, we're not talking about a clear pattern here, but there is one element that the murders of Eddie Heath, Jennifer Deighton, and Susan Story have in common. I would classify the crimes as organized."

"Not as organized with Jennifer Deighton," I pointed out. "It appears the killer attempted to disguise her death as a suicide and failed. Or perhaps he did not intend to kill her at all and got carried away with a choke hold."

"Her death before she was placed inside her car probably wasn't the plan," Wesley agreed. "But the fact is, it appears there *was* a plan. And the garden hose hooked up to the exhaust pipe was severed with a sharp tool that was never recovered. Either the killer brought his own tool or weapon to the scene, or he disposed of whatever it was he found at her house and used. That's organized behavior. But before we go too far with this, let me remind you that we don't have a twenty-two bullet or other piece of evidence that might link Jennifer Deighton's homicide with the homicides of the Heath boy and Susan."

"I think we do, Benton. Ronnie Waddell's print was recovered from a dining room chair inside Jennifer Deighton's house."

"We don't know that it was Ronnie Waddell who pumped slugs into the other two."

"Eddie Heath's body was positioned in a manner reminiscent

of Robyn Naismith's case. The boy was attacked the night Ronnie Waddell was to be executed. Don't you think there's some weird thread here?"

"Let's put it this way," he said. "I don't want to think it."

"Neither of us wants to. Benton, what's your gut feeling?"

He motioned for the waitress to bring more cognac, candlelight illuminating the clean lines of his left cheekbone and chin.

"My gut feeling? Okay. I have a very bad gut feeling about all of this," he said. "I believe Ronnie Waddell is the common denominator, but I don't know what that means. A latent print recently found at a scene was identified as his, yet we can't locate his ten print cards or anything else that might effect a positive identification. He also wasn't printed at the morgue, and the person who allegedly forgot to do so has since been murdered with the same gun used on Eddie Heath. Waddell's legal counsel, Nick Grueman, apparently knew Jennifer Deighton, and in fact, it appears she faxed a message to Grueman days before she was murdered. Finally, yes, there is a subtle and peculiar similarity between Eddie Heath's and Robyn Naismith's deaths. Frankly, I can't help but wonder if the attack on Heath wasn't, for some reason, intended to be symbolic."

He waited until our drinks had been set before us, then opened a manila envelope that was attached to Robyn Naismith's case. That small act triggered something I had not thought of before.

"I had to get her photographs from Archives," I said.

Wesley glanced at me as he slipped on his glasses.

"In cases this old, the paper records have been reduced to microfilm, the printouts of which are in the file you've got. The original documents are destroyed, but we keep the original photos. They go to Archives."

"Which is what? A room in your building?"

"No, Benton. A warehouse near the state library—the same warehouse where the Bureau of Forensic Science stores evidence from its old cases."

"Vander still hasn't found the photograph of the bloody thumbprint Waddell left inside Robyn Naismith's house?"

"No," I said as Wesley met my eyes. We both knew that Vander was never going to find it.

"Christ," he said. "Who retrieved Robyn Naismith's photos for you?"

"My administrator," I replied. "Ben Stevens. He made a trip to Archives a week or so before Waddell's execution."

"Why?"

"During the final stages of the appeals process, there are always a lot of questions asked and I like to have ready access to the case or cases involved. So a trip to Archives is routine. What's a little different in the instance we're talking about is I didn't have to ask Stevens to get the photos from Archives. He volunteered."

"And that's unusual?"

"In retrospect, I must admit that it is."

"The implication," Wesley said, "is that your administrator may have volunteered because what he was really interested in was Waddell's file—or more specifically, the photograph of the bloody thumbprint that's supposed to be inside it."

"All I can say with certainty is if Stevens wanted to tamper with a file in Archives, he couldn't do so unless he had legitimate reason for visiting Archives. If, for example, it came back to me that he had been there when none of the medical examiners had made a request, it would look odd."

I went on to tell Wesley about the breach of security in my office computer, explaining that the two terminals involved were assigned to me and Stevens. While I talked, Wesley took notes. When I fell silent, he looked up at me.

"It doesn't sound as if they found what they were looking for," he said.

"My suspicion is that they didn't."

"That brings us around to the obvious question. What were they looking for?"

I slowly swirled my cognac. In the candlelight it was liquid amber, and each sip deliciously burned going down.

"Maybe something pertaining to Eddie Heath's death. I was looking for any other cases in which victims may have had bite marks or cannibalistic-type injuries, and had a file in my directory. Beyond that, I can't imagine what anyone might have been looking for."

"Do you ever keep intradepartmental memos in your directory?"

"In word processing, a subdirectory."

"Same password to access those documents?"

"Yes."

"And in word processing you would store autopsy reports and other documents pertaining to cases?"

"I would. But at the time my directory was broken into there wasn't anything sensitive on file that I can think of."

"But whoever broke in didn't necessarily know that."

"Obviously not," I said.

"What about Ronnie Waddell's autopsy report, Kay? When your directory was broken into, was his report in the computer?"

"It would have been. He was executed Monday, December thirteenth. The break-in occurred late on the afternoon of Thursday, December sixteenth, while I was doing Eddie Heath's post and Susan was upstairs in my office, supposedly resting on the couch after the formalin spill."

"Perplexing." He frowned. "Assuming Susan is the one who went into your directory, why would she be interested in Waddell's autopsy report—if that's what this is all about? She was *present* during his autopsy. What could she have read in your report that she wouldn't have already known?"

"Nothing I can think of."

"Well, let me rephrase that. What pertaining to his autopsy would she not have learned from being present the night his body was brought to the morgue? Or maybe I'd better say the night *a body* was brought to the morgue, since we're no longer so sure this individual was Waddell," he added grimly.

"She wouldn't have had access to lab reports," I said. "But the lab work wouldn't have been completed by the time my directory was broken into. Tox and HIV screens, for example, take weeks."

"And Susan would have known that."

"Certainly."

"So would your administrator."

"Absolutely."

"There must be something else," he said.

There was, but as it came to mind I could not imagine the significance. "Waddell—or whoever the inmate was—had an envelope in the back pocket of his jeans that he wanted buried with him. Fielding wouldn't have opened this envelope until he had gone upstairs with his paperwork after the post."

"So Susan couldn't have known what was inside the envelope while she was in the morgue that night?" Wesley asked with interest.

"That's right. She couldn't have."

"And was there anything of significance inside this envelope?"

"There was nothing inside but several receipts for food and tolls."

Wesley frowned. "Receipts," he repeated. "What in God's name would he have been doing with those? Do you have them here?"

"They're in his file." I got out the photocopies. "The dates are all the same, November thirtieth."

"Which should have been about the time Waddell was transported from Mecklenburg to Richmond."

"That's right. He was transported fifteen days before his execution," I said.

"We need to run down the codes on these receipts, see what locations we get. This may be important. Very important, in light of what we're contemplating."

"That Waddell is alive?"

"Yes. That somehow a switch was made and he was released.

Maybe the man who went to the chair wanted these receipts in his pocket when he died because he was trying to tell us something."

"Where would he have gotten them?"

"Perhaps during the transport from Mecklenburg to Richmond, which would have been an ideal time to pull something," Wesley replied. "Maybe two men were transported, Waddell and someone else."

"You're suggesting they stopped for food?"

"Guards aren't supposed to stop for anything while transporting a death row inmate. But if some conspiracy were involved, anything could have happened. Maybe they stopped and got take-out food, and it was during this interval that Waddell was freed. Then the other inmate was taken on to Richmond and put in Waddell's cell. Think about it. How would any of the guards or anybody else at Spring Street have any way of knowing the inmate brought in wasn't Waddell?"

"He might say he wasn't, but that doesn't mean that anyone would have listened."

"I suspect they wouldn't have listened."

"What about Waddell's mother?" I asked. "Supposedly, she had a contact visit with him hours before the execution. Certainly, she would know if the inmate she saw was not her son."

"We need to verify that the contact visit occurred. But whether it did or didn't, it would have been to Mrs. Waddell's benefit to go along with any scheme. I don't imagine she wanted her son to die."

"Then you're convinced that the wrong man was executed," I said reluctantly, for there were few theories, at the moment, that I more wanted to disprove.

His answer was to open the envelope containing Robyn Naismith's photographs and slide out a thick stack of color prints that would continue to shock me no matter how many times I looked at them. He slowly shuffled through the pictorial history of her terrible death.

Then he said, "When we consider the three homicides that have just occurred, Waddell doesn't profile right."

"What are you saying, Benton? That after ten years in prison his personality changed?"

"All I can say to you is that I've heard of organized killers decompensating, flying apart. They begin to make mistakes. Bundy, for example. Toward the end he became frenzied. But what you generally don't see is a disorganized individual swinging the other way, the psychotic person becoming methodical, rational—becoming organized."

When Wesley alluded to the Bundys and Son of Sams in the world, he did so theoretically, impersonally, as if his analyses and theories were formulated from secondary sources. He did not brag. He did not name-drop or assume the role of one who knew these criminals personally. His demeanor, therefore, was deliberately misleading.

He had, in fact, spent long, intimate hours with the likes of Theodore Bundy, David Berkowitz, Sirhan Sirhan, Richard Speck, and Charles Manson, in addition to the lesser-known black holes who had sucked light from the planet Earth. I remembered Marino telling me once that when Wesley returned from some of these pilgrimages into maximum-security penitentiaries, he would look pale and drained. It almost made him physically ill to absorb the poison of these men and endure the attachments they inevitably formed to him. Some of the worst sadists in recent history regularly wrote letters to him, sent Christmas cards, and inquired after his family. It was no small wonder that Wesley seemed like a man with a heavy burden and so often was silent. In exchange for information, he did the one thing that not one of us wants to do. He allowed the monster to connect with him.

"Was it determined that Waddell was psychotic?" I asked.

"It was determined that he was sane when he murdered Robyn Naismith." Wesley pulled out a photograph and slid it across the table to me. "But frankly, I don't think he was."

The photograph was the one I remembered most vividly, and as I studied it I could not imagine an unsuspecting soul walking in on such a scene.

Robyn Naismith's living room did not have much furniture, just several barrel chairs with dark green cushions and a chocolate-brown leather couch. A small Bakhara rug was in the middle of the parquet floor, the walls wide planks stained to look like cherry or mahogany. A console television was against the wall directly across from the front door, affording whoever entered a full frontal view of Ronnie Joe Waddell's horrible artistry.

What Robyn's friend had seen the instant she unlocked the door and pushed it open as she called out Robyn's name was a nude body sitting on the floor, back propped against the TV, skin so streaked and smeared with dried blood that the exact nature of the injuries could not be determined until later at the morgue. In the photograph, coagulating blood pooled around Robyn's buttocks looked like red-tinted tar, and tossed nearby were several bloody towels. The weapon was never found, though police did determine that a German-made stainless steel steak knife was missing from a set hanging in the kitchen, and the characteristics of the blade were consistent with her wounds.

Opening Eddie Heath's file folder, Wesley withdrew a scene diagram drawn by the Henrico County police officer who had discovered the critically wounded boy behind the vacant grocery store. Wesley placed the diagram next to the photograph of Robyn Naismith. For a moment, neither of us spoke as our eyes went back and forth from one to the other. The similarities were more pronounced than I had imagined, the positions of their bodies virtually identical, from their hands by their sides to their loosely piled clothing near their bare feet.

"I have to admit, it's eerie as hell," Wesley remarked. "It's almost as if Eddie Heath's scene is a mirror image of this one." He touched the photograph of Robyn Naismith. "Bodies positioned like rag dolls, propped against boxlike objects. A big console TV. A brown Dumpster." Spreading more photographs on the table like playing cards, he drew another from the deck. This one was a close-up of her body at the morgue, the ragged tangential circles of human bite marks apparent on her left breast and left inner thigh.

"Again, a striking similarity," he said. "Bite marks here and here corresponding closely with the areas of missing flesh on Eddie Heath's shoulder and thigh. In other words"—he slipped off his glasses and looked up at me—"Eddie Heath was probably bitten, the flesh excised to eradicate evidence."

"Then his killer is at least somewhat familiar with forensic evidence," I said.

"Almost any felon who has spent time in prison is familiar with forensic evidence. If Waddell didn't know about bitemark identification when he murdered Robyn Naismith, he would know about it now."

"You're talking like he's the killer again," I pointed out. "A moment ago you said he doesn't profile right."

"Ten years ago, he didn't profile right. That's all I'm asserting."

"You've got his Assessment Protocol. Can we talk about it?"

"Of course."

The Protocol was actually a forty-page FBI questionnaire filled in during a face-to-face prison interview with a violent offender.

"Flip through this yourself," Wesley said, sliding Waddell's Protocol in front of me. "I'd like to hear your thoughts without further input from me."

Wesley's interview of Ronnie Joe Waddell had taken place six years ago at death row in Mecklenburg County. The Protocol began with the expected descriptive data. Waddell's demeanor, emotional state, mannerisms, and style of conversation indicated that he was agitated and confused. Then, when Wesley had given him opportunity to ask questions, Waddell asked only one: "I saw little white flakes when we passed a window. Is it snowing or are they ashes from the incinerator?"

The date on the Protocol, I noted, was August.

Questions about how the murder might have been prevented

went nowhere. Would Waddell have killed his victim in a populated area? Would he have killed her if witnesses had been present? Would anything have stopped him from killing her? Did he think that capital punishment was a deterrent? Waddell said he could not remember killing "the lady on TV." He did not know what would have stopped him from committing an act he could not recall. His only memory was of being "sticky." He said it was like waking up from a wet dream. The stickiness Ronnie Waddell experienced was not semen. It was Robyn Naismith's blood.

"His problem list sounds rather mundane," I thought out loud. "Headaches, extreme shyness, marked daydreaming, and leaving home at the age of nineteen. I don't see anything here that one might consider the usual red flags. No cruelty to animals, fire setting, assaults, et cetera."

"Keep going," Wesley said.

I scanned several more pages. "Drugs and alcohol," I said.

"If he hadn't been locked up, he would have died a junkie or gotten shot on the street," Wesley said. "And what's interesting is the substance abuse did not begin until early adulthood. I remember Waddell told me he had never tasted alcohol until he was twenty and away from home."

"He was raised on a farm?"

"In Suffolk. A fairly big farm that grew peanuts, corn, soybeans. His entire family lived on it and worked for the owners. There were four children, Ronnie Joe the youngest. Their mother was very religious and took the children to church every Sunday. No alcohol, swearing, or cigarettes. His background was very sheltered. He'd really never been off the farm until his

222

father died and Ronnie decided to leave. He took the bus to Richmond and had little trouble getting work because of his physical strength. Breaking up asphalt with a jackhammer, lifting heavy loads, that sort of thing. My theory is he could not handle temptation when he was finally faced with it. First it was beer and wine, then marijuana. Within a year he was into cocaine and heroin, buying and selling, and stealing whatever he could get his hands on.

"When I asked him how many criminal acts he had committed that he had never been arrested for, he said he couldn't count them. He said he was doing burglaries, breaking into cars—property crimes, in other words. Then he broke into Robyn Naismith's house and she had the misfortune of coming home while he was there."

"He wasn't described as violent, Benton," I pointed out.

"Yes. He never profiled as your typical violent offender. The defense claimed that he was made temporarily insane by drugs and alcohol. To be honest, I think this was the case. Not long before he murdered Robyn Naismith he had started getting into PCP. It is quite possible that when Waddell encountered Robyn Naismith he was completely deranged and later had little or no recollection of what he did to her."

"Do you remember what he stole, if anything?" I asked. "I wonder if there was clear evidence when he broke into her house that his intent was to commit burglary."

"The place was ransacked. We know jewelry was missing. The medicine cabinet was cleaned out and her billfold was empty. It's hard to know what else was stolen because she lived alone."

"No significant relationship?"

"A fascinating point." Wesley stared off at an old couple dancing soporifically to the husky tones of a saxophone. "Semen stains were recovered from a bed sheet and the mattress cover. The stain on the sheet had to be fresh unless Robyn didn't change her bed linens very often, and we know that Waddell was not the origin of the stains. They didn't match his blood type."

"No one who knew her ever made reference to a lover?"

"No one ever did. Obviously, there was keen interest in who this person was, and since he never contacted the police, it was suspected that she had been having an affair, possibly with one of her married colleagues or sources."

"Maybe she was," I said. "But he wasn't her killer."

"No. Ronnie Joe Waddell was her killer. Let's take a look."

I opened Waddell's file and showed Wesley the photographs of the executed inmate I had autopsied on the night of December thirteenth. "Can you tell if this is the man you interviewed six years ago?"

Wesley impassively studied the photographs, going through them one by one. He looked at close-ups of the face and back of the head, and glanced over shots of the upper body and hands. He detached a mug shot from Waddell's Assessment Protocol and began comparing as I looked on.

"I see a resemblance," I said.

"That's about as much as we can say," Wesley replied. "The mug shot's ten years old. Waddell had a beard and mustache, was very muscular but lean. His face was lean. This guy"— he pointed to one of the morgue photographs—"is shaven and much heavier. His face is much fuller. I can't say these are the same man, based on these photos."

I couldn't confirm it, either. In fact, I could think of old pictures of me that no one else would recognize.

"Do you have any suggestions about how we're going to resolve this problem?" I asked Wesley.

"I'll toss out a few things," he said, stacking the photographs and straightening the edges against the tabletop. "Your old friend Nick Grueman's some kind of player in all this, and I've been thinking about the best way to deal with him without tipping our hand. If Marino or I talk to him, he'll know instantly that something's up."

I knew where this was going and I tried to interrupt, but Wesley would not let me. "Marino's mentioned your difficulties with Grueman, that he calls and in general jerks you around. And then, of course, there is the past, your years at Georgetown. Maybe you should talk with him."

"I don't want to talk with him, Benton."

"He may have photographs of Waddell, letters, other documents. Something with Waddell's prints. Or maybe there's something he might say in the course of conversation that would be revealing. The point is, you have access to him, if you wish, through your normal activities, when the rest of us don't. And you're going to D.C. anyway to see Downey."

"No," I said.

"It's just a thought." He looked away from me and motioned for the waitress to bring the check. "How long will Lucy be visiting you?" he asked.

"She doesn't have to be back at school until January seventh."

"I remember she's pretty good with computers."

"She's more than pretty good."

Wesley smiled a little. "So Marino's told me. He says she thinks she can help with AFIS."

"I'm sure she'd like to try." I suddenly felt protective again, and torn. I wanted to send her back to Miami, and yet I didn't.

"You may or may not remember, but Michele works for the Department of Criminal Justice Services, which assists the State Police in running AFIS," Wesley said.

"I should think that might worry you a little right now." I finished my brandy.

"There isn't a day of my life that I don't worry," he said.

The next morning a light snow began to fall as Lucy and I dressed in ski clothes that could be spotted from here to the Eiger.

"I look like a traffic cone," she said, staring at her blaze orange reflection in the mirror.

"That's right. If you get lost on a trail, it won't be hard to find you." I swallowed vitamins and two aspirin with sparkling water from the minibar.

My niece eyed my outfit, which was almost as electric as hers, and shook her head. "For someone so conservative, you certainly dress like a neon peacock for sports."

"I try not to be a stick-in-the-mud all of the time. Are you hungry?"

"Starved."

"Benton's supposed to meet us in the dining room at eight-thirty. We can go down now if you don't want to wait."

"I'm ready. Isn't Connie going to eat with us?"

"We're going to meet her on the slopes. Benton wants to talk shop first."

"I would think it must bother her to be left out," Lucy said. "Whenever he talks with anyone, it seems she isn't invited."

I locked the room door and we headed down the quiet corridor.

"I suspect Connie doesn't wish to be involved," I said in a low voice. "For her to know every detail of her husband's work would only be a burden for her."

"So he talks to you instead."

"About cases, yes."

"About work. And work is what matters most to both of you."

"Work certainly seems to dominate our lives."

"Are you and Mr. Wesley about to have an affair?"

"We're about to have breakfast." I smiled.

The Homestead's buffet was typically overwhelming. Long cloth-covered tables were laden with Virginia-cured bacon and ham, every concoction of eggs imaginable, pastries, breads, and griddle cakes. Lucy seemed immune to the temptations, and headed straight for the cereals and fresh fruit. Shamed into good behavior by her example and by my recent lecture to Marino about his health, I avoided everything I wanted, including coffee.

"People are staring at you, Aunt Kay," Lucy said under her breath.

I assumed the attention was due to our vibrant attire until I opened the morning's *Washington Post* and was shocked to discover myself on the front page. The headline read, "MURDER IN

THE MORGUE," the story a lengthy account of Susan's homicide, which was accompanied by a prominently placed photograph of me arriving at the scene and looking very tense. Clearly, the reporter's major source was Susan's distraught husband, Jason, whose information painted a picture of his wife leaving her job under peculiar, if not suspicious, circumstances less than a week before her violent death.

It was asserted, for example, that Susan recently confronted me when I attempted to list her as a witness in the case of a murdered young boy, even though she had not been present during his autopsy. When Susan became ill and stayed out of work "after a formalin spill," I called her home with such frequency that she was afraid to answer the phone, then I "showed up on her doorstep the night before her murder" with a poinsettia and vague offers of favors.

"I walked into my house after Christmas shopping and there was the Chief Medical Examiner inside my living room," Susan's husband was quoted. "She [Dr. Scarpetta] left right away, and as soon as the door shut Susan started crying. She was terrified of something but wouldn't tell me what."

As unsettling as I found Jason Story's public disparagement of me, worse was the revelation of Susan's recent financial transactions. Supposedly, two weeks before her death she paid off more than three thousand dollars in credit card bills after having deposited thirty-five hundred dollars into her checking account. The sudden windfall could not be explained. Her husband had been laid off from his sales job during the fall and Susan earned less than twenty thousand dollars a year.

"Mr. Wesley's here," Lucy said, taking the paper from me.

Wesley was dressed in black ski pants and turtleneck, a bright red jacket tucked under his arm. I could tell by the expression on his face, the firm set of his jaw, that he was aware of the news.

"Did the *Post* try to talk to you?" He pulled out a chair. "I can't believe they ran this damn thing without giving you a chance for comment."

"A reporter from the *Post* called as I was leaving the office yesterday, " I replied. "He wanted to question me about Susan's homicide and I chose not to talk to him. I guess that was my chance."

"So you didn't know anything, had no forewarning about the slant of this thing."

"I was in the dark until I picked up the paper."

"It's all over the news, Kay." He met my eyes. "I heard it on television this morning. Marino called. The press in Richmond is having a field day. The implication is that Susan's murder may be connected to the medical examiner's office—that you may be involved and have suddenly left town."

"That's insane."

"How much of the article is true?" he asked.

"The facts have been completely distorted. I did call Susan's house when she didn't show up at work. I wanted to make certain she was all right, and then I needed to find out if she remembered printing Waddell at the morgue. I did go see her on Christmas Eve to give her a gift and the poinsettia. I suppose my promise of favors was when she told me she was quitting and I said for her to let me know if she needed a reference, or if there was anything I could do for her."

"What about this business of her not wanting to be listed as a witness in Eddie Heath's case?"

"That was the afternoon she broke several jars of formalin and retreated upstairs to my office. It's routine to list autopsy assistants or techs as witnesses when they assist in the posts. In this instance, Susan was present for only the external examination and was adamant about not wanting her name on Eddie Heath's autopsy report. I thought her request and demeanor were weird, but there was no confrontation."

"This article makes it look as if you were paying her off," Lucy said. "That's what I would wonder if I read this and didn't know."

"I certainly wasn't paying her off, but it sounds as if someone was," I said.

"It's all making a little more sense," Wesley said. "If this bit about her financial picture is accurate, then Susan had gotten a substantial sum of money, meaning she must have supplied a service to someone. Around this same time your computer was broken into and Susan's personality changed. She became nervous and unreliable. She avoided you as much as she could. I think she couldn't face you, Kay, because she knew she was betraying you."

I nodded, struggling for composure. Susan had gotten into something she did not know how to get out of, and it occurred to me that this might be the real explanation for why she fled from Eddie Heath's post and then from Jennifer Deighton's. Her emotional outbursts had nothing to do with witchcraft or feeling dizzy after being exposed to formalin fumes. She was panicking. She did not want to witness either case.

"Interesting," Wesley said when I voiced my theory. "If you ask what of value did Susan Story have to sell, the answer is information. If she didn't witness the posts, she had no information. And whoever was buying this information from her is quite likely the person she was going to meet on Christmas Day."

"What information would be so important that someone would be willing to pay thousands of dollars for it and then murder a pregnant woman?" Lucy asked bluntly.

We did not know, but we had a guess. The common denominator, once again, seemed to be Ronnie Joe Waddell.

"Susan didn't forget to print Waddell or whoever it was that was executed," I said. "She deliberately didn't print him."

"That's the way it looks," Wesley agreed. "Someone else asked her to conveniently forget to print him. Or to lose his cards in the event that you or another member of your staff printed him."

I thought of Ben Stevens. The bastard.

"And this brings us back to what you and I concluded last night, Kay," Wesley went on. "We need to go back to the night Waddell was supposed to have been executed and determine who it was they strapped in the chair. And a place to start is AFIS. What we want to know is if and what records were tampered with." He was talking to Lucy now. "I've got it set up for you to go through the journal tapes, if you're willing."

"I'm willing," Lucy said. "When do you want me to start?"

"You can start as soon as you want because the first step will involve only the telephone. You need to call Michele. She's a systems analyst for Department of Criminal Justice Services and works out of the State Police headquarters. She's involved with AFIS and will go into detail with you about how everything works. Then she'll begin mounting the journal tapes so you can access them."

"She doesn't mind my doing this?" Lucy asked warily.

"On the contrary. She's thrilled. The journal tapes are nothing more than audit logs, a record of changes made to the AFIS data base. They're not readable, in other words. I think Michele called them 'hex dumps,' if that means anything to you."

"Hexadecimal, or base sixteen. Hieroglyphics, in other words," Lucy said. "It means that I'll have to decipher the data and write a program that will look for anything that's gone against the identification numbers of the records you're interested in."

"Can you do it?" Wesley asked.

"Once I figure out the code and record layout. Why doesn't the analyst you know do it herself?"

"We want to be as discreet as possible. It would attract notice if Michele suddenly abandoned her normal duties and started wading through journal tapes ten hours a day. You can work invisibly from your aunt's home computer by dialing in on a diagnostic line."

"As long as when Lucy dials in it can't be traced back to my residence," I said.

"It won't be," Wesley said.

"And no one is likely to notice that someone from the outside is dialing into the State Police computer and wading through the tapes?" I asked.

"Michele says she can maneuver it so there's no problem."

Unzipping a pocket of his ski jacket, Wesley slipped out a card and gave it to Lucy. "Here are her work and home phone numbers."

"How do you know you can trust her?" Lucy asked. "If tampering has gone on, how do you know she's not involved?"

"Michele has never been good at lying. From the time she was a little girl she would stare down at her feet and turn as red as Rudolf's nose."

"You knew her when she was a little girl?" Lucy looked baffled.

"And before," Wesley said. "She's my eldest daughter."

9

After much debate, we came up with what seemed a reasonable plan. Lucy would stay at the Homestead with the Wesleys until Wednesday, allowing me a brief period to grapple with my problems without worrying about her welfare. After breakfast, I drove off in a gentle snow that by the time I reached Richmond had turned to rain.

By late afternoon, I had been to the office and the labs. I had conferred with Fielding and several of the forensic scientists, and had avoided Ben Stevens. I returned not a single reporter's call and ignored my electronic mail, for if the health commissioner had sent me a communication, I did not want to know what it said. At half past four I was filling my car with gas at an Exxon station on Grove Avenue when a white Ford LTD pulled in behind me. I watched Marino get out, hitch up his trousers, and head to the men's room. When he returned a moment later, he covertly glanced around as if worried that someone might have observed his trip to the toilet. Then he strolled over to me.

"I saw you as I was driving past," he said, jamming his hands into the pockets of his blue blazer.

"Where's your coat?" I began cleaning the front windshield.

"In the car. It gets in my way." He hunched his shoulders against the cold, raw air. "If you ain't thinking about stopping these rumors, then you'd better start thinking about it."

I irritably returned the squeegee to its container of cleaning solution. "And just what do you suggest I do, Marino? Call Jason Story and tell him I'm sorry his wife and unborn child are dead but I would certainly appreciate it if he would vent his grief and rage elsewhere?"

"Doc, he blames you."

"After reading his quotes in the *Post,* I suspect any number of people are blaming me. He's managed to portray me as a Machiavellian bitch."

"You hungry?"

"No."

"Well, you look hungry."

I looked at him as if he'd lost his mind.

"And if something looks a certain way to me, it's my duty to check it out. So I'm giving you a choice, Doc. I can get us some Nabs and sodas from the machines over there, and we can stand out here freezing our asses off and inhaling fumes while we prevent other poor bastards from using the self-service pumps. Or we can zip over to Phil's. I'm buying either way."

Ten minutes later we were sitting in a corner booth perusing glossy illustrated menus offering everything from spaghetti to fried fish. Marino faced the dark-tinted front door and I had a perfect view of the rest rooms. He was smoking, as were most of the people around us, and I was reminded that it is hell to quit. He actually could not have selected a more ideal restaurant, considering the circumstances. Philip's Continental Lounge was an old, neighborhood establishment where patrons who had known each other all their lives continued to meet regularly for hearty food and bottled beer. The typical customer was good-natured and gregarious, and unlikely to recognize me or care unless my picture regularly appeared in the sports section of the newspaper.

"It's like this," Marino said as he closed his menu. "Jason Story believes Susan would still be alive if she'd had another job. And he's probably right. Plus, he's a loser—one of these self-centered assholes who believes everything is everybody else's fault. The truth is, he's probably more to blame for Susan's death than anyone."

"You're not suggesting that *he* killed her?"

The waitress appeared and we ordered. Grilled chicken and rice for Marino and a kosher chili dog for me, plus two diet sodas.

"I'm not suggesting that Jason shot his wife," Marino said quietly. "But he set her up for getting involved in whatever it was that precipitated her homicide. Paying the bills was Susan's responsibility, and she was under big-time financial stress."

"Unsurprisingly," I said. "Her husband had just lost his job."

"It's too bad he didn't lose his high dollar taste. We're talking Polo shirts and Britches of Georgetown slacks and silk ties.

A couple weeks after he gets laid off, the jerk goes out and buys seven hundred bucks' worth of ski equipment and then heads off to Wintergreen for the weekend. Before that it was a two-hundred-dollar leather jacket and a four-hundred-dollar bicycle. So Susan's down at the morgue working like a dog and then coming home to face bills her salary won't put a dent in."

"I had no idea," I said, pained by a sudden vision of Susan sitting at her desk. Her daily ritual was to spend her lunch hour in her office, and on occasion I would join her there to chat. I remembered her generic-brand corn chips and the sale stickers on her sodas. I don't think she ever ate or drank anything she had not brought from home.

"Jason's spending habits," Marino went on, "leads to the shit he's causing you. He's badmouthing you like hell to anybody who will listen because you're a doctor–lawyer–Indian chief who drives a Mercedes and lives in a big house in Windsor Farms. I think the dumbass believes if he can somehow blame you for what happened to his wife, maybe he can get a little compensation."

"He can try until he's blue in the face."

"And he will."

Our diet drinks arrived, and I changed the subject. "I'm meeting with Downey in the morning."

Marino's eyes wandered to the television over the bar.

"Lucy's getting started on AFIS. And then I've got to do something about Ben Stevens."

"What you ought to do is get rid of him."

"Do you have any idea how difficult it is to fire a state employee?"

"They say it's easier to fire Jesus Christ," Marino said. "Unless the employee is appointed and got a grade off the charts, like you. You still ought to find some way to run the bastard off."

"Have you talked to him?"

"Oh, yeah. According to him, you're arrogant, ambitious, and strange. A real pain in the ass to work for."

"He actually said something like that?" I asked in disbelief.

"That was the drift."

"I hope someone is checking into his finances. I'd be interested to know if he's made any large deposits lately. Susan didn't get into trouble alone."

"I agree with you. I think Stevens knows a lot and is covering his tracks like crazy. By the way, I checked with Susan's bank. One of the tellers remembers her making the thirty-five-hundred-dollar deposit in *cash*. Twenties, fifties, and hundred-dollar bills that she was carrying in her purse."

"What did Stevens have to say about Susan?"

"He's saying that he really didn't know her, but that it was his impression there was some problem between you and her. In other words, he's reinforcing what's been in the news."

Our food arrived, and it was all I could do to swallow a single bite because I was so angry.

"And what about Fielding?" I said. "Does he think I'm horrible to work for?"

Marino stared off again. "He says you're very driven and he's never been able to figure you out."

"I didn't hire him to figure me out, and compared to him, I am certainly driven. Fielding is disenchanted with forensic medicine and has been for several years. He expends most of his energy in the gym."

"Doc"—Marino met my eyes—"you are driven compared to *anyone,* and most people can't figure you out. You don't exactly walk around with your heart on your sleeve. In fact, you can come across as someone who don't have feelings. You're so damn hard to read that to others who don't know you, it sometimes appears that nothing gets to you. Other cops, lawyers, they ask me about you. They want to know what you're really like, how you can do what you do every day—what the deal is. They see you as somebody who don't get close to anyone."

"And what do you tell them when they ask?" I said.

"I don't tell them a damn thing."

"Are you finished psychoanalyzing me yet, Marino?"

He lit a cigarette. "Look, I'm going to say something to you, and you ain't gonna like it. You've always been this reserved, professional lady—someone real slow to let anybody in, but once the person's there, he's there. He's got a damn friend for life and you'd do anything for him. But you've been different this past year. You've had about a hundred walls up ever since Mark got killed. For those of us around you, it's like being in a room that was once seventy degrees and suddenly the temperature's down to about fifty-five. I don't think you're even aware of it.

"So nobody's feeling all that attached to you right now. Maybe they even resent you a little bit because they feel ignored or snubbed by you. Maybe they never liked you anyway. Maybe they're just indifferent. The thing about people is, whether you're sitting on a throne or a hot seat, they're going to use your position to their advantage. And if there's no bond between you and them, that just makes it all the easier for them to try to get what they want without giving a rat's ass about what happens to you. And that's where you are. There's a lot of people who've been waiting for years to see you bleed."

"I don't intend to bleed." I pushed my plate away.

"Doc"—he blew out smoke—"you're already bleeding. And common sense tells me that if you're swimming with sharks and start bleeding, you ought to get the hell out of the water."

"Might we converse without speaking in clichés, at least for a minute or two?"

"Hey. I can say it in Portuguese or Chinese and you're not going to listen to me."

"If you speak Portuguese or Chinese, I promise I'll listen. In fact, if you ever decide to speak English I promise I'll listen."

"Comments like that don't win you any fans. That's just what I'm talking about."

"I said it with a smile."

"I've seen you cut open bodies with a smile."

"Never. I always use a scalpel."

"Sometimes there isn't a difference between the two. I've seen your smile make defense attorneys bleed."

"If I'm such a dreadful person, why are we friends?"

"Because I've got more walls up than you do. The fact is, there's a squirrel in every tree and the water's full of sharks. All of them want a piece of us."

"Marino, you're paranoid."

"You're damn right, which is why I wish you'd lay low for a while, Doc. Really," he said.

"I can't."

"You want to know the truth, it's going to start looking like a conflict of interests for you to have anything to do with these cases. It's going to make you come off looking worse."

I said, "Susan is dead. Eddie Heath is dead. Jennifer Deighton is dead. There is corruption in my office, and we aren't certain who went to the electric chair the other week. You're suggesting I just walk away until everything somehow magically self-corrects?"

Marino reached for the salt but I got it first. "Nope. But you can have all the pepper you want," I said, sliding the pepper shaker closer.

"This health crap is going to kill me," he warned. "Because one of these days I'm going to get so pissed I'm going to do everything at once. Five cigarettes going, a bourbon in one hand and a cup of coffee in the other, steak, baked potato loaded with butter, sour cream, salt. And then I'm going to blow every circuit in the box."

"No, you're not going to do any of those things," I said. "You're going to be kind to yourself and live at least as long as I do."

We were silent for a while, picking at our food.

"Doc, no offense, but just what do you think you're going to find out about damn feather parts?"

"Hopefully, their origin."

"I can save you the trouble. They came from birds," he said.

I left Marino at close to seven P.M. and returned downtown. The temperature had risen above forty, the night dark and lashing out in fits of rain violent enough to stop traffic. Sodium vapor lamps were pollen-yellow smudges behind the morgue, where the bay door was shut, every parking space vacant. Inside the building, my pulse quickened as I followed the brightly lit corridor past the autopsy suite to Susan's small office.

As I unlocked the door, I did not know what I expected to find, but I was drawn to her filing cabinet and desk drawers, to every book and old telephone message. Everything looked the same as it had before she died. Marino was quite skilled at going through someone's private space without disturbing the natural disorder of things. The telephone was still askew on the right corner of the desk, the cord twisted like a corkscrew. Scissors and two pencils with broken points were on the green paper blotter, her lab coat draped over the back of her chair. A reminder of a doctor's appointment was still taped to her computer monitor, and as I stared at the shy curves and gentle slant of her neat script, I trembled inside. Where had she gone adrift? Was it when she married Jason Story? Or was her destruction set up much earlier than that, when she was the young daughter of a scrupulous minister, the twin left behind when her sister was killed?

Sitting in her chair, I rolled it closer to the filing cabinet and began slipping out one file after another and glancing through the contents. Most of what I perused was brochures and other printed information pertaining to surgical supplies and miscellaneous items used in the morgue. Nothing struck me as curious until I discovered that she had saved virtually every memo she had ever gotten from Fielding, but not one from Ben Stevens or me, when I knew that both of us had sent her plenty.

Further searching through drawers and bookshelves produced no files for Stevens or me, and that's when I concluded that someone had taken them.

My first thought was that Marino might have carried them off. Then something else occurred to me with a jolt, and I hurried upstairs. Unlocking the door to my office, I went straight to the file drawer where I kept mundane administrative paperwork such as telephone call sheets, memos, printouts of electronic mail communications I had received, and drafts of budget proposals and long-term plans. Frantically, I rifled through folders and drawers. The thick file I was looking for was simply labeled "Memos," and in it were copies of every memo I had sent to my staff and various other agency personnel over the past several years. I searched Rose's office and carefully checked my office again. The file was gone.

"You son of a bitch," I said under my breath as I headed furiously down the hall. "You goddam son of a bitch."

Ben Stevens's office was impeccably neat and so carefully appointed that it looked like a display in a discount furniture store. His desk was a Williamsburg reproduction with bright brass pulls and a mahogany veneer, and he had brass floor lamps with dark green shades. The floor was covered with a machine-made Persian rug, the walls arranged with large prints of alpine skiers and men on thundering horses swinging polo sticks and sailors racing through snarling seas. I began by pulling Susan's personnel file. The expected job description, résumé, and other documents were inside. Absent were several memos of commendation I had written since hiring her and had added to her file myself. I began opening desk drawers, and discovered in one of them a brown vinyl kit containing toothbrush, tooth-paste, razor, shaving cream, and a small bottle of cologne.

Perhaps it was the barely perceptible shift of air when the door was silently pulled open wider, or perhaps I simply sensed a presence the way an animal would. I happened to look up to find Ben Stevens standing in the doorway as I sat at his desk screwing the cap back on a bottle of Red cologne. For a long, icy moment, our eyes held and neither of us spoke. I did not feel fear. I did not feel the least bit concerned by what he had caught me doing. I felt rage.

"You're keeping unusually late hours, Ben." Zipping up his toilet kit, I returned it to its drawer. I laced my fingers on top of the blotter, my movements, my speech, deliberate and slow.

"The thing I've always liked about working after hours is there is no one else around," I said. "No distractions. No risk of someone walking in and interrupting whatever it is you are doing. No eyes or ears. Not a sound, except on rare occasion when the security guard happens to wander through. And we all know that doesn't happen often unless his attention is solicited, because he hates coming into the morgue at any time. I've never known a security guard who didn't hate that. Same goes for the cleaning crew. They won't even go downstairs, and they do as little up here as they can get away with. But that point is moot, isn't it? It's close to nine o'clock. The cleaning crew is always gone by seven-thirty.

"What intrigues me is that I did not guess before now. It never crossed my mind. Maybe that is a sad comment about how preoccupied I've been. You told the police you did not know Susan personally, yet you frequently gave her rides to and from work, such as on the snowy morning I autopsied Jennifer Deighton. I remember that Susan was very distracted on that occasion. She left the body in the middle of the corridor, and she was dialing a number on the phone and quickly hung up when I walked into the autopsy suite. I doubt she was placing a business call at seven-thirty in the morning on a day when most people weren't going to venture out of their homes because of the weather. And there was no one in the office to call—no one had gotten in yet, except you. If she were dialing your number, why would her impulse be to hide that from me? Unless you were more than her direct supervisor.

"Of course, your relationship with me is equally intriguing. We seem to get along fine, then suddenly you claim that I am the worst boss in Christendom. It makes me wonder if Jason Story is the only person talking to reporters. It's amazing, this persona I suddenly have. This image. The tyrant. The neurotic. The person who is somehow responsible for the violent death of my morgue supervisior. Susan and I had a very cordial working relationship, and until recently, Ben, so did we. But it's my word against yours, especially now, since any scrap of paper that might document what I'm saying has conveniently disappeared. And my prediction is that you have already leaked to someone that important personnel files and memoranda have vanished from the office, thus implying that I'm the one who took them. When files and memos disappear, you can say anything you want about the contents of them, can't you?"

"I don't know what you're talking about," Ben Stevens said. He moved away from the doorway but did not come close to the desk or take a chair. His face was flushed, his eyes hard with

245

hate. "I don't know anything about any missing files or memos, but if it's true, then I can't hide that fact from the authorities, just as I can't hide the fact that I happened to stop by the office tonight to get something I'd left and discovered you rummaging through my desk."

"What did you leave, Ben?"

"I don't have to answer your questions."

"Actually, you do. You work for me, and if you come into the building late at night and I happen to know about it, I have the right to question you."

"Go ahead and put me on leave. Try to fire me. That will certainly look good for you right now."

"You are a squid, Ben."

His eyes widened and he wet his lips.

"Your efforts to sabotage me are just a lot of ink you're squirting into the water because you're panicking and want to divert attention from yourself. Did you kill Susan?"

"You're losing your goddam mind." His voice shook.

"She left her house early afternoon on Christmas Day, allegedly to meet a girlfriend. In truth, the person she was meeting was you, wasn't it? Did you know that when she was dead in her car, her coat collar and scarf smelled like men's cologne, like the Red cologne you keep in your desk so you can freshen up before you hit the bars in the Slip after work?"

"I don't know what you're talking about."

"Who was paying her?"

"Maybe you were."

"That's ridiculous," I said calmly. "You and Susan were involved in some money-making scheme, and my guess is that you are the one who initially got her involved because you knew her vulnerabilities. She probably had confided in you. You knew how to convince her to go along, and Lord knows you could use the money. Your bar tabs alone have got to blow your budget. Partying is very expensive, and I know what you get paid."

"You don't know anything."

"Ben." I lowered my voice. "Get out of it. Stop while there's still time. Tell me who's behind this."

He would not look me in the eye.

"The stakes are too high when people start dying. Do you think if you killed Susan that you'll get away with it?"

He said nothing.

"If someone else killed her, do you think you're immune, that the same thing can't happen to you?"

"You're threatening me."

"Nonsense."

"You can't prove that the cologne you smelled on Susan was mine. There's no test for something like that. You can't put a *smell* in a test tube; you can't save it," he said.

"I'm going to ask you to leave now, Ben."

He turned and walked out of his office. When I heard the elevator doors shut, I went down the hall and peered out a window overlooking the parking lot in back. I did not venture out to my car until Stevens had driven away.

The FBI Building is a concrete fortification at 9th Street and Pennsylvania Avenue in the heart of D.C., and when I arrived the following morning, it was in the wake of at least a hundred noisy schoolchildren. They brought to mind Lucy at their age as they stomped up steps, dashed to benches, and flocked restlessly about huge shrubs and potted trees. Lucy would have loved touring the laboratories, and I suddenly missed her intensely.

The babble of shrill young voices faded as if carried away from me by the wind, my step brisk and directed, for I had been here enough times to know the way. Heading toward the center of the building, I passed the courtyard, then a restricted parking area and a guard before reaching the single glass door. Inside was a lobby of tan furniture, mirrors, and flags. A photograph of the president smiled from one wall, while posted on another was a hit parade of the ten most wanted fugitives in the land.

At the escort desk, I presented my driver's license to a young agent whose demeanor was as grim as his gray suit.

"I'm Dr. Kay Scarpetta, Chief Medical Examiner of Virginia."

"Who are you here to see?"

I told him.

He compared me to my photograph, ascertained that I was not armed, placed a phone call, and gave me a badge. Unlike the Academy at Quantico, Headquarters had an ambience that seemed to starch the soul and stiffen the spine.

I had never met Special Agent Minor Downey, though the irony of his name had conjured up unfair images. He would be an effete, frail man with pale blond hair covering every inch of his body except for his head. His eyes would be weak, his skin rarely touched by the sun, and of course he would drift in and out of places and never draw attention to himself. Naturally, I was wrong. When a fit man in shirtsleeves appeared and looked straight at me, I got up from my chair.

"You must be Mr. Downey," I said.

"Dr. Scarpetta." He shook my hand. "Please call me Minor."

He was at the most forty, and attractive in a scholarly sort of way, with his rimless glasses, neatly clipped brown hair, and maroon-and-navy-striped tie. He exuded a prepossession and intellectual intensity immediately noticeable to anyone who has suffered through arduous years of postgraduate education, for I could not recall a professor from Georgetown or Johns Hopkins who did not commune with the uncommon and find it impossible to connect with pedestrian human beings.

"Why feathers?" I asked as we boarded the elevator.

"I have a friend who's an ornithologist at the Smithsonian's Museum of Natural History," he said. "When government aviation officials started getting her help with bird strikes, I got interested. You see, birds get ingested by aircraft engines and when you're going through the wreckage on the ground, you find these feather parts and want to figure out which bird caused the problem. In other words, whatever got sucked in was chewed up pretty good. A sea gull can crash a B-1 bomber, and you lose one engine to a bird strike with a wide-bodied plane full of people and you've got a problem. Or take the case of the loon that went through the windshield of a Lear jet and decapitated the pilot. So that's part of what I do. I work on bird ingestions. We test turbines and blades by throwing in chickens. You know, can the plane survive one chicken or two?

"But birds figure into all sorts of things. Pigeon down in poop on the bottom of a suspect's shoes—was the suspect in the alleyway where the body was found or not? Or the guy who stole a Double Yellow Amazon during the course of a burglary, and we find down pieces in the back of his car that are identified as coming from a Double Yellow Amazon. Or the down feather recovered from the body of a woman who was raped and murdered. She was found in a Panasonic stereo speaker box in a Dumpster. The down looked like a small white mallard feather to me, same type of feather in the down comforter on the suspect's bed. That case was made with a feather and two hairs."

The third floor was a city block of laboratories where examiners analyzed the explosives, paint chips, pollens, tools, tires, and debris used in crimes or collected from scenes. Gas chromatography detectors, microspectrophotometers, and mainframes ran morning, noon, and night, and reference collections filled rooms with automotive paint types, duct tapes, and plastics. I followed Downey through white hallways past the DNA analysis labs, then into the Hairs and Fibers Unit where he worked. His office also functioned as a laboratory, with dark wood furniture and bookcases sharing space with countertops and microscopes. Walls and carpet were beige, and crayon drawings tacked to a bulletin board told me this internationally respected feather expert was a father.

Opening a manila envelope, I withdrew three smaller envelopes made of transparent plastic. Two contained the feathers collected from Jennifer Deighton's and Susan Story's homicides, while a third contained a slide of the gummy residue from Eddie Heath's wrists.

"This is the best one, it seems," I said, pointing out the feather I had recovered from Jennifer Deighton's nightgown.

He took it out of its envelope and said, "This is down—a breast or back feather. It's got a nice tuft on it. Good. The more feather you've got, the better." Using forceps, he stripped several of the branchlike projections or "barbs" from both sides of the shaft and, stationing himself at the stereoscopic microscope, placed them on a thin film of xylene that he had dropped on a slide. This served to separate the tiny structures, or float them out, and when he was satisfied that each barb was pristinely fanned, he touched a corner of green blotting paper to the xylene to absorb it. He added the mounting medium Flo-Texx, then a coverslip, and placed the slide under the comparison microscope, which was connected to a video camera.

"I'll start off by telling you that the feathers of all birds have basically the same structure," he said. "You've got a central shaft, barbs, which in turn branch into hairlike barbules, and you've got a broadened base, at the top of which is a pore called the superior umbilicus. The barbs are the filaments that result in the feather's *feathery* appearance, and when they're magnified you'll find they're actually like minifeathers coming out of the shaft." He turned on the monitor. "Here's a barb."

"It looks like a fern," I said.

"In many instances, yes. Now we're going to magnify it some more so we can get a good look at the barbules, for it is the features of the barbules that allow for an identification. Specifically, what we're most interested in are the nodes."

"Let me see if I've got this straight," I said. "Nodes are features of barbules, barbules are features of barbs, barbs are features of feathers, and feathers are features of birds."

"Right. And each family of birds has its own peculiar feather structure."

What I saw on the monitor's screen looked, unremarkably, like a stick figure depiction of a weed or an insect leg. Lines were connected in segments by three-dimensional triangular structures that Downey said were the nodes.

"It's the size, shape, number, and pigmentation of nodes and their placement along the barbule that are key," he patiently explained. "For example, with starlike nodes you're dealing with pigeons, ringlike nodes are chickens and turkeys, enlarged flanges with prenodal swelling are cuckoos. These"—he pointed to the screen—"are clearly triangular, so right away I know your feather is either duck or goose. Not that this should come as any great surprise. The typical origin of feathers collected in burglaries, rapes, and homicides are pillows, comforters, vests, jackets, gloves. And generally the filler in these items comprises chopped feathers and down from ducks and geese, and in cheap stuff, chickens.

"But we can definitely rule out chickens here. And I'm about to decide that your feather did not come from a goose, either."

"Why?" I asked.

"Well, the distinction would be easy if we had a whole feather. Down is tough. But based on what I'm seeing here, there are, on average, just too few nodes. Plus, they aren't located throughout the barbule but are more distal, or located more toward the end of the barbule. And that's a characteristic of ducks."

He opened a cabinet and slid out several drawers of slides.

"Let's see. I've got about sixty slides of ducks. To be on the safe side I'm going to run through all of them, eliminating as I go."

One by one he placed slides under the comparison microscope, which is basically two compound microscopes combined into one binocular unit. On the video monitor was a circular field of light divided down the middle by a fine line, the known feather specimen on one side of the line and the one we hoped to identify on the other. Rapidly, we scanned mallard, Muscovy, harlequin, scoter, ruddy, and American widgeon, and then dozens more. Downey did not have to look long at any one of them to know that the duck we sought was being elusive.

"Am I just imagining it, or is this one more delicate than the others?" I said of the feather in question.

"You're not imagining it. It's more delicate, more streamlined. See how the triangular structures don't flare out quite as much?"

"Okay. Now that you've pointed it out."

"And this is giving us an important hint about the bird. That's what's fascinating. Nature really does have a reason for things, and I'm suspicious that in this case the reason is insulation. The purpose of down is to trap air, and the finer the barbules, the more streamlined or tapered the nodes, and the more distal the location of the nodes, the more efficient the down is going to be at trapping air. When air's trapped or dead, it's like being in a small, insulated room with no ventilation. You're going to be warm."

He placed another slide on the microscope's stage, and this time I could see that we were close. The barbules were delicate, the nodes tapered and distally located.

"What have we got?" I asked.

"I've saved the prime suspects for last." He looked pleased. "Sea ducks. And top in the lineup are the eiders. Let's bump the magnification up to four hundred." He switched the objective lens, adjusted the focus, and off we went through several more slides. "Not the king or the spectacle. And I don't think it's the stellar because of the brownish pigmentation at the base of the node. Your feather doesn't have that, see?"

"I see."

"So we'll try the common eider. Okay. There's consistency in pigmentation," he said, staring intensely at the screen. "And, let's see, an average of two nodes located distally along the barbules. Plus, the streamlining for extra good insulating quality—and that's important if you're swimming around in the Arctic Ocean. I think this is it, the *Somateria mollissima,* typically found in Iceland, Norway, Alaska, and the Siberian shores. I'll run another check with SEM," he added, referring to scanning electron microscopy.

"To scan for what?"

"Salt crystals."

"Of course," I said, fascinated. "Because eider ducks are salt-water birds."

"Exactly. And interesting ones at that, a noteworthy example of exploitation. In Iceland and Norway, their breeding colonies are protected from predators and other disruptions so that people can collect the down with which the female lines her nest and covers her eggs. The down is then cleaned and sold to manufacturers."

"Manufacturers of what?"

"Typically, sleeping bags and comforters." As he talked, he was mounting several downy barbs from the feather found inside Susan Story's car.

"Jennifer Deighton had nothing like that in her house," I said. "Nothing filled with feathers at all."

"Then we're probably dealing with a secondary or tertiary transfer in which the feather got transferred to the killer who in turn transferred it to his victim. You know, this is very interesting."

The specimen was on the monitor now.

"Eider duck again," I said.

"I think so. Let's try the slide. This is from the boy?"

"Yes," I said. "From an adhesive residue on Eddie Heath's wrists."

"I'll be damned."

The microscopic debris showed up on the monitor as a fascinating variety of colors, shapes, fibers, and the familiar barbules and triangular nodes.

"Well, that puts a pretty big hole in my personal theory," Downey said. "If we're talking about three homicides that occurred at different locations and at different times."

"That's what we're talking about."

"If just one of these feathers was eider duck, then I'd be tempted to consider the possibility that it was a contaminant. You know, you see these labels that say one hundred percent acrylic and it turns out to be ninety percent acrylic and ten percent nylon. Labels lie. If the run before your acrylic sweater, for example, was a lot of nylon jackets, then the very first sweaters that come off afterward will have nylon contaminants. As you run more sweaters through, the contaminant is dissipated."

"In other words," I said, "if somebody is wearing a down-filled jacket or owns a comforter that got eider contaminants in it when it was manufactured, then the probability is almost nonexistent that this individual's jacket or comforter would be leaking only the eiderdown contaminants."

"Precisely. So we'll assume the item in question is filled with pure eiderdown, and that is extremely curious. Usually what I'm going to see in cases that come through here are your Kmart-variety jackets, gloves, or comforters filled with chicken feathers or maybe goose. Eider is a specialty item, a very exclusive shop item. A vest, jacket, comforter, or sleeping bag filled with eiderdown is going to have very low leakage, be very well made—and prohibitively expensive."

"Have you ever had eiderdown submitted as evidence before?"

"This is the first."

"Why is it so valuable?"

"The insulating qualities I've already described. But aesthetic appeal also has a lot to do with it. The common eider's down is snow-white. Most down is dingy."

"And if I purchased a specialty item filled with eiderdown, would I be aware that it's filled with this snow-white down or would the label simply say 'duck down'?"

"I'm quite sure you'd be aware of it," he said. "The label

would probably say something like 'one hundred percent eider-down.' There would have to be something that would justify the price."

"Can you run a computer check on down distributors?"

"Sure. But to state the obvious, no distributor is going to be able to tell you the eiderdown you've collected is theirs, not without the accompanying garment or item. Unfortunately, a feather isn't enough."

"I don't know," I said. "It might be."

By noon I had walked two blocks to where I had parked my car, and was inside with the heater blasting. I was so close to New Jersey Avenue that I felt like the tide being pulled by the moon. I fastened my seat belt, fiddled with the radio, and twice reached for the phone and changed my mind. It was crazy to even consider contacting Nicholas Grueman.

He won't be in anyway, I thought, reaching for the phone again and dialing.

"Grueman," the voice said.

"This is Dr. Scarpetta." I raised my voice above the heater's fan.

"Well, hello. I was just reading about you the other day. You sound like you're calling from a car phone."

"That's because I am. I happen to be in Washington."

"I'm truly flattered that you would think of me while you're passing through my humble town."

"There is nothing humble about your town, Mr. Grueman, and there is nothing social about this call. I thought you and I should discuss Ronnie Joe Waddell."

"I see. How far are you from the Law Center?"

"Ten minutes."

"I haven't eaten lunch and I don't suppose you have, either. Does it suit you if I have sandwiches sent in?"

"That would be fine," I said.

The Law Center was located some thirty-five blocks from the university's main campus, and I remembered my dismay many years before when I realized that my education would not include walking the old, shaded streets of the Heights and attending classes in fine eighteenth-century brick buildings. Instead, I was to spend three long years in a brand-new facility devoid of charm in a noisy, frantic section of D.C. My disappointment, however, did not last long. There was a certain excitement, not to mention convenience, in studying law in the shadow of the U.S. Capitol. But perhaps more significant was that I had not been a student long when I met Mark.

What I remembered most about my early encounters with Mark James during the first semester of our first year was his physical effect on me. At first I found the very sight of him unsettling, though I had no idea why. Then, as we became acquainted, his presence sent adrenaline charging through my blood. My heart would gallop and I would suddenly find myself acutely aware of his every gesture, no matter how common. For weeks, our conversations were entranced as they stretched into the early-morning hours. Our words were not elements of speech as much as they were notes to some secret inevitable crescendo, which happened one night with the dazzling unpredictability and force of an accident.

Since those days, the Law Center's physical plant had significantly grown and changed. The Criminal Justice Clinic was on the fourth floor, and when I got off the elevator there was no one in sight and offices I passed looked unoccupied. It was, after all, still the holidays, and only the relentless or desperate would be inclined to work. The door to room 418 was open, the secretary's desk vacant, the door to Grueman's inner office ajar.

Not wanting to startle him, I called out his name as I approached his door. He did not answer.

"Hello, Mr. Grueman? Are you here?" I tried again as I pushed his door open farther.

His desk was inches deep in clutter that pooled around a computer, and case files and transcripts were stacked on the floor along the base of the crowded bookcases. Left of his desk was a table bearing a printer and a fax machine that was busily sending something to someone. As I stood quietly staring around, the telephone rang three times and then stopped. Blinds were drawn in the window behind the desk, perhaps to reduce the glare on the computer screen, and leaning against the sill was a scarred and battered brown leather briefcase.

"Sorry about that." A voice behind me nearly sent me out of my shoes. "I stepped out for just a moment and was hoping I'd get back before you arrived."

Nicholas Grueman did not offer me his hand or a personal greeting of any kind. His preoccupation seemed to be returning to his chair, which he did very slowly and with the aid of a silver-topped cane.

"I would offer you coffee, but none is made when Evelyn isn't here," he said, seating himself in his judge's chair. "But the deli that will be delivering lunch shortly is bringing something to drink. I hope you can wait, and please take a chair, Dr. Scarpetta. It makes me nervous when a woman is looking down on me."

I pulled a chair closer to his desk and was amazed to realize that in the flesh Grueman was not the monster I recalled from my student days. For one thing, he seemed to have shrunk, though I suspected the more likely explanation was that I had inflated him to Mount Rushmore proportions in my imagination. I saw him now as a slight, white-haired man whose face had been carved by the years into a compelling caricature. He still wore bow ties and vests and smoked a pipe, and when he looked at me, his gray eyes were as capable of dissection as any scalpel. But I did not find them cold. They were simply unrevealing, as were mine most of the time.

"Why are you limping?" I boldly asked him.

"Gout. The disease of despots," he said without a smile.

"It acts up from time to time, and please spare me any good advice or remedies. You doctors drive me to distraction with your unsolicited opinions on every subject from malfunctioning electric chairs to the food and drink I should exclude from my miserable diet."

"The electric chair did not malfunction," I said. "Not in the case I'm sure you're alluding to."

"You cannot possibly know what I am alluding to, and it seems to me that during your brief tenure here I had to admonish you more than once about your great facility for making assumptions. I regret that you did not listen to me. You are still making assumptions, though in this instance your assumption was, in fact, correct."

"Mr. Grueman, I am flattered that you remember me as a student, but I did not come here to reminisce about the wretched hours I spent in your classroom. Nor am I here to engage, again, in the mental martial arts you seem to thrive on. For the record, I will tell you that you have the distinction of being the most misogynistic and arrogant professor I encountered during my thirty-some years of formal education. And I must thank you for schooling me so well in the art of dealing with bastards, for the world is full of them and I must deal with them every day."

"I'm sure you do deal with them every day, and I haven't decided yet whether you're good at it."

"I'm not interested in your opinion on that subject. I would like you to tell me more about Ronnie Joe Waddell."

"What would you like to know beyond the obvious fact that the ultimate outcome was incorrect? How would you like politics to determine whether you are put to death, Dr. Scarpetta? Why, just look at what's happening to you now. Isn't your recent bad press politically motivated, at least in part? Every party involved has his own agenda, something to gain from disparaging you publicly. It has nothing to do with fairness or truth. So just imagine what it would be like if these same people possessed the power to deprive you of your liberty or even of your life.

"Ronnie was torn to pieces by a system that is irrational and unfair. It made no difference what earlier precedents were applied or whether claims were addressed on direct or collateral review. It made no difference what issue I raised because in this instance in your lovely Commonwealth, habeas did not serve as a deterrent designed to ensure that state trial and appellate judges conscientiously sought to conduct their proceedings in a manner consistent with established constitutional principles. God forbid that there should have been the slightest interest in constitutional violations on furthering the evolution of our thinking in some area of the law. In the three years that I fought for Ronnie, I might as well have been dancing a jig."

"What constitutional violations are you referring to?" I asked.

"How much time do you have? But let's begin with the prosecution's obvious use of peremptory challenges in a racially discriminatory manner. Ronnie's rights under the equal protection clause were violated from hell to breakfast, and prosecutorial misconduct blatantly infringed his Sixth Amendment right to a jury drawn from a fair cross section of the community. I don't suppose you saw Ronnie's trial or even know much about it since it was more than nine years ago and you were not in Virginia. The local publicity was overwhelming, and yet there was no change of venue. The jury was comprised of eight women and four men. Six of the women and two of the men were white. The four black jurors were a car salesman, a bank teller, a nurse, and a college professor. The professions of the white jurors ranged from a retired railroad switchman who still called blacks 'niggers' to a rich housewife whose only exposure to blacks was when she watched the news and saw that another one of them had shot someone in the projects. The demographics of the jury made it impossible for Ronnie to be sentenced fairly."

"And you're saying that such a constitutional impropriety or any other in Waddell's case was politically motivated? What possible political motivation could there have been for putting Ronnie Waddell to death?"

Grueman suddenly glanced toward the door. "Unless my ears deceive me, I believe lunch has arrived."

I heard rapid footsteps and paper crinkle, then a voice called out, "Yo, Nick. You in here?"

"Come on in, Joe," Grueman said without getting up from his desk.

An energetic young black man in blue jeans and tennis shoes appeared and placed two bags in front of Grueman.

"This one's got the drinks, and in here we got two sailor sandwiches, potato salad, and pickles. That's fifteen-forty."

"Keep the change. And look, Joe, I appreciate it. Don't they ever give you a vacation?"

"People don't quit eating, man. Gotta run."

Grueman distributed the food and napkins while I desperately tried to figure out what to do. I was finding myself increasingly swayed by his demeanor and words, for there was nothing shifty about him, nothing that struck me as condescending or insincere.

"What political motivation?" I asked him again as I unwrapped my sandwich.

He popped open a ginger ale and removed the top from his container of potato salad. "Several weeks ago I thought I might just get an answer to that question," he said. "But then the person who could have helped me was suddenly found dead inside her car. And I'm quite certain you know who I'm talking about, Dr. Scarpetta. Jennifer Deighton is one of your cases, and although it has yet to be publicly stated that her death is a suicide, that is what one has been led to believe. I find the timing of her death rather remarkable, if not chilling."

"Am I to understand that you knew Jennifer Deighton?" I asked as blandly as possible.

"Yes and no. I'd never met her, and our telephone conversations, what few we had, were very brief. You see, I never contacted her until after Ronnie was dead."

"From which I am also to understand that she knew Waddell."

Grueman took a bite of his sandwich and reached for his ginger ale. "She and Ronnie definitely knew each other," he said. "As you must know, Miss Deighton had a horoscope service, was into parapsychology and that sort of thing. Well, eight years ago, when Ronnie was on death row in Mecklenburg, he happened to see an advertisement for her services in some magazine. He wrote to her, initially in hopes that she could look into her crystal ball, so to speak, and tell him his future. Specifically, I think he wanted to know if he was going to die in the electric chair, and this is not an uncommon phenomenon—inmates writing psychics, palm readers, and asking about their futures, or contacting the clergy and asking for prayers. What was a little more unusual in Ronnie's case was that he and Miss Deighton apparently began an intimate correspondence that lasted until several months before his death. Then her letters to him suddenly stopped."

"Are you considering that her letters to him might have been intercepted?"

"There is no question about that. When I talked to Jennifer

Deighton on the telephone, she claimed that she had continued to write to Ronnie. She also said that she had received no letters from him over the past several months, and I'm very suspicious that this is because his letters were intercepted as well."

"Why did you wait to contact her until after the execution?" I puzzled.

"I did not know about her before then. Ronnie said nothing about her to me until our last conversation, which was, perhaps, the strangest conversation I've ever had with any inmate I've represented." Grueman toyed with his sandwich and then pushed it away from him. He reached for his pipe. "I'm not sure if you're aware of this, Dr. Scarpetta, but Ronnie quit on me."

"I have no idea what you mean."

"The last time I talked with Ronnie was one week before he was to be transported from Mecklenburg to Richmond. At that time, he stated that he knew he was going to be executed and that nothing I did was going to make a difference. He said that what was going to happen to him had been set into motion since the beginning and he had accepted the inevitability of his death. He said that he was looking foward to dying and preferred that I cease pursuing federal habeas corpus relief. Then he requested that I not call him or come see him again."

"But he didn't fire you."

Grueman shot flame into the bowl of his briar pipe and sucked on the stem. "No, he did not. He simply refused to see me or talk to me on the phone."

"It would seem that this alone would have warranted a stay of execution pending a competency determination," I said.

"I tried that. I tried citing everything from *Hays* versus *Murphy* to the Lord's Prayer. The court rendered the brilliant decision that Ronnie had not asked to be executed. He'd simply stated that he looked forward to death, and the petition was denied."

"If you had no contact with Waddell in the several weeks before his execution, then how did you learn of Jennifer Deighton?"

"During my last conversation with Ronnie he made three last requests of me. The first was that I see to it that a meditation he had written was published in the newspaper days before his death. He gave this to me and I worked it out with the *Richmond Times-Dispatch*."

"I read it," I said.

"His second request—and I quote—was 'Don't let nothing happen to my friend.' And I asked him what friend he referred to, and he said, and again I quote, 'If you're a good man, look out for her. She never hurt no one.' He gave me her name and asked me not to contact her until after his death. Then I was to call and tell her how much she had meant to him. Well, of course I did not abide by that wish to the letter. I tried to contact her immediately because I knew I was losing Ronnie and I felt that something was terribly wrong. My hope was that this friend might be able to help. If they had corresponded with each other, for example, then maybe she could enlighten me."

"And did you reach her?" I asked, recalling Marino's telling me that Jennifer Deighton had been in Florida for two weeks around Thanksgiving.

"No one ever answered the phone," Grueman replied. "I tried on and off for several weeks, and then, to be frank, because of timing and health fortuities relating to the pace of litigation, the holidays, and a god-awful ambush of gout, my attention was diverted. I did not think to call Jennifer Deighton again until Ronnie was dead and I needed to contact her and convey, per Ronnie's request, that she had meant a lot to him, et cetera."

"When you had attempted to reach her earlier," I said, "did you leave messages on her answering machine?"

"It wasn't turned on. Which makes sense, in retrospect. She didn't need to return from vacation to face five hundred messages from people who can't make a decision until their horoscopes have been read. And if she left a message on her machine saying that she was out of town for two weeks, that would have been a perfect invitation for burglars."

"Then what happened when you finally reached her?"

"That was when she divulged that they had corresponded for eight years and that they loved each other. She claimed that the *truth would never be known.* I asked her what she meant but she would not tell me and got off the phone. Finally, I wrote her a letter imploring her to speak with me."

"When did you write this letter?" I asked.

"Let me see. The day after the execution. I suppose that would have been December fourteenth."

"And did she respond?"

"She did, by fax, interestingly enough. I did not know she had a fax machine, but my fax number was on my stationery. I have a copy of her fax if you would like to see it."

He shuffled through thick file folders and other paperwork on his desk. Finding the file he was looking for, he flipped through it and withdrew the fax, which I recognized instantly. "Yes, I'll cooperate," it read, "but it's too late, too late, too late. Better you should come here. This is all so wrong!" I wondered how Grueman would react if he knew that her communication with him had been recreated through image enhancement in Neils Vander's laboratory.

"Do you know what she meant? What was too late and what was so wrong?" I asked.

"Obviously, it was too late to do anything to stop Ronnie's execution since that had already occurred four days earlier. I'm not certain what she thought was so wrong, Dr. Scarpetta. You see, I have sensed for quite some time that there was something malignant about Ronnie's case. He and I never developed much of a rapport and that alone is odd. Generally, you get very close. I'm the only advocate in a system that wants you dead—the only one working for you in a system that doesn't work for you. But Ronnie was so aloof with his first attorney that this individual decided the case was hopeless and quit. Later, when I took on the case, Ronnie was just as distant. It was extraordinarily frustrating. Just when I would think he was beginning to trust me, a wall would go up. He would suddenly retreat into silence and literally begin to perspire."

"Did he seem frightened?"

"Frightened, depressed, sometimes angry."

"Are you suggesting that there was some conspiracy involved in his case and he might have told his friend about it, perhaps in one of his earlier letters to her?"

"I don't know what Jenny Deighton knew, but I suspect she knew something."

"Did Waddell refer to her as 'Jenny'?"

Grueman reached for his lighter again. "Yes."

"Did he ever mention to you a novel called *Paris Trout?*"

"That's interesting"—he looked surprised. "I haven't thought of this in quite some time, but during one of my early sessions with Ronnie several years ago, we talked about books and his poetry. He liked to read, and suggested I should read *Paris Trout.* I told him I had already read the novel, but was curious as to why he would recommend it. He said, very quietly, 'Because that's the way it works, Mr. Grueman. And there's no way you're gonna change nothing.' At the time I interpreted this to mean that he was a southern black pitted against the white man's system, and no federal habeas remedy or any other magic I might invoke during the judicial review process was going to alter his fate."

"Is this still your interpretation?"

He stared thoughtfully through a cloud of fragrant smoke. "I believe so. Why are you interested in Ronnie's recommended reading list?" He met my eyes.

"Jennifer Deighton had a copy of *Paris Trout* by her bed. Inside it was a poem that I suspect Waddell wrote for her. It's not important. I was just curious."

"But it is important or you wouldn't have inquired about it. What you're contemplating is that perhaps Ronnie recommended the novel to her for the same reason that he recommended it to me. The story, in his mind, was somehow his story. And that leads us back to the question of how much he had divulged to Miss Deighton. In other words, what secret of his did she carry with her to the grave?"

"What do you think it was, Mr. Grueman?"

"I think a very nasty indiscretion has been covered up, and for some reason Ronnie was privy to it. Maybe this relates to what goes on behind bars, that is, corruption within the prison system. I don't know but I wish I did."

"But why hide anything when you're facing death? Why not just go ahead and take your chances and talk?"

"That would be the rational thing to do, now, wouldn't it? And now that I have so patiently and generously answered your probing questions, Dr. Scarpetta, perhaps you can better understand why I have been more than a little concerned about any abuse Ronnie may have received prior to his execution. You can understand better, perhaps, my passionate opposition to capital punishment, which is cruel and unusual. You don't have to have bruises or abrasions or bleed from your nose to make it so."

"There was no evidence of physical abuse," I said. "Nor did we find drugs present. You have gotten my report."

"You are being evasive," Grueman said, knocking tobacco out of his pipe. "You are here today because you want something from me. I have given you a lot through a dialogue that I did not have to engage in. But I have been willing because I am forever in pursuit of fairness and truth, despite how I may appear to you. And there is another reason. A former student of mine is in trouble."

"If you are referring to me, then let me remind you of your own dictum. Don't make assumptions."

"I don't believe I am."

"Then I must convey acute curiosity over this sudden charitable attitude you're allegedly displaying toward a former student. In fact, Mr. Grueman, the word *charity* has never entered my mind in connection with you."

"Perhaps, then, you don't know the true meaning of the word. An act or feeling of goodwill, giving alms to the needy. Charity is giving to someone what he needs versus what you want to give him. I have always given you what you need. I gave you what you needed while you were my student, and I'm giving you what you need today, though the acts are expressed very differently because the needs are very different.

"Now I am an old man, Dr. Scarpetta, and perhaps you think I don't remember much about your days at Georgetown. But you might be surprised to hear that I remember you vividly because you were one of the most promising students I ever taught. What you did not need from me was strokes and applause. The danger for you was not that you would lose faith in yourself and your excellent mind but that you would lose yourself, period. Do you think when you looked exhausted and distracted in my class that I did not know the reason? Do you think I was unaware of your complete preoccupation with Mark James, who was mediocre by your standards, by the way? And if I appeared angry with you and very hard on you, it was because I *wanted to get your attention.* I wanted you to *get mad.* I wanted you to feel alive in the law instead of feeling only in love. I feared you would throw away a magnificent opportunity because your hormones and emotions were in overdrive. You see, we wake up one day to regret such decisions. We wake up in an empty bed with an empty day stretching before us and nothing to look forward to but empty weeks, months, and years. I was determined that you would not waste your gifts and give away your power."

I stared at him in astonishment as my face began to burn.

"I have never been sincere in my insults and lack of chivalry toward you," he went on with the same quiet intensity and precision that made him frightening in the courtroom. "These are tactics. We lawyers are famous for our tactics. They are the slices and spins we put on the ball, the angles and speed we use to bring about a certain necessary effect. At the foundation of all that I am is a sincere and passionate desire to make my students tough and pray that they make a difference in this botched-up world we live in. And I feel no disappointment in you. You are, perhaps, one of my brightest stars."

"Why are you saying all this to me?" I asked.

"Because at this time in your life, you need to know it. You are in trouble, as I've already stated. You are simply too proud to admit it."

I was silent, my thoughts engaged in a fierce debate.

"I will help you if you will allow it."

If he was telling me the truth, then it was vital that I respond in kind. I glanced toward his open door and imagined how easy it would be for anyone to walk in here. I imagined how easy it would be for someone to confront him as he hobbled to his car.

"If these incriminating stories continue to be printed in the newspaper, for example, it would behoove you to develop a few strategies—"

I interrupted him. "Mr. Grueman, when was the last time you saw Ronnie Joe Waddell?"

He paused and stared up at the ceiling. "The last time I was in his physical presence would have been at least a year ago. Typically, most of our conversations were over the phone. I would have been with him in the end had he permitted it, as I've already mentioned."

"Then you never saw him or spoke with him when he was supposedly at Spring Street awaiting execution."

"*Supposedly?* That's a curious choice of words, Dr. Scarpetta."

"We can't prove it was Waddell who was executed the night of December thirteenth."

"Certainly you're not serious." He looked amazed.

I explained all that had transpired, including that Jennifer Deighton was a homicide and Waddell's fingerprint had turned up on a dining room chair inside her home. I told him about Eddie Heath and Susan Story, and the evidence that someone had tampered with AFIS. When I was finished, Grueman was sitting very still, his eyes riveted on me.

"My Lord," he muttered.

"Your letter to Jennifer Deighton never turned up," I went on. "The police found neither that nor her original fax to you when they searched her house. Maybe someone took them. Maybe her killer burned them in her fireplace the night of her death. Or maybe she disposed of them herself because she was afraid. I do believe she was killed because of something she knew."

"And this would be why Susan Story was killed, too? Because she knew something?"

"Certainly that's possible," I said. "My point is that so far two people linked to Ronnie Waddell have been murdered. In terms of someone who might know a lot about Waddell, you would be considered high on the list."

"So you think I may be next," he said with a wry smile. "You know, perhaps my biggest grievance against the Almighty is that the difference between life and death should so often turn on timing. I consider myself forewarned, Dr. Scarpetta. But I am not foolish enough to think that if someone intends to shoot me I can successfully elude him."

"You could at least try," I said. "You could at least take precautions."

"And I shall."

"Maybe you and your wife could go on a vacation, get out of town for a while."

"Beverly has been dead for three years," he said.

"I'm very sorry, Mr. Grueman."

"She had not been well for many years—in fact, not for most of the years we were together. Now that I have no one to depend on me, I have given myself up to my proclivities. I am an incurable workaholic who wants to change the world."

"I suspect that if anyone could come close to changing it, you could."

"That is an opinion not based on any sort of fact, but I appreciate it nonetheless. And I also want to express to you my great sadness over Mark's death. I did not know him well when he was here, but he seemed to be a decent-enough fellow."

"Thank you." I got up and put on my coat. It took me a moment to find my car keys.

He got up, too. "What do we do next, Dr. Scarpetta?"

"I don't suppose you have any letters or other items from Ronnie Waddell that might be worth processing for his latent prints?"

"I have no letters, and any documents that he might have signed would have been handled by a number of people. You're welcome to try."

"I'll let you know if we have no other alternative. But there is one final thing I've been meaning to ask." We paused in the doorway. Grueman was leaning on his cane. "You mentioned that during your last conversation with Waddell, he made three last requests. One was to publish his meditation, another to call Jennifer Deighton. What was the third?"

"He wanted me to invite Norring to the execution."

"And did you?"

"Well, of course," Grueman said. "And your fine governor didn't even have the manners to RSVP."

10

It was late afternoon, and Richmond's skyline was in view when I called Rose.

"Dr. Scarpetta, where are you?" My secretary sounded frantic. "Are you in your car?"

"Yes. I'm about five minutes from downtown."

"Well, keep driving. Don't come here right now."

"What?"

"Lieutenant Marino's trying to reach you. He said if I talk to you to tell you to call him before you do anything. He said it's very, very urgent."

"Rose, what on earth are you talking about?"

"Have you been listening to the news? Did you read the afternoon paper?"

"I've been in D.C. all day. What news?"

"Frank Donahue was found dead early this afternoon."

"The prison warden? That Frank Donahue?"

"Yes."

My hands tensed on the wheel as I stared hard at the road. "What happened?"

"He was shot. He was found in his car a couple of hours ago. It's just like Susan."

"I'm on my way," I said, gliding into the left lane and accelerating.

"I really wouldn't. Fielding's already started on him. Please call Marino. You need to read the evening paper. They know about the bullets."

"They?" I said.

"Reporters. They know about the bullets linking Eddie Heath's and Susan's cases."

I called Marino's pager and told him I was on my way home. When I pulled into my garage, I went straight to the front stoop and retrieved the evening paper.

A photograph of Frank Donahue smiled above the fold. The headline read, "STATE PENITENTIARY WARDEN SLAIN." Below this was a second story featuring the photograph of another state official—me. That story's lead was that the bullets recovered from the bodies of the Heath boy and Susan had been fired from the same gun, and a number of bizarre connections seemed to link both homicides to me. In addition to the same intimations that had run in the *Post* was information much more sinister.

My fingerprints, I was stunned to read, had been recovered from an envelope containing cash that the police had found inside Susan Story's house. I had demonstrated an "unusual interest" in Eddie Heath's case by appearing at Henrico

Doctor's Hospital, prior to his death, to examine his wounds. Later I had performed his autopsy, and it was at this time that Susan refused to witness his case and supposedly fled from the morgue. When she was murdered less than two weeks later, I responded to the scene, appeared unannounced at the home of her parents directly afterward to ask them questions, and insisted on being present during the autopsy.

I was not directly assigned a motive for malevolence toward anyone, but the one implied in Susan's case was as infuriating as it was amazing. I may have been making major mistakes on the job. I had neglected to print Ronnie Joe Waddell when his body came to the morgue after his execution. I recently had left the body of a homicide victim in the middle of a corridor, virtually in front of an elevator used by numerous people who worked in the building, thus seriously compromising the chain of evidence. I was described as aloof and unpredictable, with colleagues observing that my personality had begun to change after the death of my lover, Mark James. Perhaps Susan, who had worked by my side daily, had possessed knowledge that could ruin me professionally. Perhaps I had been paying for her silence.

"My fingerprints?" I said to Marino the instant he appeared at my door. "What the hell is this business about fingerprints belonging to me?"

"Easy, Doc."

"I might just file suit this time. This has gone too far."

"I don't think you want to be filing anything right now." He got out his cigarettes as he followed me to the kitchen, where the evening paper was spread out on the table.

"Ben Stevens is behind this."

"Doc, I think what you want to do is listen to what I've got to say."

"He's got to be the source of the leak about the bullets—"

"Doc. Goddam it, shut up."

I sat down.

"My ass is in the fire, too," he said. "I'm working the cases with you, and now suddenly you've become an element. Yes, we did find an envelope in Susan's house. It was in a dresser drawer under some clothes. There were three one-hundred-dollar bills inside it. Vander processed the envelope and several latents popped up. Two of them are yours. Your prints, like mine and those of a lot of other investigators, are in AFIS for exclusionary purposes, in case we ever do a dumbshit thing like leave our prints at a scene."

"I did not leave prints at any scene. There's a logical explanation for this. There has to be. Maybe the envelope was one I touched at some point at the office or the morgue, and Susan took it home."

"It's definitely not an office envelope," Marino said. "It's about twice as wide as a legal-size envelope and made of stiff, shiny black paper. There's no writing on it."

I looked at him in disbelief as it dawned on me. "The scarf I gave her."

"What scarf?"

"Susan's Christmas present from me was a red silk scarf I bought in San Francisco. What you're describing is the envelope it was in, a glossy black envelope made of cardboard or stiff paper. The flap closed with a small gold seal. I wrapped the present myself. Of course my prints would be on it."

"So what about the three hundred dollars?" he said, avoiding my eyes.

"I don't know anything about any money."

"I'm saying, why was it in the envelope you gave her?"

"Maybe because she wanted to hide her cash in something. The envelope was handy. Maybe she didn't want to throw it away. I don't know. I had no control over what she did with something I gave her."

"Did anybody see you give her the scarf?" he asked.

"No. Her husband wasn't home when she opened my gift."

"Yeah, well, the only gift from you anyone seemed to know about was a pink poinsettia. Don't sound like Susan said a word about you giving her a scarf."

"For God's sake, she was wearing the scarf when she was shot, Marino."

"That don't tell us where it came from."

"You're about to move into the accusatory stage," I snapped.

"I'm not accusing you of nothing. Don't you get it? This is the way it goes, goddam it. You want me to baby you and pat your hand so some other cop can bust in here and broadside you with questions like this?"

He got up and began pacing the kitchen, staring at the floor, his hands in his pockets.

"Tell me about Donahue," I said quietly.

"He was shot in his ride, probably early this morning. According to his wife, he left the house around six-fifteen. Around one-thirty this afternoon, his Thunderbird was found parked at Deep Water Terminal with him in it."

"I read that much in the paper."

"Look. The less we talk about it, the better."

"Why? Are reporters going to imply that I killed him, too?"

"Where was you at six-fifteen this morning, Doc?"

"I was getting ready to leave my house and drive to Washington."

"You got any witnesses that will verify you couldn't have been cruising around Deep Water Terminal? It's not very far from the Medical Examiner's Office, you know. Maybe two minutes."

"That's absurd."

"Get used to it. This is just the beginning. Wait until Patterson sinks his teeth into you."

Before Roy Patterson had run for Commonwealth Attorney, he had been one of the city's more combative, egotistical criminal lawyers. Back then he had never appreciated what I had to say, since in the majority of cases, medical examiner testimony does not cause jurors to think more kindly of the defendant.

"I ever told you how much Patterson hates your guts?" Marino went on. "You embarrassed him when he was a defense attorney. You sat there cool as a cat in your sharp suits and made him look like an idiot."

"He made himself look like an idiot. All I did was answer his questions."

"Not to mention, your old boyfriend Bill Boltz was one of his closest pals, and I don't even need to go into that."

"I wish you wouldn't."

"I just know Patterson's going to go after you. Shit, I bet he's a happy man right now."

"Marino, you're red as a beet. For God's sake, don't go stroking out on me."

"Let's get back to this scarf you said you gave to Susan."

"I *said* I gave to Susan?"

"What was the name of the store in San Francisco that sold it to you?" he asked.

"It wasn't a store."

He glanced sharply at me as he continued to pace.

"It was a street market. Lots of booths and stalls selling art, handmade things. Like Covent Garden," I explained.

"You got a receipt?"

"I would have had no reason to save it."

"So you don't know the name of the booth or whatever. So there's no way to verify that you bought a scarf from some artist type who uses these glossy black envelopes."

"I can't verify it."

He paced some more and I stared out the window. Clouds drifted past an oblong moon, and the dark shapes of trees moved in the wind. I got up to close the blinds.

Marino stopped pacing. "Doc, I'm going to need to go through your financial records."

I did not say anything.

"I've got to verify that you haven't made any large withdrawals of cash in recent months."

I remained silent.

"Doc, you haven't, have you?"

I got up from the table, my pulse pounding.

"You can talk to my attorney," I said.

*

After Marino left, I went upstairs to the cedar closet where I stored my private papers and began collecting bank statements, tax returns, and various accounting records. I thought of all the defense attorneys in Richmond who would probably be delighted if I were locked up or exiled for the rest of my days.

I was sitting in the kitchen making notes on a legal pad when my doorbell rang. I let Benton Wesley and Lucy in, and I knew instantly by their silence that it was unnecessary to tell them what was going on.

"Where's Connie?" I asked wearily.

"She's going to stay through the New Year with her family in Charlottesville."

"I'm going back to your study, Aunt Kay," Lucy said without hugging me or smiling. She left with her suitcase.

"Marino wants to go through my financial records," I said to Wesley as he followed me into the living room. "Ben Stevens is setting me up. Personnel files and copies of memos are missing from the office, and he's hoping it will appear that I took them. And Roy Patterson, according to Marino, is a happy man these days. That's the update of the hour."

"Where do you keep the Scotch?"

"I keep the good stuff in the hutch over there. Glasses are in the bar."

"I don't want to drink your good stuff."

"Well, I do." I began building a fire.

"I called your deputy chief as I was driving in. Firearms has already taken a look at the slugs that were in Donahue's brain. Winchester one-fifty-grain lead, unjacketed, twenty-two-caliber. Two of them. One went in his left cheek and traveled up through the skull, the other was a tight contact at the nape of his neck."

"Fired from the same weapon that killed the other two?"

"Yes. Do you want ice?"

"Please." I closed the screen and returned the poker to its stand. "I don't suppose any feathers were recovered from the scene or from Donahue's body."

"Not that I know of. It's clear that his assailant was standing outside the car and shot him through the open driver's window. That doesn't mean this individual wasn't inside with him earlier, but I don't think so. My guess is Donahue was supposed to meet someone at Deep Water Terminal in the parking lot. When this person arrived, Donahue rolled down his window and that was it. Did you have any luck with Downey?" He handed me my drink and settled on the couch.

"It appears that the origin of the feathers and feather particles recovered from the three other cases is common eider duck."

"A sea duck?" Wesley frowned. "The down is used in what, ski jackets, gloves?"

"Rarely. Eiderdown is extremely expensive. Your average person is not going to own anything filled with it."

I proceeded to inform Wesley of the events of the day, sparing no details as I confessed that I had spent several hours with Nicholas Grueman and did not believe he was even remotely involved in anything sinister.

"I'm glad you went to see him," Wesley said. "I was hoping you would."

"Are you surprised by how it turned out?"

"No. It makes sense the way it turned out. Grueman's

predicament is somewhat similar to your own. He gets a fax from Jennifer Deighton and it looks suspicious, just as it looks suspicious that your prints were found on an envelope in Susan's dresser drawer. When violence hits close to you, you get splashed. You get dirty."

"I'm more than splashed. I feel as if I'm about to drown."

"At the moment, it seems that way. Maybe you ought to be talking to Grueman about that."

I did not reply.

"I'd want him on my side."

"I wasn't aware that you knew him."

Ice rattled quietly as Wesley sipped his drink. Brass on the hearth gleamed in the firelight. Wood popped, sending sparks swarming up the chimney.

"I know about Grueman," he said. "I know that he graduated number one from Harvard Law School, was the editor of the *Law Review,* and was offered a teaching position there but turned it down. That broke his heart. But his wife, Beverly, did not want to move from the D.C. area. Apparently, she had a lot of problems, not the least of which was a young daughter from a first marriage who was institutionalized at Saint Elizabeths at the time Grueman and Beverly met. He moved to D.C. The daughter died several years later."

"You've been running a background check on him," I said.

"Sort of."

"Since when?"

"Since I learned he had received a fax from Jennifer Deighton. By all accounts, it appears he's Mr. Clean, but someone still had to talk to him."

"That's not the only reason you suggested it to me, is it?"

"An important reason but not the only one. I thought you should go back there."

I took a deep breath. "Thank you, Benton. You are a good man with the best of intentions."

He lifted his glass to his lips and stared into the fire.

"Please don't interfere," I added.

"It's not my style."

"Of course it is. You're a pro at it. If you want to quietly steer, propel, or unplug someone from behind the scenes, you know how to do it. You know how to throw up so many obstacles and blow out so many bridges that someone like me would be lucky to find her way home."

"Marino and I are very involved in all this, Kay. Richmond P.D.'s involved. The Bureau's involved. Either we've got a psychopath out there who should have been executed or we've got somebody else who seems intent on making us think someone is out there who should have been executed."

"Marino doesn't want me involved at all," I said.

"He's in an impossible situation. He's the chief homicide investigator for the city and a member of a Bureau VICAP team, yet he's your colleague and friend. He's supposed to find out everything he can about you and what's gone on in your office. Yet his inclination is to protect you. Try to put yourself in his position."

"I will. But he needs to put himself in mine."

"That's only fair."

"The way he talks, Benton, you would think half the world has a vendetta against me and would love to see me go up in flames."

"Maybe not half the world, but there are people other than Ben Stevens who are standing around with boxes of matches and gasoline."

"Who else?"

"I can't give you names because I don't know. And I'm not going to claim that ruining you professionally is the major mission for whoever is behind all this. But I suspect it's on the agenda, if for no other reason than that the cases would be severely compromised if it appears that all evidence routed through your office is tainted. Not to mention, without you, the Commonwealth loses one of its most potent expert witnesses." He met my eyes. "You need to consider what your testimony would be worth right now. If you took the stand this minute, would you be helping or hurting Eddie Heath?"

The remark cut to the bone.

"Right this minute, I would not be helping him much. But if I default, how much will that help him or anyone?"

"That's a good question. Marino doesn't want you hurt further, Kay."

"Then perhaps you can impress upon him that the only reasonable response to such an unreasonable situation is for me to allow him to do his job while he allows me to do mine."

"Can I refresh that?" Getting up, he returned with the bottle. We didn't bother with ice.

"Benton, let's talk about the killer. In light of what's happened to Donahue, what are you thinking now?"

He set down the bottle and stirred the fire. For a moment, he stood before the fireplace, his back to me, hands in his pockets. Then he sat on the edge of the hearth, his forearms on his knees. Wesley was more restless than I had seen him in a very long time.

"If you want to know the truth, Kay, this animal scares the hell out of me."

"How is he different from other killers you have pursued?"

"I think he started out with one set of rules and then decided to change them."

"His rules or someone else's?"

"I think the rules were not his at first. Whoever was behind the conspiracy to free Waddell first made the decisions. But this guy's got his own rules now. Or maybe it would be better to say that there are no rules now. He's cunning and he's careful. So far, he's in control."

"What about motive?" I asked.

"That's hard. Maybe it would be better for me to phrase it in terms of mission or assignment. I suspect there's some method to his madness, but the madness is what turns him on. He gets off on playing with people's minds. Waddell was locked up for ten years, then suddenly the nightmare of his original crime is revisited. On the night of his execution, a boy is murdered in a sexually sadistic fashion that is reminiscent of Robyn Naismith's case. Other people start dying, and all of them are in some way connected to Waddell. Jennifer Deighton was his friend. Susan, it appears, was involved, at least tangentially, in whatever this conspiracy is. Frank Donahue was the prison warden and would have supervised the execution that occurred on the night of December thirteenth. And what is this doing to everybody else, to the other players?"

"I should think that anyone who has had any association

with Ronnie Waddell, either legitimately or otherwise, would feel very threatened," I replied.

"Right. If a cop killer is on the loose and you are a cop, you know you may be next. I could walk out your door tonight and this guy's waiting in the shadows to gun me down. He could be out in his car somewhere, looking for Marino or trying to find my house. He could be fantasizing about taking out Grueman."

"Or me."

Wesley got up and began rearranging the fire again.

"Do you think it would be wise for me to send Lucy back to Miami?" I asked.

"Christ, Kay, I don't know what to tell you. She doesn't want to go home. That comes across loud and clear. You might feel better if she returned to Miami tonight. For that matter, I might feel better if you went with her. In fact, everybody—you, Marino, Grueman, Vander, Connie, Michele, me—would probably feel better if all of us left town. But then who would be left?"

"He would," I said. "Whoever he is."

Wesley glanced at his watch and set his glass on the coffee table. "None of us should interfere with each other," he said. "We can't afford to."

"Benton, I have to clear my name."

"It is exactly what I would do. Where do you want to start?"

"With a feather."

"Please explain."

"It's possible that this killer went out and bought some specialty item filled with eiderdown, but I'd say there's a good chance he stole it."

"That's a plausible theory."

"We can't trace the item unless we have its label or some other piece to trace back to a manufacturer, but there may be another way. Maybe something could appear in the newspaper."

"I don't think we want the killer to know he's leaking feathers everywhere. He's sure to get rid of the item in question."

"I agree. But that doesn't preclude your getting one of your journalist sources to run some trumped-up little feature about the eider duck and its prized down, and how items filled with it are so expensive that they've become a hot commodity for thieves. Maybe this could be tied in with the ski season or something."

"What? In hopes someone out there will call and say that his car was broken into and his down-filled jacket was stolen?"

"Yes. If the reporter quotes some detective who supposedly has been assigned to the thefts, this gives readers someone they can call. You know, people read a story and say, 'The same thing happened to me.' Their impulse is to help. They want to feel important. So they pick up the phone."

"I'll have to give it some thought."

"Admittedly, it's a long shot."

We began walking to the door.

"I spoke briefly with Michele before leaving the Homestead," Wesley said. "She and Lucy have already been conferring. Michele says your niece is rather frightening."

"She's been a holy terror since the day she was born."

He smiled. "Michele didn't mean it like that. She says that Lucy's intellect is frightening."

"Sometimes I worry that it's too much wattage for such a fragile vessel."

"I'm not certain she's all that fragile. Remember, I just spent the better part of two days with her. I'm very impressed with Lucy on many fronts."

"Don't you go trying to recruit her for the Bureau."

"I'll wait until she finishes college. That will take her, what? All of a year?"

Lucy did not emerge from my study until Wesley had driven off and I was carrying our glasses into the kitchen.

"Did you enjoy yourself?" I asked her.

"Sure."

"Well, I hear you got along famously with the Wesleys." I turned off the faucet and sat at the table where I'd left my legal pad.

"They're nice people."

"Rumor has it they think you're nice, too."

She opened the refrigerator door and idly stared inside. "Why was Pete here earlier?"

It seemed odd to hear Marino referred to by his first name. I supposed he and Lucy had moved from a state of cold war to détente when he had taken her shooting.

"What makes you think he was here?" I asked.

"I smelled cigarettes when I came in the house. I assume he was here unless you're smoking again." She shut the refrigerator door and came over to the table.

"I'm not smoking again, and Marino was here briefly."

"What did he want?"

"He wanted to ask me a lot of questions," I said.

"About what?"

"Why do you need to know the details?"

Her eyes moved from my face to the stack of financial files to the legal pad filled with my indecipherable penmanship. "It doesn't matter why since you obviously don't want to tell me."

"It's complicated, Lucy."

"You always say something's complicated when you want to shut me out," she said as she turned and walked away.

I felt as if my world were falling apart, the people in it scattering like dry seeds in the wind. When I watched parents with their children, I marveled over the gracefulness of their interactions and secretly feared I lacked an instinct that couldn't be learned.

I found my niece in my study sitting before the computer. Columns of numbers combined with letters of the alphabet were on the screen, and embedded here and there were fragments of what I assumed were data. She was making computations with a pencil on graph paper, and did not look up as I moved next to her.

"Lucy, your mother has had many men in and out of your house, and I am well aware of how that has made you feel. But this is not your house and I am not your mother. It is not necessary for you to feel threatened by my male colleagues and friends. It is not necessary for you to constantly be looking for evidence that some man was here, and it is unfounded for you to be suspicious of my relationship with Marino or Wesley or anyone else."

She did not respond.

I placed my hand on her shoulder. "I may not be the constant presence in your life that I wish I could be, but you are very important to me."

Erasing a number and brushing rubber particles off the paper, she said, "Are you going to get charged with a crime?"

"Of course not. I haven't committed any crimes." I leaned closer to the monitor.

"What you're looking at is a hex dump," she said.

"You were right. It's hieroglyphics."

Placing her fingers on the keyboard, Lucy began moving the cursor as she explained, "What I'm doing here is trying to get the exact position of the SID number. That's the State Identification Number, which is the unique identifier. Every person in the system has a SID number, including you, since your prints are in AFIS, too. In a fourth-generation language, like SQL, I could actually query by a column name. But in hexadecimal the language is technical and mathematical. There are no column names, only positions in the record layout. In other words, if I wanted to go to Miami, in SQL I would simply tell the computer I want to go to Miami. But in hexadecimal, I would have to say that I want to go to a position that is this many degrees north of the equator and this many degrees east of the prime meridian.

"So to extend the geographical analogy, I'm figuring out the longitude and latitude of the SID number and also of the number that indicates the record type. Then I can write a program to search for any SID number where the record is a type two, which means a deletion, or a type three, which is an update. I'll run this program through each journal tape."

"You're assuming that if a record has been tampered with, then what was changed was the SID?" I asked.

"Let's just say it would be a whole lot easier to tamper with the SID number than it would be to mess with the actual fingerprint images on the optical disk record. And that's really all you've got in AFIS—the SID number and the corresponding prints. The person's name, history, and other personal information are in his CCH, or Computerized Criminal History, which resides on CCRE, or the Central Criminal Records Exchange."

"As I understand it, the records in CCRE are matched to the prints in AFIS by the SID numbers," I said.

"Exactly."

Lucy was still working when I went to bed. I fell right to sleep, only to awaken at two A.M. I did not drift off again until five, and my alarm roused me less than an hour later. I drove downtown in the dark and listened as one of the local radio announcers gave a news update. He reported that police had questioned me, and I had refused to disclose information pertaining to my financial records. He went on to remind everyone that Susan Story had deposited thirty-five hundred dollars in her checking account just weeks before her murder.

When I got to the office, I had barely taken off my coat when Marino called.

"The damn major can't keep his mouth shut," he said right off.

"Obviously."

"Shit, I'm sorry."

"It's not your fault. I know you have to report to him."

Marino hesitated. "I need to ask you about your guns. You don't own a twenty-two, right?"

"You know all about my handguns. I have a Ruger and a Smith

and Wesson. And if you pass that along to Major Cunningham, I'm sure I'll hear about it on the radio within the hour."

"Doc, he wants them submitted to the firearms lab."

For an instant, I thought Marino was joking.

"He thinks you should be willing to submit them for examination," he added. "He thinks it's a good idea to show right away that the bullets recovered from Susan, the Heath kid, and Donahue couldn't have been fired from your guns."

"Did you tell the major that the revolvers I have are *thirty-eights*?" I asked, incensed.

"Yes."

"And he knows that *twenty-two* slugs were recovered from the bodies?"

"Yeah. I went round and round with him about it."

"Well, ask him for me if he knows of an adapter that would make it possible to use twenty-two rim-fire cartridges in a thirty-eight revolver. If he does, tell him he ought to present a paper on it at the next American Academy of Forensic Sciences meeting."

"I really don't think you want me to tell him that."

"This is nothing but politics, publicity ploys. It's not even rational."

Marino did not comment.

"Look," I said evenly, "I have broken no laws. I am not submitting my financial records, firearms, or anything else to anyone until I have been appropriately advised. I understand that you must do your job, and I want you to do your job. What I want is to be left alone so I can do mine. I have three cases downstairs and Fielding's off to court."

But I was not to be left alone, and this was made clear when Marino and I concluded our conversation and Rose appeared in my office. Her face was pale, her eyes frightened.

"The governor wants to see you," she said.

"When?" I asked as my heart skipped.

"At nine."

It was already eight-forty.

"Rose, what does he want?"

"The person who called didn't say."

Fetching my coat and umbrella, I walked out into a winter rain that was just beginning to freeze. As I hurried along 14th Street, I tried to recall the last time I had spoken to Governor Joe Norring and decided it was almost a year ago at a black-tie reception at the Virginia Museum. He was Republican, Episcopalian, and held a law degree from UVA. I was Italian, Catholic, born in Miami, and schooled in the North. In my heart I was a Democrat.

The Capitol resides on Shockhoe Hill and is surrounded by an ornamental iron fence erected in the early nineteenth century to keep out trespassing cattle. The white brick building Jefferson designed is typical of his architecture, a pure symmetry of cornices and unfluted columns with Ionic capitals inspired by a Roman temple. Benches line the granite steps leading up through the grounds, and as freezing rain fell relentlessly I thought of my annual spring resolution to take a lunch hour away from my desk and sit here in the sun. But I had yet to do it. Countless days of my life had been lost to artificial light and windowless, confined spaces that defied any architectural rubric.

Inside the Capitol, I found a ladies' room and attempted to bolster my confidence by making repairs. Despite my efforts with lipstick and brush, the mirror had nothing reassuring to say. Bedraggled and unsettled, I took the elevator to the top of the Rotunda, where previous governors gaze sternly from oil portraits three floors above Houdon's marble statue of George Washington. Midway along the south wall, journalists milled about with notepads, cameras, and microphones. It did not occur to me that I was their quarry until, as I approached, video cameras were mounted on shoulders, microphones were drawn like swords, and shutters began clicking with the rapidity of automatic weapons.

"Why won't you disclose your finances?"

"Dr. Scarpetta . . ."

"Did you give money to Susan Story?"

"What kind of handgun do you own?"

"Doctor . . ."

"Is it true that personnel records have disappeared from your office?"

They churned the water with their accusations and questions as I fixed my attention straight ahead, my thoughts paralyzed. Microphones jabbed at my chin, bodies brushed against me, and lights flashed in my eyes. It seemed to take forever to reach the heavy mahogany door and escape into the genteel stillness behind it.

"Good morning," said the receptionist from her fine wood fortress beneath a portrait of John Tyler.

Across the room, at a desk before a window, a plainclothes Executive Protection Unit officer glanced at me, his face inscrutable.

"How did the press know about this?" I asked the receptionist.

"Pardon?" She was an older woman, dressed in tweed.

"How did they know I was meeting with the governor this morning?"

"I'm sorry. I wouldn't know."

I settled on a pale blue love seat. Walls were papered in the same pale blue; the furniture was antique, with chair seats covered in needlepoint depicting the state seal. Ten minutes slowly passed. A door opened and a young man I recognized as Norring's press secretary stepped inside and smiled at me.

"Dr. Scarpetta, the governor will see you now." He was slight of build, blond, and dressed in a navy suit and yellow suspenders.

"I apologize for making you wait. Unbelievable weather we're having. And I understand it's supposed to drop into the teens tonight. The streets will be glass in the morning."

He ushered me through one well-appointed office after another, where secretaries concentrated behind computer screens and aides moved about silently and with purpose. Knocking lightly on a formidable door, he turned the brass knob and stepped aside, chivalrously touching my back as I preceded him into the private space of the most powerful man in Virginia. Governor Norring did not get up from his padded leather chair behind his uncluttered burled walnut desk. Two chairs were arranged across from him and I was shown to one while he continued perusing a document.

"Would you like something to drink?" the press secretary asked me.

"No, thank you."

He left, softly shutting the door.

The governor placed the document on the desk and leaned back in his chair. He was a distinguished-looking man with just enough irregularity of his features to cause one to take him seriously, and he was impossible to miss when he walked into a room. Like George Washington, who was six foot two in a day of short men, Norring was well above average height, his hair thick and dark at an age when men are balding or going gray.

"Doctor, I've been wondering if there might be a way to extinguish this fire of controversy before it's completely out of control." He spoke with the soothing cadences of Virginian conversation.

"Governor Norring, I certainly hope there is."

"Then please help me understand why you are not cooperating with the police."

"I wish to seek the advice of an attorney, and have not had a chance to do so. I don't view this as a lack of cooperation."

"It certainly is your right not to incriminate yourself," he said slowly. "But the very suggestion of your invoking the Fifth only darkens the cloud of suspicion surrounding you. I'm certain you must be aware of that."

"I'm aware that I will probably be criticized no matter what I do right now. It is reasonable and prudent for me to protect myself."

"Were you making payments to your morgue supervisor, Susan Story?"

"No, sir, I was not. I have done nothing wrong."

"Dr. Scarpetta." He leaned forward in his chair and laced his fingers on top of the desk. "It is my understanding that you are unwilling to cooperate by turning over any records that might substantiate these claims you've made."

"I have not been informed that I am a suspect in any crime, nor have I received Miranda warnings. I have waived no rights. I have had no opportunity to seek counsel. At this moment, it is not my intention to open the files of my professional and personal life to the police or anyone else."

"Then, in summary, you are refusing to make full disclosure," he said.

When a state official is accused of conflict of interests or any other manner of unethical behavior, there are only two defenses, full disclosure or resignation. The latter yawned before me like an abyss. It was clear that the governor's intention was to maneuver me over the edge.

"You are a forensic pathologist of national stature and the chief medical examiner of this Commonwealth," he went on. "You've enjoyed a very distinguished career and an impeccable reputation in the law enforcement community. But in the matter before us, you are showing poor judgment. You are not being meticulous about avoiding any appearance of impropriety."

"I have been meticulous, Governor, and I have done nothing wrong," I repeated. "The facts will bear this out, but I will not discuss the matter further until I speak with an attorney. And I will not make full disclosure unless it is through him and before a judge in a sealed hearing."

"A sealed hearing?" His eyes narrowed.

"Certain details of my personal life affect individuals besides me."

"Who? Husband, children, lover? It is my understanding you have none of these, that you live alone and are—to use the cliché—wedded to your work. Just who might you be protecting?"

"Governor Norring, you are baiting me."

"No, ma'am. I'm simply looking for anything to corroborate your claims. You say you are concerned with protecting others, and I'm inquiring as to who these *others* might be. Certainly not patients. Your patients are deceased."

"I do not feel that you are being fair or impartial," I said, and I knew I sounded cold. "Nothing about this meeting was fair from the outset. I'm given twenty minutes' notice to be here and am not told the agenda—"

He interrupted. "Why, Doctor, I should think you might have guessed the agenda."

"Just as I should have guessed that our meeting was a public event."

"I understand the press came out in force." His expression did not change.

"I'd like to know how this occurred," I said heatedly.

"If you're asking if this office notified the press of our meeting, I'm telling you that we did not."

I did not respond.

"Doctor, I'm not certain you understand that as public servants we must operate by a different set of rules. In a sense, we are not allowed private lives. Or perhaps it would be better to say that if our ethics or judgment are questioned, the public has a right to examine, in some instances, the most private aspects of our existences. Whenever I am about to undertake a certain activity or even write a check, I have to ask myself if what I am doing will hold up under the most intense scrutiny."

I noticed that he scarcely used his hands when he talked, and that the fabric and design of his suit and tie were a lesson in understated extravagance. My attention darted here and there as he continued his admonition, and I knew that nothing I might do or say would save me in the end. Though I had been appointed by the health commissioner, I would not have been offered the job, nor could I last long in it without the support of the governor. The quickest way to lose that was to cause him embarrassment or conflict, which I had already accomplished. He had the power to force my resignation. I had the power to buy myself a little time by threatening to embarrass him more.

"Doctor, perhaps you would like to tell me what you would do if you were in my position?"

Beyond the window rain was mixed with sleet, and buildings in the banking district were bleak against a dreary, pewter sky. I stared at Norring in silence, then quietly spoke. "Governor Norring, I would like to think that I would not summon the chief medical examiner to my office to gratuitously insult her, both professionally and personally, and then demand of her that she surrender the rights guaranteed to every person by the Constitution.

"Further, I would like to think that I would accept this person's innocence until she had been proven guilty, and would not compromise her ethics and the Hippocratic oath she had sworn to uphold by demanding that she open confidential files to public scrutiny when doing so might do harm to herself and to others. I would like to think, Governor Norring, that I would not give an individual who has served the Commonwealth faithfully no choice but to resign for cause."

The governor absently picked up a silver fountain pen as he considered my words. For me to resign for cause after meeting with him would imply to all of the reporters waiting beyond his office door that I had quit because Norring had asked me to do something that I considered unethical.

"I have no interest in your resigning at this moment," he said coldly. "In fact, I would not accept your resignation. I am a fair man, Dr. Scarpetta, and, I hope, a wise one. And wisdom dictates that I cannot have someone performing legal autopsies on the victims of homicide when this individual, herself, is being implicated in homicide or as an accessory to it. Therefore, I think it best to relieve you with pay until this matter is resolved." He reached for the phone. "John, would you be so kind as to show the chief medical examiner out?"

Almost instantly, the smiling press secretary appeared.

As I emerged from the governor's offices, I was accosted from every direction. Flashguns went off in my eyes, and it seemed that everyone was shouting. The lead news item the rest of the day and the following morning was that the governor had temporarily relieved me of my duties until I could clear my name. An editorial conjectured that Norring had shown himself to be a gentleman, and if I were a lady I would offer to step down.

11

Friday I stayed home in front of the fire, continuing the tedious and frustrating job of making notes to myself as I attempted to document my every move over the past few weeks. Unfortunately, I was in my car driving home from the office at the time the police believed Eddie Heath was abducted from the convenience store. When Susan was murdered, I was home alone, for Marino had taken Lucy shooting. I was also by myself the early morning that Frank Donahue was shot. I had no witnesses to testify to my activities during the three murders.

Motive and modus operandi would be significantly more difficult to sell. It is very uncommon for a woman to kill execution style, and there could be no motive at all in Eddie Heath's slaying unless I were a closet sexual sadist.

I was deep in thought when Lucy called out, "I've got something."

She was seated before the computer, the chair swiveled

around to one side, her feet propped up on an ottoman. In her lap were numerous sheets of paper, and to the right of the keyboard was my Smith and Wesson thirty-eight.

"Why do you have my revolver in here?" I asked uneasily.

"Pete told me to dry-fire it whenever I have a chance. So I've been practicing while running my program through the journal tapes."

I picked up the revolver, pushed the thumb latch, and checked the chambers, just to be sure.

"Though I've still got a few tapes to run through, I think I've already gotten a hit on what we're looking for," she said.

I felt a surge of optimism as I pulled up a chair.

"The journal tape for December ninth shows three interesting TUs."

"TUs?" I asked.

"Tenprint Updates," Lucy explained. "We're talking about three records. One was completely dropped or deleted. The SID number of another was altered. Then we have a third record which was a new entry made around the same time the other two were deleted or changed. I logged into CCRE and ran the SID numbers of both the altered record and the new record entered. The altered record comes back to Ronnie Joe Waddell."

"What about the new record?" I said.

"That's spooky. There's no criminal history. I entered the SID number five times and it kept coming back to 'no record found.' Do you understand the significance?"

"Without a history in CCRE, we have no way of knowing who this person is."

Lucy nodded. "Right. You've got someone's prints and SID number in AFIS, but there's no name or other personal identifiers to match him up with. And that would indicate to me that somebody dropped this person's record from CCRE. In other words, CCRE has been tampered with, too."

"Let's go back to Ronnie Waddell," I said. "Can you reconstruct what was done to his record?"

"I've got a theory. First, you need to know that the SID number is a unique identifier and has a unique index, meaning the system won't allow you to enter a duplicate value. So if, for example, I wanted to switch SID numbers with you, I'd have to delete your record first. Then, after I've changed my SID number to yours, I'd reenter your record, giving you my old SID number."

"And that's what you think happened?" I asked.

"Such a transaction would explain the TUs I've found in the journal tape for December ninth."

Four days before Waddell's execution, I thought.

"There's more," Lucy said. "On December sixteenth, Waddell's record was deleted from AFIS."

"How can that be?" I asked, baffled. "A print from Jennifer Deighton's house came back to Waddell when Vander ran it through AFIS a little over a week ago."

"AFIS crashed on December sixteenth at ten-fifty-six A.M., exactly ninety-eight minutes after Waddell's record was deleted," Lucy replied. "The data base was restored with the journal tapes, but you've got to keep in mind that a backup is done only once a day, late in the afternoon. Therefore, any changes made to the data base the morning of December sixteenth hadn't been backed up yet when the system crashed. When the data base was restored, so was Waddell's record."

"You mean someone tampered with Waddell's SID number four days before his execution? Then three days after his execution, someone deleted his record from AFIS?"

"That's the way it looks to me. What I can't figure is why the person didn't just delete his record in the first place. Why go to all the trouble to change the SID number, only to turn around and delete his entire record?"

Neils Vander had a simple answer to that when I called him moments later.

"It's not unusual for an inmate's prints to be deleted from AFIS after he's dead," Vander said. "In fact, the only reason we wouldn't delete a deceased inmate's records would be if it were possible his prints might turn up in any unsolved cases. But Waddell had been in prison for nine, ten years—he'd been out of commission too long to make it worthwhile to keep his prints on line."

"Then the deletion of his record on December sixteenth would have been routine," I said.

"Absolutely. But it would not have been routine to delete his record on December ninth, when Lucy believes his SID number was altered, because Waddell was still alive then."

"Neils, what do you think this is all about?"

"When you change somebody's SID number, Kay, in effect you have changed his identity. I may get a hit on his prints, but when I enter the corresponding SID number in CCRE, it's not his history I'm going to get. I'll either get no history at all, or the history of somebody else."

"You got a hit on a print left at Jennifer Deighton's house," I said. "You entered the corresponding SID number in CCRE and it came back to Ronnie Waddell. Yet we now have reason to believe his original SID number was changed. We really don't know who left the print on her dining room chair, do we?"

"No. And it's becoming clear that someone has gone to a lot of trouble to make sure we can't verify who that person might be. I can't prove it's not Waddell. I can't prove that it is."

Images flashed in my mind as he spoke.

"In order to verify that Waddell did not leave that print on Jennifer Deighton's chair, I need an old print of his that I can trust, one that I know couldn't have been tampered with. But I just don't know where else to look."

I envisioned dark paneling and hardwood floors, and dried blood the color of garnets.

"Her house," I muttered.

"Whose house?" Vander puzzled.

"Robyn Naismith's house," I said.

Ten years previously, when Robyn Naismith's house was processed by the police, they would not have arrived with laser or Luma-Lite. There was no such thing as DNA printing then. There was no automated fingerprint system in Virginia, no computerized means to enhance a bloody partial print left on a wall or anywhere else. Though new technology generally is irrelevant in cases that have long been closed, there are exceptions. I believed Robyn Naismith's murder was one of them.

If we could spray her house with chemicals, it was possible we could literally resurrect the scene. Blood clots, drips, drops, spatters, stains, and screams bright red. It seeps into crevices and cracks, and sneaks under cushions and floors. Though it may disappear with washing and fade with the years, it never completely goes away. Like the writing that wasn't there on the sheet of paper found on Jennifer Deighton's bed, there was blood invisible to the naked eye inside the rooms where Robyn Naismith had been accosted and killed. Unaided by technology, police had found one bloody print during the original investigation of the crime. Maybe Waddell had left more. Maybe they were still there.

Neils Vander, Benton Wesley, and I drove west toward the University of Richmond, a splendid collection of Georgian buildings surrounding a lake between Three Chopt and River roads. It was from here that Robyn Naismith had graduated with honors many years before, and her love of the area had been such that she had later bought her first home two blocks from the campus.

Her former small brick house with its mansard roof was set on a half-acre lot. I was not surprised that the site should have been ideal for a burglar. The yard was dense with trees, the back of the house dwarfed by three gigantic magnolias that completely blocked the sun. I doubted the neighbors on either side could have seen or heard anything at Robyn Naismith's house, had they been home. The morning Robyn was murdered, her neighbors were at work.

Due to the circumstances that had placed the house on the market ten years ago, the price had been low for the neighborhood. We'd discovered the university had decided to buy it for faculty housing, and had kept much of what was left inside it. Robyn had been unmarried, an only child, and her parents in northern Virginia did not want her furnishings. I suspected they could not bear to live with or even look at them. Professor Sam Potter, a bachelor who taught German, had been renting the house from his employer since its purchase.

As we gathered camera equipment, containers of chemicals, and other items from the trunk, the back door opened. An unwholesome-looking man greeted us with an uninspired good-morning.

"You need a hand with that?" Sam Potter came down the steps, sweeping his long, receding black hair out of his eyes and smoking a cigarette. He was short and pudgy, his hips wide like a woman's.

"If you want to get the box here," Vander said.

Potter dropped the cigarette to the ground and didn't bother stamping it out. We followed him up the steps and into a small kitchen with old avocado-green appliances and dozens of dirty dishes. He led us through the dining room, with laundry piled on the table, then into the living room at the front of the house. I set down what I was carrying and tried not to register my shock as I recognized the console television connected to a cable outlet in the wall, the draperies, the brown leather couch, the parquet floor, now scuffed and as dull as mud. Books and papers were scattered everywhere, and Potter began to talk as he carelessly collected them.

"As you can see, I'm not domestically inclined," he said, his German accent distinct. "I will stick these things on the dining room table for now. There," he said when he returned.

"Anything else you would like me to move?" He slipped a pack of Camels from the breast pocket of his white shirt and dug a book of matches from his faded denim jeans. A pocket watch was attached to a belt loop by a leather thong, and I noticed a number of things as he slid it out to glance at the time and then lit the cigarette. His hands trembled, his fingers were swollen, and broken blood vessels covered his cheekbones and nose. He had not bothered to empty ashtrays, but he had collected bottles and glasses and had been careful to carry out the trash.

"This is fine. You don't need to move anything else," Wesley said. "If we do, we'll put it back."

"And you said this chemical you're using won't damage anything and isn't toxic to humans?"

"No, it's not hazardous. It will leave a grainy residue—similar to when salt water dries," I said to him. "We'll do our best to clean up."

"I really don't want to be here while you do this," Potter said, taking a nervous drag on the cigarette. "Can you give me an approximation of how much time it will require?"

"Hopefully, no more than two hours." Wesley was looking around the room, and though his face was completely devoid of expression, I could imagine what was going through his mind.

I took off my coat and didn't know where to put it, while Vander opened a box of film.

"Should you finish before I get back, please shut the door and make sure it's locked. I don't have an alarm to worry about." Potter went back out through the kitchen, and when he started his car it sounded like a diesel bus.

"It's a shame, really," Vander said as he lifted two bottles of chemicals from a box. "This could be a very nice house. But inside it's not much better than a lot of slums I've seen. Did you notice the scrambled eggs in the skillet on the stove? What more do you want to pick up here?" He squatted on the floor. "I don't want to mix this up until we're ready."

"I'd say we need to move as much out of here as we can. You've got the pictures, Kay?" Wesley said.

I got out Robyn Naismith's scene photographs. "You've noticed that our professor friend is living with her furniture," I said.

"Well, then we'll leave it here," Vander said as if it were common for furniture from a ten-year-old murder scene to still be in place. "But the rug's got to go. I can tell that didn't come with the house."

"How?" Wesley stared down at the blue-and-red braided rug beneath his feet. It was filthy and curling up at the edges.

"If you lift up the edge, you can see that the parquet is just as dull and scratched underneath as it is everywhere else. The rug hasn't been here long. Besides, it doesn't look very well made. I doubt it would have lasted all this time."

Spreading several photographs on the floor, I turned them this way and that until the perspectives were right and we could tell what needed to be moved. What furnishings were original to the room had been rearranged. As much as it was possible to do so, we began to re-create the scene of Robyn's death.

"Okay, the ficus tree goes over there," I said like a stage director. "Right, but slide the couch back about two more feet,

Neils. And that way just a little bit more. The tree was maybe four inches from the left armrest. A little closer. That's good."

"No, it's not. The branches are over the couch."

"The tree's a little bigger now."

"I can't believe it's still alive. I'm surprised anything could live around Professor Potter except maybe bacteria or fungi."

"And the rug goes?" Wesley took off his jacket.

"Yes. She had a small runner by the front door and another small Oriental under the coffee table. Most of the floor was bare."

He got down on his hands and knees and began to roll up the rug.

I went over to the television and studied the VCR on top and the cable connection leading into the wall.

"This has got to go against the wall opposite the couch and the front door. Either of you gentlemen good with VCRs and cable connections?"

"No," they answered simultaneously.

"Then I'm left to my own devices. Here goes."

I disconnected the cable and the VCR, unplugged the TV, and carefully slid it across the bare, dusty floor. Referring to the photographs again, I moved it a few more feet until it was directly opposite the front door. Next I surveyed the walls. Potter apparently collected art and was fond of an artist whose name I could not quite make out, but it looked French. The sketches were charcoal studies of the female form with lots of curves, pink splotches, and triangles. One by one they all came down and I propped them against the walls in the dining room. By this point, the room was almost bare and I was itching from the dust.

Wesley wiped his forehead on the back of his arm. "Are we about ready?" He looked at me.

"I think so. Of course, not everything is here. She had three barrel chairs right over there." I pointed.

"They're in the bedrooms," Vander said. "Two in one bedroom and one in the other. Do you want me to bring them out?"

"Might as well."

He and Wesley carried in the chairs.

"She had a painting on that wall over there, and another one to the right of the door leading into the dining room," I pointed out. "A still life and an English landscape. So Potter couldn't live with her art but didn't seem to have a problem with anything else."

"We need to go around the house and close all blinds, shades, and curtains," Vander said. "If any light is still coming through, then tear off a section of this paper"—he pointed to a roll of heavy brown paper on the floor—"and tape it over the window."

For the next fifteen minutes, the house was filled with the sounds of footsteps, venetian blinds rattling, and scissors slicing through paper. Occasionally somebody swore loudly when the paper had been cut too short or the tape stuck to nothing but itself. I stayed in the living room and covered the glass in the front door and in the two windows facing the street. When the three of us reconvened and turned out the lights, the house was pitch-black. I could not even see my hand in front of my face.

"Perfect," Vander said as the overhead light went back on.

Putting on gloves, he set bottles of distilled water, chemicals, and two plastic spray bottles on the coffee table. "Here's the way we're going to work this," he said. "Dr. Scarpetta, you can spray while I videotape, and if an area reacts, just keep spraying it until I tell you to move on."

"What do you want me to do?" Wesley asked.

"Keep out of the way."

"What's in this stuff?" he asked as Vander unscrewed the caps from bottles of dry chemicals.

"You don't really want to know," I replied.

"I'm a big boy. You can tell me."

"The reagent's a mixture of sodium perborate, which Neils is mixing with distilled water, and three-aminophthalhydrazide and sodium carbonate," I said, getting a packet of gloves out of my pocketbook.

"And you're certain it will work on blood this old?" Wesley asked.

"Actually, aged and decomposed blood reacts better with luminol than do fresh bloodstains because the more oxidized the blood, the better. As blood ages, it becomes more strongly oxidized."

"I don't think any of the wood in here is salt treated, do you?" Vander looked around.

"I shouldn't think so." I explained to Wesley, "The biggest problem with luminol is false positives. A number of things react with it, such as copper and nickel, and the copper salts in salt-treated wood."

"It also likes rust, household bleach, iodine, and formalin," Vander added. "Plus, the peroxidases found in bananas, watermelon, citrus fruit, a number of vegetables. Also horseradish."

Wesley looked at me with a smile.

Vander opened an envelope and removed two squares of filter paper that were stained with dried, diluted blood. Then he added mixture A to B and told Wesley to hit the lights. A couple of quick sprays, and a bluish white neon glow appeared on the coffee table. It began to fade almost as quickly as it had appeared.

"Here," Vander said to me.

I felt the spray bottle touch my arm, and took hold of it. A tiny red light went on as Vander depressed the power button on the video camera; then the night vision lamp burned white and looked wherever he did like a luminescent eye.

"Where are you?" Vander's voice sounded to my left.

"I'm in the center of the room. I can feel the edge of the coffee table against my leg," I said, as if we were children playing in the dark.

"I'm way the hell out of the way." Wesley's voice carried from the direction of the dining room.

Vander's white light slowly moved toward me. I reached out and touched his shoulder. "Ready?"

"I'm recording. Start and just keep going until I tell you to stop."

I began spraying the floor around us, my finger nonstop on the trigger as a mist floated over me and shapes and geometrical configurations materialized around my feet. For an instant, it was like speeding through the dark over the illuminated grid of a city far below. Old blood trapped in the crevices of the parquet emitted a blue-white glow. I sprayed and sprayed, without having any real sense of where I was in relation to anything else, and saw footprints all over the room. I bumped against the ficus tree and dim white streaks appeared on the planter that held it. To my right smeared handprints flashed on the wall.

"Lights," Vander said.

Wesley turned on the overhead light and Vander mounted a thirty-five-millimeter camera on a tripod to keep it still. The only light available would be the fluorescence of the luminol, and the film would need a long exposure time to capture it. I retrieved a full bottle of luminol and, when the lights were out again, resumed spraying the smeared handprints on the wall while the camera captured the eerie images on film. Then we moved on. Lazy, wide swipes appeared on paneling and parquet, and the stitching on the leather couch was a neon hatch line incompletely tracing the square shapes of the cushions.

"Can you lift them out of the way?" Vander asked.

One by one I slid the cushions onto the floor and sprayed down the couch's frame. The spaces between the cushions glowed. On the backrest appeared more swipes and smears, and on the ceiling appeared a constellation of small, bright stars. It was on the old television that we got our first pyrophoric display of false positives, as metal around the dials and screen lit up and cable connecters turned the blue-white of thin milk. There was nothing remarkable about the TV, only a few smudges that might be blood, but the floor directly in front of it, where Robyn's body had been found, went crazy. The blood was so pervasive that I could see the edges of the parquet's inlays and the direction of the wood fibers constituting the grain. A drag mark feathered out several feet from the densest concentration of luminescence, and nearby was a curious pattern of tangential rings made by an object with a circumference slightly smaller than a basketball.

The search did not end in the living room. We began to follow footprints. At intervals we were forced to turn on lights, mix more luminol, and move clutter out of the way, particularly in the linguistic landfill that once had been Robyn's bedroom and now was where Professor Potter lived. The floor was several inches deep in research papers, journal articles, exams, and scores of books written in German, French, and Italian. Clothes were strewn about and draped over things so haphazardly it was as if a whirlwind had kicked up in the closet and created a vortex in the center of the room. We picked up as best we could, creating stacks and piles on the unmade double bed. Then we followed Waddell's bloody path.

It led me into the bathroom, with Vander at my heels. Shoe prints and smudges were scattered about the floor, and the same circular patterns that we had found in the living room fluoresced by the side of the bathtub. When I began spraying the walls, halfway up and on either side of the toilet, two huge handprints suddenly appeared. The video camera's light floated closer.

Then Vander's voice said excitedly, "Flip on the light."

Potter's powder room was, to say the least, as disreputably maintained as the rest of his domain. Vander almost had his nose to the wall as he scrutinized the area where the prints had appeared.

"Can you see them?"

"Umm. Maybe barely." He cocked his head to one side, then the other, squinting. "This is fantastic. You see, the wallpaper is this deep blue design, so nothing much is going to show to the naked eye. And it's plasticized or vinyl—a good surface for prints, in other words."

"Jesus," said Wesley, who was standing in the doorway of the bathroom. "The damn toilet doesn't look like it's been cleaned since he moved in. Hell, it's not even flushed."

"Even if he did mop up or wipe down the walls from time to time, you really can't get rid of every trace of blood," I said to Vander. "On a linoleum floor like this, for example, a residue gets down in the pebbly surface, and luminol is going to bring it up."

"Are you saying that if we sprayed down this place again in another ten years, the blood would still be here?" Wesley was amazed.

"The only way you could eradicate most of the blood would be to repaint everything, repaper the walls, refinish the floors, and pitch the furniture," Vander said. "If you want to get rid of absolutely every trace, you'd have to tear down the house and start over."

Wesley looked at his watch. "We've been here three and a half hours."

"Here's what I suggest we do," I said. "Benton, you and I can begin restoring the rooms to their normal state of chaos, and Neils, we'll leave you to do what you need to do."

"Fine. I'll get the Luma-Lite set up in here, and keep your fingers crossed that it can enhance the ridge detail."

We returned to the living room. While Vander carried the portable Luma-Lite and camera equipment back to the bath, Wesley and I looked around at the couch, the old TV, and the dusty, scarred floor, both of us somewhat dazed. With the lights on there was not so much as the slightest trace of the horror we had seen in the dark. On this sunny winter's afternoon, we had crawled back in time and witnessed what Ronnie Joe Waddell had done.

Wesley stood very still near the paper-covered window. "I'm afraid to sit anywhere or lean up against anything. Christ. There's blood all over this goddam house."

As I looked around, I pictured fading white in the blackness, my eyes traveling slowly from the couch, across the floor, and stopping at the TV. The couch's cushions were still on the floor where I had left them, and I squatted to take a closer look. The blood that had seeped into the brown stitching was not visible now, nor were the streaks and smears on the brown leather backrest. But a careful examination revealed something that was important but not necessarily surprising. On the side of one of the seat cushions that had been flush against the back-rest I found a linear cut that was, at most, three-quarters of an inch long.

"Benton, was Waddell left-handed, by chance?"

"It seems to me he was."

"They thought he stabbed and beat her on the floor near the TV because there was so much blood around her body," I said, "but he didn't. He killed her on the couch. I think I need to go outside. If this place weren't such a sewer, I'd be tempted to pinch one of the professor's cigarettes."

"You've been good for too long," Wesley said. "An unfiltered Camel would land you on your ass. Go on and get some fresh air. I'll start cleaning up."

I left the house to the sound of paper being ripped down from the windows.

That night began the most peculiar New Year's Eve in memory for Benton Wesley, Lucy, and me. I wouldn't go so far as to say the holiday was all that odd for Neils Vander. I had talked to him at seven P.M., and he was still in his lab, but that was fairly normal for a man whose raison d'être would cease to exist were the fingerprints of two individuals ever found to be the same.

Vander had edited the scene videocassette tapes to a VCR and turned copies over to me late that afternoon. For the better part of the early evening, Wesley and I had been stationed in front of my television, taking notes and making diagrams as we slowly went through the footage. Lucy, meanwhile, was working on dinner, and came into the living room only briefly from time to time to catch a glimpse. The luminescent images on the dark screen did not seem to disturb her. At a glance, the uninitiated could not possibly know what they meant.

By eight-thirty, Wesley and I had gone through the tapes and completed our notes. We believed we had charted the course of Robyn Naismith's killer from the moment she walked into her house to Waddell's exit through the kitchen door. It was the first time in my career I had retrospectively worked the scene of a homicide that had been solved for years. But the scenario that emerged was important for one very good reason. It demonstrated, at least to our satisfaction, that what Wesley had told me at the Homestead was correct. Ronnie Joe Waddell did not fit the profile of the monster we were now tracking.

The latent smudges, smears, spatters, and spurts that we had followed were as close to an instant replay as I had ever seen in the reconstruction of a crime. Though the courts might consider much of what we determined was opinion, it did not matter. Waddell's personality did, and we felt pretty certain that we had captured it.

Because the blood we had found in other areas of the house clearly had been tracked and transferred by Waddell, it was realistic to say that his assault of Robyn Naismith was restricted to the living room, where she died. The kitchen and front doors were equipped with deadbolt locks that could not be opened without a key. Since Waddell had entered the house through a window and left through the kitchen door, it had been surmised that when Robyn returned from the store, she had come in through the kitchen. Perhaps she had not bothered to relock the door, but more likely she had not had time. It had been conjectured that while Waddell was ransacking her belongings, he heard her drive up and park behind the house. He went into the kitchen and got a steak knife from the stainless steel set hanging on a wall. When she unlocked the door, he was waiting. Chances are, he simply grabbed her first and forced her through the open doorway that led into the living room. He may have talked to her for a while. He may have demanded money. He may have been with her only moments before the confrontation became physical.

Robyn had been dressed and sitting or supine on the end of the couch near the ficus tree when Waddell struck the first blow with the knife. The blood spatters that had appeared on the backrest of the couch, the planter, and the dark paneling nearby were consistent with an arterial spurt, caused when an artery is severed. The resulting spatter pattern is reminiscent of an electrocardiogram tracing due to fluctuations of arterial blood pressure, and one has no blood pressure unless he or she is alive.

So we knew that Robyn was alive and on the couch when she was first assaulted. But it was unlikely she was still breathing when Waddell removed her clothing, which upon later examination revealed a single three-quarters-of-an-inch cut in the front of the bloodstained blouse where the knife had been plunged into her chest and moved back and forth to completely transect her aorta. Since she was stabbed many more times than that, and bitten, it was safe to conclude that most of Waddell's frenzied, piqueristic attack on her had occurred postmortem.

Then this man, who later would claim he did not remember killing "the lady on TV," suddenly woke up, in a sense. He got off her body and had second thoughts about what he had done. The absence of drag marks near the couch suggested that Waddell carried the body from the couch and laid it on the floor on the other side of the room. He dragged it into an upright position and propped it against the TV. Then he set about to clean up. The ring marks that glowed on the floor, I believed, were left by the bottom of a bucket that he carried back and forth from the body to the bathtub down the hall. Each time he returned to the living room to mop up more blood with towels, or perhaps to check on his victim as he continued raiding her belongings and drinking her booze, he again bloodied the bottom of his shoes. This explained the profusion of shoe prints wandering peripatetically throughout her house. The activities themselves explained something else. Waddell's postoffense behavior was inconsistent with that of someone who felt no remorse.

"Here he is, this uneducated farm boy who's living in the big city," Wesley explained. "He's stealing to support a drug habit that's rotting his brain. First marijuana, then heroin, coke, and finally PCP. And one morning he suddenly comes to and finds himself brutalizing the corpse of a stranger."

Logs shifted in the fire as we stared at big handprints glowing as white as chalk on the dark television screen.

"The police never found vomit in the toilet or around it," I said.

"He probably cleaned that up, too. Thank God he didn't wipe down the wall above the john. You don't lean against a wall like that unless you're commode-hugging sick."

"The prints are fairly high above the back of the toilet," I observed. "I think he vomited, and when he stood up got dizzy, lurched forward, and raised his hands just in time to prevent his head from slamming into the wall. What do you think? Remorse or was he just stoned out of his mind?"

Wesley looked at me. "Let's consider what he did with the body. He sat it upright, tried to clean it with towels, and left the clothes in a moderately neat stack on the floor near her ankles. Now, you can look at that two ways. He was lewdly displaying the body and thereby showing contempt. Or he was demonstrating what he considered caring. Personally, I think it was the latter."

"And the way Eddie Heath's body was displayed?"

"That feels different. The positioning of the boy mirrors the positioning of the woman, but something's missing."

Even as he spoke, I suddenly realized what it was. "A *mirror image*," I said to Wesley in amazement. "A mirror reflects things backward or in reverse."

He looked curiously at me.

"Remember when we were comparing Robyn Naismith's scene photographs with the diagram depicting the position of Eddie Heath's body?"

"I remember vividly."

"You said that what was done to the boy—from the bite marks to the way his body was propped against a boxy object to his clothing being left in a tidy pile nearby—was a mirror image of what had been done to Robyn. But the bite marks on Robyn's inner thigh and above her breast were on the left side of her body. While Eddie's injuries—what we believe are eradicated bite marks—were on the *right*. His right shoulder and right inner thigh."

"Okay." Wesley still looked perplexed.

"The photograph that Eddie's scene most closely resembles is the one of her nude body propped against the big console TV."

"True."

"What I'm suggesting is that maybe Eddie's killer saw the same photograph of Robyn that we did. But his perspective is based on his own body's left and right. And his right would have been Robyn's left, and his left would have been her right, because in the photograph she's facing whoever is looking on."

"That's not a pleasant thought," Wesley said as the telephone rang.

"Aunt Kay?" Lucy called out from the kitchen. "It's Mr. Vander."

"We got a confirmation," Vander's voice came over the line.

"Waddell did leave the print in Jennifer Deighton's house?" I asked.

"No, that's just it. He definitely did not."

12

Over the next few days, I retained Nicholas Grueman, delivering to him my financial records and other information he requested, the health commissioner summoned me to his office to suggest that I resign, and the publicity would not end. But I knew much that I had not known even a week before.

It was Ronnie Joe Waddell who died in the electric chair the night of December 13. Yet his identity remained alive and was wreaking havoc in the city. As best as could be determined, prior to Waddell's death his SID number in AFIS had been swapped with another's. Then the other person's SID number was dropped completely from the Central Computerized Records Exchange, or CCRE. This meant there was a violent offender at large who had no need of gloves when he committed his crimes. When his prints were run through AFIS, they would come back as a dead man's every time. We knew this nefarious individual left a wake of feathers and flecks of paint, but we could surmise almost nothing about him until January 3 of the new year.

On that morning, the *Richmond Times-Dispatch* ran a planted story about highly prized eiderdown and its appeal to thieves. At one-fourteen P.M., Officer Tom Lucero, head of the fictitious investigation, received his third call of the day.

"Hi. My name's Hilton Sullivan," the voice said loudly.

"What can I do for you, sir?" Lucero's deep voice asked.

"It's about the cases you're investigating. The eiderdown clothes and things that are supposedly hot with thieves. There was this article about it in the paper this morning. It said you're the detective."

"Right."

"Well, it really pisses me off that the cops are *so* stupid." He got louder. "It said in the paper that since Thanksgiving this and that have been stolen from stores, cars, and homes in the greater Richmond metropolitan area. You know, comforters, a sleeping bag, three ski jackets, blah, blah, blah. And the reporter quoted several people."

"What is your point, Mr. Sullivan?"

"Well, obviously the reporter got the victims' names from the cops. In other words, from you."

"It's public information."

"I don't really give a shit about that. I just want to know how come you didn't mention *this victim,* yours truly? You don't even remember my name, do you?"

"I'm sorry, sir, but I can't say that I do."

"Figures. Some fucking asshole breaks into my condo and

wipes me out, and other than smearing black powder everywhere—on a day when I was dressed in white cashmere, I
might add—the cops don't do a thing. I'm one of your fucking
cases."

"When was your condo broken into?"

"Don't you remember? I'm the one who raised such a stink
about my down vest. If it wasn't for me, you guys would never
have even heard of eiderdown! When I told the cop that among
other things my vest had been taken and it had cost me five
hundred bucks *on sale,* you know what he said?"

"I have no idea, sir."

"He said, 'What's it stuffed with, cocaine?' And I said, 'No,
Sherlock. Eider duck down.' And he looked around nervous as
hell and dropped his hand close to his nine-mil. The dumb-shit
really thought there was some other person in my place named
Eider and I'd just yelled at this person to *duck down,* like I was
going to pull a gun or something. At that point I just left
and—"

Wesley switched off the tape recorder.

We sat in my kitchen. Lucy was working out at my club
again.

"The B-and-E this Hilton Sullivan's talking about was in
fact reported by him on Saturday, December eleventh.
Apparently, he'd been out of town, and when he returned to his
condo that Saturday afternoon, he discovered that he'd been
burglarized," Wesley explained.

"Where is his condo located?" I asked.

"Downtown on West Franklin, an old brick building with condos that start at a hundred grand. Sullivan lives on the first floor. The perpetrator got in through an unsecured window."

"No alarm system?"

"No."

"What was stolen?"

"Jewelry, money, and a twenty-two revolver. Of course, that doesn't necessarily mean that Sullivan's revolver is the one that was used to kill Eddie Heath, Susan, and Donahue. But I think we're going to find that it is, because there's no question that our guy did the B-and-E."

"Prints were recovered?"

"A number of them. The city had them, and you know how their backlog is. With all the homicides, B-and-Es aren't a top priority. In this instance, the latents had been processed and were just sitting. Pete intercepted them right after Lucero got the call. Vander's already run them through the system. He got a hit in exactly three seconds."

"Waddell again."

Wesley nodded.

"How far is Sullivan's condo from Spring Street?"

"Within walking distance. I think we know where our guy escaped from."

"You're checking out recent releases?"

"Oh, sure. But we're not going to find him in a stack of paper on somebody's desk. The warden was too careful for that. Unfortunately, he's also dead. I think he sent this inmate back out on the street, and the first thing he did was burglarize a condominium and probably find himself a set of wheels."

"Why would Donahue free an inmate?"

"My theory is that the warden needed some dirty work done. So he selected an inmate to be his personal operative and set the animal loose. But Donahue made a slight tactical error. He picked the wrong guy, because the person who's committing these killings is not going to be controlled by anyone. My suspicion, Kay, is that Donahue never intended for anyone to die, and when Jennifer Deighton turned up dead, he freaked."

"He was probably the one who called my office and identified himself as John Deighton."

"Could very well be. The point is that Donahue's intention was to have Jennifer Deighton's house ransacked because someone was looking for something—perhaps communications from Waddell. But a simple burglary isn't enough fun. The warden's little pet likes to hurt people."

I thought of the indentations in the carpet of Jennifer Deighton's living room, the injuries to her neck, and the fingerprint recovered from her dining room chair.

"He may have sat her in the middle of her living room and stood behind her with his arm yoked around her neck while he interrogated her."

"He may have done that to get her to tell him where things were. But he was being sadistic. Possibly forcing her to open her Christmas presents was also sadistic," said Wesley.

"Would someone like this go to the trouble to disguise her death as a suicide by placing her body in her car?" I asked.

"He might. This guy's been in the system. He's not interested in getting caught, and it's probably a challenge to see who he can fool. He eradicated bite marks from Eddie Heath's body.

If he ransacked Jennifer Deighton's house, he left no evidence. The only evidence he left in Susan's case was two twenty-two slugs and a feather. Not to mention, the guy altered his fingerprints."

"You think that was his idea?"

"It was probably something that the warden cooked up, and swapping records with Waddell may simply have been a matter of convenience. Waddell was about to be executed. If I wanted to trade an inmate's prints with someone, I'd choose Waddell's. Either the inmate's latents are going to come back to someone who is dead or—and this is more likely—eventually the dead person's records will be purged from the State Police computers, so if my little helper is messy and leaves prints somewhere, they aren't going to be identified at all."

I stared at him, dumbfounded.

"What?" Surprise flickered in his eyes.

"Benton, do you realize what we're saying? We're sitting here talking about computer records that were altered before Waddell died. We're talking about a burglary and the murder of a little boy that were committed before Waddell was dead. In other words, the warden's operative, as you call him, was released before Waddell was executed."

"I don't believe there can be a question about that."

"Then the assumption was that Waddell was going to die," I pointed out.

"Christ." Wesley flinched. "How could anyone be certain? The governor can intervene literally at the last minute."

"Apparently, someone knew that the governor wasn't going to."

"And the only person who could know that with certainty is the governor," he finished the thought for me.

I got up and stood before the kitchen window. A male cardinal pecked sunflower seeds from the feeder and flew off in a splash of bloodred.

"Why?" I asked without turning around. "Why would the governor have a special interest in Waddell?"

"I don't know."

"If it's true, he won't want the killer caught. When people get caught, they talk."

Wesley was silent.

"Nobody involved will want this person caught. And nobody involved will want me on the scene. It will be much better if I resign or am fired—if the cases are screwed up as much as possible. Patterson is tight with Norring."

"Kay, we've got two things we don't know yet. One is motive. The other is the killer's own agenda. This guy is doing his own thing, beginning with Eddie Heath."

I turned around and faced him. "I think he began with Robyn Naismith. I believe this monster has studied her crime scene photographs, and either consciously or subconsciously re-created one of them when he assaulted Eddie Heath and propped his body against a Dumpster."

"That could very well be," Wesley said, staring off. "But how could an inmate get access to Robyn Naismith's scene photographs? Those would not be in Waddell's prison jacket."

"This may be just one more thing that Ben Stevens helped with. Remember, I told you that he was the one who got the photos from Archives. He could have had copies made. The question is why would the photos be relevant? Why would Donahue or someone else even ask for them?"

"Because the inmate wanted them. Maybe he demanded them. Maybe they were a reward for special services."

"That is sickening," I said with quiet anger.

"Exactly." Wesley met my eyes. "This goes back to the killer's agenda, his needs and desires. It is very possible that he'd heard a lot about Robyn's case. He may have known a lot about Waddell, and it would excite him to think about what Waddell had done to his victim. The photographs would be a turn-on to someone who has a very active and aggressive fantasy life that is devoted to violent, sexualized thought. It is not farfetched to suppose that this person incorporated the scene photographs—one or more of them—into his fantasies. And then suddenly he's free, and he sees a young boy walking in the dark to a convenience store. The fantasy becomes real. He acts it out."

"He re-created Robyn Naismith's death scene?"

"Yes."

"What do you suppose his fantasy is now?"

"Being hunted."

"By us?"

"By people like us. I'm afraid he might imagine that he is smarter than everybody else and no one can stop him. He fantasizes about games he can play and murders he might commit that would reinforce these images he entertains. And for him, fantasy is not a substitute for action but a preparation for it."

"Donahue could not have orchestrated releasing a monster

like this, altering records, or anything else without help," I said.

"No. I'm sure he got key people to cooperate, like someone at State Police headquarters, maybe a records person with the city and even the Bureau. People can be bought if you have something on them. And they can be bought with cash."

"Like Susan."

"I don't think Susan was the key person. I'm more inclined to suspect that Ben Stevens was. He's out in the bars. Drinks, parties. Did you know he's into a little recreational coke when he can get it?"

"Nothing would surprise me anymore."

"I've got a few guys who have been asking a lot of questions. Your administrator has a life-style he can't afford. And when you screw with drugs, you end up screwing with bad people. Stevens's vices would have made him an easy mark for a dirtbag like Donahue. Donahue probably had one of his henchmen make a point of running into Stevens in a bar and they start talking. Next thing, Stevens has just been offered a way to make some pretty decent change."

"What way, exactly?"

"My guess is to make sure Waddell wasn't printed at the morgue, and to make sure the photograph of his bloody thumbprint disappeared from Archives. That was probably just the beginning."

"And he enlisted Susan."

"Who wasn't willing but had major financial problems of her own."

"So who do you think was making the payoffs?"

"They were probably handled by the same person who originally made Stevens's acquaintance and sucked him into this. One of Donahue's guys, maybe one of his guards."

I remembered the guard named Roberts who had given Marino and me the tour. I remembered how cold his eyes were.

"Saying the contact is a guard," I said, "then who was this guard meeting with? Susan or Stevens?"

"My guess is with Stevens. Stevens wasn't going to trust Susan with a lot of cash. He's going to want to shave his share off the top because dishonest people believe everybody is dishonest."

"He meets the contact and gets the cash," I said. "Then Ben would meet with Susan to give her a cut?"

"That's probably what the scenario was Christmas Day when she left her parents' house ostensibly to visit a friend. She was going to meet Stevens, only the killer got to her first."

I thought of the cologne I smelled on her collar and her scarf, and I remembered Stevens's demeanor when I'd confronted him in his office the night I was looking through his desk.

"No," I said. "That's not how it went."

Wesley just looked at me.

"Stevens has several qualities that would set Susan up for what happened," I said. "He doesn't care about anyone but himself. And he's a coward. When things get hot, he's not going to stick his neck out. His first impulse is to let someone else take the fall."

"Like he's doing in your case by badmouthing you and stealing files."

"A perfect example," I said.

"Susan deposited the thirty-five hundred dollars in early December, a couple of weeks before Jennifer Deighton's death."

"That's right."

"All right, Kay. Let's go back a bit. Susan or Stevens or both of them tried to break into your computer days after Waddell's execution. We've speculated that they were looking for something in the autopsy report that Susan could not have observed firsthand during the post."

"The envelope he wanted buried with him."

"I'm still stumped over that. The codes on the receipts do not confirm what we'd speculated about earlier—that the restaurants and tollbooths are located between Richmond and Mecklenburg, and that the receipts were from the transport that brought Waddell from Mecklenburg to Richmond fifteen days prior to his execution. Though the dates on the receipts are consistent with the time frame, the locations are not. The codes come back to the stretch of I-95 between here and Petersburg."

"You know, Benton, it very well may be that the explanation for the receipts is so simple that we've completely overlooked it," I said.

"I'm all ears."

"Whenever you go anywhere for the Bureau, I imagine you have the same routine I do when traveling for the state. You document every expense and save every receipt. If you travel often, you tend to wait until you can combine several trips on one reimbursement voucher to cut down on the paperwork. Meanwhile, you're keeping your receipts somewhere."

"All that makes good sense in terms of explaining the receipts in question," Wesley said. "Someone on the prison staff, for example, had to go to Petersburg. But how did the receipts then turn up in Waddell's back pocket?"

I thought of the envelope with its urgent plea that it accompany Waddell to the grave. Then I recalled a detail that was as poignant as it was mundane. On the afternoon of Waddell's execution, his mother had been allowed a two-hour visit with him.

"Benton, have you talked to Ronnie Waddell's mother?"

"Pete went to see her in Suffolk several days ago. She's not feeling particularly friendly or cooperative toward people like us. In her eyes, we're the ones who sent her son to the chair."

"So she didn't reveal anything significant about Waddell's demeanor when she visited him the afternoon of his execution?"

"Based on what little she said, he was very quiet and frightened. One interesting point, though. Pete asked her what had happened to Waddell's personal effects. She said that Corrections gave her his watch and ring and explained that he had donated his books, poetry, and so on to the N-double-A-C-P."

"She didn't question that?" I asked.

"No. She seemed to think it made sense for Waddell to do that."

"Why?"

"She doesn't read or write. What's important is that she was lied to, as were we when Vander tried to track down personal effects in hopes of getting latent prints. And the origin of these lies most likely was Donahue."

"Waddell knew something," I said. "For Donahue to want every scrap of paper that Waddell had written on and every letter ever sent to him, then there must be something that Waddell knew that certain people don't want anyone else to know."

Wesley was silent.

Then he said, "What did you say is the name of the cologne Stevens wears?"

"Red."

"And you're fairly certain this is what you smelled on Susan's coat and scarf?"

"I wouldn't swear to it in court, but the fragrance is quite distinctive."

"I think it's time for Pete and me to have a little prayer meeting with your administrator."

"Good. And I think I can help get him in the proper frame of mind if you'll give me until noon tomorrow."

"What are you going to do?"

"Probably make him a very nervous man," I said.

I was working at the kitchen table early that evening when I heard Lucy drive into the garage, and I got up to greet her. She was dressed in a navy blue warm-up suit and one of my ski jackets, and was carrying a gym bag.

"I'm dirty," she said, pulling away from my hug, but not before I smelled gun smoke in her hair. Glancing down at her hands, I saw enough gunshot residues on the right one to make a trace element analyst ecstatic.

"Whoa," I said as she started to walk off. "Where is it?"

"Where's what?" she asked innocently.

"The gun."

Reluctantly, she withdrew my Smith and Wesson from her jacket pocket.

"I wasn't aware you had a license for carrying a concealed weapon," I said, taking the revolver from her and making sure it was unloaded.

"I don't need one if I'm carrying it concealed in my own house. Before that I had it on the car seat in plain view."

"That's good but not good enough," I said quietly. "Come on."

Wordlessly, she followed me to the kitchen table, and we sat down.

"You said you were going to Westwood to work out," I said.

"I know that's what I said."

"Where have you been, Lucy?"

"The Firing Line on Midlothian Turnpike. It's an indoor range."

"I know what it is. How many times have you done this?"

"Four times." She looked me straight in the eye.

"My God, Lucy."

"Well, what am I supposed to do? Pete's not going to take me anymore."

"Lieutenant Marino is very, very busy right now," I said, and the remark sounded so patronizing that I was embarrassed. "You're aware of the problems," I added.

"Sure I am. Right now he's got to stay away. And if he stays away from you, he stays away from me. So he's out on the street because there's some maniac on the loose who's killing people like your morgue supervisor and the prison warden. At least Pete can take care of himself. Me? I've been shown how to shoot one lousy time. Gee, thanks a lot. That's like giving me one tennis lesson and then entering me in Wimbledon."

"You're overreacting."

"No. The problem is you're underreacting."

"Lucy . . ."

"How would you feel if I told you that every time I come visit you, I never stop thinking about that night?"

I knew exactly which night she meant, though over the years we had managed to go on as if nothing had happened.

"I would not feel good if I knew you were upset by anything that has to do with me," I said.

"*Anything?* What happened was just *anything?*"

"Of course it wasn't just anything."

"Sometimes I wake up at night because I dream a gun is going off. Then I listen to the awful silence and remember lying there, staring into the dark. I was so scared I couldn't move, and I wet my bed. And there were sirens and red lights flashing, and neighbors coming out on their porches and looking out their windows. And you wouldn't let me see it when they carried him out, and you wouldn't let me go upstairs. I wish I had, because imagining it has been worse."

"That man is dead, Lucy. He can't hurt anyone now."

"There are others just as bad, maybe worse than him."

"I'm not going to tell you there aren't."

"What are you doing about it, then?"

"I spend my every waking moment picking up the pieces of the lives destroyed by evil people. What more do you want me to do?"

"If you let something happen to you, I promise I will hate you," my niece said.

"If something happens to me, I don't suppose it will matter

who hates me. But I wouldn't want you to hate anyone because of what it would do to you."

"Well, I will hate you. I swear."

"I want you to promise me, Lucy, that you won't lie to me again."

She did not say a word.

"I don't ever want you to feel that you need to hide anything from me," I said.

"If I'd told you I wanted to go to the range, would you have let me?"

"Not without Lieutenant Marino or me."

"Aunt Kay, what if Pete can't catch him?"

"Lieutenant Marino is not the only person on the case," I said, not answering her question, because I did not know how to answer it.

"Well, I feel sorry for Pete."

"Why?"

"He has to stop whoever this person is, and he can't even talk to you."

"I imagine he's taking things in stride, Lucy. He's a pro."

"That's not what Michele says."

I glanced over at her.

"I was talking to her this morning. She says that Pete came by the house the other night to see her father. She said that Pete looks awful—his face was as red as a fire truck and he was in a horrible mood. Mr. Wesley tried to get him to go to the doctor or take some time off, but no way."

I felt miserable. I wanted to call Marino immediately, but I knew it wasn't wise. I changed the subject.

"What else have you and Michele been talking about? Anything new with the State Police computers?"

"Nothing good. We've tried everything we can think of to figure out who Waddell's SID number was switched with. But any records marked for deletion were overwritten long ago on the hard disk. And whoever is responsible for the tampering was swift enough to do full system backups after the records were altered, meaning we can't run SID numbers against an earlier version of CCRE and see who pops up. Generally, you have at least one backup that's three to six months old. But not so in this case."

"Sounds like an inside job to me."

I thought how natural it seemed to be home with Lucy. She no longer was a guest or an irascible little girl. "We need to call your mother and Grans," I said.

"Do we have to tonight?"

"No. But we do need to talk about your returning to Miami."

"Classes don't start until the seventh, and it won't make any difference if I miss the first few days."

"School is very important."

"It's also very easy."

"Then you should do something on your own to make it harder."

"Missing classes will make it harder," she said.

The next morning I called Rose at eight-thirty, when I knew a staff meeting was in progress across the hall, meaning that

Ben Stevens was occupied and would not know I was on the line.

"How are things?" I asked my secretary.

"Awful. Dr. Wyatt couldn't get here from the Roanoke office because they got snow in the mountains and the roads are bad. So yesterday Fielding had four cases with no one to help him. Plus, he was due in court and then got called to a scene. Have you talked to him?"

"We touch base when the poor man has a moment to get to the phone. This might be a good time for us to track down a few of our former fellows and see if one of them might consider coming here to help us hang on for a while. Jansen's doing private path in Charlottesville. You want to try him and see if he wants to give me a call?"

"Certainly. That's a fine idea."

"Tell me about Stevens," I said.

"He hasn't been here very much. He signs out in such an abbreviated, vague fashion that no one is ever sure where he's gone. I'm suspicious he's looking for another job."

"Remind him not to ask me for a recommendation."

"I wish you'd give him a great one so someone else would take him off our hands."

"I need for you to call the DNA lab and get Donna to do me a favor. She should have a lab request for the analysis of the fetal tissue from Susan's case."

Rose was silent. I could feel her getting upset.

"I'm sorry to bring this up," I said gently.

She took a deep breath. "When did you request the analysis?"

"The request was actually made by Dr. Wright, since he did

the post. He would have his copy of the lab request at the Norfolk office, along with the case."

"You don't want me to call Norfolk and have them make a copy for us?"

"No. This can't wait, and I don't want anyone to know that I've requested a copy. I want it to appear that our office inadvertently got a copy. That's why I want you to deal directly with Donna. Ask her to pull the lab request immediately and I want you to pick it up in person."

"Then what?"

"Then put it in the box up front where all the other copies of lab requests and reports are left for sorting."

"You're sure about this?"

"Absolutely," I said.

I hung up and retrieved a telephone directory, which I was flipping through when Lucy walked into the kitchen. She was barefoot and still wearing the sweat suit she had slept in. Groggily wishing me a good morning, she began rummaging in the refrigerator as I ran my finger down a column of names. There were maybe forty listings for the name Grimes, but no Helens. Of course, when Marino had referred to the guard as Helen the Hun, he was being snide. Maybe Helen wasn't her real name at all. I noted that there were three listings with the initial H., two for the first name and one for a middle name.

"What are you doing?" Lucy asked, setting a glass of orange juice on the table and pulling out a chair.

"I'm trying to track down someone," I said, reaching for the phone.

I had no luck with any of the Grimeses I called.

"Maybe she's married," Lucy suggested.

"I don't think so." I called Directory Assistance and got the listing for the new penitentiary in Greensville.

"What makes you think she isn't?"

"Intuition." I dialed. "I'm trying to reach Helen Grimes," I said to the woman who answered.

"Are you referring to an inmate?"

"No. To one of your guards."

"Hold, please."

I was transferred.

"Watkins," a male voice mumbled.

"Helen Grimes, please," I said.

"Who?"

"Officer Helen Grimes."

"Oh. She don't work here anymore."

"Could you please tell me where I could reach her, Mr. Watkins? It's very important."

"Hold on." The phone clunked against wood. In the background, Randy Travis was singing.

Minutes later, the man returned. "We're not allowed to give out information like that, ma'am."

"That's fine, Mr. Watkins. If you give me your first name, I'll just send all this to you and you can forward it to her."

A pause. "All *what*?"

"This order she placed. I was calling to see if she wanted it mailed fourth-class or sent ground."

"What order?" He didn't sound happy.

"The set of encyclopedias she ordered. There are six boxes weighing eighteen pounds each."

"Well, you can't be sending no 'cyclopedias here."

"Then what do you suggest I do with them, Mr. Watkins? She's already made the down payment and your business address was the one she gave us."

"Shhhhooo. Hold on."

I heard paper rustle; then keys clicked on a keyboard.

"Look," the man said quickly. "The best I can do is give you a P.O. box. You just send the stuff there. Don't be sending nothing to me."

He gave me the address and abruptly hung up. The post office where Helen Grimes received her mail was in Goochland County. Next I called a bailiff I was friendly with at the Goochland courthouse. Within the hour he had looked up Helen Grimes's home address in court records, but her telephone number was unlisted. At eleven A.M., I gathered my pocketbook and coat, and found Lucy in my study.

"I've got to go out for a few hours," I said.

"You lied to whoever you were talking to on the phone." She stared into the computer screen. "You don't have any *encyclopedias* to deliver to anyone."

"You're absolutely right. I did lie."

"So sometimes it's okay to lie and sometimes it's not."

"It's never really okay, Lucy."

I left her in my chair, modem lights winking and various computer manuals open and scattered over my desk and on the floor. On the screen the cursor pulsed rapidly. I waited until I was well out of sight before slipping my Ruger into my pocketbook. Though I was licensed to carry a concealed weapon, I rarely did. Setting the alarm, I left the house through the garage and drove west until Cary Street put me on River Road. The sky was marbled varying shades of gray. I was expecting Nicholas Grueman to call any day. A bomb ticked silently in the records I had given him, and I did not look forward to what he was going to say.

Helen Grimes lived on a muddy road just west of the North Pole restaurant, and on the border of a farm. Her house looked like a small barn, with few trees on its tiny parcel of land, and window boxes clumped with dead shoots that I guessed once had been geraniums. There was no sign in front to announce who lived inside, but the old Chrysler pulled up close to the porch announced that at least somebody did.

When Helen Grimes opened her door, I could tell by her blank expression that I was about as foreign to her as my German car. Dressed in jeans and an untucked denim shirt, she planted her hands on her substantial hips and did not budge from the doorway. She seemed unbothered by the cold or who I said I was, and it wasn't until I reminded her of my visit to the penitentiary that recognition flickered in her small, probing eyes.

"Who told you where I live?" Her cheeks were flushed, and I wondered if she might hit me.

"Your address is in the court records for Goochland County."

"You shouldn't have looked for it. How would you like it if I dug up your home address?"

"If you needed my help as much as I need yours, I wouldn't mind, Helen," I said.

She just looked at me. I noticed that her hair was damp, an earlobe smudged with black dye.

"The man you worked for was murdered," I said. "Someone who worked for me was murdered. And there are others. I'm sure you've been keeping up with some of what is going on. There is reason to suspect that the person who is doing this was an inmate at Spring Street—someone who was released, perhaps around the time that Ronnie Joe Waddell was executed."

"I don't know anything about anybody being released." Her eyes drifted to the empty street behind me.

"Would you know anything about an inmate who disappeared? Someone, perhaps, who wasn't legitimately released? It seems that with the job you had you would have known who entered the penitentiary and who left."

"Nobody disappeared that I heard of."

"Why don't you work there anymore?" I asked.

"Health reasons."

I heard what sounded like a cupboard door shut from somewhere inside the space she guarded.

I kept trying. "Do you remember when Ronnie Waddell's mother came to the penitentiary to visit him on the afternoon of his execution?"

"I was there when she came in."

"You would have searched her and anything she had with her. Am I correct?"

"Yes."

"What I'm trying to determine is if Mrs. Waddell might have brought anything to give her son. I realize that visiting rules prohibit people from bringing in items for the inmates—"

"You can get permission. She got it."

"Mrs. Waddell got permission to give something to her son?"

"Helen, you're letting all the heat out," a voice sounded sweetly from behind her.

Intense blue eyes suddenly fixed on me like gun sights in the space between Helen Grimes's meaty left shoulder and the door frame. I caught a flash of a pale cheek and aquiline nose before the space was empty again. The lock rattled and the door was quietly shut behind the erstwhile prison guard. She leaned up against it, staring at me. I repeated my question.

"She did bring something for Ronnie, and it wasn't much. I called the warden for permission."

"You called Frank Donahue?"

She nodded.

"And he granted permission?"

"Like I said, it wasn't much, what she brought for him."

"Helen, what was it?"

"A picture of Jesus about the size of a postcard, and something was wrote on the back. I don't remember exactly. Something like 'I will be with you in paradise,' only the spelling was wrong. Paradise was spelled like 'pair of dice,' all run together," Helen Grimes said without a trace of a smile.

"And that was it?" I asked. "This was what she wanted to give her son before he died?"

"I told you that was it. Now, I need to go in, and I don't want you coming here again." She put her hand on the door-knob as the first few drops of rain slowly slipped from the sky and left wet spots the size of nickels on the cement stoop.

When Wesley arrived at my house later in the day, he wore a black leather pilot's jacket, a dark blue cap, and a trace of a smile.

"What's happening?" I asked as we retreated to the kitchen, which by now had become such a common meeting place for us that he always took the same chair.

"We didn't break Stevens, but I think we put a pretty big crack in him. Your having the lab request left where he would find it did the trick. He's got good reason to fear the results of DNA testing done on fetal tissue from Susan Story's case."

"He and Susan were having an affair," I said, and it was odd that I did not object to Susan's morals. I was disappointed in her taste.

"Stevens admitted to the affair and denied everything else."

"Such as having any idea where Susan got thirty-five hundred dollars?" I said.

"He denies knowing anything about that. But we're not finished with him. A snitch of Marino's says he saw a black Jeep with a vanity plate in the area where Susan was shot and about the time we think it happened. Ben Stevens drives a black Jeep with the vanity plate '1 4 Me.'"

"Stevens didn't kill her, Benton," I said.

"No, he didn't. I think what happened is Stevens got spooked when whoever he was dealing with wanted information about Jennifer Deighton's case."

"The implication would have been pretty clear," I agreed. "Stevens knew that Jennifer Deighton was murdered."

"And coward that he is, he decides that when it is time for the next payoff, he'll let Susan handle it. Then he'll meet her directly afterward to get his share."

"By which time she's already been killed."

Wesley nodded. "I think whoever was sent to meet her shot

her and kept the money. Later—maybe mere minutes later—Stevens appears in the designated spot, the alleyway off Strawberry Street."

"What you're describing is consistent with her position in the car," I said. "Originally, she had to have been slumped forward in order for the assailant to have shot her in the nape of the neck. But when she was found, she was leaning back in the seat."

"Stevens moved her."

"When he first approached the car, he wouldn't have immediately known what was wrong with her. He couldn't see her face if she were slumped forward against the steering wheel. He leaned her back in the seat."

"And then ran like hell."

"And if he'd just splashed on some of his cologne before heading out to meet her, then he would have cologne on his hands. When he leaned her back in the seat, his hands would have been in contact with her coat—probably in the area of her shoulders. That's what I smelled at the scene."

"We'll break him eventually."

"There are more important things to do, Benton," I said, and I told him about my visit with Helen Grimes and what she had said about Mrs. Waddell's last visit with her son.

"My theory," I went on, "is that Ronnie Waddell wanted the picture of Jesus buried with him, and that this may have been his last request. He puts it in an envelope and writes on it 'Urgent, extremely confidential,' and so on."

"He couldn't have done this without Donahue's permission," Wesley said. "According to protocol, the inmate's last request must be communicated to the warden."

"Right, and no matter what Donahue's been told, he's going to be too paranoid to let Waddell's body be carried off with a sealed envelope in a pocket. So he grants Waddell's request, then devises a way to see what's inside the envelope without a hassle or a stink. He decides to switch envelopes after Waddell is dead, and instructs one of his thugs to take care of it. And this is where the receipts come in."

"I was hoping you'd get around to that," Wesley said.

"I think the person made a little mistake. Let's say he's got a white envelope on his desk, and inside it are receipts from a recent trip to Petersburg. Let's say he gets a similar white envelope, tucks something innocuous inside it, and then writes the same thing on the front that Waddell had written on the envelope he wanted buried with him."

"Only the guard writes this on the wrong envelope."

"Yes. He writes it on the one containing the receipts."

"And he's going to discover this later when he looks for his receipts and finds the innocuous something inside the envelope instead."

"Precisely," I said. "And that's where Susan fits in. If I were the guard who made this mistake, I'd be very worried. The burning question for me would be whether one of the medical examiners opened that envelope in the morgue, or if the envelope was left sealed. If I, this guard, also happened to be the contact for Ben Stevens, the person forking over cash in exchange for making sure Waddell's body wasn't printed at the morgue, for example, then I'd know exactly where to turn."

"You'd contact Stevens and tell him to find out if the envelope was opened. And if so, whether its contents made anybody suspicious or inclined to go around asking questions. It's called tripping over your paranoia and ending up with many more problems than you would have had if you'd just been cool. But it would seem Stevens could have answered that question easily."

"Not so," I said. "He could ask Susan, but she didn't witness the opening of the envelope. Fielding opened it upstairs, photocopied the contents, and sent the original out with Waddell's other personal effects."

"Stevens couldn't have just pulled the case and looked at the photocopy?"

"Not unless he broke the lock on my credenza," I said.

"Then, in his mind, the only other alternative was the computer."

"Unless he asked Fielding or me. He would know better than that. Neither of us would have divulged a confidential detail like that to him or Susan or anyone else."

"Does he know enough about computers to break into your directory?"

"Not to my knowledge, but Susan had taken several courses and had UNIX books in her office."

The telephone rang and I let Lucy answer it. When she came into the kitchen, her eyes were uneasy.

"It's your lawyer, Aunt Kay."

She moved the kitchen phone within reach, and I picked it up without moving from my chair. Nicholas Grueman wasted no words on a greeting but went straight to his point.

"Dr. Scarpetta, on November twelfth you wrote a money market account check to the tune of *ten thousand dollars cash.*

And I find no records in any of your bank statements that might indicate this money was deposited in any of your various accounts."

"I didn't deposit the money."

"You walked out of the bank with ten thousand dollars cash?"

"No, I did not. I wrote the check at Signet Bank, downtown, and with it purchased a cashier's check in British sterling."

"To whom was the cashier's check made out?" my former professor asked as Benton Wesley stared tensely at me.

"Mr. Grueman, the transaction was of a private nature and in no way has any bearing on my profession."

"Come now, Dr. Scarpetta. *You know* that's not good enough."

I took a deep breath.

"Certainly, you know we're going to be asked about this. Certainly, you must realize it doesn't look good that within weeks of your morgue assistant's depositing an unexplained amount of cash, you wrote a check for a large amount of cash."

I shut my eyes and ran my fingers through my hair as Wesley got up from the table and came around behind me.

"Kay"—I felt Wesley's hands on my shoulders—"for God's sake, you've got to tell him."

13

Had Grueman never been a practitioner of the law, I would not have entrusted my welfare to him. But before teaching he had been a litigator of renown, and he had done civil rights work and prosecuted mobsters for the Justice Department during the Robert Kennedy era. Now he represented clients who had no money and were condemned to die. I appreciated Grueman's seriousness and needed his cynicism.

He was not interested in trying to negotiate or protest my innocence. He refused to present the slightest shred of evidence to Marino or anyone. He told no one of the ten-thousand-dollar check, which was, he said, the worst piece of evidence against me. I was reminded of what he had taught his students on the first day of criminal law: *Just say no. Just say no. Just say no.* My former professor abided by these rules to the letter, and frustrated Roy Patterson's every effort.

Then on Thursday, January 6, Patterson called me at home and requested that I come downtown to his office to talk.

"I'm sure we can clear all this up," he said amicably. "I just need to ask you a few questions."

The implication was that if I cooperated, then something worse might be derailed, and I marveled that Patterson would consider, for even a moment, that such a shopworn maneuver would work with me. When the Commonwealth's Attorney wants to chat, he's on a fishing expedition that does not involve letting anything go. The same is true of the police. In good Gruemanian fashion, I told Patterson no, and the next morning was subpoenaed to appear before the special grand jury on January 20. This was followed by a subpoena duces tecum for my financial records. First Grueman claimed the Fifth, then filed a motion to quash the subpoena. A week later, we had no choice but to comply unless I wished to be held in contempt of court. About this same time, Governor Norring appointed Fielding acting chief medical examiner of Virginia.

"There's another TV van. I just saw it go by," Lucy said from the dining room, where she stood staring out the window.

"Come on in and eat lunch," I called out to her from the kitchen. "Your soup is getting cold."

Silence.

Then, "Aunt Kay?" She sounded excited.

"What is it?"

"You'll never guess who just pulled up."

From the window over the sink, I watched the white Ford LTD park in front. The driver's door opened, and Marino climbed out. He hitched up his trousers and adjusted his tie, his eyes taking in everything around him. As I watched him follow the sidewalk to my porch, I was so powerfully touched that it startled me.

"I'm not sure if I should be glad to see you or not," I said when I opened the door.

"Hey, don't worry. I'm not here to arrest you, Doc."

"Please come in."

"Hi, Pete," Lucy said cheerfully.

"Aren't you supposed to be in school or something?"

"No."

"What? Down there in South America they give you January off?"

"That's right. Because of the bad weather," my niece said. "When it drops below seventy degrees, everything shuts down."

Marino smiled. He looked about the worst I had ever seen him.

Moments later I had built a fire in the living room, and Lucy had left to run errands.

"How have you been?" I asked.

"Are you going to make me smoke outside?"

I slid an ashtray closer to him.

"Marino, you have suitcases under your eyes, your face is flushed, and it's not warm enough in here for you to be perspiring."

"I can tell you've missed me." He pulled a dingy handkerchief from his back pocket and mopped his brow. Then he lit a cigarette and stared into the fire. "Patterson's being an asshole, Doc. He wants to scorch you."

"Let him try."

"He will, and you'd better be ready."

"He has no case against me, Marino."

"He has a fingerprint found on an envelope inside Susan's house."

"I can explain that."

"But you can't prove it, and then there's his little trump card. And I swear I shouldn't be telling you this, but I'm going to."

"What trump card?"

"You remember Tom Lucero?"

"I know who he is," I said. "I don't know him."

"Well, he can be a charmer and he's a pretty damn good cop, to be honest. Turns out he's been snooping around Signet Bank and talked up one of the tellers until she slipped him information about you. Now, he wasn't supposed to ask and she wasn't supposed to tell. But she told him she remembered you writing a big check for cash sometime before Thanksgiving. According to her, it was for ten grand."

I stared stonily at him.

"I mean, you can't really blame Lucero. He's just doing his job. But Patterson knows what to look for as he rummages through your financial records. He's going to hammer you hard when you get before the special grand jury."

I did not say a word.

"Doc." He leaned forward and met my eyes. "Don't you think you ought to talk about it?"

"No."

Getting up, he went to the fireplace and nudged the curtain open far enough to flick the cigarette inside.

"Shit, Doc," he said quietly. "I don't want you indicted."

"I shouldn't drink coffee and I know you shouldn't, but I feel like having something. Do you like hot chocolate?"

"I'll drink some coffee."

I got up to fix it. My thoughts buzzed sluggishly like a housefly in the fall. My rage had nowhere to go. I made a pot of decaf and hoped Marino would not know the difference.

"How is your blood pressure?" I asked him.

"You want to know the truth? Some days, if I was a kettle I'd be whistling."

"I don't know what I'm going to do with you."

He perched on the edge of the hearth. The fire sounded like the wind, and reflected flames danced in brass.

"For one thing," I went on, "you probably shouldn't even be here. I don't want you having any problems."

"Hey, fuck the CA, the city, the governor, and all of them," he said with sudden anger.

"Marino, we can't give in. Someone knows who this killer is. Have you talked to the officer who showed us around the penitentiary? Officer Roberts?"

"Yo. The conversation went exactly nowhere."

"Well, I didn't fare a whole lot better with your friend Helen Grimes."

"That must've been a treat."

"Are you aware that she no longer works for the pen?"

"She never did any *work* there that I know of. Helen the Hun was lazy as hell, unless she was patting down one of the lady guests. Then she got industrious. Donahue liked her, don't ask me why. After he got whacked, she got reassigned to guard tower duty in Greensville and suddenly developed a knee problem or something."

"I have a feeling she knows a lot more than she let on," I said. "Especially if she and Donahue were friendly with each other."

Marino sipped his coffee and looked out the sliding glass doors. The ground was frosted white, and snowflakes seemed to be falling faster. I thought of the snowy night I was summoned to Jennifer Deighton's house, and images flashed in my mind of an overweight woman in curlers sitting in a chair in the middle of her living room. If the killer had interrogated her, he had done so for a reason. What was it he had been sent to find?

"Do you think the killer was after letters when he appeared at Jennifer Deighton's house?" I asked Marino.

"I think he was after something that had to do with Waddell. Letters, poems. Things he may have mailed to her over the years."

"Do you think this person found what he was looking for?"

"Let's just put it this way, he may have looked around, but he was so tidy we couldn't tell."

"Well, I don't think he found a thing," I said.

Marino looked skeptically at me as he lit another cigarette. "Based on what?"

"Based on the scene. She was in her nightgown and curlers. It appears she had been reading in bed. That doesn't sound like someone who is expecting company."

"I'll go along with that."

"Then someone appears at her door and she must have let

him in, because there was no sign of forcible entry and no sign of a struggle. I think what may have happened next is this person demanded that she turn over to him whatever it was he was looking for, and she wouldn't. He gets angry, gets a chair from the dining room, and sets it in the middle of her living room. He sits her in it and basically tortures her. He asks questions, and when she doesn't tell him what he wants to hear he tightens the choke hold. This goes on until it goes too far. He carries her out and puts her in her car."

"If he was going in and out of the kitchen, that might explain why that door was unlocked when we arrived," Marino considered.

"It might. In summary, I don't think he intended for her to die when she did, and after he tried to disguise her death he probably didn't hang around very long. Maybe he got scared, or maybe he simply lost interest in his assignment. I doubt he rummaged through her house at all, and I also doubt that he would have found anything if he had."

"We sure as hell didn't," Marino said.

"Jennifer Deighton was paranoid," I said. "She indicated to Grueman in the fax she sent him that there was something wrong about what was being done to Waddell. Apparently, she'd seen me on the news and had even tried to contact me, but continued to hang up when she got my machine."

"Are you thinking she might have had papers or something that would tell us what the hell this is all about?"

"If she had," I said, "then she was probably sufficiently frightened to get them out of her house."

"And stash them where?"

"I don't know, but maybe her ex-husband would. Didn't she visit him for two weeks the end of November?"

"Yeah." Marino looked interested. "As a matter of fact, she did."

Willie Travers had an energetic, pleasant voice over the phone when I finally reached him at the Pink Shell resort in Fort Myers Beach, Florida. But he was vague and noncommittal when I began to ask questions.

"Mr. Travers, what can I do to make you trust me?" I finally asked in despair.

"Come down here."

"That's going to be very difficult at present."

"I'd have to see you."

"Excuse me?"

"That's the way I am. If I can see you, I can read you and know if you're okay. Jenny was the same way."

"So if I come down to Fort Myers Beach and let you *read* me, you will help me?"

"Depends on what I pick up."

I made airline reservations for six-fifty the following morning. Lucy and I would fly to Miami. I would leave her with Dorothy and drive to Fort Myers Beach, where there was a very good chance I would spend a night wondering if I'd lost my mind. Chances were overwhelming that Jennifer Deighton's holistic health nut of an ex would turn out to be a great big waste of time.

Saturday, the snow had stopped when I got up at four A.M.

and went into Lucy's bedroom to wake her. For a moment I listened to her breathe, then lightly touched her shoulder and whispered her name in the dark. She stirred and sat straight up. On the plane, she slept to Charlotte, then wallowed in one of her unbearable moods the rest of the way to Miami.

"I'd rather take a cab," she said, staring out the window.

"You can't take a cab, Lucy. Your mother and her friend will be looking for you."

"Good. Let them drive around the airport all day. Why can't I come with you?"

"You need to go home, and I need to drive straight to Fort Myers Beach, and then I'm going to fly from there back to Richmond. Trust me. It wouldn't be any fun."

"Being with Mother and her latest idiot isn't any fun, either."

"You don't know he's an idiot. You've never met him. Why don't you give him a chance?"

"I wish Mother would get AIDS."

"Lucy, don't say such a thing."

"She deserves it. I don't understand how she can sleep with every dickhead who takes her out to dinner and a movie. I don't understand how she can be your sister."

"Lower your voice," I whispered.

"If she missed me so much, she'd want to pick me up herself. She wouldn't want someone else around."

"That's not necessarily true," I told her. "When you fall in love someday, you'll understand better."

"What makes you think I've never been in love?" She looked furiously at me.

"Because if you had been, you would know that being in love brings out both the best and the worst in us. One day we're generous and sensitive to a fault, and the next we're not fit to shoot. Our lives become lessons in extremes."

"I wish Mother would hurry up and go through menopause."

Mid-afternoon, as I drove the Tamiami Trail in and out of the shade, I patched up the holes guilt had chewed into my conscience. Whenever I dealt with my family, I felt irritated and annoyed. Whenever I refused to deal with them, I felt the same way I had as a child, when I learned the art of running away without leaving home. In a sense, I had become my father after he died. I was the rational one who made A's and knew how to cook and handle money. I was the one who rarely cried and whose reaction to the volatility in my disintegrating home was to cool down and disperse like a vapor. Consequently, my mother and sister accused me of indifference, and I grew up harboring a secret shame that what they said was true.

I arrived in Fort Myers Beach with the air-conditioning on and the visor down to shield the sun. Water met the sky in a continuum of vibrant blue, and palms were bright green feathers atop trunks as sturdy as ostrich legs. The Pink Shell resort was the color of its name. It backed up to Estero Bay and threw its front balconies open wide to the Gulf of Mexico. Willie Travers lived in one of the cottages, but I was not due to meet him until eight P.M. Checking into a one-bedroom apartment, I literally left a trail of clothes on the floor as I snatched off my winter suit and grabbed shorts and a tennis shirt out of my bag. I was out the door and on the beach in seven minutes.

I did not know how many miles I walked, for I lost track of time, and each stretch of sand and water looked magnificently the same. I watched bobbing pelicans throw their heads back as they downed fish like shots of bourbon, and I deftly stepped around the flaccid blue balloons of beached Portuguese men-of-war. Most people I passed were old. Occasionally, the high-pitched voice of a child lifted above the roar of waves like a bit of bright paper carried by the wind. I picked up sand dollars worn smooth by the surf and leached shells reminiscent of peppermints sucked thin. I thought of Lucy and missed her again.

When most of the beach was in shade, I returned to my room. Showering and changing, I got in my car and cruised Estero Boulevard until hunger guided me like a divining rod into the parking lot of the Skipper's Galley. I ate red snapper and drank white wine while the horizon faded to a dusky blue. Soon boat lights drifted low in the darkness and I could not see the water.

By the time I found cottage 182 near the bait shop and fishing pier, I was as relaxed as I had been in a long time. When Willie Travers opened the door, it seemed we had been friends forever.

"The first order of business is refreshment. Surely you haven't eaten," he said.

I regretfully told him I had.

"Then you'll simply have to eat again."

"But I couldn't."

"I will prove you wrong within the hour. The fare is very light. Grouper grilled in butter and Key Lime juice with a generous sprinkling of fresh ground pepper. And we have seven-grain bread I make from scratch that you'll never forget as long as you live. Let's see. Oh, yes. Marinated slaw and Mexican beer."

He said all this as he popped the caps off two bottles of Dos Equis. Jennifer Deighton's former husband had to be close to eighty years old, his face as ruined by the sun as cracked mud, but the blue eyes set in it were as vital as a young man's. He smiled a lot as he talked, and was beef jerky lean. His hair reminded me of white tennis ball fuzz.

"How did you come to live here?" I asked, looking around at mounted fish on the walls and rugged furnishings.

"A couple of years ago I decided to retire and fish, so I worked out a deal with the Pink Shell. I'd run their bait shop if they'd let me rent one of the cottages at a reasonable rate."

"What was your profession before you retired?"

"Same as it is now." He smiled. "I practice holistic medicine, and you never really retire from that any more than you retire from religion. The difference is, now I work with people I want to work with, and I no longer have an office in town."

"Your definition of holistic medicine?"

"I treat the whole person, plain and simple. The point is to get people in balance." He looked appraisingly at me, set his beer down, and came over to the captain's chair where I sat. "Would you mind standing up?"

I was in a mood to be agreeable.

"Now hold out one of your arms. I don't care which one, but hold it straight out so it's parallel to the floor. That's fine. Now I'm going to ask you a question and then as you answer I'm going to try to push your arm down while you resist. Do you view yourself as the family hero?"

"No." My arm instantly yielded to his pressure and lowered like a drawbridge.

"Well, you do view yourself as the family hero. That tells me you're pretty damn hard on yourself and have been from the word go. All right. Now let's put your arm up again and I'm going to ask you another question. Are you good at what you do?"

"Yes."

"I'm pushing down as hard as I can and your arm is steel. So you are good at what you do."

He returned to the couch and I sat back down.

"I must admit that my medical teaching makes me somewhat skeptical," I said with a smile.

"Well, it shouldn't, because the principles are no different from what you deal with every day. Bottom line? The body doesn't lie. No matter what you tell yourself, your energy level responds to what is actually true. If your head says you aren't the family hero or you love yourself when that's not how you feel, your energy gets weak. Is this making any sense?"

"Yes."

"One of the reasons Jenny came down here once or twice a year was so I could balance her. And when she was here last, around Thanksgiving, she was so out of whack I had to work with her several hours every day."

"Did she tell you what was wrong?"

"A lot of things were wrong. She'd just moved and didn't like her neighbors, especially the ones across the street."

"The Clarys," I said.

"I suppose that was the name. The woman was a busybody and the man was a flirt until he had a stroke. Plus, Jenny's horoscope readings had gotten out of hand and were wearing her out."

"What was your opinion of this business she ran?"

"Jenny had a gift but she was spreading it too thin."

"Would you label her a psychic?"

"Nope. I wouldn't label Jenny—wouldn't even begin to try. She was into a lot of things."

I suddenly remembered the blank sheet of paper anchored by the crystal on her bed and asked Travers if he might know what that meant, or if it meant anything.

"It meant she was concentrating."

"Concentrating?" I puzzled. "On what?"

"When Jenny wanted to meditate, she would get a white sheet of paper and put a crystal on top of it. Then she would sit very still and slowly turn the crystal around and around, watching light from the facets move on the paper. That did for her what staring at the water does for me."

"Was anything else bothering her when she came to see you, Mr. Travers?"

"Call me Willie. Yes, and you know what I'm about to say. She was upset about this convict who was waiting to be executed, Ronnie Waddell. Jenny and Ronnie had been writing to each other for many years, and she just couldn't deal with the thought of him being put to death."

"Do you know if Waddell ever revealed anything to her that could have placed her in jeopardy?"

"Well, he gave her something that did."

I reached for my beer without taking my eyes off him.

"When she came down here at Thanksgiving, she brought all of the letters he had written and anything else he had sent her over the years. She wanted me to keep them down here for her."

"Why?"

"So they would be safe."

"She was worried about somebody trying to get them from her?"

"All I know is, she was spooked. She told me that during the first week of this past November, Waddell called her collect and said he was ready to die and didn't want to fight it anymore. Apparently, he was convinced nothing could save him, and he asked her to go to the farm in Suffolk and get his belongings from his mother. He said he wanted Jenny to have them, and not to worry, that his mother would understand."

"What were those belongings?" I asked.

"Just one thing." He got up. "I'm not real sure of the significance—and I'm not sure I want to be sure. So I'm going to turn it over to you, Dr. Scarpetta. You can take it on back to Virginia. Share it with the police. Do with it what you want."

"Why are you suddenly being helpful?" I asked. "Why not weeks ago?"

"Nobody bothered to come see me," he said loudly from another room. "I told you when you called that I don't deal with people over the phone."

When he returned, he set a black Hartmann briefcase at my feet. The brass lock had been pried open and the leather was scarred.

"Fact is, you'd be doing me a big favor to get this out of my life," Willie Travers said, and I could tell he meant it. "The very thought of it makes my energy bad."

The scores of letters Ronnie Waddell had written Jennifer Deighton from death row were neatly bundled in rubber bands and sorted chronologically. I skimmed through few in my hotel room that night, because their importance all but disappeared in the light of other items I found.

Inside the briefcase were legal pads filled with handwritten notes that made little sense, for they referred to cases and dilemmas of the Commonwealth from more than ten years ago. There were pens and pencils, a map of Virginia, a tin of Sucrets throat lozenges, a Vick's inhaler, and a tube of Chapstick. Still in its yellow box was an EpiPen, a .3-milligram epinephrine auto-injector routinely kept by people fatally allergic to bee stings or some foods. The prescription label was typed with the patient's name, the date, and the information that the EpiPen was one of five refills. Clearly, Waddell had stolen the briefcase from Robyn Naismith's house on the fateful morning he murdered her. It may be that he had no idea who it belonged to until he carried it off and broke the lock. Waddell discovered he had savaged a local celebrity whose lover, Joe Norring, was then the attorney general of Virginia.

"Waddell never had a chance," I said. "Not that he necessarily deserved clemency in light of the severity of his crime. But from the moment he was arrested, Norring was a worried man.

He knew he had left his briefcase at Robyn's house, and he knew it had not been recovered by the police."

Why he had left his briefcase at Robyn's house was not clear, unless he'd simply forgotten it on a night that neither of them could know was her last.

"I can't even begin to imagine Norring's reaction when he heard," I said.

Wesley glanced at me over the rim of his glasses as he continued perusing paperwork. "I don't think we can imagine it. It was bad enough he had to worry about the world discovering he was having an affair, but his connection with Robyn would have instantly made him the prime suspect in her murder."

"In a way," Marino said, "he was lucky as hell Waddell took the briefcase."

"I'm sure in his mind he was unlucky either way he looked at it," I said. "If the briefcase had turned up at the scene, he was in trouble. If the briefcase was stolen, as it was, then Norring had to worry about it turning up somewhere."

Marino got the coffeepot and refilled everyone's cup. "Somebody must have done something to ensure Waddell's silence."

"Maybe." Wesley reached for the cream. "Then again, maybe Waddell never opened his mouth. My guess is he feared from the beginning that what he had stumbled upon only made matters worse for him. The briefcase could be used as a weapon, but who would it destroy? Norring or Waddell? Was Waddell going to trust the system enough to badmouth the AG? Was he going to trust the system enough years later to badmouth the governor—the only man who could spare his life?"

"So Waddell remained silent, knowing that his mother

would protect what he had hidden on the farm until he was ready for someone else to have it," I said.

"Norring had ten damn years to find his briefcase," Marino said. "Why did he wait so long to start looking?"

"I suspect Norring has had Waddell watched from the beginning," Wesley said, "and that this surveillance was stepped up considerably over the past few months. The closer Waddell got to the execution, the less he had to lose, and the more likely he was to start talking. It's possible someone was monitoring his phone conversation when he called Jennifer Deighton in November. And it's possible that when word got to Norring, he panicked."

"He should have," Marino said. "I personally searched through all of Waddell's belongings when we was working the case. The guy had next to nothing, and if anything belonging to him was back on the farm, we never found it."

"And Norring would have known that," I said.

"Hell, yes," Marino said. "So he's going to know there's something strange about *belongings* from the farm being given to this friend of Waddell's. Norring starts seeing that damn briefcase in his nightmares again, and to make matters worse, he can't have someone just barge into Jennifer Deighton's house while Waddell's still alive. If something happens to her, there's no telling what Waddell will do. And the worst possibility would be if he started singing to Grueman."

"Benton, " I said, "would you happen to know why Norring was carrying epinephrine? What is he allergic to?"

"Apparently, to shellfish. Apparently, he keeps EpiPens all over the place."

While they continued to talk, I checked the lasagna in the oven and opened a bottle of Kendall-Jackson. The case against Norring would take a very long time, if it could be proven at all, and I thought I understood, to a degree, how Waddell must have felt.

It wasn't until close to eleven P.M. that I called Nicholas Grueman at home.

"I'm finished in Virginia," I said. "As long as Norring is in office, he'll make sure I won't be. They've taken my life, god-damn it, but I'm not giving them my soul. I plan to take the Fifth every time."

"Then you will certainly be indicted."

"Considering the bastards I'm up against, I think that's a certainty anyway."

"My, my, Dr. Scarpetta. Have you forgotten the bastard representing you? I don't know where you spent your weekend, but I spent mine in London."

I felt the blood drain from my face.

"Now, there's no guaranteeing that we can slide this around Patterson," said this man I used to think I hated, "but I'm going to move heaven and earth to get Charlie Hale on the stand."

14

January 20 was as windy as March but much colder, and the sun was blinding as I drove east on Broad Street toward the John Marshall courthouse.

"Now I will tell you something else you already know," Nicholas Grueman said. "The press is going to be churning up the water like bluefish on a feeding frenzy. You fly too low, you lose a leg. We'll walk side by side, eyes cast down, and don't turn and look at anyone no matter who it is or what he says."

"We're not going to find a parking place," I said, turning left on 9th. "I knew this would happen."

"Slow down. That good woman right there on the side is doing something. Wonderful. She's leaving, if she can ever get the wheels turned enough."

A horn blared behind me.

I glanced at my watch, then turned to Grueman like an athlete awaiting last-minute instruction from the coach. He wore a long navy blue cashmere coat and black leather gloves, his silver-topped cane leaning against the seat and a battle-scarred briefcase in his lap.

"Now remember," he said. "Your friend Mr. Patterson decides who's going in and who isn't, so we've got to depend on the jurors to intervene, and that's going to be up to you. You've got to connect with them, Kay. You've got to make friends with ten or eleven strangers the instant you walk into that room. No matter what they want to chat with you about, don't put up a wall. Be accessible."

"I understand," I said.

"We're going for broke. A deal?"

"A deal."

"Good luck, Doctor." He smiled and patted my arm.

Inside the courthouse, we were stopped by a deputy with a scanner. He went through my pocketbook and briefcase as he had a hundred times before when I had come to testify as an expert witness. But this time he said nothing to me and avoided my eyes. Grueman's cane set off the scanner, and he was the paragon of patience and courtesy as he explained that the silver top and tip would not come off, and that there truly was nothing concealed inside the dark wood shaft.

"What does he think I have here, a blowgun?" he remarked as we boarded the elevator.

The instant the doors opened on the third floor, reporters descended with the predicted predatory vigor. My counselor moved quickly for a man with gout, his strides punctuated by taps of his cane. I felt surprisingly detached and out of focus until we were inside the nearly deserted courtroom, where

Benton Wesley sat in a corner with a slight young man I knew was Charlie Hale. The right side of his face was a road map of fine pink scars. When he stood and self-consciously slipped his right hand into his jacket pocket, I saw that he was missing several fingers. Dressed in an ill-fitting somber suit and tie, he glanced around while I preoccupied myself with the mechanics of being seated and sorting through my briefcase. I could not speak to him, and the three men had the presence of mind to pretend they did not notice that I was upset.

"Let's talk for a minute about what they have," Grueman said. "I believe we can count on Jason Story testifying, and Officer Lucero. And, of course, Marino. I don't know who else Patterson will include in this Star Chamber proceeding of his."

"For the record," Wesley said, looking at me, "I have spoken to Patterson. I've told him he doesn't have a case and I'll testify to that at the trial."

"We're assuming there will be no trial," Grueman said. "And when you go in, I want you to make sure the jurors know that you talked to Patterson and told him he has no case but he insisted on going forward. Whenever he asks a question and you respond by addressing an issue that you have already addressed with him in private, I want you to say so. 'As I told you in your office,' or 'As I clearly stated when we spoke whenever it was,' et cetera, et cetera.

"It is important that the jurors know that you are not only an FBI special agent, but that you are the chief of the Behavioral Science Unit at Quantico, the purpose of which is to analyze violent crime and develop psychological profiles of the perpetrators. You may wish to state that Dr. Scarpetta in no way, shape, or form fits the profile of the perpetrator of the crime in question, and in fact, that you find the thought absurd. It is also important that you impress upon the jurors that you were Mark James's mentor and closest friend. Volunteer whatever you can because you can rest assured that Patterson isn't going to ask. Make it clear to the jurors that Charlie Hale *is here*."

"What if they do not request me?" Charlie Hale asked.

"Then our hands are tied," Grueman replied. "As I explained when we talked in London, this is the prosecutor's show. Dr. Scarpetta has no right to present any evidence, so we have to get at least one of the jurors to invite us in through the back door."

"That's quite something," Hale said.

"You have the copies of the deposit slip and the fees you have paid?"

"Yes, sir."

"Very good. Don't wait to be asked. Just put them on the table as you're talking. And the status of your wife is the same since we spoke?"

"Yes, sir. As I told you, she's had the in vitro fertilization. So far, so good."

"Remember to get that in if you can," Grueman said.

Several minutes later, I was summoned to the jury room.

"Of course. He wants you first." Grueman got up with me. "Then he'll call in your detractors so he can leave a bad taste in the jurors' mouths." He went as far as the door. "I will be right here when you need me."

Nodding, I went inside and took the empty chair at the head of the table. Patterson was out of the room, and I knew this was one of his gambits. He wanted me to endure the silent scrutiny of these ten strangers who held my welfare in their hands. I met the gazes of all and even exchanged smiles with a few. A serious young woman wearing bright red lipstick decided not to wait for the Commonwealth's Attorney.

"What made you decide to deal with dead people instead of the living?" she asked. "It seems a strange thing for a doctor to choose."

"It is my intense concern for the living that makes me study the dead," I said. "What we learn from the dead is for the benefit of the living, and justice is for those left behind."

"Don't it get to you?" inquired an old man with big, rough hands. The expression on his face was so sincere that he seemed in pain.

"Of course it does."

"How many years did you have to go to school after you graduated from high school?" asked a heavyset black woman.

"Seventeen years, if you include residencies and the year I was a fellow."

"Lord have mercy."

"Where all did you go?"

"To school, you mean?" I said to the thin young man wearing glasses.

"Yes, ma'am."

"Saint Michael's, Our Lady of Lourdes Academy, Cornell, Johns Hopkins, Georgetown."

"Was your daddy a doctor?"

"My father owned a small grocery store in Miami."

"Well, I'd hate to be the one paying for all that schooling."

Several of the jurors laughed softly.

"I was fortunate enough to receive scholarships," I said. "Beginning with high school."

"I have an uncle who works at the Twilight Funeral Home in Norfolk," said someone else.

"Oh, come on, Barry. There really isn't a funeral home called that."

"I kid you not."

"That's nothing. We got one in Fayetteville owned by the Stiff family. Guess what it's called."

"No way."

"You're not from around here."

"I'm a native of Miami," I replied.

"Then the name Scarpetta's Spanish?"

"Actually, it's Italian."

"That's interesting. I thought all Italians was dark."

"My ancestors are from Verona in northern Italy, where a sizable segment of the population shares blood with the Savoyards, Austrians, and Swiss," I patiently explained. "Many of us are blue-eyed and blond."

"Boy, I bet you can cook."

"It's one of my favorite pastimes."

"Dr. Scarpetta, I'm not real clear on your position," said a well-dressed man who looked about my age. "Are you the chief medical examiner for Richmond?"

"For the Commonwealth. We have four district offices. Central Office here in Richmond, Tidewater in Norfolk, Western in Roanoke, and the Northern Office in Alexandria."

"So the chief just happens to be located here in Richmond?"

"Yes. That seems to make the most sense, since the medical examiner system is part of state government and Richmond is where the legislature meets," I replied as the door opened and Roy Patterson walked in.

He was a broad-shouldered, good-looking black man with close-shorn hair that was going gray. His dark blue suit was double-breasted, and his initials were embroidered on the cuffs of his pale yellow shirt. He was known for his ties, and this one looked hand painted. He greeted the jurors and was tepid toward me.

I discovered that the woman wearing the bright red lipstick was the foreman. She cleared her throat and informed me that I did not have to testify, and that anything I said could be used against me.

"I understand," I said, and I was sworn in.

Patterson hovered about my chair and offered a minimum of information about who I was, and elaborated on the power of my position and the ease with which this power could be abused.

"And who would there be to witness it?" he asked. "On many occasions there was no one to observe Dr. Scarpetta at work except for the person who was by her side virtually every day. Susan Story. You can't hear testimony from her because she and her unborn child are dead, ladies and gentlemen. But there are others you will hear from today. And they will paint for you a chilling portrait of a cold, ambitious woman, an empire builder who was making grievous mistakes on the job. First, she paid for Susan Story's silence. Then she killed for it.

"And when you hear tales of the *perfect crime,* who better able to carry it off than someone who is an expert in solving crimes? An expert would know that if you plan to shoot someone inside a vehicle, it would behoove you to choose a low-caliber weapon so you don't run the risk of bullets ricocheting. An expert would leave no telling evidence at the scene, not even spent shells. An expert would not use her own revolver—the gun or guns that friends and colleagues know she possesses. She would use something that could not be traced back to her.

"Why, she might even *borrow* a revolver from the lab, because, ladies and gentlemen, every year the courts routinely confiscate hundreds of firearms used in the commission of crimes, and some of these weapons are donated to the state firearms lab. For all we know, the twenty-two revolver that was put against the back of Susan Story's skull is, as we speak, hanging on a pegboard in the firearms lab or downstairs in the range the examiners use for test fires and where Dr. Scarpetta routinely practices shooting. And by the way, she is good enough to qualify for any police department in America. And she has killed before, though to give her credit, in the instance I'm referring to her actions were ruled to be self-defense."

I stared down at my hands folded on top of the table as the court reporter played her silent keys and Patterson went on. His rhetoric was always eloquent, though he usually did not know when to quit. When he asked me to explain the fingerprints recovered from the envelope found in Susan's dresser, he made such a big production of pointing out how unbelievable my explanation was that I suspected the reaction of some was to wonder why what I'd said *couldn't* be true. Then he got to the money.

"Is it not true, Dr. Scarpetta, that on November twelfth you appeared at the downtown branch of Signet Bank and made out a check for *cash* for the sum of ten thousand dollars?"

"That is true."

Patterson hesitated for an instant, his surprise visible. He had counted on my taking the Fifth.

"And is it true that on this occasion you did not deposit the money in any of your various accounts?"

"That is also true," I said.

"So several weeks before your morgue supervisor inexplicably deposited thirty-five hundred dollars into her checking account, you walked out of Signet Bank with ten thousand dollars cash on your person?"

"No, sir, I did not. In my financial records you should have found a copy of a cashier's check made out to the sum of seven thousand, three hundred and eighteen pounds sterling. I have my copy here." I got it out of my briefcase.

Patterson barely glanced at it as he asked the court reporter to tag it as evidence.

"Now, this is very interesting," he said. "You purchased a cashier's check made out to someone named Charles Hale. Was this some creative scheme of yours to disguise payoffs you were making to your morgue supervisor and perhaps to others? Did this individual named Charles Hale turn around and convert pounds back into dollars and route the cash elsewhere—perhaps to Susan Story?"

"No," I said. "And I never delivered the check to Charles Hale."

"You didn't?" He looked confused. "Then what did you do with it?"

"I gave it to Benton Wesley, and he saw to it that the check was delivered to Charles Hale. Benton Wesley—"

He cut me off. "The story just gets more preposterous."

"Mr. Patterson . . ."

"Who is Charles Hale?"

"I would like to finish my previous statement," I said.

"Who is Charles Hale?"

"I'd like to hear what she was trying to say," said a man in a plaid blazer.

"Please," Patterson said with a cold smile.

"I gave the cashier's check to Benton Wesley. He is a special agent for the FBI, a suspect profiler at the Behavioral Science Unit in Quantico."

A woman timidly raised her hand. "Is he the one I've read about in the papers? The one they call in when there are these awful murders like the ones in Gainesville?"

"He is the one," I said. "He is a colleague of mine. He was also the best friend of a friend of mine, Mark James, who also was a special agent for the FBI."

"Dr. Scarpetta, let's get the record straight here," Patterson said impatiently. "Mark James was more than a, quote, *friend* of yours."

"Are you asking me a question, Mr. Patterson?"

"Aside from the obvious conflict of interest involved in the chief medical examiner's sleeping with an FBI agent, the subject is nongermane. So I won't ask—"

I interrupted him. "My relationship with Mark James began in law school. There was no conflict of interest, and for the record, I object to the Commonwealth's Attorney's reference to whom I allegedly was sleeping with."

The court reporter typed on.

My hands were clasped so tightly my knuckles were white.

Patterson asked again, "Who is Charles Hale and why would you give him the equivalent of ten thousand dollars?"

Pink scars flashed in my mind, and I envisioned two fingers attached to a stump shiny with scar tissue.

"He was a ticket agent at Victoria Station in London," I said.

"*Was?*"

"He was on Monday, February eighteenth, when the bomb went off."

No one told me. I heard reporters on the news all day and had no idea until my phone rang on February 19 at two-forty-one A.M. It was six-forty-one in the morning in London, and Mark had been dead for almost a day. I was so stunned as Benton Wesley tried to explain, that none of it made any sense.

"That was yesterday, I read about that yesterday. You mean it happened again?"

"The bombing happened yesterday morning during rush hour. But I just found out about Mark. Our legal attaché in London just notified me."

"You're sure? You're absolutely sure?"

"*Jesus, I'm sorry, Kay.*"

"They've identified him with certainty?"

"With certainty."

"You're sure. I mean . . ."

"Kay. I'm at home. I can be there in an hour."

"No, no."

I was shivering all over but could not cry. I wandered through my house, moaning quietly and wringing my hands.

"But you did not know this Charles Hale prior to his being injured in the bombing, Dr. Scarpetta. Why would you give him ten thousand dollars?" Patterson dabbed his forehead with a handkerchief.

"He and his wife have wanted children and could not have them."

"And how would you know such an intimate detail about strangers?"

"Benton Wesley told me, and I responded by suggesting Bourne Hall, the leading research facility for in vitro fertilization. IVF is not covered by national health insurance."

"But you said the bombing was way back in February. You just wrote the check in November."

"I did not know about the Hales' problem until this past fall, when the FBI had a photo spread for Mr. Hale to look at and somehow learned of his difficulties. I'd told Benton long ago to let me know if there was ever anything I could do for Mr. Hale."

"Then you took it upon yourself to finance in vitro fertilization for strangers?" Patterson asked as if I'd just told him that I believed in leprechauns.

"Yes."

"Are you a *saint*, Dr. Scarpetta?"

"No."

"Then please explain your motivation."

"Charles Hale tried to help Mark."

"Tried to help him?" Patterson was pacing. "Tried to help him buy a ticket or catch a train or find the men's room? Just what is it that you mean?"

"Mark was conscious briefly, and Charles Hale was seriously injured on the ground next to him. He tried to move rubble off Mark. He talked to him, took off his jacket, and wrapped it around . . . He, uh, tried to stop the hemorrhaging. He did everything he could. There was nothing that would have saved him, but he wasn't alone. I am so grateful for that. Now there will be a new life in the world, and I am thankful I could do something in return. It helps. There is at least some meaning. No. I'm not a saint. The need was mine, too. When I helped the Hales, I was helping me."

The room was so quiet it was as if it were empty.

The woman wearing red lipstick leaned forward a little to get Patterson's attention.

"I expect Charlie Hale is way over there in England. But I wonder if we could subpoena Benton Wesley?"

"It's not necessary to subpoena either one of them," I answered. "Both of them are here."

When the foreman informed Patterson that the special grand jury had refused to indict, I was not there to see it. Nor was I present when Grueman was told. As soon as I had finished testifying, I had begun frantically looking for Marino.

"I saw him come out of the men's room maybe a half hour ago," said a uniformed officer I found smoking a cigarette by a water fountain.

"Can you try him on your radio?" I asked.

Shrugging, he unfastened his radio from his belt and asked the dispatcher to raise Marino. Marino did not respond.

I took the stairs and broke into a trot when I got outside. When I was in my car, I locked the doors and started the engine. I grabbed the phone and tried headquarters, which was directly across the street from the courthouse. While a detective in the squad room told me that Marino wasn't in, I drove through the lot in back looking for his white Ford LTD. It wasn't there. Then I pulled into an empty reserved place and called Neils Vander.

"You remember the burglary on Franklin—the prints you recently ran that matched up with Waddell?" I asked.

"The burglary in which the eiderdown vest was stolen?"

"That's the one."

"I remember it."

"Was the complainant's ten print card turned in for exclusionary purposes?"

"No, I didn't have that. Just the latents recovered from the scene."

"Thank you, Neils."

Next I called the dispatcher.

"Can you tell me if Lieutenant Marino is marked on?" I asked.

She came back to me. "He is marked on."

"Listen, please see if you can raise him and find out where he is. Tell him this is Dr. Scarpetta and it's urgent."

Maybe a minute later the dispatcher's voice came over the line. "He's at the city pumps."

"Tell him I'm two minutes from there and on my way."

The gas pumps used by the city police were located on a bleak patch of asphalt surrounded by a chain-link fence. Filling up was strictly self-service. There was no attendant, no rest room or vending machines, and the only way you were going to clean your windshield was if you brought your own paper towels and Windex. Marino was tucking his gas card in the side pouch where he always kept it when I pulled up next to him. He got out and came around to my window.

"I just heard the news on the radio." He couldn't contain his smile. "Where's Grueman? I want to shake his hand."

"I left him at the courthouse with Wesley. What happened?" I suddenly felt light-headed.

"You don't know?" he asked, incredulous. "Shit, Doc. They cut you loose, that's what happened. I can think of maybe two times in my career that a special grand jury hasn't returned with a true bill."

I took a deep breath and shook my head. "I guess I should be dancing a jig. But I don't feel like it."

"I probably wouldn't, either."

"Marino, what was the name of that man who claimed his eiderdown vest was stolen?"

"Sullivan. Hilton Sullivan. Why?"

"During my testimony, Patterson made the outrageous accusation that I might have used a revolver from the firearms lab to shoot Susan. In other words, there is always a risk involved if you use your own weapon because if it's checked and it's proven that it fired the bullets, then you've got a lot of explaining to do."

"What's this got to do with Sullivan?"

"When did he move into his condo?"

"I don't know."

"If I were going to kill someone with my Ruger, it would be pretty clever of me to report it stolen to the police before I commit any crimes. Then if for some reason the gun is ever recovered—if, for example, the heat is on and I decide to toss it—the cops might trace the serial number back to me, but I can prove through the burglary report I filed that the gun was not in my possession at the time of the crime."

"Are you suggesting Sullivan falsified a report? That he staged the burglary?"

"I'm suggesting you consider that," I said. "It's convenient that he has no burglar alarm and left a window unlocked. It's convenient that he was obnoxious with the cops. I'm sure they were delighted to see him leave and weren't about to go the extra mile and get his fingerprints for exclusionary purposes. Especially since he was dressed in white and bitching about the dusting powder everywhere. My point is, how do you know that the prints in Sullivan's condo weren't left by Sullivan? He lives there. His prints would be all over the place."

"In AFIS they matched up with Waddell."

"Exactly."

"If that's the case, then why would Sullivan call the police in response to that story about eiderdown we planted in the paper?"

"As Benton said, this guy loves to play games. He loves to jerk people around. He skates on the edge for kicks."

"Shit. Let me use your phone."

He came around to the passenger's side and got in. Dialing Directory Assistance, he got the number of the building where Sullivan lived. When the superintendent was on the line, Marino asked him how long ago Hilton Sullivan had purchased his condominium.

"Well, then, who does?" Marino asked. He scribbled something on a notepad. "What's the number and what street does it face? Okay. What about his car? Yeah, if you've got it."

When Marino hung up, he looked at me. "Christ, the squirrel doesn't own the condo at all. It's owned by some businessman who rents it, and Sullivan started renting it the friggin' first week in December. He paid the deposit on the sixth, to be exact." He opened the car door, adding, "And he drives a dark blue Chevy van. An old one with no windows."

Marino followed me back to headquarters and we left my car in his parking place. We shot across Broad Street, heading toward Franklin.

"Let's hope the manager hasn't alerted him." Marino raised his voice above the roar of the engine.

He slowed down and parked in front of an eight-story brick building.

"His condo's in back," he explained, looking around. "So he shouldn't be able to see us." He reached under the seat and got out his nine-millimeter to back up the .357 in the holster under his left arm. Tucking the pistol in the back of his trousers and an extra clip in his pocket, he opened his door.

"If you're expecting a war, I'll be glad to stay in the car," I said.

"If a war starts, I'll toss you my three-fifty-seven and a couple speed loaders, and you damn better be as good a shot as Patterson's been saying you are. Stay behind me at all times." At the top of the steps, he rang the bell. "He's probably not going to be here."

Momentarily, the lock clicked free and the door opened. An elderly man with bushy gray eyebrows identified himself as the building superintendent Marino had spoken to earlier on the phone.

"Do you know if he's in?" Marino asked.

"I have no idea."

"We're going to go up and check."

"You won't be going up because he's on this floor." The superintendent pointed east. "Just follow that corridor and take the first left. It's a corner apartment at the very end. Number seventeen."

The building possessed a quiet but tired luxuriousness, reminiscent of old hotels that no one particularly wants to stay in anymore because the rooms are too small and the decor is too dark and a little frayed. I noted cigarette burns in the deep red carpet, and the stain on the paneling was almost black. Hilton Sullivan's corner apartment was announced by a small brass 17. There was no peephole, and when Marino knocked, we heard footsteps.

"Who is it?" a voice asked.

"Maintenance," Marino said. "Here to change the filter in your heater."

The door opened, and the instant I saw the piercing blue eyes in the space and they saw me, my breath caught. Hilton Sullivan tried to slam shut the door, but Marino's foot was wedged against the jamb.

"Get to the side!" Marino shouted at me as he snatched out his revolver and leaned as far away from the door's opening as he could.

I darted up the corridor as he suddenly kicked the door open wide and it slammed against the wall inside. Revolver ready, he went in, and I waited in dread for a scuffle or gunfire. Minutes went by. Then I heard Marino saying something on his portable radio. He reappeared, sweating, his face an angry red.

"I don't fucking believe it. He went out the window like a damn jackrabbit and there's not a sign of him. Goddamn son of a bitch. His van's sitting right out there in the lot in back. He's off on foot somewhere. I've sent out an alert to units in the area." He wiped his face on his sleeve and struggled to catch his breath.

"I thought he was a woman," I said numbly.

"Huh?" Marino stared at me.

"When I went to see Helen Grimes, he was inside her house. He looked out the door once while we were talking on the porch. I thought it was a woman."

"Sullivan was at Helen the Hun's house?" Marino said loudly.

"I'm sure of it."

"Jesus Christ. That don't make a damn bit of sense."

But it did make sense when we began looking around Sullivan's apartment. It was elegantly furnished with antiques and fine rugs, which Marino said belonged to the owner, not to Sullivan, according to the superintendent. Jazz drifted from the bedroom, where we found Hilton Sullivan's blue down jacket on the bed next to a beige corduroy shirt and a pair of faded jeans, neatly folded. His running shoes and socks were on the rug. On the mahogany dresser were a green cap and a pair of sunglasses, and a loosely folded blue uniform shirt that still had Helen Grimes's nameplate pinned above the breast pocket. Beneath it was a large envelope of photographs that Marino went through while I silently looked on.

"Holy shit," Marino muttered every other minute.

In more than a dozen of them, Hilton Sullivan was nude and in poses of bondage, and Helen Grimes was his sadistic guard. One favorite scenario seemed to be Sullivan sitting in a chair while she played the role of interrogator, yoking him from behind or inflicting other punishments. He was an exquisitely pretty blond young man, with a lean body that I suspected was surprisingly strong. Certainly, he was agile. We found a photograph of Robyn Naismith's bloody body propped against the television in her living room, and another one of her on a steel table in the morgue. But what unnerved me more than any of this was Sullivan's face. It was absolutely devoid of expression, his eyes cold the way I imagined they would be when he killed.

"Maybe we know why Donahue liked him so much," Marino said, sliding the photographs back inside their envelope. "Someone was taking these pictures. Donahue's wife told me the warden's hobby was photography."

"Helen Grimes must know who Hilton Sullivan really is," I said as sirens wailed.

Marino peered out the window. "Good. Lucero's here."

I examined the down vest on the bed and discovered a downy white feather protruding from a minute tear in a seam.

More engines sounded. Car doors slammed shut.

"We're out of here," Marino said when Lucero arrived. "Make sure you impound his blue van." He turned to me. "Doc? You remember how to get to Helen Grimes's crib?"

"Yes."

"Let's go talk at her."

Helen Grimes did not have much to say.

When we got to her house some forty-five minutes later, we found the front door unlocked and went inside. The heat was turned up as high as it would go, and I could have been anywhere in the world and recognized the smell.

"Holy God," Marino said when he walked into the bedroom.

Her headless body was in uniform and sitting in a chair against the wall. It wasn't until three days later that the farmer across the road found the rest of her. He didn't know why anyone would have left a bowling bag in one of his fields. But he wished he had never opened it.

EPILOGUE

The yard behind my mother's Miami house was half in the shade and half in the gentle sun, and hibiscus grew in a riot of red on either side of the back screen door. Her Key Lime tree by the fence was heavy with fruit when virtually all others in the neighborhood were barren or dead. It was a fact I failed to understand, for I had not known it was possible to criticize plants into good health. I thought you had to talk nicely to them.

"Katie?" my mother called from the kitchen window. I heard water drumming into the sink. There was no point in answering.

Lucy knocked out my queen with a castle. "You know," I said, "I really hate playing chess with you."

"Then why do you keep asking me?"

"*Me* asking *you*? You force me, and one game is never enough."

"That's because I keep giving you another chance. But you blow it every time."

We were sitting across from each other at the patio table. The ice in our lemonades had melted and I felt a little sunburned.

"Katie? Will you and Lucy go out after a while and get the wine?" my mother said from the window.

I could see the shape of her head and the round outline of her face. Cupboard doors opened and shut; then the telephone sounded its high-pitched ring. It was for me, and my mother simply handed the cordless phone out the door.

"It's Benton," the familiar voice said. "I see from the papers that the weather's great down there. It's raining here and a lovely forty-five degrees."

"Don't make me homesick."

"Kay, we think we've got an ID. And by the way, someone went to a lot of trouble. Fake identifications—good ones. He was able to walk into a gun store, and rent a condo, with no questions asked."

"Where'd he get his money?"

"Family. He's probably had some stashed. Anyway, after going through prison records and talking to a lot of people, it seems that Hilton Sullivan is an alias for a thirty-one-year-old male named Temple Brooks Gault from Albany, Georgia. His father owns a pecan plantation and there's a lot of money. Gault's typical in some ways—preoccupied with guns, knives, martial arts, violent pornography. He's antisocial, et cetera."

"In what ways is he atypical?" I asked.

"His pattern would indicate that he's completely unpredictable. He doesn't really fit any profile, Kay. This guy's off the charts. If something strikes his fancy, he just does it. He's consummately narcissistic and vain—his hair, for example. He highlights it himself. We found the bleach, rinses, and so on in his apartment. Some of his inconsistencies are, well, weird."

"Such as?"

"He was driving this beat-up old van that was once owned by a housepainter. Doesn't appear Gault ever washed it or bothered to clean it out, not even after he murdered Eddie Heath inside the thing. We've got some pretty promising trace, by the way, and blood that's consistent with Eddie's type. That's disorganized. Yet Gault also apparently eradicated bite marks and had his fingerprints changed. That's as organized as hell."

"Benton, what is his history?"

"A manslaughter conviction. Two and a half years ago he got angry with a man in a bar and kicked him in the head. This was in Abingdon, Virginia. Gault, by the way, has a black belt in karate."

"Any new developments on locating him?" I watched Lucy set up the chessboard.

"None. But for all of us involved in the cases, I'll say what I've said before. This guy's absolutely without fear. He's very much guided by impulse and is, therefore, troublesome to second-guess."

"I understand."

"Just make sure you exercise the appropriate precautions at all times."

There were no appropriate precautions against someone like this, I thought.

"All of us need to be alert."

"I understand," I said again.

"Donahue had no idea what he unleashed. Or better put, Norring didn't. Though I don't believe our good governor handpicked this dirtbag. He just wanted his damn briefcase and probably gave Donahue the necessary funds and told him to take care of it. We're not going to get any hard time for Norring. He's been too careful and too many people aren't around to talk." He paused, adding, "Of course, there's your attorney and me."

"What do you mean?"

"I've been clear—in a subtle way, of course—that it would be a damn shame if something got leaked about the briefcase stolen from Robyn Naismith's house. Grueman had a little tête-à-tête with him, too, and reports that Norring looked a little queasy when it was mentioned that it must have been a harrowing experience when he drove himself to the ER the night before Robyn's death."

By checking old newspaper clips and talking to contacts in various ERs around the city, I had discovered that the night before Robyn's murder, Norring had been treated at Henrico Doctor's emergency room after administering epinephrine to himself by injection in his left thigh. Apparently, he had suffered a severe allergic reaction to Chinese food, cartons for which I recalled from police reports had been found in Robyn Naismith's trash. My theory was that shrimp or some other shellfish had inadvertently gotten mixed in with spring rolls or something else he and Robyn had eaten for dinner. He had begun to go into anaphylactic shock, had used one of his

EpiPens—perhaps one he'd kept at Robyn's house—and then had driven himself to the hospital. In his great distress, he had left without his briefcase.

"I just want Norring as far away from me as possible," I said.

"Well, it seems he's been suffering health problems of late and has decided it would be wise to resign and look for something less stressful in the private sector. Perhaps on the West Coast. I'm quite certain he won't bother you. Ben Stevens won't bother you. For one thing, he—like Norring—is too busy looking over his shoulder for Gault. Let's see. Last I heard, Stevens was in Detroit. Did you know?"

"Did you threaten him, too?"

"Kay, I never threaten anyone."

"Benton, you're one of the most threatening people I've ever met."

"Does that mean you won't work with me?"

Lucy was drumming her fingers on top of the table and leaning her cheek against her fist.

"Work with you?" I asked.

"That's really why I'm calling, and I know you'll need to think about it. But we'd like you to come on board as a consultant to the Behavioral Science Unit. We're just talking a couple of days a month—as a rule. Of course, there will be times when things get a little crazy. You'll review the medical and forensic details of cases to assist us in working up the profiles. Your interpretations would be very useful. And besides, you probably know that Dr. Elsevier, who has been serving as our consulting forensic pathologist for the past five years, is retiring as of June one."

Lucy poured her lemonade on the grass, got up, and began stretching.

"Benton, I'll have to think about it. For one thing, my office is still in shambles. Give me a little time to hire a new morgue supervisor and administrator and get things back on track. When do you need to know?"

"By March?"

"Fair enough. Lucy says hello."

When I hung up, Lucy looked defiantly at me. "Why do you say something like that when it isn't true? I didn't say hello to him."

"But you desperately wanted to." I got up. "I could tell."

"*Katie?*" My mother was in the window again. "You really should come in. You've been outside all afternoon. Did you remember to put on sun block?"

"We're in the *shade,* Grans," Lucy called out. "Remember this *huge* ficus tree back here?"

"What time did your mother say she was coming over?" my mother asked her granddaughter.

"As soon as she and what's-his-name finish screwing, they'll be here."

My mother's face disappeared from the window and water drummed in the sink again.

"Lucy!" I whispered.

She yawned and wandered to the edge of the yard to catch an elusive ray of sun. Turning her face to it, she closed her eyes.

"You're going to do it, aren't you, Aunt Kay?" she said.

"Do what?"

"Whatever Mr. Wesley was asking you to do."

I began putting the chess game back in its box.

"Your silence is a very loud answer," my niece said. "I know you. You're going to do it."

"Come on," I said. "Let's go get the wine."

"Only if I get to drink some."

"Only if you're not driving anywhere tonight."

She slipped her arm around my waist and we went inside the house.

BODY OF EVIDENCE

Patricia Cornwell

A reclusive writer is dead. And her final manuscript
has disappeared . . .

Someone is stalking Beryl Madison. Spying on her and making
threatening, obscene phone calls. Terrified, Beryl flees to Key West –
but on the very night she returns to her Richmond home, Beryl
inexplicably invites her killer in.

Now Dr Kay Scarpetta must take on a case that is as convoluted as it
is bizarre. Why would Beryl open the door to someone who brutally
slashed and then nearly decapitated her? Did she know her killer?
Adding to the intrigue is Beryl's enigmatic relationship with a prize-
winning author and the disappearance of her own manuscript.

As Scarpetta retraces Beryl's footsteps, an investigation that begins in
the laboratory with microscopes and lasers leads her deep into a
nightmare that soon becomes her own.

'Head-under-the-bedclothes tension' *The Times*

'A great writer . . . read these books only in broad daylight'
Daily Mail

978-0-7515-4443-5

POSTMORTEM

Patricia Cornwell

A serial killer is on the loose in Richmond, Virginia. Three women have died, brutalised and strangled in their own bedroom. There is no pattern: the killer appears to strike at random – but always early on Saturday mornings.

So when Dr Kay Scarpetta, chief medical officer, is awakened at 2.33 am, she knows the news is bad: there is a fourth victim. And she fears now for those that will follow unless she can dig up new forensic evidence to aid the police.

But not everyone is pleased to see a woman in this powerful job. Someone may even want to ruin her career and reputation . . .

'Terrific first novel, full of suspense, in which even the scientific bits grip'
The Times

978-0-7515-4439-8

PREDATOR

Patricia Cornwell

Florida is full of human predators from the animals who thrive in its humid heat to the humans that stalk the air-conditioned malls, and they all give Dr Kay Scarpetta the opportunity and the means to do what she does best – persuading the dead to speak to her.

In the icy chill of Boston, Benton Wesley is working on a secret project involving convicted killers. It is a project which gives Scarpetta deep disquiet, as does the behaviour of her niece, Lucy, who is spending too much time in cheap bars looking for casual pick-ups.

The Academy is called when a woman's body is found in Boston. She has been tortured, sexually abused, her body tattooed with handprints. The same sort of handprints Lucy had seen on the flesh of her latest pick-up . . .

'Sensationally plotted, with a twist at the end that will leave you gasping for breath' *Daily Express*

978-0-7515-4414-5

BOOK OF THE DEAD

Patricia Cornwell

The 'book of the dead' is the morgue log, the ledger in which all cases are entered by hand. For Kay Scarpetta, however, it is about to have a new meaning.

Fresh from her bruising battle with a psychopath in Florida, Scarpetta decides it's time for a change of pace. Moving to the historic city of Charleston, South Carolina, she opens a unique private forensic pathology practice, one in which she and her colleagues offer expert crime scene investigation and autopsies to communities lacking local access to competent death investigation and modern technology. It seems like an ideal situation, until the murders and other violent deaths begin.

A woman is ritualistically murdered in her multi-million-dollar beach home. The body of an abused young boy is found dumped in a desolate marsh. A sixteen-year-old tennis star is found nude and mutilated near Piazza Navona in Rome.

Scarpetta has dealt with many brutal and unusual crimes before, but never a string of them as baffling, or as terrifying, as the ones before her now. Before she is through, that book of the dead will contain many names – and the pen may be poised to write her own.

'Patricia Cornwell is the queen of gritty, grisly, crime fiction writing and her latest offering doesn't disappoint. *Book of the Dead* will keep you gripped throughout'
Heat

978-0-7515-3405-4

FROM POTTER'S FIELD

Patricia Cornwell

It's Christmas and a naked body is discovered in Central Park . . .

Although a holiday for most, the festivities always seem to heighten the alienation felt by society's criminals; and that usually means more work for Dr Kay Scarpetta, Virginia's Chief Medical Examiner and consulting forensic pathologist for the FBI.

The body is found propped against a fountain in a bleak area of New York's Central Park. The unknown female's apparent manner of death points to a modus operandi that is chillingly familiar: the gunshot wound to the head, the sections of skin excised from the body, the displayed corpse – all suggest that Temple Brooks Gault, Scarpetta's nemesis, is back at work.

Calling on all her reserves of courage and skill, and the able assistance of colleagues Marino and Wesley, Scarpetta must track this most dangerous of killers, in pursuit of survival as well as justice – heading inexorably to an electrifying climax amid the dark, menacing labyrinths of the New York subway.

'Cornwell is on magnificent form' *Evening Standard*

978-0-7515-3046-9

sphere

If you have enjoyed this book, you can find out
more about Patricia Cornwell's books
on her website

www.patriciacornwell.com

Or you can follow her on Twitter

@1pcornwell

And feel free to follow

@LittleBrownUK
@TheCrimeVault

To buy any Patricia Cornwell books
and to find out more about all other Little, Brown
titles go to our website

www.littlebrown.co.uk

To order any Sphere titles p & p free in the UK,
please contact our mail order supplier on:

+ 44 (0)1832 737525

Customers not based in the UK should contact the same
number for appropriate postage and packing costs.